# HER RADIANT CURSE

# HER RADIANT CURSE

*LEGENDS OF LOR'YAN*

## ELIZABETH LIM

Alfred A. Knopf
New York

THIS IS A BORZOI BOOK PUBLISHED BY ALFRED A. KNOPF

Visit us on the Web! GetUnderlined.com

Educators and librarians, for a variety of teaching tools, visit us at RHTeachersLibrarians.com

*Library of Congress Cataloging-in-Publication Data*
Names: Lim, Elizabeth, author.
Title: Her radiant curse / Elizabeth Lim.
Description: First edition. | New York : Alfred A. Knopf, [2023] | Series: Legends of Lor'yan | Audience: Ages 12 up. | Summary: "Two sisters, one as beautiful as the moon and the other monstrous, must fight to save each other when a betrothal contest goes wrong."—Provided by publisher.
Identifiers: LCCN 2023013676 (print) | LCCN 2023013677 (ebook) | ISBN 978-0-593-30099-2 (hardcover) | ISBN 978-0-593-30100-5 (library binding) | ISBN 978-0-593-30101-2 (ebook)
Subjects: CYAC: Sisters—Fiction. | Blessing and cursing—Fiction. | Betrothal—Fiction. | Contests—Fiction. | Fantasy. | LCGFT: Fantasy fiction.
Classification: LCC PZ7.1.L5523 He 2023 (print) | LCC PZ7.1.L5523 (ebook) | DDC [Fic]—dc23

ISBN 978-0-593-71002-9 (international ed.)

The text of this book is set in 11.25-point Sabon MT Pro.
Interior design by Michelle Crowe
Orchid flower illustration: suwi19/stock.adobe.com
Snake illustration: val_iva/stock.adobe.com

Printed in the United States of America
10 9 8 7 6 5 4 3 2 1
First Edition

*For Diana, my fellow fantasy nerd and the big sister I always wished for.*

*For Amaris, one of my oldest and dearest friends, also plothole-catcher extraordinaire.*

*For Eva, treasured friend who's believed in me from the very first book.*

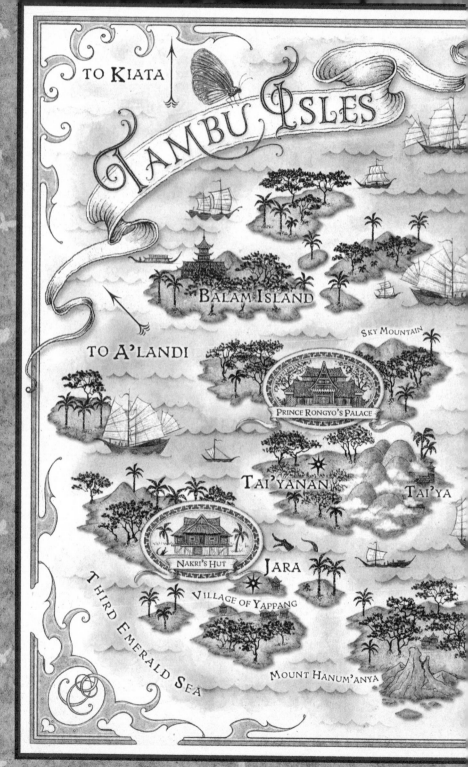

PAKKIEN ISLAND

SUNDAU

Temple of Dawn
Puntalo Village    Angma's Rock

CHANNI'S HOME

Sundau Strait

FOURTH EMERALD SEA

Bonemaker's Arena

SHENLANI

KING MEGUH'S PALACE

# HER RADIANT CURSE

I was not born a monster.

People forget that. The cruel ones sneer and tell me I'm demon spawn. They think the words will hurt me, but they are closer to the truth than they know.

It is the kind ones who lie. "You have a good heart, like your sister," they say in their pitying tones. "Deep down, you are beautiful—like your sister."

I am nothing like my sister.

Across the islands, her birth is a legend. Many come from near and far for a glimpse of her beauty, and our neighbors have made good coin telling her tale—how on a moonbow night seventeen years ago, my father faced a terrible choice: to save his wife, who lay dying on a moth-ridden cot, or his newborn daughter, whose pink cheeks, silken curls, and divine glow had already enraptured everyone who saw her.

Adah chose his wife. He snatched my sister from the midwife's arms and ran into the jungle to sacrifice her to Angma, the Demon Witch. There, on a flat rock beside a crooked tree, he left my sister to die.

Yet even as a baby, my sister gave off a golden light, which mesmerized the Demon Witch such that she could not devour her. And so, the next day, Adah found my sister where he had left her, laughing and singing among the birds and the frogs, and she was returned to us.

The story has a touch of fairy tale, which is why the villagers love recounting it. But it does not explain what happened to my face . . . because that is not how it *really* happened.

It is true that from the moment my sister was born, she was so radiant she outshone the stars, and her smile could soften even the hardest heart. It is also true that Adah faced that terrible, fateful choice. To save my mother, he *did* try to sacrifice a child. Only it was not my sister that he took into the jungle.

It was me.

# CHAPTER ONE

There was no moon or moonbow when my sister was born. Contrary to the stories, she arrived late in the morning, close to noon. I remember, because the sun was in my eyes, and its glaring heat needled my skin until I bubbled with sweat.

I was very young and playing outside, poking the ants crawling up my ankles with a stick, when the sun suddenly receded—and I heard screams. *Mama's* screams.

They were faint at first. Thunder had begun to rumble, swallowing the brunt of her cries. The loud cracks in the sky did not frighten me; I was already used to the island's fickle winds and the low howls that rolled from the jungle at night. So I stayed, even as rain unfolded from the sky and the chickens ran for cover. The dirt under my toes became mud, and the warm, humid air chilled. The ants drowned as the water climbed up my ankles.

Adah had told me not to come inside until I was called, but the rain was getting harder. It came down in sheets, soaking my shirt and sandals and drumming against my skull. It hurt.

Kicking off my sandals, I clambered up the wooden stairs to our house and ran inside to the kitchen. I shook my hair free of rain and tried to warm myself by the fire, but only a few embers remained.

"Adah?" I called, shivering. "Mama?"

No answer.

My stomach growled. Up beside the cooking pot was a plate of cakes Mama had steamed for me yesterday. They'd made her hands smell like coconut and her nails shine, sticky with syrup.

"Channi's cakes are ready!" she would always call when they were done. "Don't eat too much at once, or the sugar flies will come sweeping into your belly for dinner."

She didn't call for me today.

I stood on my tiptoes and stretched my arms high, but I wasn't tall enough to reach the plate.

"Mama!" I cried. "Can I have cake?"

Mama had stopped screaming, but I heard her breathing hard in the other room. Our house was very small then, with only a curtain separating the kitchen from Mama and Adah's bedroom.

I stood on my side of the curtain. Its coarse muslin chafed my nose as I breathed against it, trying to see what was happening on the other side.

Three shadows. Mama, Adah, and an old woman—the midwife.

"You've another daughter," the midwife was telling my parents. "Channi has a baby sister."

A sister?

Forgetting Adah's warning and my hunger, I ducked under the curtain and crawled toward my parents' bed.

There Mama lay, propped up on a pillow. She looked like a fish, all translucent and pale, her lips parted but not moving. I barely recognized her.

Adah was hovering over her, and the restless look on his face soured quickly as Mama locked her fists around the edges of the bed—as if she were about to start screaming again.

Instead, she let out a gasp, and a gush of red swelled through the blankets.

"She's bleeding!" Adah cried to the midwife. "Do something!"

The midwife lifted the blankets and went to work. I'd never seen so much blood before, and especially not at once. Not knowing it was my mother's life flowing out of her, it almost looked beautiful. Vibrant and bright, like a field of ruby hibiscuses.

But Mama's face, twisted in pain, kept me quiet.

Something was wrong.

I stood rooted to my corner, unseen. I wanted to hold Mama's hands. To see if they still smelled like coconuts and if the sugar syrup had seeped into the lines of her palms like always—and tasted sweet when I kissed her skin. But all I smelled was salt and iron: blood.

"Mama," I breathed, stepping forward.

Adah grabbed my arm and pulled me away from the bed. "Who let you in here? Get out."

"It's all right," said Mama weakly. She turned her head to face me. "Come, Channi. Come meet your sister."

I didn't want to meet my sister. I wanted to talk to Mama. I reached to squeeze her fingers, wan and blue, but the midwife intercepted me and thrust my sister into my face.

Most newborns are ugly, but not my sister. Her black hair was long enough to touch her shoulders; it was smoother than glass, and softer than a young bird's feathers. Her complexion was gold and bronze at the same time, with a kiss of pink on her plump, glowing cheeks and smiling lips.

Yet most enchanting of all was the light that emanated from her, brightest around her chest, as if a sliver of the sun were lodged inside her tiny heart.

"Isn't she a beauty?" the midwife whispered. "Hundreds of babies I've delivered—you included, Channi. Out of them all, only your sister laughed when she came into this world. Look at her smile. I tell you, kings and queens will bow down to that smile one day." She touched my sister's chest, her palm covering that strange glow inside her. "And this heart! Never have I ever seen a heart like this. She's been graced by the gods."

"Vanna," Mama whispered. Pride rippled in her voice. "We'll call her Vanna."

*Golden.*

I reached for my sister's tiny hand. She was warm, and I could feel her little heart pitter-patter against my finger. For someone who'd been alive only a few minutes, she smelled sweet, like mung beans and honey. All I wanted to do was hold her close and press my nose against her soft cheeks.

"Enough," said Adah sharply. "Channi, go back outside. Now."

"But, Adah," I said, feeling small, "the rain."

"Get out."

"Let her stay," Mama said, biting back another scream. Clearly, the pain was returning. "Let her. I don't have long."

I didn't understand what Mama meant then, or why Adah wiped his eyes with his arm. He folded onto his knees beside the bed and muttered prayer after prayer to the gods, promising to be a better husband if only Mama would live. The midwife tried to comfort him, but he jerked away.

Shadows fell over his face. "Give me the baby."

His look frightened me more than Mama's screams. I'd never felt much for my father; he was always working in the rice paddies while Mama took care of me. But he'd never been cruel. He loved my mother, and I thought he loved me too. This was the first time I'd heard him speak so sharply, with an edge that bit.

The midwife noticed too. "Khuan, let's not be rash. I'll take care of your wife. You go to the temple and pray."

My father would not listen. He seized my sister, and alarm flared in Mama's tired eyes.

"Khuan!" she rasped. "Stop."

Against Adah's wide, hulking frame, Vanna looked no bigger than a mouse. But my sister must have cast the same spell over my father that she had cast over me, for once he cradled her in his arms, she began to glow, brighter than before.

It was like magic, the way Adah softened. He stroked her

hair, black as obsidian. He kissed her cheeks, pink like her lily-bud lips. He stared in awe at her skin, which shone gold like the sun.

Then his shoulders fell, and he gave her back to the midwife. "Feed her."

Mama wheezed with relief. "Come, Channi. Mama will hold you."

Before I could go to her, Adah snatched me up, hooking a strong arm around my waist. He threw me over his shoulder, so hard that I gasped instead of screamed.

In three long strides, we were out of the house, and quickly the midwife's shouts faded behind us, consumed by the rain and thunder. He ran through the thick of the jungle.

I kicked and shouted, "Adah! Stop!"

Fear spiked in my heart. I did not know where he was taking me, and Mama wasn't coming after us. The rain had grown stronger, and it battered my face with such force I thought I might drown from it. I beat at Adah's back with my small fists, but this only irritated him. His grip tightened as he continued running.

In the jungle the rain weakened. All I could see were flashes of green and brown. I'd never been in the forests before, and for a moment I forgot to be afraid. Instead, I gazed in wonder at the trees with toothlike leaves, flowers large enough to swallow me whole, and vines that looked like snakes hanging from the sky. Gnats buzzed, mosquitoes bit Adah's neck, and mud splashed under his sandals.

Suddenly, Adah fell back in surprise, almost crushing

me. A magnificent red serpent hung from one of the trees, its long, forked tongue drawn out to hiss at us.

Adah propped himself up on his elbows, and I clung to his neck as the serpent bared its fangs.

"Let her go," it said.

Adah did not seem to understand. He got up, grabbing me by the waist so tightly I let out a little gasp, and shuffled away from the creature.

The serpent followed. It did not speak again; instead, it wrapped its body around my father's ankle.

Adah screamed and kicked his foot frantically, almost dropping me as he struggled. He grabbed a fallen branch and started beating the snake.

"Don't hurt it!" I squealed. "Adah!"

Freed from the serpent, my father ran faster than before, pounding deeper into the jungle.

The rain had ended. Mist layered the trees, and faint gold sunlight streaked across the graying sky. I only noticed because Adah ran hard and had to stop often, his chest shaking as he breathed. His back was slippery, and my hair became drenched with his sweat and odor. At some point, I craned my neck up for fresh air.

"Where are we going?" I asked.

"Quiet."

The chill in Adah's voice startled me, and I fell silent.

At last we came to a valley with a great clove tree at its center, ringed by flat white rocks. Elsewhere in the jungle, trees wrestled for space, their branches snarling against one another for a mere brush of the sun's nurturing light. But this crooked tree was alone. Not even gnats or dragonflies or mosquitoes dared to encroach here. As soon as we approached, they flittered away from Adah's skin, done with him.

Adah set me down on the largest rock. Rain and sweat glistened in his beard.

"Stay here," he said.

"Are you coming back?"

"I will come for you in the morning."

He would not look at me as he said this.

"Adah. . . ." I began to cry. "Don't go!"

"Stay, Channari."

At the sound of my full name, I made a whimper and crouched obediently.

The rock's face was cool and dry, shaded by the tree's canopy. As Adah turned back the way we'd come, I gathered my knees to my chest. In the distance I saw a family of monkeys climbing a tree. One of them had a baby on her hip, and I thought of Mama on that bed, screaming. Mama had never allowed me to enter the jungle before. Why was I here now?

"Adah!"

He'd left. The bushes still rustled, betraying his proximity, but no matter how I howled *"Adah! Adah!"* he did not come back for me. I was alone.

Well, not completely alone.

Birds chirped unseen in the trees. Centipedes and other mites skittered across the dirt around the clearing. Then the serpent—the same one that had attacked Adah earlier—appeared.

I backed away from it fearfully as it slithered across the rock. Its eyes glittered like emeralds, and its bright red scales were stark against the watery sunlight.

"Come with me," said the snake.

I flinched, but not because the idea of a talking snake surprised me. I'd heard enough about magic and demons not to be frightened by such creatures. What made me hesitate was that this snake had tried to bite Adah. I couldn't trust him.

"Go away."

"Follow me," the snake said. "Angma is coming."

Though I was very young, a chill swept down my spine when I heard that name. Mama had told me about Angma, always in the same cautionary tone she used to warn me when Adah was in a foul mood.

"Long ago," she'd begin, "Angma was a human witch whose daughter was stolen from her. In her rage, she was transformed into a fearsome demon, wandering the earth in search of her daughter. She devoured babies to maintain her immortality and strength, and sometimes, when a child was offered freely, she would grant a favor in return."

Such as saving my mother's life—or so Adah must have hoped.

I was too young to understand what "sacrifice" meant. I didn't know why I should be afraid of Angma. So I ignored the snake's warning.

"Adah said for me to stay here," I said stubbornly.

"Suit yourself," hissed the snake. He paused. "Just don't look into her eyes."

He slid off the rock and disappeared.

It wasn't long before a shadow cloaked the clove tree, and all the music of the jungle—the twittering birds, chirping insects, and rustling monkeys—was silenced.

I looked around me. A shadow darted from behind one of the bushes.

"Adah?" I called out again.

I climbed off the rock, digging my toes into the moist dirt. Tiny pebbles pricked my feet. If only I hadn't kicked off my sandals at home!

"Adah?"

A beast purred behind me, and I whirled around. A tiger!

She moved languidly, knowing I was trapped. Even if I tried to run, she would catch up in fewer than five paces. Her powerful legs were longer than my entire body, and her fur was copper, like the statues at the Temple of Dawn, streaked with bolts of black.

There was something odd about this tiger. I had never seen one in real life before, but I had seen the sculptures in the village, the paintings and scrolls hanging in the temple. I had seen the pelts that hunters brought back to the village to sell, and they looked nothing like this tiger's.

It wasn't just that the tiger breathed smoke from her nostrils, or that she had sharp ivory tusks like an elephant and a sheath of ancient white hair that cascaded down her striped back. It was the glow of her fur, both dark and radiant at the same time, like shadows burning under moonlight. It made me feel cold.

"So," rasped the tiger. Her voice was low and guttural. It reverberated against the dirt beneath me and nearly made me jump. "Your father has left you to me."

Shadows swelled from wherever the tiger moved, enveloping me as she drew close. She smelled strong, though I could not recognize the scent. It was not of the trees or flowers or anything I had experienced before. A spice, maybe.

My eyelids grew heavy.

"You're a bit old," the tiger continued, sniffing me. "Your father was supposed to bring your sister. The baby." Her shadow eclipsed me. "The pretty one."

I rubbed my eyes, awash in sleepiness. My fear of the tiger gone, I glanced at the stone before me. Flat and smooth: perfect for taking a short nap.

The tiger roared. "Look at me, child! Where is your sister?"

I stared stubbornly at the ground. I hadn't paid attention to the snake's warning to run, but his warning not to look into the tiger's eyes made sense. I disliked the way she was yelling. When Adah yelled this way, he would strike me as soon as I glanced up.

The tiger was so close now, the air quavered with her breath. She exhaled on me, a cloud of black curling smoke.

"Look at me," she said again as I coughed. "Look at me, or I swear I will break your neck."

Slowly, I lifted my gaze to meet hers. Her whiskers were

taut and sleek, bone-white against her black-striped cheeks. Her eyes were the most vivid yellow I'd ever seen. Like the turmeric powder Mama made me eat when my stomach hurt but which only made it hurt more.

Blood trickled out of my nostrils, and I could not move. In the tiger's eyes, my reflection showed a streak of my hair whitening at my temple. The blood from my nose turned black.

My knees buckled in fear, and behind me the snake darted out of his hiding place. He was a flicker of red, so quick I barely saw him glide toward me. He flashed his fangs, and for an instant I thought he was going to attack the tiger.

Instead, he bit me on the ankle.

His fangs sank into my flesh, into my muscle and bone. I let out a gruesome howl, one I barely recognized as coming from my lungs. All of me quaked, and hot bursts of searing pain ripped across my flesh as if I'd been lit afire.

The snake retracted his fangs, and the pain abated slightly. A wave of cold swept over me. Sweat still dribbled down my temples, but now I shivered.

I'd forgotten about the tiger. She leaned forward, laying one sharp claw on the rock, and growled at the snake. "What are *you* doing here?"

The snake slid forward, creating a barrier between the tiger and me. He flared his hood. "Leave her alone. She isn't the child you've been waiting for."

"What does it matter to you whether I eat her or not? Move aside."

"Mother Angma," the snake said respectfully, "I would

advise you to let this child go. Her blood is worth nothing to you now."

The snake gestured to my ankle with his tongue. Already a painful lump had formed, and strange green streaks limned my veins. Great Gadda, it hurt!

The tiger let out a furious growl. She whipped her tail at the snake, catching him and flinging him into the bushes. Then she whirled back to me, ready to unleash her fury. But as she watched me trying to limp out of the clearing, her anger vanished.

She blocked me from leaving. "Poor, poor girl. You think he has saved you, don't you?"

No. I didn't think anything other than how my leg hurt, how the world was spinning, and how I wanted to go home. How I missed Mama.

I tried to run past the tiger. A bad idea.

She pressed a paw to my chest, her yellow eyes swirling with lurid enchantment. "The Serpent King has poisoned your blood," she said viciously, "and so I shall curse your face. You will never look at it without feeling pain."

Strange, that in the moment that should come to define me, I felt so little. Only a tingle across my face, then a thick, suffocating pressure that rose to my neck, as if there were an invisible string cutting off my breath. Then nothing.

Nothing but a premonitory shiver that tracked down my spine as shadows spun beneath the tiger's fur, and her eyes . . . changed. They were still yellow, still mesmerizing. But her pupils had gone from black to a bright and violent red. Like blood.

"Bring your sister to me before her seventeenth birthday," she said in a quiet, lethal tone, "and I will undo my curse. If not, I will come for you both—and you will wish you had died."

Then, with one great leap, she bounded into the jungle. She was gone.

It felt a long time before the snake slithered back into view. Everything was blurry, but in the dense mess of green, I could easily make out his red scales and glittering eyes.

I didn't care if the tiger had wounded him. Or what curse had befallen me. "You hurt me," I accused.

"I had to bite you," replied the snake. "Otherwise, Angma would have devoured you. But now my poison runs through your blood. If she tries again to eat you, it will harm her."

I didn't like his reasoning.

When I touched my ankle, the green streaks transferred onto my fingers. They wouldn't rub off, either, no matter how hard I tried. "It hurts."

"The pain will go away," the snake said, sounding apologetic. He paused. His mouth stayed open, and though I did not know how snakes spoke, I got the sense he wanted to say more. Instead, he asked, "What's your name, little one?"

"Channi," I whispered. "Channari."

If a snake could smile, this one did. His mouth curved as he flicked out his thin, forked tongue. "Moon-faced."

Mama and Adah had named me Channari because I was born under a full moon, and when I arrived my eyes were wide and open, catching its silver light. But I wasn't about to tell that to a stranger. A snake, no less.

"What's *your* name?" I asked.

His smile faded. Only then did I see the claw marks on his scales, raw and pink in the jaundiced sunlight. Many years later I would learn that when a snake dies, he can see the future, for a brief instant. And that this snake, who had sacrificed his life to protect me, was the king among his kind.

"My name doesn't matter," he said. "For you, you need Hokzuh. Say his name."

"Hok . . . Hok . . . zuh."

"Remember it. He'll come looking for you one day, when you are older."

Before my eyes, the snake's skin turned white, his scales becoming like tiny sea pearls studded along his body. His head was still lifted, while the rest of his body curled, slowly shriveling and going limp. "You'll need him."

"Why?"

"One sister must fall for the other to rise," he replied, so softly that I almost didn't hear. He folded his head into the center of his coiled body, eyes closing. "Sleep now."

I didn't want to, but the poison in my blood gave me no choice. Already my head felt leaden, and as the ground spun faster and faster, I had to cover my face. My leg tingled until I could no longer feel it, and the numbness swept up from my ankle to my brow.

"Sleep," the Serpent King whispered one last time. Then he too slept. Except unlike me, he would not wake up.

When I awoke, I was home, nestled in my little bed by the cooking pot. I lifted my head. The throbbing pain in my arms and legs was gone, replaced by a numbing sensation behind my cheeks, but even that was fading.

I crawled up to Mama's bedside. In her arms, little Vanna was asleep.

*The pretty one,* I remembered.

Mama stirred. When she saw me, she let out a small gasp. Fear leapt into her eyes and made her voice shake. "Ch-Ch-Channi, what happened to your face?"

I blinked, confused. "Is it dirty, Mama?"

"No. No." Mama swallowed. I tried to see my face in her pupils, but it was dark. The sun had fallen, and we were too poor to burn candles at night.

When she spoke again, she was calmer. "Never mind your face. Come."

She cupped my cheek in her cold, sallow hand. I held it close, feeling how weak she was, how brittle her fingers were against my skin.

I snuggled beside her. Her pulse was so faint I had to press my ear to her chest to hear it. I glanced over at Vanna, still sleeping peacefully. Still glowing, though the light was softer than it had been earlier, when she'd just been born. A tinge of envy washed over me, imagining that I'd have to share Mama in the future.

But then Vanna opened her eyes. She smiled at me, reaching out her tiny fingers to touch my cheeks.

"Look there," Mama whispered. "Vanna opened her eyes. For you."

*I* was the first person or thing she ever saw.

Vanna laughed then, an adorable little giggle that made my heart flutter. That was the moment I fell in love with my sister, the moment I swore I wouldn't let the Demon Witch take her. Not ever.

"Will you promise to watch over her, Channi?" Mama asked. "To protect her always?"

I almost jumped. Had Mama read my mind?

"Yes, I promise." I reached out and held Vanna's tiny hand, squeezing as hard as I dared. *I'll protect you.*

The light in Vanna's chest flashed, and a shot of warmth emanated from her fingertips, so unexpected and powerful that it sent a jolt through my entire body.

"You see? Even the gods know now that you two are bound." Mama leaned back with a feeble smile. "A promise is not a kiss in the wind, to be thrown about without care. It is a piece of yourself that is given away and will not return until your pledge is fulfilled. Understand?"

This was a saying from her village that she'd taught me long ago. "I understand," I said, even though I didn't really.

"Good." Mama inhaled. "Now, let the baby sleep."

Obediently, I let go of Vanna and climbed up the bed to Mama's side. Even though Mama was tired and worn, to me she was still the prettiest woman in the world. She had the warmest, brownest eyes. They weren't large or wide, and her eyelashes weren't long or thick, but they were honest eyes. Honest eyes to match her proud, honest nose and lips.

I glowed whenever anyone said I looked like her.

Bringing me close, Mama caressed my hair and began to sing:

> *Sitting among the stars is my beautiful moon-faced girl.*
> *Channi, my beautiful moon-faced girl.*

Her music calmed me, and I forgot about the fear in her eyes when she'd seen my face. I forgot about Angma's promise to kill my sister and me. My thoughts drifted far away, and my muscles softened.

For the last time, I fell asleep to the sound of Mama's voice.

In the morning, she was dead. And no one called me beautiful again. Not for a long, long time.

# CHAPTER TWO

*Seventeen years later*

It is the perfect morning to hunt a tiger.

Last night's rain still shimmers over the earth, and all around, bouquets of jasmine and moon orchids have blossomed. I'm counting on their perfume to mask my scent—or at the very least to bury it until I attack.

While the dawn light fans across the jungle, I steal under a veil of mist and hold my breath. The tiger is emerging from her den.

She is thin. Likely hungry. But that doesn't mean she's weak. Her striped fur is burnished with the luster of youth, and her muscles bulge as she stalks silently through the grass. She'll head to the nearest pond for a drink, then hunt for breakfast.

But not if I get to her first.

Lanky, wet grass prickles my feet as I close the distance between us. I roll the end of my fighting stick in my palm. A few more steps and I'll be within range.

*Not every tiger is one of Angma's demons,* interrupts a voice in my head. *You really think she doesn't see you hiding in the mist?*

There's only one being on the entire island that would dare disturb me while I'm hunting, and I don't have to look down to know there is a freckled green snake circling my feet.

*Don't you remember the last time you wrestled a tiger?* he says. *You're lucky you got out without any scars. Imagine adding a scratch or two to your face—*

I greet my friend with a venomous glare.

*Just some advice,* he says.

*Which I don't need.* I stride forward, eyes on the tiger. *I won't hurt her if she isn't a demon. But I need this, Ukar. It's good practice.*

*Is it "good practice" if you end up as breakfast?*

*You're* more likely to end up as breakfast than I am, I scoff. I am not game, not when poison sings in my blood.

Every creature that breathes knows that. Even mosquitoes do not prick my skin for blood. One sniff, and they understand that I am not prey. That a taste of me will kill.

Only the snakes are immune to my poison, as I am to theirs. The Serpent King's bite linked me to them, allowing me to understand their tongue and even exchange thoughts. "Lady Green Snake," they call me affectionately. They practically raised me and have taught me their wisdom, their lore, their ways. They are my brothers and sisters. My friends.

Ukar, in spite of his constant hectoring, is my best friend.

*I thought you said you weren't coming into the jungle today,* he remarks.

*Leave me alone. I'm trying to concentrate.*

Keeping to the bushes, I crouch low and creep closer to my target. I've been waiting all summer to find a tiger, and I am not about to let her get away.

Ukar follows me, making an annoying crackling sound as he slithers over some wet ferns. I glare at him again.

The snake glares back, tail shaking. *Give it up. If that tiger were Angma, she wouldn't be rambling around the pool, passing wind every few paces to make her mark. You've searched every leaf in this jungle for the Demon Witch. She isn't here.*

Ignoring Ukar, I quicken my pace, taking a series of calculated steps forward. Not a twig snaps, and the leaves whistle like they're being played by the wind. I've grown into a spry and bony thing, with wide-set eyes and sloped shoulders far stronger than they look. I'm reedy enough to disappear behind the trunk of a teak tree and limber enough to climb it without rope. If not for my face, I'd look as plain as any girl of nineteen. But there is always my face.

My face, with its green-brown scales, which Adah forces me to cover with a mask whenever I am home. My face, which makes grown men shriek in terror and has robbed me of any human friendship other than my sister Vanna's. My face, which has trapped me somewhere between beast and woman.

Right now, my face has its advantages: it blends perfectly with the green ferns and vines, allowing me to move unseen—until I am two leaps behind the tiger.

She has reached the watering hole, a crystalline pond in which I can see spotted frogs swimming. She bends, majestically tucking her legs behind her, and lowers her head for a drink. She is a magnificent creature.

No horns, no white hair, no reek of cold wickedness about her.

But the way of demons is to deceive, and the most formidable ones can take on the shape of nearly any beast. So no matter how sure I am, I will not know for certain if she is Angma . . .

. . . until I see her eyes.

I ready the stick in my hand. *Keep your gaze up, Channi. Always up.*

The reminder has nothing to do with the possibility that the tiger might have Angma's demon eyes. It's to avoid the water.

I advance toward the pond. It's ironic that the villagers forbid children from entering the jungle to protect them from tigers, so they play by the sea, splashing and swimming with the colorful fish and tortoises. But I would rather face a thousand tigers than the monster that is my reflection.

To see *that* instead of the girl I should have been: one with black braids, brown eyes, a soft nose, and full lips. . . . I thought the pain would ease over the years, but it hasn't. It's only become more deeply entrenched, stitched into my very soul.

I suck in a breath. Luckily, I've gotten good at not looking down.

*Enough of this, Channi,* chides Ukar. *You're going to get yourself killed—*

I scoop him up with my stick and toss him far from imminent danger. Without wasting a second, I leap out of the ferns and onto the tiger's back.

She snarls with surprise. She's not used to being ambushed. I have only seconds before her shock turns into anger, and then into brutal, tremendous strength.

I cling to her torso, squeezing as hard as I can. Even though she isn't fully grown, she is easily twice my size. I feel her muscles ripple under her shoulders, her blood rushing under the heat of my cheek. She rises onto her hind legs and roars, making my ears ring.

If I want to know the truth, I've no choice but to look down. Honey-yellow eyes, dilated now from our fight, glare at me in the pool's reflection. They're flat and angry and dull. And their pupils are black.

*Guess she's not a demon after all,* I realize as she flings me into the pool.

My world shrinks, and water beats against my eardrums. I flail for the surface. Gasping for air, I pull myself out with my stick—and clamber for the bank.

I don't get far. Sharp teeth snap at my neck. I duck, and the tiger's jaws clamp down around my fighting stick instead. Its pieces blow past my shoulder while I dart left, narrowly evading the next strike.

The tiger's fast, but I know how to move, thanks to years of chasing monkeys trying to filch cakes from my pockets, years of rooting rat and spider demons out of their caves, years of evading the hard thwacks of Adah's cane.

Before she can pounce on me again, I let out my fiercest cry. She throws her head back and snorts.

25

"I'm not done yet," I say through my teeth.

Then, retrieving my knife, I slash my palm and hold it before her.

Her claws retract. She snarls but ceases her taunting. As the blood pools around the gash, the scent of its poison is magnified a thousandfold. The tiger knows it is more lethal than any sword.

Our fight fizzles into a stare-down. The tiger circles me, but my eyes never leave hers. I don't even dare blink. I hold my hand up, letting the blood trickle down my forearm onto the dirt.

Finally, she roars. A deafening, wrathful roar that I surely deserve. Then she runs off into the jungle, disappearing into the mist.

Once she's gone, I practically collapse. My heart thunders in my ears, which are still ringing from the tiger's roar. My chest hurts so much it feels like my heart and my lungs are at war. I want to throw up, but instead, a laugh bubbles out of my throat.

I melt onto the earth, all but cackling as the sun dries my hair and clothes.

Ukar finds me. His scales blend with the dirt, and I almost don't see him. Only descendants of the Serpent King can change their colors, and Ukar loves flexing this ability to catch me off guard.

*Using your blood was a cheat,* he chides. *You said you wouldn't do that anymore.*

I roll my eyes. "I won, didn't I?"

*Recklessly, and without honor.*

"Demons don't have honor."

*Not all demons are the same.*

I shrug. "I'm alive. I needed the practice."

*The whole forest will be nattering about this. There's a code, you know. Already some of us don't like that you've been given free rein of the island. You shouldn't be picking fights. Especially not with tigers.*

"I don't like tigers," I say, brushing dirt off my arm. "You know that better than anyone."

*And I don't like man. My kin are the oldest in the jungle, descended from the great dragons themselves—until man hunted them all into hiding. But you don't see me attacking your kind every chance I get.*

I chuckle, but inside a tight pressure rises to my chest. "It's three days until Vanna's birthday. When the Demon Witch comes for her, I need to be ready."

*No tigress can prepare you for a match against Angma.* Ukar frowns, looking as displeased as a snake can look. *I could have told you that before you ruined yet another tunic and fouled the earth with your blood. I'll have to ask my kin to clean it up.*

My laugh dries up in my throat. "I'm sorry."

*No, you're not.*

I'm not, it's true. I meant what I said about needing the practice. Reminded of the blood on my palm, I rip my sleeve with my teeth and wrap the strip of cloth around my cut. I don't bother with a knot; the wound's already closing.

*You might be strong enough to wrestle a tiger, Channi, but you'll need more than brawn to defeat Angma.*

I know. I need Hokzuh, whoever—or whatever—he is. All these years I've searched, I've never found a trace of him.

"Was that the last tiger in the jungle?" I ask, shaking away my thoughts.

*You mean, the only one left you haven't assaulted?* Ukar pauses dramatically. *Yes.*

I twist my lips. "That's unfortunate."

Ukar lets out a hiss. It's soft and sibilant, the equivalent of a snake's sigh. *Prudence and vigilance—that's what I'd hoped the jungle would teach you. Not a thirst for vengeance—*

"It's defense, not vengeance."

*—besides, isn't it bad luck to hunt on your sister's selection day?*

"It'd be worse bad luck for a tiger to kill the entire village on my sister's selection day," I retort.

*Unlikely. The tiger fed yesterday.*

"How do you know that? She looked hungry."

*Tigers always look hungry. She won't hunt for at least three days. By that time, your sister will be long gone. You wouldn't care if the tiger ate your village then.*

Always a killjoy, my best friend. I glower at him, mostly because I know he's right. Also because I don't need a reminder that Vanna is leaving. I don't want one.

*Heed the lesson and go home. Your father will be wondering where you are. Especially today.*

"This is my home."

*You know what I mean.*

I grit my teeth. Adah's house is not my home. The jungle is. It's here—where I can fling off my mask and let the sun touch my cheeks, where I am surrounded by so much green that I can barely see the sky. Only here do I feel truly awake, truly alive, and truly free. Only here do I forget that I am a monster.

Ukar does not heed my impassioned thoughts. *The sky is already an hour stained with light. You'll be in trouble if he finds that you're gone.*

"I'll get back in time to finish my chores. Besides, I'll be the last thing on Adah's mind this morning, what with Vanna being married off." I grimace. *Auctioned* off, though no one seems to want to call it that.

I sweep tree branches aside angrily. I don't know which sickens me more: that a dozen kings are coming for the chance to make Vanna their concubine, or that Adah's been tinkering at his abacus all month, calculating how much he'll make by selling her off.

*Shouldn't you be with her, then?* says Ukar. *Instead of stirring up trouble in the jungle?*

The lump in my throat hardens. "I'm more worried about Angma than some pompous, overdressed, over-feathered king."

*You mean, you're not invited.*

Curse Ukar for knowing me so well.

*That's never stopped you before. I tell you a thousand times not to hunt tigers, and you do it anyway.*

Yes, but it's different when I'm in the jungle. Ukar often forgets that. I never do.

"You think Angma will be early?" I ask quietly. "You think she'll show up at the auction?"

*No. The winds of Sundau have been free of her magic ever since my king passed. If she remembers to kill you, it will not be today.*

"Oh, she'll remember," I mutter. I touch my cheek, recalling Angma's promise to spare me and to lift the curse from my face if I give her my sister.

I'd rather gut myself with my own nails than betray Vanna, but I can't help the deep yearning that knots itself in my chest.

Before Ukar senses it, I drop a small kiss on his head. "You're still not coming?"

*I'll be there for you when you need me to fight Angma. But to watch your sister be paraded about like some prize to be won? I have no desire to witness such a spectacle.*

Fair enough.

I start for Adah's house, picking up my knees and running as fast as I can up the low, rolling hills, past the rice fields and cassava farms. The rush of blood to my head helps distract me from the apprehension that rises to my throat. No matter what Ukar says, I'm certain that the tiger was a warning sent by Angma. That the Demon Witch *is* back.

And she is waiting for me.

# CHAPTER THREE

The Channi of the jungle and the Channi who lives in her adah's house are two very different girls. One races barefoot in the jungle, a queen of the wild, content and free. The other sits on a broken stool, peeling taro root all day.

I sit on that broken stool now, surrounded by four walls. I've never liked walls, and I dislike the walls of Adah's house most of all. They prevent me from seeing the sun. They bake the air and keep out the freshness after a rainstorm. They cage me in and hide me, like a mask on top of my mask, holding me in place so I cannot run away.

"Walls protect us from rain and heat and tigers," Vanna said once, trying to comfort me. "Sometimes even from each other."

I didn't agree, but to keep her from worrying about me and Adah, I nodded.

Deep down I know that if not for Vanna, I'd have left Adah's house long ago. Maybe I'd have sought out the dragons in the sea and gone to live in a palace of coral. Maybe I'd have found the Nine-Eyed Witch of Yappang and discovered some way to lift this curse from my face. Most likely I'd have gone to live with the snakes and become a true queen of the jungle.

Because of Vanna, I stayed. I haven't forgotten my promise to Mama that I would protect her—from Angma or anyone who wishes her harm.

Even if she doesn't want my protection.

Crows squawk across the sky, and koels make desperate mating calls from the trees. I peel off my tattered pants and wipe the jungle's musk off my face.

My stepmother doesn't come to find me, as she normally does when she wakes. Vanna doesn't come to find me, either.

I crack eight eggs into a pan and fry them. Heat shoots up in my face, and I add a dash of cumin and ginger before sliding the eggs onto four separate plates.

Sticking my head out of the window, I shout, "Breakfast!"

No one pays me any heed, for a golden light is flashing from Vanna's open window, and my sister's delighted squeal rings across the compound.

"Lintang!" I hear her cry. "Thank you, thank you! It's the most beautiful dress I've ever seen. I love it."

Frothy pink dresses and bracelets and hairpins—that's what makes my sister's light shine. We are so different that sometimes I cannot believe we are related.

There's a rush of footsteps and the sliding of doors, then Vanna appears in the courtyard.

The sight of her never fails to stun me. Her black hair, soft as waterbird feathers, cascades down her back in a silken sheet, and her eyes, framed by thick dark lashes, are bright with excitement. The mysterious light in her chest, which has grown more brilliant since she was a baby, emanates through the layers of her robes.

Our stepmother embraces her, and Adah is there too. He's smiling with his mouth open. He's in a good mood. They all are.

A sparrow demon sits on my windowsill, its wings fraying with smoke. I feed it a chili pepper for breakfast. Then, as it flies away, satiated, I cut a pepper of my own and scrape its seeds onto my eggs. My belly growls, hungry from my morning hunt. Even if no one else eats, I will.

I wolf down my breakfast, letting the spice warm my tongue as I listen to Vanna laugh. The sound is music, sweeter than the songbirds at dawn—and worlds away from the Demon Witch's vengeful promise.

Vanna's laugh swirls round and round as she dances in her new dress. Lintang spent weeks embroidering moon orchids and butterflies onto the skirt, for once able to convince my stingy adah to buy the finest dyed threads for her to work with. As Vanna spins and twirls, a rainbow arches across the low hills behind us. Even the gods know better than to let it rain today.

I suspect that they've fallen under her power too. For when Vanna is happy—when that strange light inside her glows brightest—I swear she outshines the sun. Her radiance touches every living creature around her, from Adah and Lintang to the butterflies and the lizards, the flowers and the trees. I myself am beaming.

33

Vanna blows me a kiss when Lintang isn't looking. I smile, tapping my feet to the beat of her dance until she suddenly stops.

"Enough dancing! You'll tire yourself."

It's Adah. He's rounding the orchard toward the kitchen, and I quickly shut the curtain before he glimpses me. I'm to stay hidden, in case one of Vanna's suitors visits our house before the binding selection this morning. Any sight of me, and Adah has promised to whip me so hard my backside will be the same texture as my face. A difficult thing to do, but Adah is strong for a man. Not as strong as I am, but he doesn't know that.

I've already swept all the floors and dusted every corner. The only task left is to make cakes—Vanna's request. I scoop the cassava I grated last night into a bowl and test its consistency with my fingers. Not enough moisture, so I sprinkle in a spoonful of water, then set about gathering the other ingredients.

I've made this recipe so many times that my hands move without thinking and the batter becomes alive to me, like clay in a potter's hands. Mama's cake is the only thing I have left of her. The sound of her voice, the soft outline of her face—they're all scraps of memories that I'm desperate not to lose.

Sometimes I wish Vanna looked more like her. But my sister looks nothing like any woman who walks this earth.

And neither do I.

"I'm going to get my veil, Adah," I hear Vanna say. "I'll be right back."

Her voice is high with excitement. She's a good actress, and I'm sure she's convinced the entire village that she's thrilled to be the center of something as demeaning and ridiculous as a binding selection. But she can't convince me.

I'm contriving ways I can get out of the kitchen to talk sense into her and warn her about Angma when I hear someone behind me. The footsteps are light and rhythmic with a bounce. I'd know them in my sleep.

I don't turn around, even when I see the shadow of two outstretched arms reaching for my ribs. Instead, I speak: "I thought you said you were going to look for your veil."

Vanna groans. "You have the hearing of a bat."

"And you have the cunning of a mule. I'm not falling for that trick again."

"I wasn't going to frighten you this time. Just tickle you." My sister wiggles her fingers menacingly and reaches for my side.

I evade her easily. "I'm trying to work."

"How can you think about chores *today* of all days?"

"Not everyone gets the morning off for your selection," I reply. "Though I *am* shocked that you're awake. Usually you're snoring in your bed until noon."

Vanna crosses her arms indignantly. "I do not snore."

"Tell that to the crows on the roof." I turn to her, hiding a smile. "They'd disagree."

"Not funny." Vanna pretends to be upset, but she can't help smiling too. "Must you always be such a grouch?"

"Yes."

Vanna sticks out her tongue, and I let slip a tender smile.

Specks of sugar dot her nose, and her black hair is tangled about her shoulders from spinning. I would not change anything about her but the light flaring from her heart.

We still don't know what it is. Our shaman says she's blessed with the Light of Gadda, but he'd say anything to attract more coin to his temple. Part of me wonders whether it's the light that Angma covets. Why Vanna is special.

"You should come outside," says Vanna, unaware of my thoughts. "You're always hiding in here."

"I have chores to do, unlike you. You requested cakes, remember?"

"Can I have a taste?" She tries to dip her finger into the batter, but I give her hand a light smack with my spoon.

"Not so fast. I still have to add pandan and coconut milk and—"

"White sesame," we say at the same time.

Mama's mystery ingredient. It took me years to figure out what it was, and it's a secret only Vanna and I share.

"Will the cakes be finished soon?" Vanna asks. "Mother's waiting to braid my hair, and you know how she doesn't like me eating too many sweets."

My smile vanishes, and I set down the mixing bowl with a thud. "You're old enough to eat whatever you want. And Lintang's not our mother. She's our stepmother."

"She's the only mother I know." Vanna's arms fall with a tinkle, gold and silver bangles pinging on her wrists. "I wish you didn't hate her so much."

"I don't *hate* Lintang. She just . . . isn't our mother." I raise the bowl of batter. "*This* is our mother."

Vanna arches both eyebrows. "The cakes?"

"The smell." I inhale deeply. "Mama's hands smelled like coconut."

Vanna leans forward, greedy for any morsel of information about our mother, and I wish I had more to share with her than a few cakes. I wish I had more than a Demon Witch and her curse. But alas.

"Vanna," I begin, "do you remember the story I used to tell you when we were little?"

My sister knows exactly where this is going. She lets out a sigh and crumples onto a stool. "About Angma and the snake that cursed your face?"

"*Angma* cursed my face," I say, correcting her. "Listen to me: your birthday is three days away. Angma promised to come and—"

"She isn't going to kill me," Vanna interrupts. "You were two years old."

"Closer to three."

"Don't you think it's possible you imagined all this? I know you believe you can talk to snakes, and you think your face is some horrible curse, but—"

"But what?" I say, deathly quiet.

I can hear the words she was about to say: *but maybe you were born this way.*

I wasn't born this way.

My sister realizes she's gone too far. She bites down on her lip, then says, "I want you to be happy."

My jaw tightens. I turn my back to her, sprinkling too much pandan juice into the batter. "I *am* happy."

"You can't be happy while you nurture this obsession with Angma. I thought you'd forgotten about it in all the preparation for the selection ceremony, but then I saw you go out this morning. You were in the jungle hunting tigers again, weren't you?"

I reach for the paring knife that's behind the coconuts. How did she make this conversation be about me? I'm supposed to be warning *her* about Angma.

"Look outside, Channi. There isn't a cloud in the sky. Don't you think, with my birthday so near, there would be some sign of the Demon Witch? A swarm of termites or bats? A storm, at least. When was the last time anyone saw her? She's only a legend—even Adah says so."

I hide a grimace. Adah will say anything to set his conscience at ease.

But it's true. Angma hasn't appeared in years. Maybe she isn't a threat anymore and I've become obsessed with hunting a ghost. Maybe. But I'm not willing to take the chance.

With my back to Vanna, I slip the knife into my pocket.

"I know you've been unhappy," she is saying. "Things will get better after today. You'll see. The selection is a boon for both of us. Adah thinks I'll marry a king—perhaps even an emperor." She greets a butterfly that's landed on her shoulder. "We'll start a new life together. In a palace."

In the past, whenever we've talked about her binding selection, it always ends in an argument. But today I'm silent. I want to understand how she justifies it to herself.

"Imagine it," Vanna goes on. "We'll be fancy ladies taking strolls in the garden in our silk gowns, and musicians will have to sing whenever we return to our villas. We'll gossip about who's romancing whom, we'll host poetry contests and decorate cakes with fresh lilies and orchids—"

Honestly, I'd rather gouge out my scales one by one than spend my life cloistered in some castle, idly gossiping and decorating cakes with flowers. Yet seeing Vanna so hopeful makes me want such things, if only to please her. Such is my sister's power. Such is my love for her.

But I am, as she said earlier, a grouch.

"I *am* imagining it," I say, "and you forget one important factor, sister. *My face*."

Vanna comes close, and she tucks my stripe of white hair behind my ear. "I never forget about your face, Channi," she says tenderly. "I've learned to see past it. Just as I know everyone else will."

There's a firm press to her words, like she's determined to make this so. Normally, I wouldn't doubt her. Her radiance is powerful. When she learns to master its power, she might hold an entire army in her thrall.

But she'll not be able to change a single mind about me. I know this because I am as monstrous as she is beautiful. Our power is equal in that way.

The butterfly on her shoulder grows jittery, alarmed by my nearness. Vanna tries to console it with a few soft words. I should take a step back, but I don't. The butterfly flutters out the window, and my sister and I are alone once more.

"Help me with the batter," I say, before our silence grows

an edge. "You add the coconut milk. I'll take care of the sugar."

While Vanna obeys, I reach for the small sack of sugar in the corner of the shelf. Sugar's expensive, but thanks to my sister, we have more than anyone else in Sundau. When we were poor, I used to collect sap from palm flowers to make Mama's cakes. It'd take me hours for only a few drops, but I never minded. The chore was my favorite; I loved the excuse to be outside—and I wanted Vanna to have something to remember Mama by.

Then one day, a lost merchant docked his boat not far from our hut. He'd misread his map and ended up in Sundau instead of the main islands. When he saw Vanna, glowing like the sun while she ate cakes beside the reedy quay, he dropped to his knees and bowed as if she were a goddess incarnate.

That same day, he delivered a barrel of sugar to our door, asking only that Vanna speak a few words of blessing for his business. Then he left, and Adah clasped Vanna's shoulders proudly. "So it begins," he told her.

I thought Adah was being delusional. But it turned out I was the fool, not he. Soon more merchants came, docking at Sundau and bringing reams of rose-dyed silk, tins of tea from the far ends of the Spice Road, porcelain cups and plates, and stacks of gold coins, which Lintang secretly buried in the courtyard so the neighbors wouldn't steal them (and Adah couldn't gamble them away at tiles).

Thanks to Vanna, everything changed. Adah no longer needed to work on the cassava farm, and I didn't have to collect sap anymore. We moved into a house with a courtyard, and no one missed our old lives, our old hovel by the jungle. Except me.

The batter is nearly ready, and I breathe in its sweet aroma, thankful that at least my cakes haven't changed.

It's tradition for Vanna and me to add the secret ingredient last, together. At the same time, we each toss a pinch of white sesame into the batter. Vanna doesn't waste a second trying to get a taste, and this time I don't stop her.

"Mmm." She licks the batter off her finger. "I don't know how you do it."

"Good?"

"Divine. Now hurry and steam them so I can eat a dozen before the ceremony."

I chuckle. I'm not indifferent to praise, and a part of me puffs up with pride as I start dividing the batter. "You should have a contest where all your suitors make cakes. I wonder who would win."

Vanna flushes. She tries to hide it by turning to the window, which only makes her feelings more obvious.

"Is there someone you *want* to win?"

There's a falter in her countenance, but she covers it up quickly. "The richest one, of course," she responds automatically, "with the biggest palace."

It's an answer Adah's trained into her, and I'm curious if she'll follow through. Secretly, I suspect she has a lover. The other day, I found a note in her pocket, folded into thirds.

*You are the light that makes my lantern shine,* it read.

It's a beautiful turn of phrase, like a line from a poem.

It makes me respect whoever wrote it for her. I only hope Adah doesn't find out.

"There's Prince Rongyo," I say. "He's supposed to be your age."

"Adah didn't invite princes, only kings."

I set the cakes into the steamer, close the lid. "What if the richest is King Meguh?"

Vanna tenses. The color in her cheeks drains away, and I immediately regret asking.

"Meguh is old," she replies. "It wouldn't be so bad. He'll probably die within a few years, and then I'll be rich and free."

I hope King Meguh is having breakfast as we speak, and choking to death on a slagfruit seed.

I lower my voice. "Vanna, are you sure this is what you want? To be auctioned off like a . . . a prize sow?"

"I am not a sow."

"You know that's not what I mean."

"It's tradition for a girl to have a dowry—so why not a man?" Vanna interrupts, on the verge of snapping. "Why shouldn't Adah pick the most generous one? The money will go to the temple, to the future of Puntalo Village—"

"I couldn't care less about Puntalo Village," I say over her. "I care about *you*. Vanna, the last selection ceremony was a hundred years ago. It's obscene that you should have one."

She bites down on her lower lip to stop its trembling, and bunches the fabric of her dress in her hand. "The selection is our chance for a better life."

"Vanna . . . ," I say. I know my sister. She wears a mask of her own, except hers is that of the perfect young lady everyone expects her to be. Modest and meek, without a thought for herself. She's trying so hard to be perfect, to please everyone, and yet, in doing so, she is forgetting herself. "Enough about me. Is this what you want?"

Vanna lets go of her skirt. "Princesses are still traded away for lands and alliances. Is that so different? I want to get out of Sundau, and this is the best way." The light inside her grows cloudy, and her expression darkens. "Don't bother trying to convince me otherwise. Adah and I have discussed it. I will be a great lady. Maybe even a queen. And when I am, I'll be able to do anything I wish."

She sounds so sure that her future will be better than her past. I wish I had the same certainty, but kings do not make queens of peasant girls.

"Marriage isn't the only way to become a great lady," I say. "Look at you. You are radiant, you are powerful. Do you not understand how much people love you and want to please you? If only you'd learn to wield that light. . . ."

My words trail off as Vanna covers her heart with her hands. Light still spills through the seams between her fingers. "I know what you're thinking. If you were in my place, you'd have mastered it. You'd never let anyone determine your fate." She looks up at me, and her voice falls soft. "But I'm not as brave as you are."

For the first time I see that she's frightened. My shoulders drop.

I'm not a perfect sister. I've been envious of Vanna, even

resented her at times. Yet great beauty is not always a gift; it can be as much a curse as great ugliness. Better than anyone, I understand the burden she bears.

"At least tell Adah you need more time," I say gently. "He won't deny you. Make the suitors prove themselves. Ask for things no one can procure: ten thousand mosquito hearts on silver platters, a bridge of gold connecting our home to the sun, a—"

"I don't want to postpone the selection. The longer I stay here, the longer I stay a child. I'm not a child anymore."

"Vanna . . ."

She lifts her chin. "I'm going to become a queen, and you're going to come live with me in my palace. We'll bicker over trivial things and grow old together." She clasps my hand, and her heart beams. "You've always protected me, Channi. Let me do something for you. We'll sail across the world and find a way to break the curse on your face. I swear it."

*I thought you didn't believe it was a curse,* I almost say. There's a twinge in my chest I can't ignore. Vanna can look past my face better than anyone, but never once has she asked me what *I* want.

I force a smile. "Until then I guess we're stuck with my snake eyes."

Vanna smiles back, not hearing the bitterness creeping into my voice. "They'll be useful in court. You can use them to mesmerize my enemies."

I can't look her in the eye. "If I had that power, I'd just make everyone forget I'm here."

The light in Vanna's heart dies a little. She opens her mouth to say something cheering, but Adah calls for her from outside: "Vanna! What's taking you so long? Lintang wants to braid your hair."

My sister turns to me, an unspoken apology creasing her brow. "Save some cakes for me, and then get changed. Please? We're going soon."

As she leaves, I wipe my hands dry, ignoring how they tremble.

---

When the cakes are ready, I set a dozen aside for Vanna, two for me, and three on a clay plate. I place it in front of Mama's shrine, which I keep by my cot across the kitchen.

Adah used to pray to her when he thought I wasn't looking. The moments I spied him kneeling at her altar were the only times I ever felt respect for my father. But they grew fewer and further between, until he stopped altogether a few years ago.

I still pray, every day. I crouch by the shrine, lighting a fresh bundle of incense and placing it in the tin cup next to a figurine of Mama. I carved it when I was younger, when I could still remember the lines of her face, her eyes, her smiling lips. It used to be bigger than both my hands . . . but now that I'm grown, I can hold the entire statue in one.

*What's the matter, my moon-faced girl?* I would imagine Mama saying. *What do you wish for?*

When I was younger, I wished to escape my curse. So

many times, I took a knife to my face, biting down on a cloth and holding in my screams while I tried to nick off my scales, as if they were mere thorns on a flower. But overnight, the cuts would heal, and I'd see the monster in the mirror again. Trapped.

Now that I am grown, I have a different wish. A secret wish I've buried so deep I dare not say it aloud.

I wish that one day someone will love me. Someone will look me in the eyes without fear or pity. Someone will take away the loneliness etched in my heart so that I will know what it's like to be loved. So I can laugh without tasting the bitterness on my tongue once the sound fades.

I bend my head so Mama won't see the tears pooling in my eyes.

"Help me watch over Vanna today, Mama," I whisper, rubbing my thumb over the statue's face. I press my forehead to the ground. "Help keep her safe from Angma, from Meguh, from anyone who would wish her harm."

I wave the incense at Mama's altar, realizing I didn't ask her to protect me too. But there's no need.

I'm already a monster. What fear need I have of the Demon Witch?

# CHAPTER FOUR

An elephant trumpets outside, making the kitchen's gables tremble. It's not a sound one hears often on this side of the island, so I peek out the window—and my heart hums with dread.

King Meguh is here.

He rode an elephant the last time he came. A hairy little male barely taller than Adah, with ears that fanned out like wings, and a crown of reddish hair above its eyes. Vanna had doted on its long eyelashes and fed it mangosteens from her hand; the fruit's pink flesh stained the little elephant's tongue.

I didn't have the heart to tell her I'd found the calf abandoned the next day, just outside the jungle, with Meguh's purple banner draped over its back. I'd tried to help it, but Meguh's bodyguards had hacked off its ivory tusks and left it there to die. There was nothing I could do. So I sang to it, the gentlest song I could, and I sliced my palm and fed it my blood for a swift, merciful death. I'll never forget how mournful its young eyes looked, full of all the sorrow in the world—before they closed forever.

I have never been more ashamed to be human.

Lintang calls for Vanna, and I immediately slide the kitchen door shut, more afraid of King Meguh than of Adah's threats to beat me if I am seen. There is something cruel about Meguh's eyes—poets bend the truth and say they are soft as brushstrokes, but to me they are knives. Merciless and sharp. I've heard about the menagerie he keeps in his palace—hundreds of creatures caged solely for his pleasure—and the arena he's built to watch grown men kill one another. I see how his servants quail every time he looks at them, and how blue and yellow bruises peek out of their purple sleeves.

Everyone says Vanna ought to pick him. Meguh is the wealthiest king in the Tambu Isles: his island is belted by volcanoes rich with gold, and he has been generous, sending gifts every year.

But I worry. Life with him could be worse than death at the hands of the Demon Witch.

Outside, Vanna is singing, no doubt at Meguh's request. Her sweet voice entices birds and butterflies to her side, the purest proof of the divinity within her. Lintang is busy too, guiding the king's servants as they carry gifts to the main house. That leaves Meguh alone with Adah.

They were strolling in the garden, but now they've stopped to sit on a bench near the kitchen, not far from where Vanna is still singing. I crack the curtains open a little and lean forward to eavesdrop. Meguh's voice is brassy and deep; it booms through the wooden walls.

"Khuan, you insult me," he is saying. "Have you reason to doubt my intentions?"

"You are not the only king who's tried to win my daughter, Your Majesty. I only wish to make it fair. I would not want Vanna to be the cause of a war between—"

"It's that shaman of yours, isn't it?" Meguh interrupts. "Let me guess—he foresaw such a war between the sovereigns and devised the contest to keep things *fair*. How convenient that such a contest also showers his temple with gold."

That is exactly what happened, but Adah avoids answering. Years of dealing with Vanna's suitors has polished his speech. Instead, he says, "I could arrange it, if you were to make my daughter your wife—"

"I already have a queen," Meguh cuts him off curtly.

My ears perk up. It's said that Queen Ishirya is much adored by the fierce and brutal king, that she is the goddess of love, Su Dano, incarnate. I heard Lintang tell Vanna once that Ishirya is the real power behind Meguh's throne. I don't believe this story. Seeing the way Meguh struts about our island, I can hardly imagine him bowing down to anyone.

He must not win.

"Do not forget your place, Khuan," Meguh continues. "Your daughter's beauty may be divine, but her blood is common, no matter how your shaman says she is touched by the gods."

"My daughter is *descended* from the gods," Adah says. His tone wavers between thin and civil. "She glows with the light of Gadda and—"

"Now, now, Khuan. I mean no offense. Vanna is special. That much is clear. But my queen is the source of my gold, and without my gold, you wouldn't invite me here—now, would you?"

Adah smiles uneasily while Meguh bursts into laughter. His laugh is an ugly sound; it reminds me of the broken bell that peals from the Temple of Dawn every morning, harsh and unbalanced. I hear it even from the jungle.

As he laughs, I shake my head, thinking of how little I understand men. As I take out a cloth to catch a stray lizard that's going after my plate of Mama's cakes, I notice Meguh's beady eyes rake over my sister. I shudder with revulsion as he licks his lips, and my hand instinctively grips the hilt of my paring knife. I'll gut him if he ever harms her.

"I thought Bonemaker's Arena was the source of your gold," Adah is saying.

"Only recently," Meguh replies, stroking the giant white stone around his neck. It hangs from a heavy gold chain, like a moon enslaved. "You must come see it one day. I've even brought my best fighter with me, in case the contest for your daughter's hand needs to be settled in a more . . . *old-fashioned* way."

Adah's smile thins. A fight is the last thing he wants. This selection is supposed to be about gold, not bloodshed. "I have no doubt that you'll win her."

"I know, I know. You're simply trying to keep the peace, Khuan. I can appreciate that."

I curl my lip, disgusted with both Meguh and my father. In my hand, the lizard squirms free, leaping for the plate by Mama's shrine and burying itself in a sugary pillow of cake.

"Get away from there," I whisper. "That's disrespectful."

I lurch after the lizard, trying to grab it by its tail, but I might as well catch a fly with my fingernails. It hops onto the head of Mama's statue, and as its legs kick up, Mama falls back and rolls off the shrine—

She lands with a quiet thud.

Outside, Meguh rises from the bench. He tips his chin in my direction. "What was that?"

I duck, pressing my back against the wall. I dare not move, not even to close the curtains. The lizard scampers free, hopping out of the crack between the curtains.

"Th-th-that?" Adah splutters. "I didn't hear anything."

"Sounds like you're hiding something."

"No. No. That . . . that was nothing. Probably a monkey."

"I'm certain I saw someone." Meguh's voice grows closer, and I sink deeper into a shadow. "I heard you have another daughter, Khuan. One who is rather . . . unique."

I stiffen. *Unique* is not a word commonly used to describe me.

"I'd rather not speak of her, Your Majesty."

King Meguh's curiosity is piqued. "So it's true: she's a monster."

I don't need to hear Adah's response. I lift myself slowly and peek out at my father and the king.

Adah makes me hide whenever one of Vanna's suitors comes to call so the sight of me won't diminish my sister's

51

value. But with Meguh, I sense there's more to it. With the others, Adah will lock me in the rice barn or banish me to the kitchen. When Meguh calls, it's Lintang, not Adah, who comes for me. She doesn't make me hide—she makes me leave the house altogether.

*Quickly now,* she'll tell me. *Off to the jungle.*

Adah never sends me to the jungle.

*But what about my chores?*

*Never mind that. Go. Don't come back until the torch on the gate has been lit.*

The first time, I was confused. I thought I was being punished, but Lintang is never cruel to me, even though her kindnesses are rare. Not until years later, when I first saw Meguh, did I understand that she pitied me. That was when I started to stay.

"Come now, relax." Another laugh rumbles from Meguh's bulging throat. "You're about to be a rich man."

Their voices grow distant, and I hear the elephant trumpet once more as the servants prepare the mount. I creep forward as Vanna and Lintang escort the king out of the courtyard. My sister bows to Meguh, and his servants bestow on Adah more gifts and flowers. But as King Meguh climbs onto the back of his elephant, he steals another glance in the direction of the kitchen.

In the direction of *me*.

I duck again, but not fast enough. I catch a flash of his merciless black eyes through the stripe of my open window— like a hunter intent on finding his prey.

My heart hammers as I drop to the ground. I dare not

breathe, not until the noise from Meguh's parade of servants fades. Only then do I peek up. The light hurts my eyes, but the king of Shenlani is indeed gone, his last servant rounding the bend from the courtyard into the village.

I shut the curtain and collapse into a corner, hugging my knees to my chest as dread mounts inside me, knotted tight and tense.

Gadda be kind, I pray that Meguh did not see me.

# CHAPTER FIVE

When my heartbeat steadies, I leave the kitchen and find Adah tending to his white stallion, a gift from Meguh last year.

Time has weathered my father's face, and wrinkles crease the area around his eyes. He stoops when he walks, and Lintang often threatens to tie a wooden rod to his spine so he'll stand straight.

He needs no reminder today. Anyone can tell how eagerly he anticipates the rank and fortune his radiant daughter is about to bring him. He's wearing his best tunic, and his beard's been trimmed. Today, a brighter future awaits him.

Even though he's in a good mood, sweat slicks my temples as I approach him, and it is not just from the humidity.

I try to temper the emotions I have for my father, but it's hard. When we lived in our old house, he would make me go out into the fields to scare away the crows pecking at our banana tree. All I had to do was show my face, and the birds exploded into the sky in terror.

I've never forgotten how eerily their shrieks sounded like my own.

At least this new house has no banana trees. It faces east and does not have stilts, since there is little flooding on this side of our island. There is a courtyard, a rice barn, a free-standing hut that we use as the kitchen, and two separate buildings—one for sleeping, and one for entertaining. The move was very exciting for Vanna and Lintang, but I still miss our old place by the jungle, the hut we lived in before Adah cared more about money than his daughters.

Vanna is far from earshot, praying at the courtyard shrine with Lintang, but I keep my voice quiet anyway, almost a mumble: "Adah."

Adah is stroking his stallion's mane. I half expect him to pretend I'm not here, but he sets the brush aside and says, "I've told you never to go outside without your mask on."

A flash of anger stabs my chest. I smother it and drag my mask out of my pocket. It is plain, unlike the skin I wear. The rough wood clings to the ridges on my scales, sticky with humidity, but what I hate most is how hard it is to breathe when I'm wearing it. There's only a thin slit for my mouth, and nothing for my nose, which is flat against my skull anyway—like a snake's.

Adah carved it for me soon after I was cursed. He spent days pounding the bark and sanding the wood down until it was smooth. Back then, it was too big, and I had to tie it around my head with a string. Still, though I despise it, it's a reminder that he once cared.

It was so long ago it's almost a dream, but I still remember the relief in his eyes when he first saw me the morning Mama died. "You're alive," he had breathed, rushing to embrace me. "Angma didn't take you."

I remember how that relief slowly curdled into horror, and how he washed my face again and again, growing rougher with each attempt. I remember how he struggled to look at me with tenderness, and how, eventually, he gave up. When the rest of the village came to shun me, it was easier for him to join them than it was to defend his own daughter. And now here we are.

My mask is on. I breathe in and try again. "Adah."

"What is it?"

"I'd like to go to Vanna's binding selection."

Adah stiffens. It is perhaps the only trait my father and I share, how we both become agitated in the same way. His jaw locks, and his shoulders go straighter than the horizon.

When our eyes meet, the narrow slits of my pupils are reflected in his. I do not look away. Whatever power I can claim over Adah, I will take. And I will not be the first to look away.

He flinches and averts his gaze. "You are forbidden to enter the village."

"But—"

"It's for your own good." He's trying to contain his anger, unlike most days. "No one's seen you in years. They've almost forgotten about you."

"I'll keep quiet," I insist. "I'll stand behind someone's tent, out of sight."

"No is no."

"Vanna wants me there. No one will notice me."

At that, Adah raises a square hand. Fury hardens his eyes, and I go still, waiting for him to strike. But Vanna is too close. She'd see.

The tassels on his sleeve sway as he lowers his arm.

"Do you really think no one would notice *you*?" he says harshly. "King Meguh nearly saw you just now. That face of yours could have cost your sister everything. Everything!"

Emotions cling to my throat. I can't breathe. "Why is it always about my face?"

"It's who the fates have made you. A monster."

My tongue itches to tell him he's the monster, not me. But I don't argue. I fear that if I do, I will cry. And I promised myself long ago I would never weep in front of my father.

It's because of Vanna that he tolerates me. I know that every time I disappear into the jungle he wishes that I would never come back. But I do, only to feel the pain again and again of a wound that will not close. To feel the hope that Adah will one day open his eyes and remember I am his daughter too.

Adah and I face off, locked in our second standstill of the day, when Vanna calls out from the shrine in the courtyard. "Look, look!" she squeals.

My sister's voice knifes through the tension between us, and Adah goes to her. She's twirling into the courtyard with moon orchids in her hair—her favorite flower, matching the embroidered ones on her skirt.

"Aren't they beautiful?" she exclaims, touching her braids.

"Now you are a woman," Lintang says, picking a stray leaf off Vanna's shoulder before ushering her to the gate. "Careful down the steps. The mud from the rains last week still hasn't dried. Don't step on the carpet with your wet feet."

Vanna glances back, noting the distance between Adah and me before I retreat to a shadowed corner. A crease furrows her smooth brow, and to Lintang's dismay, my sister hurries toward me. She touches my shoulders. "Channi, why are you hiding like this? Come. Come."

She tries to nudge me to the front, but Adah won't allow it. "Get back inside, Channi."

Vanna blocks me. "Why should she go back inside? I want her to come."

"Hurry, Vanna. You'll be late." He lifts a confused Vanna onto the stallion. It nickers and kicks, spying me in my corner. Horses do not like snakes, and that includes me.

"Channi is coming," says Vanna. She whirls on Adah. "Or I will—"

"You will what?" Adah is irritated at Vanna, but his eyes are on me. "You won't go?"

My stepmother casts me a harrowed glance, as if it's my fault that she'll have to make peace and lie to Vanna. "Enough, Vanna," she soothes my sister. "Of course Channi is coming. Adah will take you to the village first. I'll walk behind you, and Channi will follow once she's finished washing the courtyard stones."

I hate myself for not speaking up, but Adah and Lintang are happiest when they forget I exist, and Vanna is happiest when everyone else is happy. So I force a smile and watch them leave. Vanna waves from her horse and blows me a kiss, but I pretend not to see. It hurts less that way.

My eyes drift to the little houses down the pebbled path. Many of our neighbors hurry out of their homes to join Vanna's entourage.

"Good luck with the contest, Vanna!" they shout.

"Khuan, your daughter grows prettier every day!"

"Find her a rich one, Khuan!"

The voices grow faint, and once Adah, Lintang, and Vanna disappear down the slope of the dirt road, I take off my mask and let my face breathe.

"Pathetic, Channi," I mumble at myself. "Pathetic."

I kick the wall, hating Adah, the binding selection, and Vanna for going along with it. Hating myself for being a coward.

Puntalo Village isn't far. I *could* go. I used to sneak out when I was younger, while Adah and Lintang worked at the cassava farms. I would ask anyone, *everyone,* what they knew of Angma and if they'd heard of Hokzuh.

The last time I went, Adah caught me. As punishment, he dragged me to the river and threw me in. I couldn't swim, and he waited—almost too long—before fishing me out.

"If I catch you going to the village again," he warned me as I coughed up river water, "next time I won't save you."

For the rest of the day, he locked me in the rice barn, and he forbade Vanna from visiting. My sweet little sister came anyway, with hardboiled eggs she'd snuck into her pockets from dinner. While I gobbled them down, she hugged me.

"You shouldn't disobey Adah," she said. "It only angers him."

How serious she sounded, as if *she* were the older one, not me.

"But Angma—"

"You can't protect me if Adah hurts you," she said. She'd kept one egg, still hot, and carefully rolled it over my bruises and swollen eyes. "Don't let him hurt you. I need you, Channi."

*I need you, Channi.*

Words that undo me, even when I am only remembering them.

In the following weeks, Vanna took me to the river. Every morning, with the patience of the goddess Su Dano, she taught me to float, to work through the fear of my reflection, to swim.

For so many years, I've been focused on saving her life. I forget how many times, in little ways, she's saved mine.

I grab my mask and put on my sandals. It doesn't matter whether Angma will show herself today, or whether she will wait for Vanna's birthday. Angma is not the only monster that walks this earth.

My sister needs me, and I will not let her down.

# CHAPTER SIX

It is midmorning, and I dart across the wide street, pressing my hood over my head as I move from shadow to shadow. So far, no one has noticed me. I need to keep it that way.

There must be over a thousand people crammed into Puntalo's tiny market—the entire village and then some. Everyone is dressed in their finest. Women wear lilies around their necks and begonias in their hair, and the men have brightened their sun-faded tunics and pants with beaded necklaces and brass bangles. Crisp knots of pandan leaves hang from every stall; they serve to repel roaches as well as freshen the air. I can hardly smell the horse dung that carpets the dusty streets.

I weave my way deeper into the market. Today is different, even if it doesn't look different. The local peddlers and merchants have all laid out their wares—baskets of curries and spices, copper pans of ginger rice and shrimp noodles, along with spiky durians, ripe bananas, and hairy rambutans piled on coarse blankets—but no one is shouting them out to entice potential buyers. The entire market is frozen, and everyone clusters in the center courtyard, waiting for a glimpse of the kings, for a glimpse of my sister.

Before I lose my nerve, I climb a stack of fruit crates and hoist myself up the pole of an empty merchant stall. After I lift my legs onto the awning, I duck my face out of sight.

*What a coward you are,* my inner voice rebukes. *You're not afraid of tigers, but you fear a bunch of harmless villagers?*

The reason's obvious. When I was younger, boys and girls my age would throw pebbles whenever they saw me, snickering and hooting when they hit. During monsoon season, they'd gather outside my kitchen and sing:

> *Channi, Channi, Monster Channi.*
> *Rain and wind and gloom all day.*
> *When the sun sees your face,*
> *It goes away. . . .*

I can run faster than a sunbird flies. I can throw a knife behind my head and still hit the target. I can nick off my scales and have them heal overnight. Yet I can't stop the pain that such taunts bring.

Which is why my heart leaps with dread when a young man calls from below: "I would rethink that hiding spot if I were you."

I recognize the voice, and my stomach pinches when I look down and confirm its owner: a scrawny young shaman with lank black hair and a bright orange scarf over his shoulder.

Oshli.

I flatten myself against the roof's awning. *Gods be merciful, make him go away.*

The gods are not merciful. Oshli crosses his arms and all but stakes himself in front of my tent. "Shouldn't you be at the temple with your sister and your parents?"

"No."

"Why not?"

My face folds. He knows why not.

"Come, Channari, I'll take you to the front myself. They're about to start."

It's unlike Oshli to be so considerate. Usually it's a game between us: who can ignore the other better.

"What are you doing here?" I ask. "Shouldn't you be with your father?"

"That's my business." Oshli's teeth are locked, and his arms hang stiffly at his sides. "Will you stop hiding up there and come down? Vanna would want you at her side."

"You go. She seems to prefer *you* when we're in the village."

Oshli makes no reply, but his lips twist unhappily, informing me that something's amiss between them.

Interesting. The roof creaks under my weight as I edge forward, just a little. "Did you quarrel?"

"I told her she's a fool to go through with this," Oshli says, somehow both ignoring my question and answering it. "I told her to run away. Now she won't speak to me."

"Of course she won't speak to you," I retort. "Vanna's waited her whole life for today. Why would she run away?" I can't resist adding the barb: "To be with you?"

Oshli's expression turns dark.

It's a low blow, but I don't care. It's no secret he's in love with Vanna. Thankfully, my sister is too sensible to fall for a penniless, unsmiling shaman half a head shorter than her. Still, I'm irked that she likes him and that, at least in public, he's supplanted me as her best friend and confidante.

"What do you want from me?" I ask. "To talk some sense into her? To stand by her side while the kings bid for her hand? It's *your* father who's leading this damned show. *You* do something about it."

"I'm trying. Why do you think I'm talking to you?" His dark eyes rake over my hiding place. He shakes his head. "Forget it."

He stalks off. With his back to me, he throws a barb of his own: "I thought you loved her."

I watch him go, my heart hardening against the sting of his words. Old memories resurface: of him throwing rocks at my face, of him putting flowers in Vanna's hair and laughing with her as though I didn't exist. That fool wants to question my love for Vanna? He deserves neither my thought nor my time.

Still, I hate that his words rattle me, echoing in my ears until the marketplace's blessed noise drowns them out. A horn is blaring. It draws my attention to the Temple of Dawn, where the priests are clearing a way through the crowds. The procession of suitors is about to begin.

I didn't think I'd be nervous, but my breath goes shallow. This is it, the start of Vanna's selection ceremony. The event could be as short as a day; if it were up to me, it would take months. However long it takes, in the end everything will be different.

I hide my face behind a lantern and sit up, suddenly missing Ukar. I wish he were here.

*I'll be there for you when you need me to fight Angma,* he said. *But to watch your sister be paraded about like some prize to be won? I have no desire to witness such a spectacle.*

Neither do I.

But what a spectacle it is.

Eleven kings have come, carried forth on silver litters and gilded palanquins and in carriages drawn by fine Caiyan stallions. In the back, smiling smugly, as if he considers himself the grand finale, is King Meguh on his elephant.

My stomach burns at the sight.

"King Hoa Tho of Pakkien Island," announces High Priest Dakuok, Oshli's father. He is several suitors behind. "King Leidaya of Balam Island!"

On it goes. Here is more royalty than most will see in a lifetime, but I'd bet Adah is disappointed with the turnout. He was expecting dozens of suitors from across the world: the khagans of A'landi, the emperor of Samaran, the kings of Balar, and perhaps even the high queen of Agoria herself.

So far, there is only one suitor from beyond the isles. He's arrived with a meager entourage of two servants, and he walks instead of rides in a carriage or a litter. The other kings are already scoffing at him.

Steadily the royals make their way to the Temple of Dawn. Constructed entirely of stone, it's shaped like the tip of a spear: rounded along the sides but pointed at the top. From my vantage, it's piercing a cloud in the sky, and sunlight sieves down upon the stone walls. Or maybe that's Vanna's light.

While her suitors line up at the bottom of the temple steps, Vanna glides out from behind an orchid-festooned door and at last makes her appearance.

A wispy veil obscures her face. Its color matches the faded gold carved into the temple walls. At her sides are Adah and Lintang. Adah sports a prosperous bulge in his belly, and Lintang stands proudly beside him, jade disks dangling brightly from her ears as she holds her chin high.

I feel a tug on my heartstrings. With Vanna in the center, they appear a beautiful family. No one would guess someone was missing.

At my father's other side is High Priest Dakuok. His eyebrows have gone gray since the last time I saw him, but they are as slippery as ever, like eels that cannot stay still.

"Behold the fairest of all!" he cries over the marketplace. "Vanna Jin'aiti of Sundau, chosen of the gods. See how she glows with the light of the very sun."

The commotion fades as Vanna steps forward. Many have never seen her before, and even under the brilliant sun the light in her chest shimmers with a heavenly intensity. The anticipation of her unveiling grows with every second. Many in the crowd drop to their knees, while the kings in the front lean forward, like gnats drawn to a flame.

It's repugnant. Obscene. If Vanna were anyone but my sister, I would leave in disgust.

But she *is* my sister, and I watch on, unable to tear my gaze away.

"Great rulers of Tambu and beyond," Dakuok says, summoning the royals' attention. "Many of you have heard of the Golden One's radiance . . . and disbelieved it. But witness for yourselves the light shining from her heart. The luminous Vanna is blessed not only with divine beauty but also by the gods of prosperity. Her song will turn your rains into silver. Her touch will turn the sands of your shores into gold!"

Dakuok is more showman than priest, and I roll my eyes at anyone who'd believe his lies. If Vanna has such power, why is our temple in a state of disrepair and our island so poor it does not even have a proper port?

"Show us her face!" clamors the crowd.

"Yes, show us her face!"

"Patience," Dakuok responds. "Patience." He smiles. "From the moment I saw her as a mere baby, I knew that the Golden One was a goddess reborn, a celestial maiden fallen from Heaven. For any mortal to claim her hand, they must first prove themselves worthy."

I hear snorts and sniffs from the direction of the royals. Kings are not used to being told they are unworthy.

"Great rulers," says Dakuok, "before we begin these proceedings, I would ask a trifling favor of you. On behalf of this sacred island of Sundau, I ask that you swear a vow before Heaven and Earth to honor the results of the Golden One's selection contest, and that you will not have dispute with whoever should win her hand."

The snorts and sniffs turn into roars of laughter.

"Do you think that your girl's so special we'll fight a war over her?" a suitor jeers.

"We haven't even seen her!"

"Exactly," muses Dakuok loudly. He angles himself toward Vanna. "You haven't seen her."

I might hate Oshli's father, but he is more meticulous and foresighted than most kings. Everyone's anticipation doubles, even mine.

"*I* have seen her," yells Meguh from atop his elephant, "and I will swear!"

The kings quickly change their tunes. If Vanna is good enough for Meguh, then she is good enough for them. One by one they agree to Dakuok's request. Last to swear is the foreign king with the tiny retinue, whose voice is so soft that it's barely audible.

When it is done at last, Adah nods at my sister. Her light shimmers nervously, but slowly she comes forward on the dais, the hem of her bright skirts brushing against the floor.

She lifts her veil.

It is like opening a window and seeing the first sun after a long monsoon. Her radiance floods the temple, chasing away every shadow, illuminating every dark corner. Even those who have seen her before gasp.

"The stories are true!" everyone whispers. "Hair, blacker than the richest lacquer. Lips, pink as the begonia blossoms in spring. Skin, kissed with gold."

Perfection.

The kings are humbled, and their snide remarks die on

their lips. The entire village takes a collective breath. Except me. I exhale, releasing the air inside me.

This is it, I realize. The final moment that my sister Vanna, the Golden One, is a mere rumor, the topic of far-flung gossip tossed from one island to the other. From now on, she will be a legend.

I reach for the paring knife in my pocket and press its blade to one of the wooden poles holding up the tent. Slowly, patiently, I scrape upward, beginning to shape a spearpoint.

Over the years, I've learned to carry a weapon everywhere I go. Even in my dreams.

Call it prescience, call it vigilance; like Dakuok, I too know how to think ahead.

And when it comes to my sister, I will not take any chances.

# CHAPTER SEVEN

"You see I do not lie," declares Dakuok, looking smug. "The Golden One is beyond compare. Come now, great kings— show us how you are worthy."

The temperature of the assembly has changed. Breathless anticipation has now turned into a feverish frenzy, and the kings converge on the wooden steps leading up to the temple.

One after another, they saunter up to Vanna, and their servants leave gifts: barrels of wine, platters of gemstones and jade disks, spices worth their weight in silver, satin and brocade and silks in the most expensive, dazzling colors.

Vanna receives each presentation with grace. To everyone, she is the picture of serenity, but I know better. For all the gifts of her beauty, it brings torment as well. Her entire life, she has been guarded, with little freedom except the hours we steal together. Today, especially, she must feel the pressure. Each time someone approaches, inspecting her as though she were a ship or a sculpture rather than a living, breathing girl—there's a snag in her smile and a falter in her light.

I know my sister has a spine. By the time the fifth king steps up to be introduced, thank Gadda she finds it.

"Tell me about yourself," she says, her light trembling as she strides forward. "I don't need to know how wealthy you are, how many servants you have, or what gifts you have brought. Tell me instead, Your Majesty: What do you love?" She clasps her hands to keep them from shaking. "Why should I select you?"

This king stares, taken aback, as though he didn't realize she could speak. Then he puffs up with pride, misunderstanding Vanna's attention for interest.

"I am the sovereign of the Phan Isles," he replies. "I've eighty horses in my stables, and the finest collection of teas in all of Tambu. My palace is the size of your village—that is why you should choose me."

Vanna frowns. "I asked about you, not your kingdom. Who are *you*? Why do you come today?"

"Vanna!" Lintang grasps my sister's wrist, and I can read her lips: *What's gotten into you?*

Vanna stiffens, and she schools her expression back into its doll-like serenity. "Forgive me, Your Majesty. I was merely curious. I am grateful for your presence here."

She retreats with a bow, returning to her place beside Lintang. Her head is down, but her eyes are up, roaming across the assembly of villagers. Is she looking for me?

"I'm here," I whisper, daring to wave from my tent.

She doesn't see me. Her gaze goes to the cordon of young shamans separating the villagers from the temple. I can't tell if she finds Oshli among them. She sinks into a shadow and folds her hand over her chest, covering her light.

Gadda help me, I wish I were there with her.

She doesn't speak again, but the next suitors answer her questions anyway. One says that he likes music, and he actually sings for us, a pleasant ditty that has a few tapping their feet. Another is very religious and says he would build Vanna a golden shrine in her honor. Dakuok glances at the horizon, a sign that he is tiring of all the banter. At this rate, maybe the selection *will* take months.

Then comes King Meguh. He seems intent on rivaling Vanna's light, the rubies and emeralds on his fingers flashing as he dismounts from his elephant and cuts in front of Emperor Hanriyu for the stairs.

He saunters up, patting the white moonstone as it swings across his torso. Nine attendants trail him, carrying violet-ribboned baskets. No, violet-ribboned *cages*. I hear birds flapping against the rattan fibers, and the multi-voweled cry of a monkey.

Then his last gift, a lidded clay pot, comes into view.

My throat goes tight, and the roof under my body vibrates with my anger. I can feel snakes suffocating inside, tangled and trapped, their bodies so entwined they're like the threads in Lintang's embroidery basket.

"I figured you'd had enough of silks and spices," says King Meguh, flaunting his familiarity with Dakuok and Adah. "So I bring one of the great treasures from Shenlani."

An attendant carefully lifts the lid.

"From my personal menagerie," Meguh announces. "A

gift to the island of Sundau, in honor of the extraordinary beauty found in its daughter, Vanna Jin'aiti."

The most stunning serpents I've ever seen spring out of the pot, their vibrant azures and yellows rivaling the flowers sewn onto Vanna's dress.

My sister leaps back in fear, and two attendants brandish flaming torches at the snakes, who shudder and coil back into the pot.

*Lady Green Snake,* they hiss. *Help us. Free us.*

My teeth saw side to side. These are not garden snakes, nor are they the typical serpents one would find while traipsing through the jungle.

They're vipers. Rare ones. Poisonous ones.

A shiver spikes down my spine. King Meguh collects rare creatures. And Vanna is the rarest, most beautiful creature of all.

"Behold their exquisite markings," he is saying. "Their skin is worth more than gold." He smiles. "Like you, Vanna."

I feel singed by hatred. I seize the spear I've made, about to snap it off the tent. If Meguh comes even close to winning the contest, I will deliver him the same fate I have prepared for Angma.

But thankfully—or regrettably, depending on how you look at it—Meguh steps aside.

I let go of the spear.

"What about you, swan king?" Dakuok regards the last suitor—the only foreigner, Emperor Hanriyu. "You've not said a word."

At least three kings have cut in front of Hanriyu, yet he

made not a sound or complaint. Many will take that to be a weakness, but I'm intrigued. He stands out by wearing white, a simple robe unadorned by gold or jewel. While the other kings strut like peacocks before my sister, he is rooted to his place on the dais, black eyes distant like a spirit—half here and half not.

"I am Emperor Hanriyu of Kiata," he says in stilted, formal Tambun. He speaks slowly, clearly having rehearsed these words. It impresses me that he's bothered to learn our language. "My country is a week's sail north of your island. It is beautiful here, but warmer than I expected." He pats his neck with a folded handkerchief. "Forgive me if I am unaccustomed."

One of his servants carries a small carving of what I think is a swan. I've only heard of such a creature; its feathers are white as coconut flesh, with a long neck and doleful eyes that mirror the emperor's own. Except this one has a striking red crown on its head.

Vanna is equally curious. "What manner of bird is this?" she asks.

"In my land, we call it the bird of happiness. A crane."

"It's beautiful."

"They oft visit my home in the winter," Hanriyu replies. "The sight of one always brings me great joy. It is something I love."

My sister softens. "I think I can see why. Thank you for sharing this with me."

"Your statue is a paltry tribute to my daughter's radiance," Adah interrupts rudely. "You are from a faraway land, Your Majesty. Why should Vanna choose you?"

Hanriyu takes a moment to gather his words. "I'd heard that the Lady Vanna was radiant, but I did not expect it to be . . . literal. There is no enchantment in Kiata, you see."

My ears perk up. No magic in Kiata? Does that mean there are no demons there? Such a place is hard for me to imagine.

The emperor goes on, "My empress recently passed, leaving me with six young sons and a baby daughter." His voice grows hoarse; the wound in his heart is still raw. "She asked that I remarry so our children might have a mother, with the request that my new wife be kind and generous with her love. I'd heard the Lady Vanna was as benevolent as she was beautiful, so I'd hoped she might consider."

"You propose to marry my daughter?" Adah's interest is piqued. None of the other kings have promised marriage yet.

"I would wish to know her first," replies Hanriyu carefully, "and her me."

"That is not how things work here," Dakuok cuts in. "Vanna is a goddess incarnate, not a simple village girl. Her hand belongs to whoever can offer the most."

Vanna's brow creases with confusion. "My hand belongs to whomever I like the most." She turns to the priest. "I thought this was what we agreed. That *I* will choose."

"You speak out of turn, Golden One," Dakuok says curtly, shuttling Vanna back to her place. "Now, swan king . . . you were proposing to make the Golden One your queen? What tribute do you offer for that honor?"

Hanriyu looks unsettled. He glances at his fellow kings, who are smirking at his naïveté, then at Vanna, whose light has dulled to a flicker.

"I cannot make a proposal under such circumstances," he confesses at last. "I had anticipated that the Lady Vanna would choose her own suitor, but I see that I am mistaken, and it is best that I withdraw. Please, however, keep my gift as a token of my admiration."

Dakuok dismisses him with a wave, and Vanna bunches up her skirt in her fists. She's angry, but she's been trained to hold back her emotions. The last thing she'd do is make a scene.

This Kiatan king seems kind, and when he mentioned his children his eyes brightened. *A man who cares deeply about his children is a man I instinctively respect. A man entirely unlike my adah.*

*Then again, Kiata is an ocean away, so far that the sun is pale, and the rain is cold and white. I can't imagine Vanna thriving there, when she herself is warmth and light. She would be miserable.*

"The initial gifts are presented," Dakuok announces, waving his ceremonial staff, "and all the suitors are introduced. Now, we shall—"

"Wait," says Vanna.

"—invoke the gods to see whose stars best align with the Golden—"

"Wait!"

Dakuok lowers his staff. He smiles through his irritation. "Yes, Golden One?"

"I . . . I'd like time to consider the noble suitors who have come today." She exhales, then turns to the remaining kings on the platform. "Let us call for a respite. I'd like to speak to each of you in private and learn to know you, as His Majesty Emperor Hanriyu suggests."

"A prudent suggestion," says Dakuok. He places a hand on Vanna's shoulder. "But these are kings, not messenger boys. Do you understand, Vanna? Their realms need them, and already they show you great esteem by coming to our humble island. They have not the time to chatter with you."

Vanna twists away from the priest. "Perhaps they should. If I were in search of a queen, I would wish to know her."

"Therein lies the difficulty, Golden One." Dakuok lets out a sigh. "Your Majesties, who here is in search of a queen?"

The only response is a long and baleful silence.

It is in this moment that Vanna's strength crumbles. Dakuok and Adah have filled her head with fantasies of becoming a great lady, practically assuring her that she will be a queen. But reality is cruel.

Our family has no status or influence; we prosper only off the generosity of Vanna's admirers. Her sole value is the light in her heart and the tales Dakuok has crafted about its divinity and beauty. But as much as any might covet her, they also fear her, for her mysterious glow and its power. No king in his right mind would offer her a throne beside him.

Her light goes dim.

"You see?" Dakuok says. "The Lady Vanna is tired. Let us finish the selection quickly."

Vanna jerks. "That's not what I asked for—"

"Let us bid with gold."

Gold is a language the kings understand. Suddenly the selection ceremony takes a sharp and dangerous turn.

"I offer a thousand golden riels!" shouts one.

"Two thousand."

"Five thousand."

"Be generous with your gifts, Majesties," clucks Dakuok, "and be respectful. The lady is the Golden One, a daughter of the gods!"

"Ten thousand."

"Fifteen thousand, along with four Caiyan mares."

So on it goes. I stop watching the kings and focus on Vanna. When she isn't fidgeting with her skirt, she touches the flowers in her hair, as if they'd been pinned too close to her scalp. The light in her heart continues to flicker, no matter how she tries to still it.

Within minutes the price is at forty thousand, a sum greater than Adah had hoped for.

"Forty thousand?" Dakuok repeats. "King Narth'ii offers forty thousand in honor of the divine Vanna Jin'aiti. Will any other match his generosity?"

The bids continue. Vanna leans against Lintang, looking feeble. The way this is going, she will not be a queen as she'd hoped, but the mistress of a king.

I try to catch her attention, to signal that she could end this. But her earlier attempts to intercede have cowed her. I can read what she's thinking: that the gods of luck have always favored her, and so long as she wishes hard enough, she has a way of getting what she wants.

For her sake, I hope she gets her wish today. I only pray it will be everything she dreamed of, and not a nightmare.

King Meguh has not spoken, but his reticence is not due to uneasiness. It is a tactic. He's calculated for this moment, for when the kings have reached their highest offer and have no more in their purses to give.

His shout splinters the air. "Seventy thousand golden riels."

I nearly tumble off the roof. Seventy thousand golden riels? That is a tremendous sum, enough to buy an entire island.

Adah and Dakuok exchange a look, and my father starts to declare that King Meguh has won.

*No, no, no.* I tug at the sharpened pole, trying to work it free of the tent's canvas. I could easily spear Meguh in the heart from here. But then I'd be captured, and Vanna would be vulnerable to the Demon Witch.

I find Oshli among the villagers, his gaze already on mine.

*Do it,* he mouths.

My mind is made up, and Meguh is a breath away from being impaled—when a commotion breaks out at the other end of the square. The crowd parts as an unmarked palanquin appears in the square, heralded by a fanfare of drums and flutes.

"Wait!"

A handsome young man steps out of the palanquin, a thick and heavy gold chain slung across his chest. Neither Adah nor I recognize him, but Meguh does, and his expression turns tight with wrath.

I loosen my grip on the pole. It seems the gods of luck have come through for Vanna after all, conjuring a royal procession out of thin air to save her.

"I am Crown Prince Rongyo of Tai'yanan," announces the young man, slightly breathless, "and I offer my kingdom."

# CHAPTER EIGHT

The prince's announcement ripples across the marketplace. He stands there, holding out his gold chain as if to prove his title, and makes a slight bow to Adah. "I would marry your daughter," he declares. "She will be queen."

Adah's jaw hangs agape, and my sister brightens, her glow seeping through the layers of her robes.

"A bit young to choose your queen, aren't you?" King Meguh jeers. "The Lady Vanna deserves a king, not a prince. She deserves temples built in her honor. Are you sure your mother would agree to this, boy?"

"I am old enough to make my own decisions."

Meguh persists, "What are you, fifteen years?"

"Sixteen."

"Ah." Meguh stretches his hand toward Adah and Dakuok. "Sixteen years old, without the blessing of his mother to make such a ludicrous offer—"

"I am the crown prince of Tai'yanan," Rongyo says, shutting down Meguh's taunts. He doesn't sound like a mere boy anymore. "The only heir of the late beloved King Wan. In a year, I will be crowned. My word is good."

Rongyo steals a glance at Vanna. He looks younger than his age, especially next to Meguh and Leidaya, who both sprout gray in their beards. A few pimples dot the prince's boyish face, and his jaw has not finished squaring into manhood. Yet it is a pleasant face, and he seems like a pleasant young man.

If I were Vanna, I'd choose him . . . and on the way to his kingdom, I'd drug him with a dose of spindlebeard, steal his ship, and sail it to the far ends of Cipang or Agoria, where the lands are so vast that even destiny can be fooled.

It's a fantasy, I know, but it feels good to hope.

Adah and Dakuok are murmuring to each other. I knot my hands together, hoping they will have the sense to accept Rongyo's offer.

Finally, the shaman steps forward. "The crown prince of Tai'yanan offers marriage." He turns to the first in the line of competitors. "King Tayeh, can you match the offer?"

"I would marry her, but . . ." Tayeh hesitates. "But, no, I cannot match Prince Rongyo's offer."

"King Leidaya?"

Again, no.

"King Hoa Tho?"

One by one, the suitors resign and step off the temple's podium. All except Meguh.

"What about you, King Meguh?"

Meguh straightens. He is shorter than Rongyo but somehow seems to take up more room on the dais. Next to him, Rongyo looks like a reed. And Meguh is ready to break him.

Meguh's voice booms, "I cannot offer marriage, but I *can* promise one hundred thousand golden riels."

The buzzing in the marketplace shrivels into silence.

Dread prickles my gut. Prince Rongyo's kingdom is rich, but not as rich as Meguh's. Not half as rich as Meguh's. And he is not yet the king.

"I will match King Meguh," Rongyo says quietly. "In a year, when I am king, I will pay one hundred thousand golden riels."

Meguh snorts. "Take my word, the boy prince doesn't have that sort of coin. My offer is good, Khuan—you'll have the gold in a week."

Adah's still hesitating, which is a good sign. I pray his love for Vanna is stronger than his greed.

"Don't choose either of them!" a familiar voice shouts from the crowd. Even without looking, I know it's Oshli.

Vanna flinches as everyone's attention goes to the orange-scarfed shaman.

I hold my breath. This is her chance to say something. To use her light and close down the selection ceremony, if she wishes. She could do it; she has the power.

But she doesn't.

"For the good of Sundau, I will be a queen," she says firmly. Her voice rings across the entire courtyard, but her eyes are on Oshli. "The fates will make it so."

Oshli turns abruptly, shouldering through the crowds

for the road out of Puntalo Village. As he disappears around the bend, Vanna drags her attention back to the selection.

She touches Adah's arm. Her lips are moving, but I can't make out what she's saying. I hope she's telling him to accept Prince Rongyo's offer—that the throne of a queen is worth more gold than Meguh and his servants can dig in a lifetime.

Adah whispers something to Dakuok, who shakes his head, clearly disagreeing. Before Adah can stop him, he raises his staff high up in the air to command everyone's attention.

"We will settle this the way our ancestors did," announces the shaman. "Resolution by conflict. A contest of warriors."

Meguh's mouth curves into a wide smile, and I nearly choke with fury. This isn't fair. Dakuok knew that Meguh brought a warrior with him!

Prince Rongyo, unaware of his disadvantage, straightens. He carries no weapons, but he is young and lean—he must think he has a fair chance of winning the match.

"I accept," he tells Meguh. "Swords or spears?"

Meguh erupts with laughter. "Not against me," he booms. "Against my champion."

Twelve of his servants emerge from behind the temple, and it takes all twelve to roll forth an enormous box covered by a blue sheet. Confused, the villagers draw back, making room for this new arrival.

I'm confused too. It must be a cage. But why would Meguh's champion be confined?

Meguh descends the temple steps into the square. With a flourish, he removes the cloth. "Behold!"

The air goes still. Gasps pulse across the marketplace, little pops of horror and shock—and wonder. The villagers crowd around the box, murmuring excitedly.

Vanna's gone pale. She turns to Adah, pleading with him, but he shakes her away. She turns to the crowds, silently beseeching. But no one pays her any heed, except me. *Channi,* I can almost hear her whisper. *Channi, help me.*

I can't see what's in the box. I crane my neck, to no avail, then rise to my knees for a better view. It *is* a cage, and there's a beast inside, its back to all. It's turning. Turning.

My hand jumps to my mouth, and I let out a belated gasp.

"A dragon," I whisper.

The crowd backs away in fear, while I lean forward. It's been a long time since I've been awestruck, but this dragon is magnificent. A natural fighter. A shock of tangled black hair obscures his face, but I can see that he has legs and arms like a human and that he stands upright like us. But unlike us, he's got knife-sharp talons and iron-thick scales, gleaming blue-green or black depending on the light. And wings! The tales I've heard of the great sea dragons never mentioned wings.

Rongyo approaches the cage. He may know the princely arts of combat, but any fool can see he is no warrior.

Meguh's beast will rip him into shreds.

My mind careens. If Rongyo loses this fight, then Vanna will become King Meguh's concubine. I can't let that happen.

With a loud crack, I snap off the tent pole I carved into a spear. The awning beneath me rips, and before I fall, I hear myself yelling, "I will fight for my sister!"

# CHAPTER NINE

*I will fight for my sister.*

As soon as the words slide off my tongue, my stomach lurches. It's the only warning I get before the tent collapses, and I roll off onto a mound of hard, bristly coconuts.

I shoot up to my feet, but instead of checking for bruises, I scrabble for my wooden mask. It's fallen behind a hawker's stand.

Hurriedly I press it to my face, then spin toward the temple. But it's too late.

Villagers corner me against a wall. "Demon!" they screech, jabbing at my face with their fingers. "Demon!"

I could easily evade them, strike down the two on my left with a swing of my makeshift spear, and kick my way through the three in front of me. But I'm frozen. I've fought all manner of beasts and demons without so much as a trace of fear in my heart. Why am I afraid now? What is it about being despised by my own kind that makes me forget my instincts and behave like prey?

"Demon!" the villagers continue yelling. "Monster!"

The dragon is forgotten. My sister too. More villagers gather near, and the gasps multiply across the marketplace.

I stiffen against the wall and use my spear to push forward through the throng.

"Don't hurt her!" a child shouts. It's a little girl of five or six—too young and innocent to think me a monster. My chest goes tight. I could hug her as she cries for me. Then her mother pulls her away, and I begin to drown.

Faces. So many faces. I can't tell them apart but for the whites of eyes, the paired flares of nostrils, the crooked teeth. Fingers grab my ankles and my wrists, nails raking across my skin. I hurl them off and start to run, but the crowd's become a mob. Faces mass around me, and bamboo fans beat at my back.

"Why isn't this *thing* in a cage?"

"A snake demon! Chain it up!"

"Kill her! Burn her!"

Everywhere I turn, more faces. They've become a wall, the noses and eyes and ears and mouths. A wall I can't break apart with my fists.

Red tassels swing. Dakuok's priests. They're batting the mob with their ceremonial sticks, trying to push the villagers back. I've lost my spear and reach for the knife in my pocket, but I don't take it out.

Tigers I know how to fight. Crocodiles and bears too. Even the scarce demons that dare show themselves outside the dark. But children and old women and men—my own kind? In front of Vanna?

If I fight back, things will get worse. If I wield my knife, there is a good chance blood will be spilled. My blood too. Its poison is a secret I've kept with the greatest care. If the villagers learn what it can do, it will be the end of me.

So I let them spit and shout at me. Fruits smash against my head; pebbles nick my arms. I hurry toward Vanna. Words will not hurt me, but stones and knives will. My skin is not as thick as it looks.

My mask falls off again and is trampled under the storm of a hundred feet. I make the mistake of looking back for it, and while I'm distracted, someone loops a rope around my waist.

So much for not using my knife. I slice at the rope, but others swing over my head faster than I can cut.

"Stop!" I shout as they begin dragging me. "Stop it!"

Above my own cries, I hear Vanna's.

"Let her go!" my sister screams. The light in her heart blazes. She cannot control it. "They're hurting her!"

Prince Rongyo's guards break into the crowd, trying to fish me away from the danger, but the mob is too great. They can't get to me.

Vanna's voice fades beneath the roar of angry shouting. My ears are ringing, my body's abuzz from the tumult. Then, somewhere at the bottom of the din, I hear a familiar rustling.

*Channi, Channi . . .*

Meguh's vipers. I cannot see them, for they are trapped in their clay pot, hissing and rattling—*feeling* my distress.

*Free us,* they urge. *Free us, and we will help you.*

How? My fingers scrape the ground for something—

anything. *I can't*, I think. *That'll only make it worse. I must fight alone.*

Or so I intend. I easily fend off the men carrying me away, but new men take their place. There are too many. "Monster!" they shout. "Demon!"

*You cannot fight them alone,* the vipers insist. *Let us help you, our queen.*

*Our queen.* The Serpent King never named a successor after he died, but because he gave his life for me, and poisoned my blood to make it deadlier than any other snake's, many consider me his rightful heir. They would die to protect me, if needed.

I take in the blur of angry faces, the raised scythes and fistfuls of stone. Maybe I do need help.

I stop fighting and start grasping at pockets, satchels, baskets. Straw hats and coin purses are of no use to me. I need something bigger. A durian would be ideal. A coconut will do.

There's one rolling on the ground. I strain for it, stretching until I can clasp it between my fingers. Then I throw. Never has my aim been truer.

Meguh's pot shatters, piercing the mantle of noise, and the vipers spill free.

Like soldiers, they lurch to defend me—they weave toward me, crawling up my arms and legs until my attackers drop me in terror.

The villagers yelp and back away. I'm quite a sight, wreathed in snakes, with vipers hissing out of my hair, striking at any who dare come close.

The coils of rope chafe my arms, and as I slide them off, I breathe shakily. *Thank you.*

*Give the command, and we will execute King Meguh and his men,* one viper says. *We will do so with pleasure.*

Tempting. But there are too many people here. Too many children who might get hurt if Meguh's men were to retaliate.

*No,* I reply, holding in a cough. *You've helped enough. Go, be free.*

*Very well, Lady Green.*

Weaving through the fallen crates and smashed fruit, they make their escape.

Before long, Rongyo's guards arrive. They clear a space in the middle of the square, and as I wipe the dust from my eyes, Vanna rushes to my side.

Panic and concern crease her brow. She's shaking me, words tumbling out of her lips. I can barely understand them.

My skin still aches, phantom ropes burning my flesh, even though I am safe. Every part of me hurts, to be honest, but what propels me out of my delirium is the need to check myself for one thing.

Blood.

I've bruises and welts all over, but no blood was drawn.

My worry dissolves with relief. I bite the inside of my cheeks to keep my voice steady. "I'm fine."

While Vanna helps me to my feet, I keep my head down. Everyone has already seen my face, so I shouldn't care if they see it again. But my cheeks cannot help smarting with shame, even while Vanna guides me toward the temple.

"That *thing* is your sister?" one of the suitors shouts.

"Gadda's grief!" spits King Hoa Tho. "You thought to hide *this* from us, shaman? If the Golden One's family is cursed, I want no part of it."

Others quickly agree. Only Emperor Hanriyu does not fling insults upon me. He is taller than he looked from afar, and he offers me a handkerchief. The gesture catches me off guard, and I take it gingerly.

The silk is soft. I bring it to my face, inhaling a floral scent I cannot recognize. It's crisp and not too sweet. I breathe it in again because I like it and want to remember it, then dab my cheek—a mistake, for a spot of dirt soils the delicate cloth. "Serpents of Hell," I start. "I'm sorry, I . . ."

"There's no need to apologize," says Hanriyu. "Please, keep it."

He speaks as though he's caused me offense, not the other way around. Usually I'd attribute such words to pity, but there's a sincerity to his voice that I actually believe.

I fold the handkerchief in one hand. "Thank you."

"You are welcome." The emperor bows his head politely, and then he leaves to offer his well-wishes to Prince Rongyo and Vanna. He slips away, unnoticed by anyone except me.

A twinge of disappointment winds about my heart. It's a feeling I don't expect after such a fleeting encounter with the foreign king, but I'm no stranger to it. Disappointment is a consequence of hope, and there is always a ghost of hope in my soul, no matter how I wish I could purge it. I stuff the handkerchief into my pocket.

Dakuok and his priests are calming down the villagers, who have started gathering around the dragon, marveling at his wings and strangely human physique. As they start placing bets on whether Rongyo can defeat him, I'm quickly forgotten.

Is it the cage that makes them admire him and revile me? Would I be an attraction like the dragon if I were chained and imprisoned? My mind likes to torture itself with such questions, but I know better than to seek the answers.

I start going after Prince Rongyo to remind him of my offer to fight, when I see Meguh ascending the temple stairs.

He's staring at me. With curiosity.

With unbridled want.

He makes himself an obstacle in my path, and never have I missed my mask so acutely.

"So . . . you are Khuan's other daughter," he says, smiling widely. His voice is silkier than the handkerchief in my pocket. It's the same tone he uses with Vanna, and that makes me shudder. "Impressive stunt with the snakes."

I bare my teeth at Meguh. "I will fight for my sister."

At my side, Vanna steps forward, attempting to refuse my offer, but Meguh waves her away—as if I interest him more. That's a first.

His gaze bores into mine. "You can't even handle a few villagers. How do you think you can defeat my dragon?"

"Watch me."

I sound more confident than I look. Anyone can see my hands are still shaking.

I pull myself to my full height. "Understand this: I do not fight for Prince Rongyo, but for my sister. If I win, Vanna will walk free of this selection."

Vanna grabs my hand and presses fiercely into my palm. "You can't, Channi. I won't let you fight. It's too dangerous."

My gaze drifts to Adah, stomping down the stairs until he stands wrathfully behind my sister. His mouth is bent into a fierce scowl, and though he won't meet my gaze, the way his fists curl, closed tight like flytraps, tells me all I need to know.

*Go away, you stupid girl,* his look is saying. *You're going to ruin everything.*

I won't go away. I'm not afraid of him. Unlike Dakuok, Adah doesn't wield any power. He won't act out in front of Vanna's suitors. He won't do anything to lose face.

I twist out of Vanna's grip and bow before Prince Rongyo. He keeps his expression stony, but his eyes give him away. Hope quavers in them, particularly when they regard my sister.

Vanna and Rongyo are the same face of one coin. They are gentle and kind, their smiles sweet because they have never tasted the bitterness of life. Their eyes are bright because they prefer to see the good in the world, rather than the truth.

I am the other side of that coin. The darkness lurking under their light.

Rongyo hesitates, not knowing what to say, so I step forward, without his permission. I must be drunk on adrenaline from the mob, for I am bolder in this moment than I've ever been in my life. I say, "Do you accept me as your champion?"

"You are a brave soul," he begins, "but you are only a—"

"A girl? Do not underestimate me. I want to fight." I stare him down. "If you do not accept me as your champion, I will fight anyway."

"You heard the snake," says Meguh. "She wants to fight. Let her."

Rongyo grits his teeth, but he nods. "First blood will determine the winner."

"That is not the way it is done," Meguh says. "They fight to the death."

"You put forth the challenge. I choose the rules. First blood."

"Very well." Meguh sighs, and I worry he gives in too easily. "Then it will be a short fight."

The first thing I do is hike up my skirt so I can move faster. One does not wear a dress when brawling with a dragon.

A stage is created for us in the center of the square. Bets are being made, all on the dragon. Meguh's twelve servants gather, holding thick iron chains as they prepare to unbolt the dragon.

Someone thrusts a scythe into my hand. It's a clumsy weapon. I would have much preferred a spear or a dagger, but no one except King Meguh was expecting to see a duel today, so it's the best I am offered.

I prepare my stance, fix my gaze on my opponent. His wings are folded in front of his face, obscuring it. I want to see his eyes when he's let free, to see if he is a prisoner like the vipers or Meguh's champion, as the king brags. No matter. Either way I will not hold back. I will win.

The cage door falls upon the earth with a deafening thud.

And the battle for my sister begins.

# CHAPTER TEN

Across the square, the dragon's great wings unfurl, blanketing me in their shadow. I ignore the gasps that echo behind me. No one in Sundau has ever seen a dragon—the giant lizards in the jungle that prey on monkeys and goats and snakes may be called dragons, but they are not the fabled serpents of sea and sky.

I get my first good look at my opponent. He has the face of a dragon—wildly unkempt eyebrows and crooked horns—along with a winding tail, but he stands like a human, with two arms and legs clothed in coarse cotton. The crowd begins to chant, "Dragon! Dragon!" Yet there is something rather un-dragon-like about him. Unfortunately, this is not the time to decipher what.

I focus on finding a weakness. Sapphire-green scales ripple across his limbs and torso. The colors are like the sea at dawn, when the sun tickles the waters with light fresh from Heaven. Even their beauty is a weapon; they stipple his flesh, making it difficult to pin down a vulnerable spot. His wings are fearsomely long, spiked along the edges, and webbed like a bat's.

I can tell what Meguh—what *everyone*—is thinking. That I'm a scrawny, pathetic girl. No match for his prize dragon.

I can't help thinking the same.

We circle each other. My mind's never worked so fast, trying to pick out his weaknesses and strengths. His left leg is shackled to his cage, which will slow him down. Speed is on my side, then. I fix my gaze upward at his chest, marred by scars of all colors, at all stages of healing. Then I look at his arms, curiously inked with lines of script. Then at his eyes, with their broken pupils and mismatched colors. One limpid blue, one fiery red. So divergent they might as well be on opposite poles of the world.

I'm unconsciously matching the rhythm of his gait, and once I realize it, I mutter an inward curse. The crowd's making bets on how long I'll last, not whether I'll win. Right now, the wager's a minute. Two, if we keep circling each other like this.

I resent these odds.

The dragon's red eye flickers, the only warning I have before he flies forward.

I swing the scythe, and the curved blade sings as it arcs through the air. But I don't even get close. I was wrong about his speed. Even with his leg shackled, the dragon's startlingly fast. He darts about like lightning, bursting from the darkness in shocks of shadow and light.

More bets go on the dragon's side. Meguh wears an oily grin.

*Stop looking at Meguh!* I yell at myself. *Focus!*

The dragon's wing strikes from behind. I've been punched before, slapped and knocked off my feet by beast and man, but nothing prepares me for the staggering force of his wing against my back. I'm flying forward, hot wind whipping the air, villagers scrambling to get out of my way.

I fall against a merchant's cart. For a second, I can't feel my spine, can't breathe. My chest burns. *Breathe.* I dig my nails into my thighs, summoning my grit. *Fight.*

For Vanna.

I pull myself up. The dragon's already waiting, one wing outstretched, as if in invitation, and one thick eyebrow lifted. He must have thought I was so inferior that one strike would end me. But I sense that he's reassessing my skills. I know that if I were him, I'd want to draw out the fight so I wouldn't have to go back into that cage.

My blood would even out this battle, but with Meguh watching, I'm reluctant to reveal that valuable secret of mine. I wonder if the dragon can smell my poison. Maybe he knows how deadly my blood is, that a drop will sear even his thick hide. Maybe that's why he's keeping his distance.

I only have two advantages: I am small, and I am not chained. Against a lesser foe, this might make a difference, but he is far stronger than I am, and far larger. His wings give him an unfair reach, and his scales are a natural shield.

"Fight!" the crowd chants, growing bored of us circling each other. "Fight!"

Meguh's guards draw their swords, pushing the dragon deeper into the arena. I keep my distance, still watching. *Always know your enemy before attacking,* Ukar has told me a thousand times. *Chances of success are multiplied with wisdom.*

The guards jab their swords toward the dragon again, and I seize the chance to launch at him, angling my scythe at the fleshy part of his side.

The dragon spins to deflect my blade, his wings crashing down on my back. I dive, skidding forward in the dirt, and deliver a thwack to his ankle with the butt of my scythe.

He stumbles, and I shoot to his flank. I bring down my weapon with a heavy blow and a low roar from my throat. But my scythe scrapes earth instead of dragon. He's so fast I catch only a flash of teeth, hooked like a snake's, before he pivots away, wings throwing me to the side.

I land on a bent knee, my breath going out in a cough.

Something buzzes in my mind. *You fight well for a girl.*

I look up, startled to hear the dragon's voice inside my thoughts.

*Impossible.*

*Not impossible. Serpents and dragons are cousins— didn't you know?*

I do know, but this connection still surprises me. So does his voice. It's not as rough as I expected, considering the way he fights, but it's not smooth, either. It's deep and gruff. And smug.

*Get out of my head,* I demand.

*The more you resist, the more you'll get hurt.*

I bristle at his words. *We'll see.*

With that, his touch on my mind is gone.

Our fight resumes, except the dragon doesn't waste time circling me anymore. My strength surprised him; he expected to simply throw me off, pin me down, and nick my skin with a pointed nail. He didn't expect me to hold my own against him.

I'll count that as a victory.

We run at each other. Me, a dozen steps. Him, only three.

Every time I attack, he dances two beats ahead, evading my blow and delivering one of his own.

He's been a silent opponent, unlike me with my cries and grunts. But when I start slashing at his wings, and nearly slice off a webbed edge, he lets out an angry, earth-shattering roar.

He knocks the scythe out of my hand and flings me to the other side of the marketplace. This time I land on my stomach, no merchant's cart to punctuate my fall. Blood gushes into my mouth, and I feel my teeth with my tongue. Half a tooth is broken off. I swallow it, blood and all.

The crowd kicks me back into the arena. "Finish her, dragon! Trample the snake girl!"

I won't give him the chance. My fists fly, powered by anger and the need for vengeance. But the dragon is no filthy-mouthed village boy. Fighting him is like fighting a crocodile and a tiger all at once. Against his strength, I can hold my own—as long as I am careful. But I am no match for his speed or his wings.

He blocks me with his claws, but when I don't stop, he pivots, and the chain tied to his ankle bites into my calf, sending me reeling back.

I wedge one foot against a broken wagon wheel as I regain my balance. It's only by luck that he hasn't drawn blood from me. Those talons on his feet are sharp as knives, and the hooked spikes on his elbows look just as deadly.

The next attack catches me by surprise from behind. A wing slams me, knocking me to the ground, while the dragon's arm comes smashing down to finish me off.

I roll, barely scraping away. I'm a patchwork of welts and bruises, and the wounds I incurred while fighting against the mob earlier are catching up with me.

Unless I find a way to get past his defenses, this duel is as good as over.

Gathering my courage, I charge. This time, instead of attacking me, the dragon leaps up. The rush of air from his wings sends me reeling onto my heels.

Then it dawns on me: the dragon is trying to escape. Meguh's servants shout at one another, their sandals digging into the dirt, faces scrunching red as they pull on the dragon's chain to keep him grounded.

His wings spread open, wider than they were before. It's the first time I've had a clear view of his back, seen the welts ribboning down his spine, the chipped scales and thick, gruesome scars on the flesh between his wings.

Pity rushes unexpectedly to my chest, but it's short-lived. If he escapes, then Meguh will find some other excuse for Vanna to be his. I cannot let that happen.

I join Meguh's servants, grabbing the dragon's chain and wrenching him down. The dragon fights. His wings beat faster. But with my added strength, the servants are able to pluck him from the sky and pull him back to earth.

The dragon lands with a thud. He sends me a baleful look.

*Only cowards run,* I taunt. *Fight.*

Slowly, reluctantly, the dragon pulls himself up. Seeing the fight—the spark of ferocity—flee from his eyes, something in me changes.

I have no grievance against him, and I don't want to hurt him anymore.

He's a monster. Like me.

Trapped. Like me.

Unfortunately, he has no idea of my change of heart. He leaps into the air again, eliminating the distance between us in a breath. His wings were black a second ago, but now they are bluer than the ocean on the clearest day, almost mesmerizing—a tidal wave about to crash.

My mind sharpens back into battle mode, and I swoop left an instant before he would've reduced me to dust.

I land hard on my side. Pain stabs through my hip bone, and I feel something edged underneath—a rock maybe.

Through the pain, I force myself up. My skirt is torn, which is when I see—and remember—my paring knife!

Its blade is thin, meant for skinning mangoes and extracting coconut meat. But it'll do.

The dragon lunges. Out of desperation, I feint to the right. He's left an opening to his ribs, a mistake a warrior like him should know better than to make. In my frenzy of thoughts, I don't question whether he's made it on purpose. I have an opening. I seize it.

I rush forward, slamming my entire body into his ribs. I weigh little compared to him, but the force of my rush makes him stagger. Thrusting the knife at his leg, I slice just above his knee.

His wings snap into a fold over his back, but he doesn't cry out, as a man would.

He bleeds silently, landing on one knee.

Wind ruffles my hair, tickling the sweat beading on my nape. Behind me, Dakuok declares, much to everyone's astonishment, that I am the winner.

# CHAPTER ELEVEN

The fight is over, but I cannot move. I am still shocked by the abruptness of my victory.

I glance at the dragon, taking in the intricate webbing of his wings, the sheen of his scales, the blood flowing from his knee.

Funny, I expected him to bleed red, as a human does. As I do. But his blood is as black as ink. A reminder that he's anything but human. That, skilled as I may be, he is a hundred times the warrior I am. Yet he left that opening. . . .

He let me win. Why?

The dragon's eyes flick to mine. With a flip of my stomach I remember that, like Ukar, he can hear my thoughts.

*Thank you,* I say.

He doesn't respond. A soldier emerges from the crowd. He is holding a blue-feathered dart, and he shoots it into the dragon's neck.

The dragon sags to the ground, wings falling so fast that a few villagers scream and tear away.

As Meguh's servants drag him back into his cage, pity

blooms inside me. This is the first time I've recognized a little of myself in someone else besides Vanna.

The villagers are applauding. Minutes ago, they were shouting for my death. Now they part for Prince Rongyo, who approaches with an outstretched hand. On his palm is my wooden mask, cracked but still intact.

Wordlessly, I take it from him. His attendants surround me. I'm fanned and lifted onto a rattan chair, and the little gold bells sewn onto the attendants' vests tinkle as they carry me to the temple dais.

My sister's face fills my vision. She takes my hand, a flush high on her cheeks from running. "You did it, Channi." Tears stream down her face, and she grabs my hand, drowning me in her light. "Thank you. Thank you."

I'm too tired to speak, but I am content to see Vanna so happy. Slowly, the blood rushes back into my face. I slide my paring knife under my skirt, its weight heavy on my hip.

I am rank with sweat, and there is dirt all over me. Lintang nudges Vanna away, but my sister doesn't let go of my hand.

"Well done for a demon girl," Dakuok says, patting my shoulder. I shrug him off, but he is still smiling at me. "I am glad you won. Perhaps you can be of some use after all."

In the near distance, Meguh is conceding victory to Prince Rongyo. I hear the words "snake" and "dragon" and a rumble of unpleasant laughter from Meguh's belly, but the rest is lost. All I want is to drink a jugful of water and lie down for hours.

Prince Rongyo extends a hand to me. "I am in your

debt, Channari. Please permit my servants to tend your wounds."

I ignore him and dust off my tattered skirt, unused to such attention—from a prince, no less. "I'm fine."

The prince is persistent. "At least allow one of my servants to carry you home."

"We thank you most graciously for your concern, Your Highness," Adah interrupts, "but Channari is capable of walking home alone."

Adah starts pushing me along, but even in my exhaustion I won't budge. I'm not going anywhere until the selection is over.

"Understand this, Prince," I say to Rongyo. "I have not won her for you. I have won for her the right to choose." I turn to my sister. "End this. Let's go home."

Vanna's eyes go back and forth from me to Rongyo and back to me. She's torn. She doesn't know this prince, but he's everything she hoped for—handsome and young and, so far, good-natured. It's as if she wished him into being.

That's when I realize I've won one battle only to lose another.

Rongyo, curse him, takes both Vanna's hands. "Choose me," he says softly. "You have my word, before the witnesses of the island of Sundau, that the day I am crowned king, so too will you become my queen."

Vanna looks up at him. "I will choose you." A firm pause. "*If* you will grant me one favor."

"Anything."

She raises her voice so all may hear: "Allow my sister to accompany us to Tai'yanan."

My eyes fly up as Adah gasps in disapproval. Sweat trickles down my temples, and I watch the prince blink as he mentally formulates his reply. He'll refuse in a nice way. Then the crowds will cheer, and Vanna will come home—

"I should be honored to welcome your sister to my palace."

I choke on my own spittle. *"What?"*

Vanna releases Rongyo's hands and takes mine. "You're coming, Channi!" She beams giddily, as though we are children again. "We'll be together, just as I promised."

Her joy is overwhelming, and while she squeezes my fingers, I catch King Meguh whispering something into Dakuok's ear. Apprehension coils inside me, but I push it away. The entire village has witnessed Vanna make her choice. There is nothing Meguh can do.

"Will you come now, Channari?" the prince asks kindly. "The servants on my ship can tend to your injuries."

It seems I don't have a choice. I start along, until Dakuok intercepts me. "May I assist?" he asks, bowing so low his wooden necklace touches the ground. "The Temple of Dawn is right here, and my priests and priestesses would be honored to tend to Channari's wounds."

"You?" Vanna turns on Dakuok. "You nearly killed her!"

"Forgive me, I did not recognize her. I did not realize she was the Golden One's sister."

"That's a lie—"

"Vanna," cautions Lintang. With a glance, our step-mother reminds her that we are still in the public eye. "The temple is more suitable for healing Channi than the prince's ship. It is a generous offer. She will be in good hands."

"She'll be in the best hands," Dakuok says smoothly. "Look how tired she is, how hurt. The ship will be too far for her. I will take her to the temple and then see her safely to the port. You have my word on it."

I glare at Dakuok, not trusting him at all. But what can he do? Lock me up? No, Prince Rongyo is expecting me on his ship. Maybe the priest is simply feeling generous in his joy that Sundau will soon be one snake fewer.

Rongyo makes a hesitant nod. "My servants will fetch you an hour before dusk. Is there anything you'd like them to retrieve from your home?"

That's when it finally hits me. I'm *leaving* Sundau. I'm *leaving* my jungle.

I need to tell Ukar.

Ignoring the prince, I urgently turn toward the trees. Most of the serpents I freed have fled the marketplace, but a few remain within reach.

*Find Ukar,* I entreat them. *Tell him it's over, and I'm leaving Sundau.*

Adah touches my shoulder—an act that startles me back into my present surroundings. "She has some clothes, Your Highness," he is answering. "Not much else. My wife and I will bring them."

My father won't look at me, but he is less angry than I expected. "It is settled," he tells Dakuok. "Clean her up."

Dakuok makes a grand gesture of placing his scarf over me.

"I'll see you soon, Channi," says Vanna. "This is the beginning for us." Her light fans across the temple; I've never seen her so happy. I should be happy too.

As I said, Vanna has a way of getting what she wants. Soon she will be a princess of Tambu, and one day the queen. Poets will write about her for centuries, and musicians will compose songs about her long after she is dead.

It's everything she's ever wished for, and it will make a splendid tale for generations to come. A tale of dreams and love and hope that children will clamor to hear before they sleep.

But this is not Vanna's tale.

It is mine.

*It's late, and Adah reeks of wine as he stumbles into the courtyard with Vanna and Lintang holding him upright by the shoulders. My sister's selection is half a year away, and Adah and Dakuok spend many evenings feasting in anticipation of the riches she is soon to bring.*

*"Good night, Adah," says Vanna. "Good night, Mother." She goes to her room and blows out her candle. Her window goes dark; soon, Adah and Lintang's does too.*

*But I know she isn't asleep.*

*Before long, the kitchen doors creak open and my sister tiptoes inside, gracefully navigating by the light of my simmering soup pot. She slides next to me on my cot and quickly throws my quilt over herself. "I brought presents."*

*By "presents," she means "supper." Out of her purse she takes two wings of beggar's chicken, stuffed with claypot rice, still wrapped in a lotus leaf, still warm. I bask in the smell.*

*Vanna watches me eat. She looks tired, and I can't blame her. During the day, while I'm supposedly doing my chores and keeping hidden, she has lessons in the temple. Singing, dancing, reading, writing, embroidery—everything a great lady supposedly needs to know.*

*Usually, she bubbles to life when we're together. She'll show me what she's learned, even teach me from her lessons, even though I have little interest in how to say such and such in formal Tambun or make my writing look curly and elegant. We'll share a midnight feast with whatever she's managed to scrounge.*

*Tonight she's different. Withdrawn.*

*I'm not training to become a great lady, so I can talk with my mouth full: "What happened?"*

*She combs her fingers through my hair and starts to braid a lock. "I was just thinking how lucky I am to have a sister."*

*I tilt my head. "If you're so lucky, why do you sound so sad?"*

*"I love our nights like this," she says quietly. "Getting to talk to you without Adah around. Sharing what we've done with our day."*

*I hear what she leaves unsaid: Pretending like we aren't worlds apart because of how we look.*

"Do you think," she says, "that we'll still have nights like this after I leave Sundau?"

"You don't have to leave Sundau. You could stay."

"Stay?" she echoes. "On this tiny speck of the earth, where you can walk from one end to the other in half a day? Where the jungle makes up most of the land, and we've only one real town and a few scattered huts on the beaches—"

"We used to live in one of those huts," I remind her.

"I know. But the world is vast. I don't want to stay here forever." Her voice rises, filled with a passion I've rarely heard. "I want to sail the Emerald Seas and hear the yawn-birds of the Suma Desert. I want to climb the thousand steps to Gadda's Temple on Jhor. You know I've never even left Sundau before?"

*Yes, I know. More than once I've stolen boats and tried sailing us to the continent, where the gods are different and the lands so broad you could live a hundred lifetimes without seeing a demon. But every time, high seas and violent winds stopped us. Angma might have vanished, but I can feel the power of her curse thwarting me at every turn.*

"You won't miss it here?"

*Vanna turns wistful.* "Of course I'll miss it. I'll miss the reedy quay where we used to jump up and down, waving at ships and trying to get them to stop over. I'll miss the peddlers with the stale coffee biscuits and those jars of salty dried mystery fruit, all cut up to look like mushroom slivers."

"I still don't know what the fruit was," I say, chuckling. "But we were addicted for years."

"I'll miss the moon orchids you bring me on my birthday," says Vanna softly. She's finished braiding my hair. "Will you come with me, Channi?" she asks then. "Wherever I go, will you be there too?"

"You know that's out of the question. Adah won't—"

"Never mind Adah. Even if he says no, I'll send for you." She bites down on her lip. "Will you come if I do?"

I haven't thought much about our lives past Vanna's seventeenth birthday, but that isn't the only reason I hesitate. As much as my sister yearns to leave Tambu, I'm the opposite. I yearn to stay, to retreat into the wilds and never come out.

But it is the hardest thing, saying no to Vanna. She is the root of all my suffering in that way, but she is also the bringer of my greatest joys. When she is happy, I am too.

I wrap my arms around her and we press our cheeks together, the way we used to do when we were little. Her cheek was always too warm, mine always too cold. Together, I'd say, we were just right.

"Whenever you need me," I promise, "I will be there."

Vanna hugs me. There's relief in her eyes, as though she was afraid that I'd say no.

To this day, I wish I'd asked her why.

# CHAPTER TWELVE

I'm too tired to protest when Dakuok and his priests steer me into the Temple of Dawn. Thick clouds of incense assault my nostrils, and my senses dull as I'm led past chamber after chamber.

An old priestess brings me a shallow bowl of water. I suck it down greedily. The dryness in my throat vanishes, and the drink slakes my misgivings about coming into the temple. When I'm finished, the priestess beckons, and against my common sense, I trail her deeper inside the temple.

The last time I was here, I was a child. I would come early in the morning, before other worshippers arrived to pray, and pick a spot in the darkest corner. There, I prayed to Gadda. His statue is enormous, surrounded by daily offerings of fruit and wine.

I wanted to look like the other girls in Puntalo, but I thought a normal face would be too much to ask for. *I wish for a nose,* I begged instead. *Let it be wide or narrow, straight or hooked, small or big. I won't be picky. But let it be a nose.*

I pause before the prayer room, almost certain I'll find Oshli among the priests praying to Gadda to bless Vanna and Rongyo's union. But Dakuok's son isn't here.

Next I pass the courtyard of ancestor worship, where Adah used to pray to Mama before he forgot about her. Bronze bells hang above me, and lizards scamper along the temple's wooden beams. By the time we reach the end of the hallway, all I can think about is a stool to rest my aching feet.

Every muscle hurts, and there are bruises as big as oranges on my ribs. I always thought of myself as a warrior, but compared to the dragon, I am barely fit to stand on my own two feet. Why did he let me win?

I shiver, remembering Meguh's face when I won the duel, all pinched and tight, like he'd skewer the dragon alive if he had a spear big enough.

The dragon will be punished, that much I know.

Guilt prickles my conscience, and I don't like it. I'm not used to feeling indebted to a stranger, much less a dragon.

At last the priestess leads me across the temple's courtyard to a squat house behind the pond. A bath has been drawn inside. "I'll return with fresh clothes," says the old woman.

"I prefer my own."

The priestess doesn't argue. "And I'll bring ointment."

Dakuok's generosity makes me frown. Prince Rongyo's won, I remind myself. Maybe Dakuok regrets betting on Meguh and is trying to curry favor by being kind to me.

I undress quickly, draping my tunic over my knife before

the priestess comes back. A silk handkerchief falls out of my pocket—the one from the Kiatan emperor. I hold it in my palm, and it unfolds like a lily in bloom. I've never owned anything so soft, so graceful.

The spot of my blood is dried, no longer poisonous. But I wash it off anyway.

I wonder if I'll see Hanriyu at the port. Whether he'll tell his seven children about his strange trip to Tambu, and how he'll have to continue his search to find them a new mother. I might not know him or his family, but I know what it's like to lose a mother.

For his children's sake, I hope he finds them someone, someone with a gentle heart to love them as he does, and I hope she will be better than Lintang was to me.

I tuck the handkerchief back into my pocket.

Slowly, I sink into the wooden tub. Although the water is only lukewarm, it scalds the burns and scrapes on my skin. I grimace through the pain. It's a sign that I'm healing. Already the welts on my arms have evened out, and my bruises have faded to a brownish yellow.

I scrub myself clean, taking extra care with my left ankle—where the Serpent King bit me seventeen years ago. The bite festered for days, turning my veins green. Adah wouldn't pay for the local doctor to look at it. Secretly, I think that after seeing my face he was hoping I'd die.

But my ankle healed, even if my face did not. Today, the skin is smooth, except for two puncture wounds. Only in my dreams does it ever hurt.

The old priestess awaits with ointment for my burns. Her

face is so wrinkled I cannot tell if she's smiling or frowning, and she squints at my approach.

The ointment smells strongly of turmeric, and it stings. For both reasons, I cringe. "Don't move," she warns. "It'll hurt more if you do."

I grasp my knees, holding myself still. Her fingers steadily smear medicine across my arms, and I hope I don't have any open cuts. Even if she is one of Dakuok's priestesses, I would hate for my blood to burn through her skin and possibly kill her.

"It was brave," she says, talking to get my mind off the pain, "what you did for your sister. You were nearly killed."

As if I need the reminder.

"Is Oshli here?" I ask, changing the subject. He'd want to say goodbye to Vanna.

The priestess ties the skirt around my waist, makes a neat bow on the side. "His father has asked him to help put the marketplace back in order, after today's proceedings. He'll be away the rest of the afternoon."

My chest goes tight and old resentments flare. *Find him,* I mean to say. *Tell him that Vanna's leaving.* But I don't. I owe Oshli nothing.

I put on my mask, and when the priestess isn't looking, I tuck my paring knife back under my skirt. We're finished, and I follow her back to the front of the temple.

*Channi? Channi, where are you?*

At the sound of Ukar's voice, I perk up. He doesn't sound far.

*I'm in the building past the courtyard,* I reply. *Wait there. I'm coming.*

I quicken my pace, but just ahead is Dakuok, waiting in the main prayer room, under the shadow of Gadda's statue. When he spies me, he flashes a wide smile. Tea stains yellow his teeth, and from how red and puffed up his cheeks are, I can tell that he's about to say something self-important.

I try to sidestep him, but he offers me a thin handful of joss sticks, and gestures for me to light them with the candle before the altar. The smell is spicy, a waft of cinnamon and jasmine and smoke. I open my mouth to catch a fresh breath.

I doubt Dakuok will take my refusal well, but still I say, "Prince Rongyo is waiting for me."

"The prince is a good, religious boy. I'm sure he would allow you to pray one last time with your father's shaman."

Gadda's enormous shadow looms over me. He is bald, as he is in every statue, with a kind, toothless smile under his beard and a round belly. For a god of mercy, he hasn't been very merciful to me. No wonder I've never liked him much. Still, my curse is not his fault, so I bow three times, stab the joss sticks into the burner, and turn to leave.

Dakuok's priests, appearing from the chamber's anterooms, block my exit. They're muttering words of enchantment, and though they are third-rate sorcerers at best, I can feel the wards they're putting up around the temple to trap me inside.

I tense. "Let me go. The prince is waiting."

Still kneeling before Gadda, Dakuok chuckles. "I will never understand your sister's attachment to you."

"Let me go," I repeat.

"You nearly incited a riot, Channari," says Dakuok, as if I could forget. "You must understand that Vanna can't have you at her side while she is queen. What will the prince's people think? No, your destiny lies elsewhere." The candles behind him flicker as he rises from his prayer. "Fortunately for you, Channari, you have your own buyer."

I hate how he keeps saying my name. But I hate most of all that he has my attention. "My own buyer?"

It's the reaction he wants. He watches the muscles of my arms go taut as the truth sinks in. And stings.

He sneers. "Did you really think your father would let you live in the palace with Vanna?"

I don't answer. Adah is cruel, but he wouldn't sell me. Not like this. . . . Would he?

*Run, Channi!* Ukar cries from the distance, but his warning barely registers.

Anyway, I can't run. Adah's betrayal has turned my legs to jelly and my nerves to ice. I think of Mama lying on the bed, of Adah howling when she died. The blood blooming and blooming on the sheets, and my last night of thinking I was her moon-faced girl.

"He was always going to send you away," Dakuok goes on. "He kept you only because of Vanna. But now she's leaving, and as a future queen, she won't have time to think of you, her wretched, monstrous sister. You see, Channari, there's no use for you anymore."

Hate boils inside me. I remember every time Dakuok has encouraged the village boys and girls—even his own son—to throw rocks at my back, has pushed the idea into Adah's and Lintang's heads that Vanna be auctioned off.

I ram two of Dakuok's priests into each other, clapping their heads together like thunder. Then I reach for the paring knife on my hip—and drive the blade across Dakuok's face.

He screams. High and shrill, like a child. The sound makes me falter, for I would never hurt a child. But when I hold him down, my palm pressing against his two slippery eyebrows, my rage rushes in again and spurs me to action. I press my knife down harder, as if I'm scraping sap from a tree.

He has impressive lungs. Some of the candles shudder from his howls, and a few even go out. Finally, when my knife slices across his lip, he goes silent. I think he faints from the shock.

That's enough. I need to run.

The doors are bespelled, so I can't get past. But like I said, Dakuok and his priests are third-rate magicians, and they didn't enchant the windows. I smash through the wooden lattice and vault into the courtyard.

I run straight, and before long I see the gate. I can hear the birds outside squawking, I can smell the heat of the afternoon beyond the temple's cool walls. Only a few more steps and I will be free.

It never occurs to me that I should have asked who Adah sold me to. Because deep down, I already know. . . .

"How many priests does it take to catch a snake?" rumbles a familiar voice.

King Meguh sidles to the front of the temple, surrounded by a troop of men that block the gate. He claps, as though my escape attempt were a performance and I have entertained him.

His men have swords at their sides and bronze shields strapped to their backs, but none of them makes a move to draw their weapons. I should find that odd, but I'm too preoccupied by Dakuok's damned priests.

"The snake girl's disappeared!" one shouts.

I don't need to look to know where Ukar is. I can feel him, slowly slithering above us, crawling along a wooden beam. We've hunted together for years, Ukar and I, and now that King Meguh has arrived, Ukar's counting on me to keep him busy. When the time is right, he will swoop down from the ceiling and bite Meguh's neck, paralyzing him.

And I will deliver him the death he deserves.

I mark the closest guard as my first target. The urgency of my task forces my mind to work quickly, and I launch my attack. I fell the man with one hit, then move to the next guard, and the next. Soon I'm halfway across the courtyard, inching closer to my victory and escape.

Except I don't see the dragon.

In a whir of blue, he smashes through the rafters, dropping down before me. Debris rains, wooden tiles collapsing from a roof in one of the covered walkways. Meguh and his guards have already moved to the sides. This was planned.

I shield myself with my arm, try to fan away the dust obscuring my vision. Where did the dragon go?

A wing slams into my side, answering my question. My knife flies from my hand and I crash against the wall, toppling the statues around me. I duck under an altar before I'm crushed.

There, I suck in a desperate breath. I can feel Ukar hanging from a wooden beam, offering to help. I don't look at him, for fear the dragon might notice. I can handle this alone.

The dragon's waiting for me to get up. Like earlier, I can feel that our minds are connected, as if tied by some invisible string. I tap into his thoughts. *Stop this. We can help each other.*

His response is to land a punch in my ribs. I double over, the wind knocked out of my lungs. He was definitely holding back earlier. I'm sure of it; he let me win.

Well, he's not letting me win now. Something is off. Something is different about him this time.

He grabs me by the shoulders. I kick, I bite. But his skin is tough as a crocodile's hide, and my teeth do not even draw blood.

I twist around in his grip so I'm facing him. In the jungle, I've often felt small compared to the trees, the winding vines, the falling waters. But never have I felt as helpless as I do now: being forced to size myself up to this dragon, to confront the interminable breadth of his wings and his dominating height, the dark expanse of his face, with those two strange eyes. And it arrives at last: what is different since last we fought.

His movements are confident, unfettered. Because—

He's no longer chained.

Meguh is beaming as he sees the realization dawning on my face—that the dragon wasn't imprisoned at all, that he might not be a prisoner, but a . . . a . . .

*You,* I blast into his mind, *you're . . . you're in league with Meguh!*

The dragon's mismatched eyes lower to meet mine. I swing up for another kick, but it's pointless. As before, I barely have time to blink before his head comes bashing into my skull.

I jerk to the side, dodging the brunt of the strike. Even then, the whole world goes ringing, and I clench my jaw as my head throbs, overwhelmed by a febrile heat. Gods, I wish it were my breath, not my blood, that were poison. Oh, the hell I would unleash if that were the case!

I spit at the dragon, then turn to spit at Meguh. But the king plucks off my wooden mask. And at the sight of me, he does something no one has ever done before.

He lets out a low, approving whistle.

The sound makes the fire in my gut go out. I'm suddenly cold, suddenly afraid.

"A true wildling," he murmurs in my ear. "You'll be the prize of my collection."

Dakuok appears at Meguh's side. The arc of my blade is carved into his skin, like one of the swooping letters Vanna's tutors used to make her practice. It must hurt hellishly.

"Be careful," the priest rasps. His eyes glitter with hate. "She's a demon, that one."

"Fortunately, I have experience with demons." Meguh throws the priest a disgusted look. "Clean yourself, old man."

Chastened, Dakuok wipes at the blood dripping down his face. He straightens his robes too, which are rumpled from our earlier encounter.

"Better," says Meguh. He's found my knife, and he taps it idly against his palm. "Now . . . what will you tell her father if I take her?"

"Doesn't matter. Khuan will be glad to be rid of her."

Dakuok knows just how to hurt me. His words about my father sting—because I know they're true.

Meguh grunts. "Makes me wonder what he did in his past life to father such children. One the greatest beauty this world has seen, and the other a monster." The king chortles, and Dakuok joins him. The dragon doesn't make a sound. Neither do I. I can't even call out to Ukar, for fear that the dragon might hear me and tattle to Meguh.

I'm on my own, and I fight to lurch free. The dragon has to use both hands to hold me still. A small victory. At least I'm not *that* much weaker.

Meguh's laughter fades, and he glances at me struggling against the dragon. When he addresses Dakuok next, his voice takes a darker tone: "What will you tell Prince Rongyo?"

"That she ran away into the jungle. Who would blame her? They'd make a mockery of her in Rongyo's court."

"True enough. It's a deal, priest."

The king flicks a hand, and one of his manservants passes Dakuok a heavy pouch of coins.

Dakuok's eyes light up with glee, and he bows low. "The wards are lifted, so you may depart, Your Majesty," he says. "I will return to my prayers."

"Indeed you shall." Meguh abruptly raises his chin, and his guards tackle the shaman.

"What are you—" Dakuok's cry turns into an ugly grunt. He stretches hopelessly for a bronze bell hanging from the ceiling.

But Meguh falls upon him, with a little knife raised high. *My* knife. One thrust down, and Dakuok drops flat against the ground. His panicked eyes turn to me. He is already graying. He garbles something I can't understand. A plea for my help, perhaps? Or a command to his priests outside. I'll never know.

Meguh takes the knife out of Dakuok's belly and slits the old man's throat.

I don't want to watch, but I can't turn away. The priest is choking on his own blood. His eyes roll back in his head, and his once-slippery eyebrows form a wrinkled knot. Then his muscles release, and he finds peace.

"A holy man should not be so mercenary," King Meguh says, retrieving his heavy pouch of gold coins and tsking at the dead shaman. "Disgraceful, putting on an auction to raise money for the temple. Don't you think, Channari?"

I don't have time to respond. From above, Ukar falls over the dragon's eyes and bites him in the arm so he'll release me.

*Go, Channi!* Ukar cries as the dragon flings him against the wall.

I run. Meguh's guards try to chase me, but I'm faster than any of them. I'm not, however, faster than the dragon.

One step from the door, his shadow is upon me. His hand slaps over my mouth, sharp nails grazing my cheek. I ram my elbow up to his chin and jam my bone into his neck. I will kill him—I will kill all of them—before I become Meguh's prize.

"Finish her, Hokzuh!" Meguh shouts from behind.

At that, my head snaps up. My eyes bulge; my heart leaps in my chest.

Hokzuh?

No, it can't be. I must have imagined it.

For years, I've searched for the owner of that name. The name that the Serpent King promised would help me.

Serpents of Hell, my curiosity gets the better of me and I glance back at the dragon. It's a mistake that costs me everything.

Meguh's guards surround me. One yanks me back by my hair, and another gags me with a cloth, tying it so tight my temples throb. Then the dragon raises his arm like a club.

The last thing I see is Ukar, slithering up a guard's leg and coiling himself under the shield on his back.

# CHAPTER THIRTEEN

I spring up in the darkness, and my head thumps against a low ceiling. A string of colorful expletives spills from my mouth, but the words come out muffled.

Right, I'm gagged. I'm Meguh's prisoner.

There's a hemp sack over my head. Explains the darkness. I yank it off and untie my gag.

The new air clears my head, and I blink my eyes into focus. Four walls hold me in.

Just like home. Except the room's swaying—back and forth, back and forth. The rhythm's unrelenting, and if I watch the walls too long, I can feel my stomach start to rise to my throat.

Wonderful. Just wonderful.

I am on a ship.

So much for going to Tai'yanan with Vanna, for being welcomed in the palace as the princess's honored sister. So much for protecting Vanna from the Demon Witch.

My chest tightens with despair. I must be halfway to Shenlani now, seas away from Rongyo's kingdom.

A thick coil of rope lies on the ground. It has been gnawed, which explains my free hands and feet. Ukar couldn't have done this, could he?

"Ukar?" I call out.

No answer, but as I speak, I taste a bitter note on my tongue. A sedative of some sort.

*Nice try, Meguh.* I lick my lips clean of the poison. It will have no effect on me.

I get up. My sandals sink into something soft and moist on the floor, too rank to be dirt. Disgust pools in my gut. At least the pain in the back of my head, where that dragon struck me, is dulling.

That dragon, Hokzuh.

The name makes my breath burn in my lungs, singeing my composure. I've searched years for him. Searched the jungle, the fields, the valleys and low hills all over the island. Some days I even brought Vanna, carrying her on my back after rubbing camphor oil over her smooth skin so it wouldn't attract mosquitoes. She helped me yell, "Hokzuh! Hokzuh!"

*He'll come looking for you one day, when you are older. You'll need him,* the Serpent King had said. I never had a chance to ask him what he'd meant, but I assumed this Hokzuh would break my curse and help me fight Angma. I assumed he'd be an ally.

I ball my fists.

The world rocks, and chains rattle down the slanted floor. I use the walls to steady myself.

*Clank*—I jerk back with a painful grunt. Metal bites

into my neck, cold and unforgiving, and I choke as I fall against the wall.

My fingers scrabble at the weight around my neck. There's a damned collar there. Bronze. My eyes are as sharp as a snake's, even in the dark, so I can tell from the sheen it casts over the wooden walls and over my thighs as I struggle to rip it off. No use. I'll need a key to get it off. Or an axe.

Behind my neck is a shackle fastener, sticking out of the collar like a hook. A thick metal chain slinks down my spine, and I follow it to where its end meets the anchor in the wall. *There!* I crouch and press my feet against the wall, digging my elbows into my thighs and wrapping the chain around my arms until it burns into my skin. With all the power in my body, I pull.

Little by little, the anchor grinds free, writhing through the wooden wall like a mouse clawing its way out. Then in a rush it flies out and crashes at my feet.

*Careful,* hisses a familiar voice. *Fool, do you want the guards to come back?*

Ukar slithers through the hole I made in the wall, his cool scales brushing against my ankles. I've never been so relieved to see anyone in my life.

"How did you bite through my ropes?" I whisper.

*The rats did it in exchange for me not eating them. But now I'm hungry.*

I almost laugh, though Ukar's not in the mood for humor.

*I gather that the dragon betrayed you. If I'd known a dragon was pretending to be Hokzuh, I'd have warned you earlier.*

His voice is so vehement that I sit up. "Warned me about what?"

*Dragons. They're our cousins, so we don't seek strife with them—especially since they mostly keep to their own realms. But we would never ever trust them.*

This I didn't know. "Why not?"

*Because of the first dragon—Hanum'anya. He betrayed us.*

Ukar won't say more; the grudge is one that the snakes have buried long since anyone can remember.

"You can't blame all dragons for the sins of one."

*Can't I?* Ukar is a champion at holding grudges. *It seems yours isn't trustworthy, either.*

He has a point there. "You don't think he's Hokzuh?"

*My father would never prophesy a dragon coming to your aid. Never.*

There's no use debating this with him. "Let's just try to get out of here."

Ukar eyes the metal anchor at my feet. I pick it up. There's nothing I can do about getting my collar off, so I will have to carry this cursed chain around.

*You might as well stay in your cell. Where can you go with that chain weighing you down? The sea? You'll drown.*

"What happened to your optimism, Ukar?"

*Don't forget,* he adds, smirking at how I lumber about, *you're not a very good swimmer.*

My head hurts too much to argue. I throw my chain over my shoulder. I feel naked without any weapon, so it'll have to do. "Where's the door?"

*Behind you.*

I immediately spy the crack in the wall Ukar entered through. He's unbolted the door from outside, and I push.

Beyond my cell is the ship's cargo hold. Cages swing from the ceiling—some wooden, others wrought of iron. Birds cheep from baskets that are covered by blankets, and I hear a growl or two from one corner of the room. But no snakes.

No Hokzuh.

To think how indebted I felt to him after the duel! Now I regret I gave him only a scrape on his knee. I won't make that mistake twice.

Ukar stands alert on his tail. *They're coming.*

I hear the footsteps a beat later.

I spring for a dark corner as the ship lurches but stumble into the wall just as two guards enter. The tall one blocks the exit hatch, and he swings a torch toward his companion, who's younger and has a long flat nose and floppy ears, like a rat.

No more spying. I pretend to be unconscious, lest the torches catch the glint of my yellow eyes.

The guards don't even notice me. The tall one passes the door I escaped from, not even noting I carelessly left it ajar. His torch tilts at the largest cage, and a flash of blue-green snags my attention.

Hokzuh.

I tense. So he *is* here. Shouldn't he be above deck with King Meguh, peeling him longan fruits and swatting away mosquitoes?

The guards throw him something, and Hokzuh sniffs.

"You call this a meal? I smell fish upstairs. Bring me some of that."

"You're in no position to make requests. Be lucky there's even meat on these bones."

"Come now, that's no way to treat King Meguh's champion."

The tall guard spits. "You lost. To a scrawny snake-eyed brat."

"Maybe because I'm so ill-fed."

"Maybe because you tried to escape. You know the rules, dragon, and you tried to break them. Meguh's displeased with you. I wouldn't want to be in your place when we reach Shenlani."

"The queen will understand," Hokzuh says silkily. "Now, let me out. It isn't polite to keep royalty in cages."

"Royalty?" The tall guard snickers and turns to his companion (whom I'll call Ratface). "Still thinks he's the king of the dragons, doesn't he?"

"He's just acting this way to get out of a beating." Ratface draws closer to the dragon's cage, and my eyes follow.

Hokzuh has definitely been punished. Dried blood crusts his scaled cheeks, and one eye is bruised. I cannot see his back, but I'd wager it's covered with new lash marks.

Ukar slinks across the ground, darting me an impatient look. *What are you waiting for?*

I hesitate, unable to ignore the twinge in my chest. What if the dragon . . . what if he's really the Hokzuh I've been waiting for?

Ukar flicks his tongue, exasperated. *That thing is one of King Meguh's beasts.*

*He could help us.*

*He could betray us.*

Still clinging to that ancient grudge, Ukar. But based on Hokzuh's record so far, he probably isn't wrong.

Crouching lower, I steal into the shadows, behind the stairs up to the hatch.

Meanwhile, Hokzuh springs to his feet in his cage and grabs the guard's wrist. Bones crack, and the dragon smothers Ratface's scream with his arm.

"You'll pay for that!" says the tall guard, taking out his whip. It slices the air with a visceral crackle before it comes down, lashing against the dragon's hide.

The dragon doesn't holler. Instead, he looks right at me, those two mismatched eyes boring into mine.

My heart stops, and my foot knocks against a cage. Birds chirrup to life, wings flapping.

*Serpents of Hell!* I curse. I drop to my knees and hide behind the cage, hoping no one heard.

The tall guard heard. "What was that?"

Dread curdles my stomach. I need to get moving, but my muscles won't work. Hokzuh saw me. He's *still* looking at me.

Ratface is on the floor, writhing in pain, but it's not long before he starts to clamber to his feet.

*I claim the big one,* Ukar says, getting straight to business.

Which leaves me Ratface.

I can't go far with the chain weighing me down, so I jump

on his back as if he's the tiger I fought yesterday. His nails dig into my arms, imprinting little sickles. He tries to throw me off, but I cling tighter. I don't let go, not until I drive his head into the wall, and he melts onto the deck.

Ukar's guard is also unconscious, sprawled over a wooden barrel. Ukar's venom doesn't kill like my blood does, but it can paralyze a man for days.

"How many more above?" I ask Ukar, taking the guard's whip.

"Too many for you to handle alone," Hokzuh replies. Gone is the mocking tone he took with the guards.

*At least seven more,* Ukar replies. Dislike simmers between him and Hokzuh, and he ignores the dragon completely. *I can tackle one undetected. Two, if the first doesn't scream. But that will leave you to fend off the rest.*

Not great odds. I pick a key off Ratface's belt and try it on my collar. It isn't a fit.

"Only Ishirya can remove that collar," says Hokzuh.

"The queen?"

"It isn't Meguh you should be worried about," he says darkly, with a nod. "Toss me the key."

He doesn't wait for me to oblige. His tail sweeps at my ankle, swift and slender as a rope. As I fall, he snatches the key and unlocks the cage door. To my bafflement, he remains inside, letting out a long sigh as his wings uncurl through the opened door.

"What are you?" I demand. "Meguh's prisoner or—"

"You won't win by trying to escape the ship," he interrupts. "You need to stay until we get to Shenlani."

133

I'm done with the dragon's nonsense. I throw the whip over my shoulder. "If you won't help, then Ukar and I will get out on our own."

Hokzuh grabs my arm. "I *am* helping you."

I whirl to view him. During the tense minutes that I fought him in the marketplace, I'd memorized the way he moved. Graceful and fleet of foot, his wings like two lethal extensions of his arms.

In the cage, he doesn't look half as fearsome. His red eye is less virulent, less murderous.

But I'm no fool.

"I'll take my chances alone." I twist out of his grip and leap for the hatch.

I've forgotten how fast he is. In three beats, I have my hand on the door. In four beats, Hokzuh is out of his cage, has leapt to the top of the stairwell, and is blocking me from exiting.

"What will you do after you overtake the guards?" he whispers harshly. "Even if you can fight them all off and subdue Meguh, where will you go? Do you know how to sail a ship?"

*No.* "Do you?" I retort.

"Yes." Hokzuh unfolds his wings. "I can help you. Just not here."

His hand is on my arm again, and I'm startled that I didn't notice how it got there. I shake him off. "You expect me to believe it'll be easier to escape Shenlani than this ship?"

"Yes."

I don't get to demand why. "What's all that noise?" someone above us bellows. Footsteps thump closer. "What's taking you so long?"

Hokzuh leaps back down into the hold, but I stay at the door. It swings open, and I hit the new intruder neatly in the groin before kicking him off the stairs. Let the dragon deal with him.

I hurry onto the deck. There's laughter and music coming from the front of the ship, enough to cover the sound of my violence. I hope.

The noise is coming from a tent in the middle of the ship, marked by bright orange lanterns and a line of servant girls carrying platters of curried vegetables and spiced rice. The smells make my belly stir.

"There," I murmur. "Meguh must be there."

*What exactly is your plan?* Ukar asks.

I grind my teeth. *Attack Meguh. Hold him hostage until someone gives me the key to my collar.*

*Then swim to Tai'yanan?* Ukar says dryly.

It's a terrible plan, but I can't think of anything better. Except maybe killing Meguh instead of holding him hostage. Yes, that would be better.

I slink close to the tent, keeping away from the pools of torchlight. My face blends with the green banners hanging over the canvas. When a snake hunts, it is an invisible predator, waiting for the perfect opportunity to strike, and that is the method I take now. I seek my targets—three guards standing ten yards away. Ukar is already slithering behind one . . . gliding up his spine . . . and silently smothering him with his tail.

Before the other two notice, I sweep behind them and knock their heads together. I don't bother watching as they crumple to their knees. Holding my chain close, I climb up a stack of crates for a better vantage. I almost have a clear view of Meguh when I hear Ukar cry out, and my blood goes cold.

Below, guards spill out of the tent. I should stay hidden, shouldn't make a sound. But it's impossible.

Because Meguh has Ukar.

"What a spectacular snake," the king purrs, admiring my friend. Ukar's color shifts uncontrollably—the way it does when he is afraid. "I've never seen one like him."

I vault down, launching myself at Meguh. The guards quickly protect him, and I swing my chain at them, aiming at their blocky knees and ankles. While they fall, I raise my dagger, about to send it flying at Meguh's heart.

I never get to throw it.

To my horror, two black wings form a shield in front of the king. Hokzuh alights on the deck.

I jab at his throat, but he grabs my chain and chokes the dagger out of my hand. He flips it neatly in his grasp, pointing it at *my* throat.

Defeated, again.

"So much fire," Meguh says, seating himself on his throne. "You're sturdier than you look, girl. Very different from the fragile creature that is your sister." He leans back against a surfeit of silk cushions. "You'll do for now."

I spit in his face.

With a laugh, Meguh wipes his cheek with a silk scarf, which he then stuffs into my mouth. I try to bite down on his thick fingers, but I barely taste the metal of his rings before his hand is back at the platter of longans beside his cushioned throne.

The guards pull me by the arms. Something in my shoulder pops, and I roar with pain.

For the second time, Hokzuh strikes me in the head.

# CHAPTER FOURTEEN

A splash of cold water jolts me awake.

"Get up," a guard grumbles, kicking my shins. Under his arm is a wooden bucket. "Up."

I barely make out his wide nose and dirty knuckles before he tosses the rest of the bucket at my face. A pile of clothes lands at my feet.

"Get changed," he says before scuttling out of my cell, eager to leave as quickly as possible. Snickers sound outside the door, and I guess that the guards drew sticks to see who'd have to wake me.

*Cowards.* I shiver as the water drips, muddying the dirt under my feet.

Dirt . . . meaning I'm not on a ship anymore.

Sunlight slants through a narrow window, drawing a yellow stripe over my lap. I press my cheek against the window, but I can't see much other than the outline of Mount Hanum'anya, far in the distance under a mantle of clouds.

Mount Hanum'anya, the cradle of demons. Its shape is

that of a dragon's head, jaws snapping at the clouds. The sight is a stab to my gut.

I'm in Shenlani.

*Ukar?* I call out, but there's no response.

Ukar is my best friend, closer to me than anyone, human or snake. On Sundau, he could call for me from one side of the jungle and I would hear him.

Surely, if he is anywhere on this island, he must hear me now. He must.

*Ukar!*

I yank at my collar. The chain is clipped to a wooden pole in the corner of my cell. The metal gnaws at my palms, leaving painful indents, but it doesn't budge. I crumple onto the cot behind me, flea-bitten and stained with smears of old blood.

I don't want to wear Meguh's clothes, but mine are drenched. Curiously, they don't look like prisoner's garb: I've been given a long silk tunic decorated with purple hibiscus flowers and artfully painted leaves. There's a matching skirt, a sash—and a new mask too.

I dress quickly, but rather than tie on the sash, I hide it under my sleeve. I'd use my own hair to strangle the guards if I could. Thoughtful—but careless—of Meguh to provide me with a weapon.

Lastly, I pick up the mask. It's heavier than what I'm used to. The wood is thicker and is painted the color of flesh, with fat red lips and eyelids shaded a lurid purple. Meguh's color.

I feel sick just looking at it, and I hurl it into the corner. It hits the wall, and on the other side, footsteps clomp. The guards are back.

It's the captain this time, judging from the gold trim along his vest. He's burlier than the boy they sent earlier, and he's got an impressive ivory-hilted sword on his hip. When he sees me, he laughs.

"Never seen a snake in a dress before," he says.

Behind my back, I start unrolling the sash from my wrist. I won't need much of it to strangle his thick neck, but I'll need to be swift.

"Get over here. You've been invited to dinner with the king and queen."

Now that's unexpected.

I'd ask why, but I have other business. I launch myself at the captain, looping my purple sash around his neck.

Unfortunately, the man has good reflexes. His hand goes to his sword the instant I pounce, and he slices my sash into ribbons. I get a kick in the ribs and stifle a yelp.

"Careful," he says. He points his sword at my chin, the blade scraping into the hard ridges of my scales. "The king doesn't oft have a taste for snake meat, but he might make an exception for your little pet."

A brittle understanding dawns on me. "Where is Ukar?" I demand.

"He's been put away for safekeeping." The captain smirks. "You'll get him back, if you're good."

I stop listening. *Ukar!* I cry out. *Ukar, my friend. Where are you?*

Still no answer.

My stomach burns. No wonder they didn't bother tying

my wrists or binding my ankles. There's no need. As long as Ukar is Meguh's prisoner, I won't leave.

The captain unclips my chain, and my shoulders drop from suddenly losing the extra weight. His smirk grows. "Put on your mask or you'll scare the serving girls."

I obey, but as he wraps a scrap of the sash over my eyes, I imagine the ways I could wipe that smile off his face. All end with me breaking his jaw.

I'm led through a labyrinth of passageways, blindfolded. I try to count my steps and remember things—like how the smoke of smoldering banana leaves stings my nostrils before we make a sharp right, or how the dirt under my bare feet becomes smooth sanded wood, then grass, then paved stone. But it's a long walk, and it's hard to remember what you cannot see in a land where you've never been.

The captain doesn't warn me when there are stairs or rocks, and he laughs every time I stumble. I'm too focused on my escape to care. Only in nightmares have I imagined that my first steps away from home would be in Shenlani.

The wind becomes cool and crisp, harkening the arrival of dusk. Soon, the light seeping through my blindfold turns gray, like ash.

At last I hear the sound of dulcimer and bells. The music swells as I approach, joined by the buzz of male chatter.

I'm pushed onto a flat cushion, my blindfold is removed, and I find myself in the heart of King Meguh's royal dining chambers.

Sitting next to Hokzuh.

# CHAPTER FIFTEEN

"I see you got the new mask," he slurs. "Like it?"

The dragon has had too much to drink. I count five empty cups stacked by his wine jug and a thicket of metal goblets behind them.

"Not feeling sociable, are we?" he says. A trail of milky palm wine dribbles down his chin, staining his vest, which is ripped and too small. His black hair has been tamed and braided, but his claws remain sharp, untrimmed. It takes him two tries before he can pick up a cup. "Well, cheers."

He thrusts it at me, and my reflection glares back from the goblet.

I quickly look away. My new mask makes me look like a theater dancer: round doll eyes with thickly drawn brows and lashes, a fixed red grin. I despise it.

I tuck my legs beneath the table. Hokzuh and I are seated in a corner, and his wings take up six seats instead of one. I'm glad for it, since it spaces us out from the glittering crush of courtiers. Meguh's court. I can smell the lacquer on their fans, the oil in their slick hair. This is my Ninth Hell.

I clench the edge of my silk-covered chair, trying to keep my emotions from betraying my hand. Here, I'm not Channi of the jungle or Channi of Adah's house anymore. I'm a different Channi—an imprisoned, hostage Channi, wearing a mask that isn't hers. I feel clumsy and out of place, and stupid—oh so stupid—for sitting still and playing Meguh's game.

What can I do?

"Drink," mumbles Hokzuh, thumping a metal goblet in front of me. "The wine's good. Strong."

I don't want to drink. I want to scream and hold a knife to Meguh's jowls until he tells me where Ukar is. But I can't even do that. The king isn't here. His chair is empty, as is the queen's beside it. So I'll start with Hokzuh.

"Are you aiming to pass out before the night begins?" I remark. "It won't be half as fun for me to slit your throat if you're unconscious."

Hokzuh wipes his mouth with the back of his hand. "So violent, Channi. I can see we're going to be good friends."

"Do *not* call me Channi."

There are no knives at our table, so I reach for the wooden spoon on my right. I wonder how much damage I can do with it before Hokzuh breaks my arm, like he broke the guard's on the ship. He's not wearing a collar. No chains, either.

He reaches for the jug of wine to pour himself yet a new cup, and I surreptitiously observe him make the slightest flinch when he extends his left shoulder. Maybe a strain from our fight, maybe from the guards.

"Hope you're hungry," says Hokzuh pleasantly. "Food's almost here."

"I'm not eating Meguh's food."

"Yes, you will. You'll eat to get your strength." He belches, and my glare turns deadly. "Snakes and dragons hate being hungry more than anything. And you *smell* hungry."

"I don't smell like anything."

"You smell like poison," Hokzuh says, which makes me go still. "Oh, you didn't think I noticed? I might not have a long tongue like your friend to sense smells, but—"

I stab my spoon into the fleshy part of his forearm, digging into muscle, then bone. "Where is Ukar?" I growl.

Hokzuh makes a show of setting his cup down and, using his free hand, adjusting his sleeve so the spikes on his elbows don't tear the cloth. *You should've listened to me on the ship,* he says silently. *Now if you want your friend back, you're going to have to play Meguh's game.*

Before I can ask what he means, a gong is struck. The air swims with its resonance, and under the veil of fading chatter, Hokzuh twists my hand off his arm. He catches the spoon before it falls, and places it squarely on his side of the table.

"This isn't over," I hiss at him. "If you ever get in my head aga—"

*Look up.*

King Meguh has arrived. His headdress, purple and gold and wide as a peacock's tail, bobs across the room. I crane

144

my neck for a better look, but Hokzuh grabs my chain, making me fall back onto my cushion.

*Don't do anything stupid,* he says harshly.

I don't have to. Meguh himself stops at my seat, and his guards pluck me up by my chain, raising their swords to my chin.

"For many years now," declares Meguh, "I've gone to Sundau to visit a rare and beautiful creature, born of the sun. The Golden One." He pauses poetically. "I'd hoped to bring that girl back to Shenlani, so her beauty might grace our kingdom. But I returned with something even better: her sister." He leans close, dropping his voice to heighten the drama: "Behold the secret horror of Sundau—hidden for years behind the blazing light of the Golden One. A warrior as hideous as her sister is beautiful." He pulls off my mask. "Channari, the Lady Serpent of Tambu!"

A hush falls over the court, and even the musicians go silent.

I raise my chin defiantly, though inside I'm burning with anger, with humiliation. No one can look away from me, and I know they're all wondering the same thing. *What is she?*

I don't care anymore about the swords at my chin. I lunge at Meguh.

To be fair, I didn't have a chance. Two days without food has weakened me, and these guards are the king's best. The captain I tried to strangle earlier is here, and in a blink, his whip is lashing out at me.

145

My body hits the floor. I do not scream, even as the lash bites into my skin again and again.

"Witness her ferocity," King Meguh says, clapping slowly. "When I first encountered her, I thought to add her to the royal menagerie, but no—she's a fighter. Tomorrow, my friends, we will see this serpent lady . . . in the arena!"

At that, the nobles burst into applause, drowning out what Meguh says next. It could be a death sentence, for all I care.

*Strike me again,* I think. One more lash and my skin will break, and it will be the guards who will scream.

"That is enough," purrs a new voice.

The gong is struck a second time as a beautiful woman appears. The queen, flanked by two female guards. Servants wave giant feathered fans to cool the air for her, and a chill creeps down my nape.

The queen's walk is like lilies floating across a pond—so fluid I can't tell one step from the other. As she passes me, a cloud of perfume assails my nostrils. It's floral, with hints of orange and musk, but there's a note of something that doesn't belong. Something acrid and gray. Something I've smelled before. Before I can place it, my eyelids grow heavy.

A sudden lethargy washes over me. My vision blurs, and I can barely make out this woman, supposedly with the heart and face of Su Dano.

"Did you rest well, my queen?" Meguh asks, his voice larded with affection.

"Well enough. Won't you let our guest enjoy her dinner?"

That voice. Low and smooth like the blow of a conch

shell. Something about it is familiar, etched deep into my memory.

I squint to see the queen, but she is a haze of candlelight and gold. Odd, everywhere else I look is clear. Meguh kicks me with a slippered foot. "Get up."

The giant moonstone swings against his belly as he speaks. I imagine forcing it down his gullet and strangling him until he turns as purple as his scarf.

The music resumes. A dancer dressed as a tiger entertains the nobles on the other side of the table, her magnificent pelt glistening under the candlelight. Two other dancers surround her: a princess and a soldier; they must be reenacting a Shenlani tale that I don't know. I try to catch scraps of the story, but dinner has arrived.

Tall pyramids of saffron rice, capped with folded banana leaves, appear on the table, followed by porcelain platters of skewered meats perfumed with coconut, and copper bowls of shrimp and fish curries so fragrant my nostrils tingle with pleasure.

Too bad I've lost my appetite.

My back and my ribs are still burning, making it hard to breathe. I can't even sit up straight without wincing. In that small way—even though I'll be fine in the morning—Meguh has won, and I hate it.

The nobles make a game out of throwing peanuts at me, not stopping even when Hokzuh glares at them. The dragon, curse him, pushes my plate toward me.

"Leave me alone," I rasp. "You're no friend of mine."

"You need to eat. You're fighting tomorrow."

"Is that what you are to Meguh? One of his prize fighters?"

Hokzuh doesn't reply. Maybe he isn't as drunk as I thought.

"I saw the guards beat you on the ship," I mutter. "Was that for show? Why bother letting me win in Puntalo if you were just going to hand me to Meguh?"

"I told you I'd help you. But you didn't listen." He reaches for my arm. "Listen to me now. We need to treat your back."

I twist away. "I'm fine."

"Don't scream." It's all the warning he gives before he lifts his wing, using it as a screen so no one sees—and pours his cup of wine down my back. The pain is dazzling, and I jerk up, knees hitting the table.

He holds me down. "Best not to get an infection before the fight," he explains belatedly. "Trust me, I've seen it."

Next he blots my skin with a napkin. For someone who's tried to kill me more than once, he's surprisingly gentle. I've seen his claws; he's taking great care not to hurt me, and I can barely feel his fingers brush against my skin.

"All done," he says, lifting his wing. "You'll thank me tomorrow."

I'm breathing hard. My wounds are burning from the wine, but it's the sort of heat that I know is good for me. I'd never admit it, though. "I'll be out of here before tomorrow."

"Famous last words." Hokzuh raises an inked arm, nods at the neat rows of script that swathe his scaled hide. "Every line is the name of someone I've killed in the arena."

There have to be well over a hundred names, but I betray

neither fear nor awe. "Meguh carved them into your arm," I state. It's not a question. "What are the words in red?"

"The names of demons."

My interest spikes. There are demons in the arena? "But demons can't be killed—"

"Eat first."

Hokzuh dives into the platter the servants left for us. I reach for a skewer, but I don't bite.

"It's not poisoned," he says, amused by my hesitation. "You should be hungry."

It's not poison I'm worried about. I pick through the dishes in front of us and look at what the others are eating. Chicken, not snake. Spinach and cassava leaves, not snake.

Not Ukar.

Finally, I bite into a drumstick. The chicken is moist, still hot, so I suck in a puff of air. As I chew, the spices linger on my tongue, whetting my hunger. Slowly my appetite returns, but I refuse to look like I'm enjoying myself. I refuse to owe Meguh anything.

But to Hokzuh I mutter, so low I hope he doesn't hear, "Thank you."

His ear perks, and a corner of his mouth tugs upward. He heard.

I eat and eat, filling myself with strength. I am on my third bowl of rice when the nobles suddenly stop throwing peanuts, and the dancers fall into a deep bow.

Queen Ishirya has risen from her seat. Strange, how I'd forgotten about her until now. She moves like a shadow, gliding elegantly to where the dancers performed. Something about her eyes arrests me. I've never seen eyes like them on a human before: they are ancient like old gold, like the heart of a flame, like—

The queen swivels her head, catching me neatly in her snare. She smiles.

That same lethargy washes over me again. Quickly, before it's too late, I splash wine over my face. And breathe.

I breathe again.

No one else seems to notice. Not the servants, not King Meguh, I'd wager not even Hokzuh.

I'm trembling all over, and I throw a glance at the dragon. Gold flecks shimmer in his pupils. They weren't there a moment ago, but he's not the only one. *Everyone's* eyes shimmer, as if clouded over with a glittering haze.

Golden dust swirls across the chamber, but Meguh and his nobles eat as if nothing has happened. The musicians keep playing, and the horn makes the same peaceful drone as before. What do I do?

If Ukar were here, he'd tell me not to be so human and impulsive. He'd tell me to calm down and think through my next step. But Ukar is *not* here, which makes me angry as well as human and impulsive. And dead certain this is not a mistake.

I shoot up, charging at the queen.

I get close enough to see my reflection in the black pearls dangling at her earlobes, in the lariat of opals and rubies hanging from her neck, and in those blazingly familiar pupils.

Then I'm intercepted. One of her bodyguards grabs my wrist. Her skin is unnaturally cold. Damp, too, like a corpse.

I'm thrown, and I hear my spine thud against stone. The bodyguard cocks her head at me when I grunt. She sounds disappointed that I didn't break.

She's about to throw me again, when Hokzuh arrives, his eyes still spangled with gold. Using his wings, he bats the bodyguard aside and plucks me up with one claw. He pins me against the wall, and I brace myself. My ribs are bruised, my back is swollen, I've had no time to heal. I'm not in any shape to fight.

To my surprise, he pulls his punch. He holds me against the wall, his wings blocking everyone's view as his fist knocks into stone instead of my bones.

I look up at him, confused. *Hokzuh,* I say. *What are you—*

He leans forward, so close that our breaths mingle; I can see the silvery lines between his scales and the cuts on his pink-gray lips. I can smell the sweat on his brow. *Never attack the queen,* he says.

Then he lets me drop.

The nobles are on their feet, calling for me to be lashed again. Their mouths are half full, and food flies everywhere. It's disgusting, but I can't stop watching. Their eyes no longer glow. Neither do Queen Ishirya's.

In my delirium, I almost wonder if I imagined it all. Almost.

Meguh rushes to the queen's side. "Are you hurt, my dove?"

"No, no." Ishirya bestows on her husband a winsome laugh. "I'm amused."

"By the snake?" Meguh peers down at me, pinned to the wall.

"A fierce little thing, isn't she?" Ishirya's shoulders shake with mirth, and though I keep my eyes resolutely lowered, I feel her gaze on me. "You've done well to bring her here. But where is the sister?" A pause. "The pretty one."

*The pretty one.* Three words that overturn my world. Only one person has ever described my sister as such. The words in my mind, over and over, drowning out the excuse that Meguh is making about Vanna.

My stomach pinches, and the color drains from my face, making me cold.

"You look unwell, Channari," says the queen. When did she get so close? She rests her hand on mine. Her nails are sharp and press against my wristbone. "It must be difficult for you to be so far from your sister. I've heard you two are close."

I don't move. Am I the only one who can see through her? Everyone here adores her, even the servants. I imagine she is the one who pleads with Meguh not to beat them, who sees to it that they are bandaged and taken care of while she whispers sweet poison into the king's ear.

Hokzuh was right. It *is* the queen who rules Shenlani.

She instructs the servants to bring me water. "Come, sit with me. Won't you reconsider my generosity?"

No wonder Queen Ishirya is often compared to Su Dano. To everyone in the room, it sounds like an invitation to peacefully rejoin dinner. But I know better.

I'll never betray Vanna. "Never."

Her smile fades, and she clucks her tongue dramatically—as if my vehemence has stung her. I could laugh at the absurdity of it, but the way everyone moves to defend Ishirya is a sour taste of her power.

The guards circle me.

"Escort her to her room," Ishirya says, pretending to sound troubled. "The poor thing has had too much to eat. She'll need rest before the fight tomorrow."

The smell of her sharpens in my nostrils, and I am brought back to that fateful day in the jungle. As I am led away, I become sure that Queen Ishirya is a demon, and not just any demon . . .

She is Angma.

# CHAPTER SIXTEEN

I cannot sleep.

Every time I close my eyes, I think of Angma, barely a thousand steps away, deceiving the entirety of Shenlani under the guise of its beloved queen. No wonder I could never find her. Ukar was right; all this time she wasn't even on Sundau.

I'm tense all over, every muscle in my body gone stiff. *Ukar!* I try calling out.

Never an answer, no matter how far I stretch my thoughts. But he is alive, somewhere. I'd know if he weren't.

Digging is hopeless. Kicking the walls and the door only rattles my neighbors, who don't need much encouragement to hate me.

"Hope you're ready to die, snake hag," they jeer. "No girl's ever survived the Bonemaker."

I ignore the taunts. After a while I give up trying to escape. I count the mice and listen to the other prisoners snore.

There's no point in running away. The person I need to kill is here.

A lone stripe of moonlight illuminates my cell, and

Mount Hanum'anya's fearsome silhouette fills my view. I try for the hundredth time: *Ukar?*

Silence. Then—

*Go to sleep.*

I inhale a sharp breath. Not Ukar.

*Hokzuh?* I say, cautiously.

A beat. *Go to sleep,* he says again. *You'll wake the others . . . and they need their rest.*

He sounds tired. I wonder how long he had to stay at the dinner after I left. I wonder why he is here, sleeping in a dirty cell, when he is Meguh's great champion.

*The queen,* I say. *You said she's the real ruler of Shenlani. Did you know she's—*

*What were you thinking, attacking the queen?* he asks brusquely, cutting me off. *If you want to live, stay away from her. Now go to sleep.*

*What do you know about her—*

*Go to sleep.*

He severs our connection, and I let out a frustrated grunt.

I lie down. Anger winds itself around my chest, constricting each breath. But the dragon has a point: I need rest to heal my injuries. I need rest to face tomorrow.

I close my eyes. "A fierce little thing, isn't she?" Angma had said.

Tomorrow, I will show her just how fierce I can be.

Gadda help me, I will burn this whole island down if I must.

I am not alone when I wake.

Two young servants hover over my body. They're so close I can smell betel leaves on their breath, the sandalwood oil on their skin. A brush tickles the side of my neck, cool and wet as it traces up my cheekbones. They're painting me!

"What are you doing?" I try to bolt up, forgetting the chains that shackle me.

I snarl and punch and kick, but the servants are braver than most. Probably having been instructed upon pain of death to ignore my struggles, the girl avoids looking at my face and concentrates on her work, and the boy glances nervously behind him, at the guards supervising this spectacle.

Iron cuffs lock my ankles together, so I prop myself up on my elbows. The servants changed me into a garish costume while I was sleeping. Around my arms are vines fresh from the rainforest, and there are wooden beads in my hair, which has been plaited and coiled above my temples. As a finishing touch, I've been fitted with a headdress inlaid with gilded serpents.

"There," says the girl, sweeping a cold stroke over my shoulder. The paintbrush is damp with bright yellow ink, and I can only imagine what horror she's made of me. "Finished."

I glance down. Stripes! Of all the ways she could have vandalized my skin, she's painted tiger stripes on my arms. Desperately I try to rub the paint off, but the prison guards yank my chains until my arms fall to my sides.

The boy holds up a wooden box and opens the lid. "A present from Queen Ishirya, for your first fight."

It's another mask. I don't know what happened to the

one Meguh gave me yesterday, but this one looks like it was made with far greater care. The surface is smooth and shiny, the edges covered with rich ruby snakeskin. Its touch makes my skin crawl.

"What is this?" I demand.

"Your battle attire," replies a new voice.

It belongs to Queen Ishirya herself. A servant hastily un-rolls a carpet so that she need not soil her feet with the filth of my cell. I take her in, from her violet satin slippers to the cocoon of silk draped over her shoulders. She looks so frag-ile as a human, with her middle-aged skin and the fine lines fanning around her eyes. One would hardly imagine a tiger underneath.

At the incline of her chin, the servants know to leave.

"My, my, Channari," says Ishirya. "How beautiful you've become."

The words are meant to disarm me, and I hate that they do. "I know who you are."

"Do you, now? Then you know it is rude to refuse a gift from your queen."

"You are not my queen," I seethe. "You are Angma!"

Her lips curve into a gentle smile. "Careful, Channari. I have cut out tongues for lesser slights. Be grateful I am compassionate."

I try to grab her neck, but Queen Ishirya's eyes become two golden yolks. Her black hair billows out of her head-dress, lifted by an invisible wind as it turns bone-white, and her perfect teeth grow into fangs. At last, the tiger I've been searching for.

The glimpse of her true self is so startling, so riveting, that I don't remember to look away—until it's too late. Her haze bores into me, glassy pupils fixated on my own. How they shimmer, like the ridges of a gold coin in the summer light.

I can no longer move.

*Angma.* I curse inwardly. My hands won't curl into fists, and I cannot strangle the Demon Witch with anything else. "How?"

She tilts her head, the dangling pearls on her headdress pinging. "I take it you haven't heard the tale. It is quite popular in Shenlani, if not as famous as the story of your sister's birth.

"Princess Ishirya was once considered the future of her kingdom, so bright and charming and kind that her father rewrote the law and made her—a *woman*—his successor. Now, a terrible tiger had been ravaging Shenlani, killing children and young innocents. The king worried for his precious daughter's safety and promised that any man who could capture this tiger—with eyes like gold—would marry the princess and one day become king."

The hairs on the back of my neck bristle. This is a story she's told countless times, a story that has been embraced by the court and transcribed into song and dance. I remember the dancer with the tiger's pelt. Why did I not pay more attention during dinner?

Angma continues with the tale. "So it happened that one day a poor soldier came across this tiger in the jungle. This tiger with eyes like gold." Her smile grows. "He captured it and brought it to the king, who made good on his word and had Princess Ishirya wed the soldier. Sadly, the king perished soon after, and Ishirya, now the queen—began to suffer dreams that it was the tiger who'd caused her father's death. To make amends, she freed it from its cage. But the creature turned on her."

Angma tilts her head. "Ishirya screamed for her soldier husband, who came and killed the tiger." She licked her lips. "As she rushed into his arms, grateful to have been saved— she buried her face in his shoulder. He never saw how her eyes had changed . . . gold, like the tiger's."

"You!" I realize in horror. "*You* were the tiger. You killed the king, and then Ishirya. You stole her body—"

"And became a queen," Angma finishes for me.

All these years, I'd thought Angma was hiding because she was weak. How wrong I was. She'd been biding her time, squirreling her strength and resources.

"How about your story, Channari?" Angma whispers into my ear. She inhales, taking in the scent of my blood. "You haven't changed. Still as venomous as ever."

"Why not kill me?" I ask. "If you've been here this whole time, why wait until now?"

"Oh, Channari, Channari," says Angma, cupping my cheek. Her palm is warm and smooth. "I'd never planned to kill you. Just your sister. Your sweet, beautiful little sister."

My blood thrums in my ears, but no matter how I struggle, I cannot move.

"You've never told Vanna about the bargain I offered you, have you?" she says. "You're afraid of what she'd say.

Afraid that she'd tell you, in her selfless way, to sacrifice her and break your curse."

What is Angma getting at? "It's my choice. Not hers."

A laugh rasps out of Angma. "Ever the good older sister."

"What do you want with her, anyway?" For seventeen years, I've wondered. "Why can't you let her go?"

"You made a promise to your mother to protect your sister—but at what cost? You don't deserve this punishment, Channi. Give your sister to me, and you will have the face you were meant to have. You will be human again." She pauses with intent. "You will look like your mother again."

*You will look like your mother again.*

How can she know just the words that will destroy me? I grind my teeth, trying to tamp down my surge of emotions. The memories.

Sometimes, when I'm feeling brave and stare in the mirror, when I'm able to look past the band of yellow around my pupils, I imagine I see Mama's eyes in my own—the way I used to, before I was cursed. I imagine I've inherited her honest nose and mouth, and I've become that beautiful moon-faced girl she used to call me.

What I would give to see Mama again. To look like her again.

Angma knows I'm cornered. Her voice goes tender. "It only takes one word, Channi. One word, and you'll have the face you were meant to have. Your mama's eyes."

It stuns me how much I want that. I would give anything for that.

Anything but Vanna.

"You will never have my sister," I whisper. "Never."

Angma's face shimmers, veins turning gold. "There is darkness in you, Channari. Beautiful, beautiful darkness. Did you think, after I left my mark on you, that I wouldn't see behind your secrets? I heard you every time you came to the rock where I cursed you. Every time you begged for me to take your sister away—"

"I would never."

"—and give you the face you should have had."

"Enough!" I shout. "You lie. If I've gone to the rock, it's to summon you back—to kill you!"

Angma is smiling as if she's already won. In a way, she has. I'm shaken, my thoughts rattling.

She backs into the sunlight fanning through the window, and her hair turns black once more. Her fangs are gone, and her eyes are a clear, warm brown.

She ties my mask behind my head and tightens the string. "You'll need a name. What is it they call you in the jungle? Ah yes: Lady Green Snake."

I flinch that she should know. The nestlings gave me the name years ago, thinking I was a big snake. It's stuck ever since, and even grown on me. But on Angma's lips it sounds like a mockery.

"Lady Green Snake," she muses. "It doesn't quite have that ring that we need, but I've another idea." She touches the streak of white in my hair. "I've heard that the Serpent King never named an heir. How tragic. I've always thought it should be you, Channi. We shall announce you as the Serpent Queen."

I balk. "I'm not the—"

"The queen?" Angma leans close, cutting me off with a whisper. "Neither am I."

That silences me, and she claps for her bodyguards. "Take her out."

The women lurch to life. They're the same two that flanked Angma yesterday, the ones with cloudy, ashen eyes and lips so pursed they might as well be sewn shut. Their hands are as cold as snakeskin, despite the heat rising in the air, and they jerk me to my feet, dragging me out the cell door by my arms.

"I'll see you outside," says Angma with a wave.

I don't struggle anymore. I figure if I'm expected to fight in the arena, Angma will either have to unlock my chains or give me a weapon. I am too valuable to go into combat empty-handed. Once I am armed, I will slay the Demon Witch.

Even if it costs me my life.

# CHAPTER SEVENTEEN

Drums pound the instant I step out into Bonemaker's Arena. It's very dramatic, as is the retinue of guards escorting me. I can't tell if that's symbolic of how dangerous I am or if it's all for show.

The whole capital must be here. Thousands spectate from wooden benches under wide palms, ringed by an iron fence to protect them from the fighters. Tambu has a long tradition of champions dueling for honor, but never for sport. This place is an atrocity.

I'm dragged forward. More than once, something cracks under my sandals. Fragments of sun-bleached bones and skulls protrude from the earth, buried under scattered weeds. Beyond the arena's fence is a high wall of sea cliffs, jutting out like stone teeth. There's nowhere to run.

Meguh and Ishirya are finishing their public prayers, and though I can't fathom what god would listen to the Demon Witch without striking her down, her somber countenance fools the crowds easily. To them, she is the most pious of queens.

The drums roll and the crowd cheers as she ascends a winding staircase to the gilded pavilion she shares with Meguh. "Our brave queen!" they shout in adulation.

This is an island of idiots, I decide.

Then again, are they so different from the fools who worship my sister?

One of the guards holds up a bronze key and unlocks my collar.

As the chain falls, I catch it in one hand. I could easily take down the guards . . . but then what? Angma sits high above the arena, with a line of archers behind her. Each has drawn their bow, with an arrow pointed at my head.

"Her Majesty is merciful," the guard says when I drop the chain. "She wishes me to tell you that if at any time you wish to yield, she will listen."

I spit on the ground. "I will never yield."

"Then die well, Lady Snake."

The guards depart, leaving me alone in the arena.

Cursing at my predicament, I face the spectators. They are chanting to see my face, and I get the impression it's rare that a female lasts long in the arena.

Who am I to fight?

"Dragon Prince! Dragon Prince!" the crowd chants.

Meguh wouldn't throw me into a death match against Hokzuh, would he?

He's the king of Shenlani. He can do whatever he wants.

King Meguh rises from his seat and spreads his arms wide. "I hear your cries!" he shouts. "Battles within Bone-maker's Arena are to the death. Our Serpent Queen is new to Shenlani. There is plenty of time to pit her against the Dragon Prince."

He clasps his hands, and as a cloud eclipses the sun, his eyes become speckled with gold, with Angma's magic. My blood turns cold. Colder still when the captain of the guard passes him a lidded basket.

Meguh raises the basket high for all to see. Whatever is inside shakes and hisses. "Now, Serpent Queen. The rules are simple. Fight to survive. Win to save the life of your friend."

"Ukar," I breathe.

At last I feel his touch on my mind. It's faint.

*Channi,* he rasps weakly. *The menagerie.*

The frailty of his voice guts me. Ukar never sounds weak. Never. No wonder he couldn't call to me earlier.

*I'm coming,* I swear to him. *I'll save you.*

The captain takes the basket and disappears behind the line of archers. To the menagerie, as Ukar said. I follow him with my eyes as long as I can.

The drums are getting faster and louder. The arena gate growls open.

I'm tossed a spear. I expected the weapons they provided to be crude, like the fighting sticks and short lances I fashioned back home. But this spear has been crafted by a master.

Its weight feels natural in my hand and instantly becomes an extension of my arm. Though the shaft is worn, black paint crusting off the smooth ash wood, the blade is sharp on its twin edges. Shiny, which tells me plenty. Either the weapon's new or it's been wielded only by losers. I'm guessing the latter.

I hold the spear upright, as keen as the spectators around me to know who I'll be fighting. Or *what*.

A cold draft tickles my ankles, so slight I don't notice its ill portent. Until a furred tail whips out of the shadows.

It's thick as a wolf's. Then, as my opponent rotates into view, come the horns. Horns positioned to tear my bones from my body. A bear's head pierces the darkness, but obviously it is no ordinary bear. It has curved fangs and three glittering red eyes—a demon!

The crowds roar with approval.

The demon prowls, restrained by a long chain. From the neck down, it has the spotted body of a leopard, with thick, muscular legs and horse hooves for feet. It reeks of rotting flesh, and even from this distance, I suck in my breath.

I don't even get a chance to prepare.

In one leap it's halfway across the arena. I barely scrape away in time.

My instincts are on full alert. The demon snaps at my legs, and I counter with my spear, but the creature is too fast. It meets my weapon with its horns and rams me backward. The soles of my sandals burn as they skate across the dirt. My back crashes down onto the ground with a crack.

"Fight! Fight!" the crowd shouts. *"Fight!"*

The demon's chains rattle, the only warning before it charges again. I duck this time, sliding underneath it and plunging my spear up through the soft flesh of its neck.

The demon lets out a high-pitched shriek, and I crawl onto my knees, expectant of victory. But the crowd's not cheering. They're laughing.

Are they the idiots, or am I?

The demon rears. Worms and beetles and smoke pour out of the hole I've made in its neck, but the beast isn't dying. Using its claws, it pinches the shaft of my spear and slides the weapon out. The wet sound makes my stomach churn.

New, hideous flesh forms over the wound, and the demon raises my spear while releasing an earthshattering battle cry. I've made it angry.

I utter every foul word and curse I know and run for the gate, banging my fists against the iron barricade.

The guards think I'm trying to escape, and jab at me with the ends of their swords. "Get back inside. Fight, coward!"

I ignore them, narrowly avoiding their blades as I try to climb the gate. In the distance, Meguh yells a command to the archers. Arrows fly, several landing perilously close to my head.

The warning is clear. If I don't fight, I die.

But if I fight, I die anyway.

I hang on the gate, taking these seconds of reprieve to think. Only magic can kill a demon, and I've no charms, no weapons of enchantment. How do I defeat an opponent that is immortal?

With my blood.

It's my last resort. It won't kill the demon, but it'll certainly stun it.

I glance over my shoulder, wondering why the creature hasn't come after me yet. People are throwing rocks at it, and my chest goes tight.

Instead of chasing me, the demon picks at its chain with my spear. Its hooves and claws don't have the dexterity to wield the weapon, and it keeps dropping the spear before it reaches the linked iron. Watching the demon, I feel my terror cool into something unexpected.

Compassion.

I've battled my share of demons back on Sundau. I picked a fight with every one I saw.

*Let them be,* Ukar would say. *Not every demon is Angma's ally. They're not dangerous if you leave them alone.*

Sadly, that isn't an option here.

My decision's made, and I pinch my nails into my arm. Pain ripples in a white-hot flash, and I wince as my flesh opens, blood gushing warm against my skin. With one quick sweep, I coat my hands and drop back into the arena.

Hoots and jeers from the crowd alert the demon to my return, and it swivels, rising onto its hind legs. It charges, razor-sharp horns aimed at my guts. My imagination races forward in time, to my future as a carcass swinging from those horns.

I grab a handful of stones and old bones, priming them with poison—then hurl them at the demon.

A stone strikes the demon in the shoulder; the next one gets it in the eye. The effect is immediate. The creature seizes in pain, and I leap onto its back, grabbing my spear.

"Work with me," I speak into its ear. "We are both captives. Together, we can be free."

Its red eyes roll all the way back, meeting mine. I cannot read what it's thinking at all.

"Work with me," I repeat. I lift my spear just a little. My poison loses potency as my blood dries, and under Shenlani's wrathful sun, the stains I've left on the demon's fur are already crusty.

Which means, unless my gamble pays off, I'm going to end up a giant smear of red on the arena grounds.

"I will free you," I promise, "if you will help me kill the queen and take me to Ukar."

*Not the queen,* insists the demon in my mind. *She is too strong. Take the king instead.*

"But—"

*The king.*

There's no time to argue. "I have your promise?"

Immortals are bound to their promises, and the demon plucks a near-invisible red string from behind my neck with a single claw and loops it around our hands. A piece of my soul, to seal the oath.

With that, the deal is struck, and all that's left is to make my victory look convincing. I twirl my spear and stab its blade between the demon's eyes.

The demon gurgles, foam rippling from its mouth. Its legs collapse underneath me, and hooves skid as the rest of it falls.

I catch my breath, keeping to the fence's shadow and out

of the blistering sun. Sweat stings the cuts on my skin, and my clothes cling to me, slick with mucus and blood.

"I've won!" I shout, raising my spear in triumph while the crowd cheers.

Then, as fast as I can, I act. From afar, it'll look like I'm impaling the demon by the throat. But really, I'm hacking at its collar. With all my strength, I stab. Worms and smoke peel out of the demon's neck, and I mutter a silent apology to it before I apply more brutal force.

At last, the chain breaks.

*Onto my back,* utters the demon, whose wounds are already healing. *Quickly.*

I don't waste a second, and together we leap high, bounding across the arena. Meguh's shouting, the spectators are fleeing. Chaos is in bloom, and the demon loves it.

I ready my spear as we charge toward the gilded pavilion. For a fraction of a second I aim at Angma, not the king. But the demon is right. I have a chance to slay an enemy; I must not waste it on the one that cannot be killed by sword or spear.

One chance, one throw.

As we draw closer, I think of the story Angma told me: of the soldier who won Ishirya's love. That soldier was Meguh. I wonder what he was like, if he was cruel to begin with or if his years living with a demon warped him into the monster he is. But I don't wonder too long.

I launch my weapon into the air. Loaded with years of hatred, it flies straight and true—and pierces Meguh in the heart.

Just like I've dreamed for years, he stumbles, already white with shock. Time brakes, and every memory I have of Meguh comes flooding back. The young elephant, the vipers, all the creatures he's ever killed and tortured: avenged. All the terror he's brought into my sister's life—and mine: avenged. My only regret is that his agony will be quick, but I am a smart hunter, not an indulgent one. Dead is dead.

My spear juts out of his chest, and death claims him mid-breath. The moonstone around his neck pools red with his blood.

He's the first man I've ever killed.

"Get her!" Angma screams.

The demon and I don't wait. We leap over the barricades.

A hundred bowstrings twang to life. The air tenses, and I glance behind my shoulder, expecting to find a wave of arrows arcing after us. But my gaze lands on a hulking blue-green figure ramming past the arena gates.

There is gold in Hokzuh's eyes as his wings unfold, casting a wide silhouette over the cliffs and stone teeth.

For the first time, I am afraid of him. I know without a doubt that he is after us, sent to get revenge. And he will not stop until I am dead.

# CHAPTER EIGHTEEN

The Kumala Sea sounds like thunder. Or maybe that's just my heart. As we race away from the arena, the waters thrash against the cliffs, and I hardly breathe until we are bounding over land once more.

We make it to the menagerie, and the demon tosses me off its back. The red string around its claw and my hand dissolves into the air. Without so much as a goodbye, the demon bounds away, and it's gone in two blinks.

I hurry past the cages, and I can't help but wonder if one was meant for me.

I creep past three sentries guarding a leopard. It's moaning with hunger, too weak to even flex its jaws. The guards laugh and poke it with a dry stalk of bamboo. There's a piece of meat skewered in the middle of the stick, tauntingly out of reach.

I wish I had time to snap their necks. That'll have to wait.

Hiding behind the large teak trees shading the menagerie, I sneak beyond the leopard, past the elephants languishing in their mud-baked trench, toward a pit framed by a fence of sago leaves. Inside, I'll find allies.

I approach the pit of vipers. Over a hundred of them, brilliantly red and green and gold, knotted against each other, writhing.

*Lady Green Snake!* they greet in chorus. Snakes are legendary gossips, and they've heard what I did for their brothers and sisters in Sundau. *You have to free us!*

The pit is deep, the walls glazed with a slippery glass the snakes cannot climb. I snap a branch off the closest tree and lean it against the side so they can slither out. Each thanks me with a quick flick of the tongue.

"Which way to Ukar?" I ask.

The snakes tip their heads to the left of the leopards. Towering high above a line of banana trees is a pointed dome painted white as an eagle's scalp.

*The aviary,* respond my friends. *He's in the aviary.*

My nostrils flare. "Take care of the guards," I tell them.

While the snakes scatter to obey, a lump hardens in my throat. Of course, the aviary. The one place my poor, fearsome Ukar will be prey.

I follow the sound of screeching birds.

The aviary walls are high, latticed with diamond-shaped holes. Sharp beaks pierce through the slats, and I hope I am not too late.

"*Ukar!*" I shout, racing around a marble pathway to find the entrance. As I turn the bend, the aviary's two doors slide open with a snap. My breath, short and quick until now, hitches.

"So," says a cruel voice, "you're still alive."

The doors slam shut, but the captain of Meguh's guard doesn't advance out into the menagerie. He dangles Ukar by the tail, holding him perilously close to a ravenous-looking hawk pecking through the latticed holes of the aviary walls.

My heart ices with fear, with fury.

"Meguh is dead," I say through locked teeth. "You will be too, if you don't let him go."

The captain doesn't flinch at my threat—or at the news about his king—but he does glance to the sky, at the dark outline of a dragon fast approaching. The sight makes him sneer. "My queen wouldn't like that."

"Let him go," I hiss.

"Or what?" He dangles Ukar lower.

My friend is in no shape for a fight. The spots on his skin are dull, his eyes cloudy. He hisses at the hawk in a desperate attempt to stave off the predator. But his mouth is bound shut; he cannot bite.

*Ukar, stay very still. I'm going to free you.*

"Let him go," I repeat. My voice goes low, delivering a solemn oath. "Or I'll kill you."

The captain makes that smirk I hate so much. Then he drops Ukar into the hawk's waiting clutches.

*"No!"* I lunge, but the captain blocks me with his body, and the hawk pulls Ukar through a hole into the aviary.

I rush the captain, but he is faster than he looks. His sword comes out, blazing silver against the white walls, and flashes at my torso. I jump back, mind reeling. Pulse racing.

He gloats with his eyes. I swear, he is not going to best me—I will not be anyone's trophy.

He kicks me against the aviary wall, and the starved birds within stab at my calves before they taste the poison and shrink back.

Another swing comes, but this time I lean into the strike, taking the captain by surprise. He didn't expect a girl to take a hit on purpose. His mistake. The impact of the hit is reduced; it still hurts, but I'll end up with barely a bruise. Meanwhile, the captain won't be so lucky.

I grab his sword arm. His eyes bulge as I choke the blade out of his hand. It clatters against the stones under our feet.

He's mine now. I claw at his face, my fingers digging into the hollows of his cheek.

He turns purple, a shade more violent than the rich mulberry of his vest. He grasps for the dagger on his hip, the long blue veins on his arm bulging as he tugs it off his belt. Poor captain, I butt him in the head and break his jaw just like I fantasized. He drops the dagger.

His eyes become defiant yet pleading. There's something else too—something I've seen before, only not to such a ferocious degree.

Horror.

I turn his face away from mine, and my arm hooks around his neck. Part of me knows I'm making up for what I wanted to do to Meguh and that I should stop myself, but I can't. I begin to choke him, squeezing my elbow around his thick, throbbing neck. The muscles in his neck contract and fight, his shoulders seize up, and blood drains from his head, paling his skin bone-white.

I squeeze harder.

Harder.

His lungs give up the fight, and one last wheeze escapes his body.

He falls, heavy with death, and I let myself sink with him. I've just killed a man with my bare hands. But I feel nothing, no tarnish on my soul or conscience—only regret that this is not how I killed King Meguh.

I toss the captain's corpse aside and grab his sword from the marble path. Then I tear into the aviary.

Birds scatter from the trees when I enter, squawking loudly. I snarl at them.

They swipe their talons at my flesh and snap their beaks at my fingers. I cannot fight them all with one lone sword, so I let them come. The wild-eyed birds that taste my blood drop lifeless onto the ground. My path is clear, and I brandish my sword at those who still dare approach.

"Ukar!" I shout. "Ukar, where are you?" I know he's still alive. "Ukar!"

*Here . . . ,* rasps Ukar's voice, as faint as gauze. *Behind the nest.*

I look up to one of the gnarled trees. The remains of a nest are lodged between two branches, and Ukar is wedged underneath. He's coiled his body, wrapping himself tense and thick as a shell. It is his best defense, but it won't last for long.

Gingerly, I ease him out of the tree and lower him into

my arms. Then I jump down and race out of the aviary, smashing the doors shut behind me.

I collapse behind a fountain, cradling my friend.

"Ukar, Ukar . . ." I press a kiss to his forehead.

Ukar curves against me. His scales have turned gray; he is in his resting state. His tail is battered, marred with bites and talon marks, and when I remove the band that binds his mouth, his tongue hangs slack. He doesn't even have the strength to greet me, and when I touch my mind to his, I feel only a cold, numbing pain.

"Rest," I whisper, wrapping him gently around my neck to make sure he's comfortable. "Heal."

I'm on my feet again, but I've taken too long.

A shadow crosses the sun, plummeting toward me. Hokzuh is here.

I spring up, charging at him with my sword, but he bats me aside with his wing. He twists the sword from my grasp and throws it into the bushes.

I stagger back, bracing myself for another fight. But instead of killing me, as Angma commanded, Hokzuh blinks, and the gold swirling in his eyes fades. His red eye glitters bright.

He says, with a disarming smile, "Clever, using the demon to help you escape. You've earned my respect, Lady Green Snake."

He doesn't even give me a second to be confused. He slings Ukar and me over his shoulder, and we accelerate into the sky.

# CHAPTER NINETEEN

We shoot high above the Kumala Sea, reaching the clouds in a matter of heartbeats, and as the adrenaline rushes to my head, I learn that I am not fond of heights. Neither is Ukar. He wraps his body around my neck so tight I can hardly breathe. This is good, I suppose, for it prevents me from vomiting over Hokzuh's shoulder.

"I thought you were going to kill me!" I shout. "Your eyes, they were—"

"If I wanted to kill you, you'd be dead," he says bluntly. "No more talking. You're weighing me down enough as it is."

Right then, a barrage of arrows blows past us like a swarm of locusts.

"Left!" I scream, slamming my weight into his wing so his body tilts left. "Higher!"

Another wave of arrows clips the underside of the clouds. Hokzuh veers upward until we're so high that frost rimes my nose and the palace looks like a toy, small enough for me to pinch between my fingers.

I don't know the extent of Angma's magic, but the darkening sky and gathering winds cannot be a coincidence. We're dragged back down through the clouds, caught in an invisible net.

Below, the murky outline of a ship penetrates the mist. Suddenly the ship glows, and its purple sails are illuminated by an orange halo. It's cannon fire.

The blasts come fast and relentless. Hokzuh swerves. He strains to fly us higher, beyond the cannons' trajectory. But the wind is too strong. We jolt across the sky, jagging across the clouds—until our luck runs out.

A cannon blast scrapes the edge of Hokzuh's left wing. Smoke explodes everywhere, and I inhale pure sulfur. I can't breathe. Can't see. All I can hear is the pain in Hokzuh's roar.

He keeps flying. His wing crackles, bits of rubbery flesh singed off.

My mind is racing. He can't outfly the ship like this, and when he tires—when he slows down—Angma will take us. She'll tail us until we reach Tai'yanan, if she has to. The only way we'll lose her is by destroying her ship.

"Fly us closer."

It's a ridiculous idea, and the dragon rightfully ignores it, which forces me to act. Reaching over his shoulder, I strain to fold his wings closed.

"What are you—"

"*Shut up.*" I knee him in the ribs and keep his wings pinned together.

As we plunge for the sea, Hokzuh begins to understand my plan.

"Closer," I repeat, loosening my grip on his wings. "Above the sails."

"You're going to get us killed."

I pretend not to hear and carefully wrap Ukar around Hokzuh's shoulders. "I'm going to jump. Take care of Ukar."

Before Hokzuh can object, I grip the batten and pull myself up into the purple sails. The wind blusters, the fabric sags under my weight—

And I fall.

I fumble at the sails, trying to grip one of the beams that cuts across the mast. At the last moment, I kick against roiling fabric, and my legs clench together to seize it still.

I catch my breath, but unfortunately I've been spotted.

"Get her!"

Arrows tear after me, puncturing the sails, as I drop down onto the deck. In my periphery, Hokzuh circles back, diverting the archers' attention so I can dash across the ship. My target is the brass lanterns hanging from the forecastle. They'll do nicely for what I have in mind.

Fog thickens the air, and I can barely see Hokzuh's wings. But men are shrieking in every direction, bodies splash into the sea, and swords clatter against the deck. A useful ally, this dragon.

I'm almost at the lantern when two female soldiers slip out of the fog. I've encountered their cloudy eyes and bony shoulders before: Queen Ishirya's bodyguards.

"Where is Angma?" I demand.

In unison, they blow a shimmery mist from their lips.

It dusts my eyelids, soft as a veil. Everything slows; time is suspended.

Maybe if I didn't bear Angma's mark, I would be fooled. But I can see the threads of magic that stitch together her net, and I will not be ensnared.

I claw at my face, fighting off the mist. I shake free of it, lunging for the lanterns.

Before I can unhook one, a bodyguard seizes my arm. Her grip is strong enough to crush my bones, and as I try to twist away, the mist embraces her.

Her skin turns translucent, revealing a horrible clockwork of muscle and vein pulsing under her flesh. Sheets of white hair sprout from her arm, fanning out like wings. Her eyes are no longer cloudy but black and ravenous, and when she finally shows her teeth, they are serrated—and stained with blood.

She's a suiyak!

Suiyaks are former witches. *Mosquitoes from Hell*, Ukar calls them, because they fly like they're jumping, the way a mosquito moves, in quick bursts. They also feed on blood.

Her nails dig into my arm, and I resist the urge to kick her away. Angma must not have told her servants about me. My blood surfaces onto my skin, bubbling red and burning through her nails. With a shriek, the suiyak drops my arm.

Suiyaks never travel alone. As her shriek resonates across the sky, another one appears. This time I am ready. I sweep her away with my arm, using the bloodied side. My poison hisses upon contact, searing ashen flesh. While she flails, I yank an arrow from the railing and plunge it into her chest. A gurgled cry strains out of her throat. I throw her overboard, and she disappears into the fog.

The other suiyak is still here. She's been watching me, observing. When I spin to face her again, she leaps into the air, simply hanging there. I brace myself, but she doesn't charge. She smiles, mist hissing from her nostrils, then she melts into the fog like her sister.

I have a feeling I'll see them again.

*Hurry, Channari!* Hokzuh shouts. *I'm feeling unwelcome at this party.*

Hurrying, I glance over my shoulder for one of the brass lanterns swinging from the rails. I bend over to unhook one.

From behind comes a yank on my hair, then the cold sting of metal on my neck.

Angma, holding the spear I threw at King Meguh. "Yield to me."

Gone is the low flute of her voice. Her command is a rasp, and though magic glazes her eyes, I still notice that in the short time since I've last seen her, her hair has gone gray, bone-white stripes translucent on her neck and cheeks.

"Yield," Angma demands.

"Never." I swing the lantern at her head, and as she staggers, I clap the tip of the spear between my hands. The point bites into my skin, drawing blood, but I don't need blood to end this. That's just to make it hurt. I thrust my knee up, knocking the spear out her grasp. Then I thrust its blunt end into her heart.

Her skin goes instantly white, and her pupils turn red, bright as the blood streaming down her queenly robes.

"Save the queen!" guards cry. "Hurry!"

I drop my lantern, and its oil spills over the deck, trailing fire in all directions. Flames roar to life, traveling swiftly across the ship, and a wall rises, separating Angma and me from her soldiers.

I kneel beside her. This is the moment I've prepared for, the moment I've trained endlessly for. I will not fail.

I press my fingers to her lips, forcing the blood on my skin onto her tongue. I expect her eyes to lose luster, for my poison to take her life quickly. But instead, her flesh starts to peel away under my thumbs, her black hair, her nose and lips crumbling like dough. Within seconds, she is but brittle bone and ash. Then that too crumbles under my fingers, and I draw back in horror—as a white-haired tiger emerges.

The transformation is riveting. It begins with the fur, which coats her hands, traveling down her arms and her back as powerful muscles bulge from her limbs and her body swells. With a soft thud, she falls onto all fours. A tail winds out of her rear, and whiskers pierce her cheeks, taut and pearlescent against the ebony-black stripes twining across her back. Last come the shadows radiating from her fur. They are the night unfolding, a boundless and depthless abyss, and wherever they touch, the waters fall dark.

*You will give me your strength,* she purrs wordlessly.

The command spreads across the ship, and three of the

archers shooting at Hokzuh whirl. Their faces go slack as they stride numbly toward Angma. One of them even catches fire on the way, but he doesn't scream. He doesn't even whimper.

"My strength is yours, my queen," he murmurs before Angma grabs him. In a blink, all that is left of the man is the blood staining her ivory teeth and a scrap of purple sleeve.

Bile rises to my throat as she turns on another guard, repeating the gruesome sacrifice to renew her strength.

I have to stop this. I grip my spear, the blood still wet on my fingertips. Then I find my rhythm, my courage—and charge.

I'm one step, one breath, one strike from impaling her heart when Hokzuh cuts in from above and wrenches me into the sky.

"No!" I scream. "Let me go!"

*Enough, Channi!* It's Ukar. He twists his head over Hokzuh's shoulder. *What did I tell you about being impulsive? She's too strong.*

I look down at the ship, but it's already blurred into the fire.

My mouth tastes like smoke. "I almost had her."

"You were almost killed," Hokzuh corrects me, "and you almost got *us* killed with you. That was selfish. And like the snake said, impulsive."

I grit my teeth, replaying my battle with Angma in my head. Though I won't admit it, I know they're right.

The wound on my hand is still bleeding, and I rip a piece of my sleeve to wrap it. Hokzuh may understand the language of the snakes, but he is not one, and he's not immune to my venom.

There are arrows in his wings, and though he doesn't show it, I can tell he's in pain. As the last of the sun melts into the sea, we coast below the moon. Its edges are sharp tonight, and the sky bleeds the precise red of Angma's eyes.

# CHAPTER TWENTY

Sometime after dusk, Hokzuh stumbles upon a fin-shaped island and drops me onto its beach. The sand is moist, and it feels heavenly against my wind-burned skin. Ukar is already searching for a place to burrow and heal, while Hokzuh lies unmoving.

I crawl toward him. "Hokzuh?" *Hokzuh?*

The dragon doesn't respond. His back is to me, muscles wound tight as he releases a breath. Under the thin moonlight, his blood inks the sand. I reach over to inspect one of his wings. An arrow is lodged in the muscled ridge, practically stitching two of the pleats together. Before he has a chance to object, I pull it out.

He jerks away from me with a snarl.

"You have seven arrows in your wings, two in your back, and another in your thigh," I point out. "You want to stay like that? You look like a pincushion."

He snarls again, then jolts up before I can get any closer.

He's breathing hard, shoulders heaving.

His wings won't fold over his back like they did before. They stick out, one crooked and the other sagging. A tear in his right wing is especially bad.

"I used to make an ointment for Vanna that would help her wounds heal faster," I say, doing my best to mask the worry in my voice. "It's dark now, but I'll gather the herbs in the morning. I'll use my spear for now to splint your wing—"

"I don't need some silly girl's herbs and potions. Just help me into the water."

An odd request, but he's adamant.

I'm tired, and he's heavy, but I manage to drag him to the edge of the sea. I can see the reflection of my hands as I help, and I avert my gaze. This is as close to the sea as I will get. I sit, cross-legged on the sandy bank, as he lowers himself into the water with his elbows.

Hokzuh doesn't comment on my reluctance to go near the water. "So you're not strong enough to lift me," he notes instead, sounding calmer now. "I was wondering about that."

"I *could* lift you," I retort. "I just don't want your sweat all over my clothes." I smell myself and make a face. "Gods, I reek."

Hokzuh wrinkles his nose in agreement.

"I was worried when they sent that demon out in the arena," he says, after a brief stretch of silence. "A bit sloppy with your footwork, but you're fast. And strong. *Very* strong." He shakes his head, like he still can't believe it.

"Are you enjoying your bath?" I say tartly.

"Very much," he replies. "This isn't a bad island for resting a few days. It'll be a while before I can fly again."

I shoot up to my feet. "Not too long, I hope. My sister's birthday is in two days."

Hokzuh shrugs. "So?"

"The Demon Witch is going to kill her."

Hokzuh cocks his head at the sea. From here, we can still see smoke from Angma's ship. "I think your Mother Witch has other problems right now."

"Demon Witch," I correct.

"Angma isn't a demon."

"Yes, she is."

"No," says Hokzuh. "She's a witch. The *demon* in her name's meant to mislead and instill fear. As it has." His red eye glints, and something tells me to trust what he has to say about demons.

I dig my nails into the sand. "Then how does she wield such power? You saw how she mesmerized the court, how she controlled Meguh. I've never heard of a witch with such ability."

Hokzuh splashes his face with water, rubbing his eyes clean before he finally answers: "Your Angma has something that belongs to me. It's given her great power, though not without great inconvenience." He smirks. "She can't sustain a human body for long. I'll bet she was fond of Ishirya's, but now that's a pile of dust—thanks to you. She'll be a tiger until she finds a new one."

He wrings his long hair dry, and it flares behind him like

a flame. "That must be why she wants your sister," he says. "A younger, fresher body. And soon to be a queen, or so I hear."

I ball my hands into fists. "That's not going to happen. Once your wings heal, you're taking me to her."

"Am I, now? Shouldn't it be you who's in my debt?" Hokzuh's gaze bores into me. "I saved you from Angma. If not for the mess you made, I'd know where my pearl is by now."

"Your dragon pearl?" My eyebrows knit with revelation. "You don't have one?"

*That explains much,* says Ukar with a sniff.

I glare. "*You're* supposed to be resting."

*All dragons have a pearl,* Ukar insists. *Unless they've been exiled from the sea and the heavens.*

Hokzuh's red eye glows. "Mine was taken from me at birth. Split in half and tossed to the far ends of Lor'yan."

*Split in half?* Ukar shoots out his tongue like an arrow. *Impossible.*

"You think I lie?" Hokzuh's eye flares bright in challenge.

*No, no.* Ukar backs off, his tail curling in. But secretly he and I exchange a look. We are thinking the same thing: that Hokzuh is only half-dragon, and half something else entirely.

"Are you saying that Angma has part of your pearl?" I ask.

"She found it over a century ago. It fused with her heart and has given her great power."

*Impossible,* says Ukar again. *My kin have known Angma for generations, since . . . since—*

"Since I was born," interrupts Hokzuh. "Angma isn't nearly as old as stories make her out to be."

"But she is immortal now, isn't she?" I ask. "Or is that part of the legend wrong too?"

"Depends on how you look at it. Angma wished to be immortal, and my pearl made her so, but not exactly in the way she envisioned." Hokzuh smiles balefully. "Seems it has a sense of humor, like me."

I shudder, remembering how Angma ate human flesh and blood to regain her strength. If that is the price of immortality, I'd happily pass.

Still, a flare of hope rises to my chest. If Hokzuh can take his pearl from her, the damage she's wrought with it will be undone. That means Vanna will be safe—and maybe . . . maybe my own curse will be broken.

I turn to the dragon. It takes all my restraint to sound indifferent, to act as if he needs me and not the other way around. "You've been searching a hundred years for your pearl?" I remark. "That's a long time. Doesn't seem like you've made much progress."

Hokzuh sends me a glare. "I've been searching for seventeen years. I slept a century after I was born; I awoke only shortly before my dragon half found its way to earth."

Seventeen years. I shiver without knowing why.

"Even so," I say. "It sounds like you could use help. How about you take me to my sister, and in exchange I'll make sure you get your pearl back from Angma."

*Channi!* Ukar hisses. *Do not make a deal with a dragon.*

I kick sand over the snake. *Hush.*

Hokzuh's reaction gives away his thoughts. For me, a puny human, to ask such a favor is ludicrous. But then his brow creases. He's remembering the potency of my blood. . . .

"Your blood," he says. "It works against her?"

"It worked against Angma as Ishirya," I admit. "I don't know what power it will have against Angma as a tiger."

"Her tiger form is the only one that matters. The others are shells."

"I know that, but—"

*Channari's blood carries the venom of the last Serpent King,* Ukar cuts in, always a busybody, even when he's injured. *Not another sovereign has been chosen since he bit her. Her blood is the greatest poison known to Lor'yan.*

"I am familiar with the magic of Sundau's serpents," says Hokzuh, "and their poison."

*Then you know that not even Angma is immune to it,* Ukar replies pointedly. He burrows into the sand. *And neither are you.*

A muscle twitches in Hokzuh's enormous jaw. "Seems I've got no choice, then. Very well, I'll take you to your sister. I won't be able to fly, but we can charter a boat in the morning, should reach Tai'yanan in time if we get one.

"Or . . ." He cocks his head. "We *could* pay the witch of Yappang a visit."

My eyes widen in recognition. "The Nine-Eyed Witch?"

"Why so surprised? We've landed on her island."

"I didn't think she was real."

"If your Angma exists, why wouldn't she?" Hokzuh

laughs at my astonishment. "Old Nakri ought to have *some* disgusting concoction to fix up my wings." He yawns. "We can discuss her tomorrow. It's late. Even monsters like us need sleep."

It *is* late. The tide is rising higher, and the sea laps at my toes, cold enough that a shiver loosens down my spine.

Buried in the sand, Ukar is already sleeping. Hearing his quiet, steady breathing, I breathe easier too. I could use some rest. But not as much as Hokzuh.

"Thank you, by the way," I say, low enough I'm not sure if Hokzuh will hear. "For coming back for me in Shenlani."

The dragon hears. His tone is gruff, but gentle: "You're welcome."

With a nod, I head up a sandy dune.

"Where are you going?" he asks.

"I'll keep watch."

"For what, crocodiles? They like to stay by the witch."

I don't respond. It isn't crocodiles or the Nine-Eyed Witch of Yappang I'm worried about, and Hokzuh knows it. Stubbornly, I stake a spot on the sloping dune where I can watch for Angma.

I don't know how long I stay awake watching the stars blink, bright as Vanna's heart, but there's no sign of Angma or her suiyaks. The world is still, with only the distant percussion of the wind in the trees lulling me to sleep.

I resist as long as I can. For the first time in years, I allow hope to creep into my heart. Maybe I will break this curse on my face and save my sister. Maybe everything will be fine, in the end. I can live the rest of my days with my family, the way I've dreamed.

With those thoughts to soothe me, the knots in my muscles melt into the sand, and I fall into a sea of dreams.

⁓

I've had this dream a thousand times. It begins with the jungle calling for me, but I'm a different Channi. A Channi who waves hello to the other girls in the marketplace, a Channi who's terrified of snakes and spiders and lizards that jump faster than she can run. A Channi who does not heed the jungle's calls because she cannot hear them.

My arms are full of starfruits and paper-wrapped rice noodles and fish, and as I come home, Adah takes the basket from me.

"Channi," he says, "let me help you with that." The note of tenderness in his voice and the way he looks at me, straight in the eye without flinching, remind me that this is but a dream. I don't care. This is the Adah I've yearned for. This is the life I've craved in secret. I'm happy to linger, even if I know it isn't real. "The cakes are almost ready. Your favorites."

I follow the smell of coconut cakes into the kitchen. Inside, I find a woman who looks like me, only rounder around the waist and hips, and with earthy eyes and a freckled, sunburned nose.

Her hair is grayer than I remember, and strokes of silver

brush her hairline, but I would know that face anywhere. It is my favorite face.

Mama's arms fold over me. "My Channi," she whispers in her singsong voice. "My moon-faced girl. Why are you staring at me like that?"

In her eyes, I am beautiful, with smooth, tanned skin and a normal nose and mouth. And I do not remember having a sister.

"Is this real, Mama? You, me, Adah. We're a family."

"Of course it's real."

I press my face against her neck, searching for the beat of her heart—steadier than the temple drums at dawn. Her nails are sticky with sugar, and there's flour in her hair and in the lines of her palms.

Here, my dream often ends, and I wake up with a blissful smile on my face, truly content for a few moments before the truth sinks in.

But this time, the dream drags on. A dark cloud skulks across the sky, and suddenly the kitchen roof flies apart. Ash rains down, smothering our house, the trees, the grass. The air grows thick, and Mama and Adah cough.

I cough too. As I cover my mouth with my sleeve, I look up from Mama's arm—willing the storm to stop. But it doesn't. Strange. Normally, I control my dreams.

Mama holds me tighter, but something feels wrong. Her hands have gone pale, her fingers shriveling. And her nails—they're claws!

"No!" I cry out, pushing Mama away. She isn't Mama at all, but Angma.

Around me, my home vanishes. The jungle swallows me, and suddenly I'm falling, down and down through a tunnel of trees and vines and ash.

I land on my back, on a flat moss-covered stone. A place I know all too well. The place where it all began.

"You miss your mama, don't you?" Angma says, returning to my side. She caresses my cheek with a soft paw. "If only your father had brought me the right daughter seventeen years ago, I would have saved your dear mama. You would have grown up happy. Loved."

I recoil, but against my will I want nothing more than to go back to that alternate life. The one I dream of so often. Gods, I wish I weren't so easy to tempt.

"But alas," Angma continues. "Not even the greatest magic can change the past."

There's a trace of sorrow in her voice—it's the first time she's sounded even remotely human. I catch myself with a jolt. I must not be fooled by Angma's deceptions.

My spear materializes in my hand. In my dreams, I never miss a target. But this is my dream no longer.

I shoot up. Before I can stab the spear into her heart, she clicks her tongue—and my weapon vanishes.

I jump back to retreat, but Angma grabs me by my neck. Years and years of training, and just like that, I am caught.

"Rash as always, Channi," she murmurs with a chuckle. "I see Hokzuh told you about his pearl. You think taking it back will kill me? You think it will break my curse?

"You forget I made you a promise. Right here, on this

195

very rock, I gave you the face of a monster. And I swore to you that I wouldn't undo it—unless you bring me Vanna."

The hairs on the back of my neck bristle. I'm beginning to see where she's going with this.

"Corrupt the pearl may be," she says, "but even it is bound to the power of a promise."

All the hope I've hoarded in my heart crumples as I realize what she's saying. "I don't care about my curse," I seethe. "I don't care about my face. I will kill you."

Angma laughs and laughs. She's seen into my dreams, and now she will wield them against me.

In the glassy surface of her eyes, I see my reflection— the reflection of the girl I become in dreams. Then all at once it vanishes. Scales crack open my smooth skin, hard and ridged and green. My eyes turn yellow and constrict like a snake's, my rosy cheeks go hollow, and my nose flattens until it is no more.

"Stop!" I cry out. This is my dream. Why can't I control it? Why can't I end it?

"Two days," Angma hisses. Her breath is hot on my skin. "Bring me your sister, or I will come for you. This is your last chance, Channari. Do not make your father's mistake."

Above, the sun devours itself from within. Its rim is the first to singe, crumbling like parchment being fed to the fire. Darkness envelops the earth, and as Angma's claws sink into my chest, my scream tears the whole world into pieces.

# CHAPTER TWENTY-ONE

I wake, gasping.

Above me, a young sun rises. Thank Gadda, it is whole and luminous, too self-important to care about some cursed girl's nightmares. It warms the sand beneath me, but I'm still cold. I'm numb all over, and my veins are blue from clenching my fists. Deep in my chest is a sharp, biting throb where Angma tried to kill me.

*It was just a dream*, I tell myself. But I don't believe it.

The taste of ash in my mouth is too real, and my ears are still ringing with the sound of Angma's growls.

She spoke the truth in my dreams. Of that, my certainty is engraved in my bones.

I can't have both, I realize with stinging clarity. My sister *and* my face. I can pick only one.

The choice is easy. I've spent seventeen years with a curse that would sap the hope of the strongest of men, nearly my whole life looking like a monster. It won't be too different living the rest of it like this. I would happily pay that price to save Vanna's life.

Even so, I feel a pang inside me that won't go away.

For a few precious hours I thought I could have everything. The truth is like a bandage removed too soon from its wound. No balm will ever heal the scars.

*Are you all right?*

The voice startles me. At my side, Hokzuh blinks a bleary blue eye open.

*Normally I can sleep through a monsoon*, he says, *but you . . . you were screaming.*

He actually looks worried. The blue of his eye is clearer than the sky, and though his face is covered in sea-green scales, there's something human about his concern.

Seeing it makes my stomach flip. I purse my lips tight. "It was nothing. Just a nightmare."

"I'm no stranger to bad dreams," he says seriously. His voice comes out hoarse. "If you want to talk about it, or about what happened at Bonemaker's—"

"It was nothing," I say again, more firmly than I mean to. I drop my shoulders then, and I add, softly, "Go back to sleep. You need it."

Hokzuh doesn't argue. He tips his head back into the sand and murmurs, "Just know you're not alone, Channari."

*You're not alone.* I don't expect such comfort from the half-dragon. I'm so startled I don't know what to say. It doesn't matter, because within seconds he's snoring again.

I shake my head at him, partly envious, and partly touched that he asked after me.

A ball of dry moss tumbles over the sand, leading my

gaze westward beyond the beach. As it wheels away, a little hope finds its way back into my heart.

Maybe the witch of Yappang will have answers. Maybe she'll know how to defeat Angma.

I sit up slowly and dust sand off my belly. A spider is crawling over my lap, its fast, hairy feet prickling as it crosses the hills of my legs. I'm surprised it would dare venture so close with Ukar sleeping by my side, but that's when I notice my friend is gone.

"Ukar?"

*Here.* He's circling Hokzuh mistrustfully, his tail shaking every time the dragon whistles in his sleep. Even injured, the snake cuts a menacing figure.

*How about I bite off a scale or two?* Ukar asks. *There's bound to be a village on this island. We can sell his scales for a pretty boat, sail away—*

"No biting. He's hurt."

*Don't defend him just because he's the prophesied Hokzuh. My father wouldn't send a dragon to aid you against Angma. It isn't possible.*

"Why not? You said yourself that dragons and serpents are related."

*That doesn't mean we trust each other.*

"Maybe it's time to get rid of old prejudices."

*Says the girl who hates all tigers because of Angma.*

For someone who nearly died yesterday, Ukar's mouth has lost none of its bite. That almost makes me smile.

Before he asks why I'm in such a brooding mood, I hike

up my skirt and make for the trees. "Come on, let's get supplies before the dragon wakes up."

～

Once I step inside the jungle, a wave of longing comes over me. As my heels sink into the damp earth, I'm overcome by the urge to lose myself among the trees, to disappear into this sea of green and forget that Angma is hunting my sister.

Ukar and I venture deeper into the forest. Monkeys follow in the trees, yammering at us with a variety of grunts and hisses.

"They don't like me," I murmur.

*They don't know you. Just move faster. They won't go past the ravine.*

I hurry, like Ukar suggests, but I'm still troubled. In Sundau's jungle, my face frightens few. All creatures in the wild can sense their enemies, and they should know not to fear me. When we pass the ravine, and the monkeys recede, I ask my friend, "What was that all about?"

Ukar pounces on a lizard, swallowing it quickly before he answers, *They say Angma is looking for a girl with a snake face.*

I go very still. "Angma is here?"

*No. But she's sent a call throughout Tambu looking for you.* He pauses, ambushing a ten-legged spider demon creeping out of the shadows. As he swallows, his scales flicker red before dulling to match the grainy earth. *She's offering a reward for anyone who'll turn you in.*

"What's the reward?"

*A blood bond—to live as long as she does.*

Plenty would find that an ample prize. Thankfully, not the snakes. They're cleverer and wiser than most. Too clever by far to want to live forever.

Still, I'm on edge. "Do you think what Hokzuh said about her is true? That she's human—and that his pearl has made her what she is?"

*I don't think he was lying.*

Neither do I. In all the stories, Angma began as a witch. She wished for immortality, but her spell went terribly wrong.

"In her hunger, she unwittingly devoured her own daughter," I murmur. "In despair, she stalked the thousand islands of Tambu, seeking a way to undo her curse, but she could not. With each year that passes, she becomes more demon than human."

If it's true that Hokzuh's pearl made her what she is and gave her a demon's appearance and a demon's hunger, then I almost feel sorry for her. Almost.

*The tiger is her only form that does not age,* Ukar says, *but it needs to feed to remain vigorous. She relies on people like your father, desperate enough to bring new blood for her to consume.*

"Like babies?" I say flatly.

*She eats adults too,* Ukar replies. *But she prefers the young. They sustain her longer.*

I know about Angma. That she takes the young only if they are brought to her. That the reason she's been waiting for Vanna to grow up and hasn't killed her yet is because of the daughter she once lost. The tragic, nameless girl who was mistakenly slain when her mother became possessed by a demon.

In this twisted way, Angma has honor. Sometimes I wonder if she's still human enough to grieve. Whether that is why, for every child a parent sacrifices to her, she will grant a wish.

Well, nearly every child.

*If only your father had brought me the right daughter seventeen years ago*, she'd taunted me, *I would have saved your dear mama. You would have grown up happy. Loved.*

Mama is gone and I can't bring her back, but I can save Vanna.

No matter what it costs, I will save Vanna.

Birds have gathered above us, speeding through the trees. I track their flight to a pond.

"Up ahead," I say to Ukar abruptly, "we'll find the herbs we need." Without waiting for him, I run.

Camphor and gingerroot I find easily beside the pond. Lizards and frogs enjoy a morning swim, and Ukar eyes them hungrily. There's a telling bulge in his neck when I find him minutes later, after collecting my herbs, and I loop him over my arm before he gets greedy.

Spindlebeard is trickier to locate. It's a thorny bush of

drooping white flowers that grows like a weed back home, but birds adore feasting on its buds and roots, which makes it near impossible to find a mature plant.

It takes me over an hour to track down a clump, hidden behind a fallen tree. I pluck as much as is respectful and tie the stalks together with a thin vine.

Most know spindlebeard for its thorns. They're poisonous. One prick, and your muscles go soft. One taste, and your mind goes numb, falling into a deep sleep. Sometimes for days.

What most *don't* know is that when you crush the thorns with the flowers in a certain way, their respective poisons blend into a paste that speeds up healing. The snakes taught me that.

Sometimes, poison is a medicine in disguise.

"That should be enough," I say, tucking the spindlebeard into a pouch I've fashioned from ripping my skirt.

*Take some extra thorns,* says Ukar dryly. *In case you need to subdue the dragon.*

"Ukar, if you really don't trust him, *you* could bite him."

*That would be a waste of venom.*

Ukar stifles a yawn. He always gets sleepy after he bites; he just doesn't like to admit it.

*I still think you should leave the dragon behind,* he goes on. *We can steal a boat, sail to Tai'yanan on our own.*

"I get why you might not trust Hokzuh. But *every* dragon?"

*It's a long story. An old story.*

"We have time before we get back to the beach. Tell me."

*You remember I told you that Hanum'anya betrayed my kind?*

"I do."

*That's all you need to know.*

I glare at my friend. We've arrived at a small clearing, and I leap up on a rock. "Look," I say, gesturing at the sea. "I can see Hanum'anya's snout from here." I lift Ukar so he too can see the scrap of faraway mountain.

"Tell me the story or I'll knot you over this branch." I hoist him onto a tree. "You'll have to look at Hanum'anya all day until you set yourself free."

Ukar hisses with deep displeasure. *You know how he came to be that rock?*

"Yes." Since the snakes rarely speak of Hanum'anya, I had to learn from other humans. Long ago, he tried to over-throw the creator god Niur and failed. As punishment, Niur seized his dragon pearl, banished him from Heaven, and turned him into a mountain.

While Hanum'anya's scales hardened into stone, he saw his pearl hanging from the heavens—a taunt from Niur. He reached for it, so that its magic might guide him home. But his pearl was too far, and it was too late.

A mountain he became, with smoke and fire spitting from his jaws—his final struggle immortalized for all eternity in the middle of the Kumala Sea.

Usually I don't believe the legends, but the shape of the dragon's head glowering at the sky is indisputable.

"Tell me why the snakes despise him so," I say. "Please."

Ukar relents with a sigh, and I settle him back on my shoulder.

*In the ancient times, we snakes had wings,* he begins. *We glided through the clouds with the gulls and the sparrows, and in the water, we used our wings to swim among the turtles and the sea maids.*

*We snakes had magic in our blood. Powerful magic.* He pauses to proudly remind me: *Sundau was the first island created, you know. All your shamans have forgotten this. For centuries, the snakes of Sundau—my kin—were considered sacred beings.*

"Something you've told me only a hundred and one times," I say wryly. I pretend to yawn. "That's why the serpent sovereign is always chosen from your line."

Ukar harrumphs. *There's more to it than that. My kin are oldest of all the snakes of Tambu. We are descended from Hanum'anya's Great Betrayal.*

I tilt my head, curious now. "What's that?"

*See? You don't know everything.*

"If I don't, it's because you didn't teach me."

Another harrumph. *One day, Hanum'anya, first ruler of the sky dragons, came to my kind. "Greetings, cousin," he said. "I'm planning a gift for the great god Niur and have need of your wings. May I borrow them?"*

*My foremother, the Serpent Queen, was no fool. She refused. But Hanum'anya was persistent. "Come, permit me to borrow your wings. I shall make them better than before."*

*"We are content with our wings as they are."*

205

"But you cannot fly high enough to reach the sky dragons in Heaven, nor can you swim deep enough to Ai'long, realm of the sea dragons. Lend them to me, and when I return them, no realm shall be unknown to you, mortal or immortal. It is all to your benefit. What say you?"

The Serpent Queen thought long and hard. "You may borrow our wings," she said finally. "But I must have your promise."

"Of course."

So Hanum'anya borrowed our wings, but the dragon had lied on two accounts. First, he didn't use the wings to create a gift for Niur. Quite the opposite. Ukar's scales turn dark as a cloud crosses the sun. Haven't you wondered why Mount Hanum'anya is also called the Demons' Cradle?

"I can't honestly say I've thought much about it."

Ukar lets out an exasperated sigh. Vanna would have made a better student than you. He stole our wings to construct an army of new creatures. Monsters that might overthrow Niur.

"Demons," I breathe, suddenly understanding. The oldest, most powerful demons could fly.

Yes. Ukar hisses with displeasure. We rue our role in their creation and how it has shaped our name in all eyes.

I think of how I often curse by saying Serpents of Hell. I won't do it again. "But you were tricked."

Only snakes know the truth. Hanum'anya and his heirs spread their own story. That is why many across Lor'yan despise snakes and find us untrustworthy.

"What's the other way that Hanum'anya lied?"

He worded his promise cleverly, so he'd have to grant

*us access to all the realms only after he returned our wings.*
*He never did.*

"So you don't trust dragons." I roll my eyes. "That was one dragon, and hundreds, if not thousands, of years ago."

*Legends always have a spark of truth. Dragons are not to be trusted. Those with demon blood least of all.*

Ukar's waiting for me to agree, to keep heading north for the other end of the jungle to seek a village and a boat. But I can't.

I think about how concerned Hokzuh looked this morning when I woke from my nightmare. There was an understanding in his eyes and a moment of shared torment and vulnerability that I've never felt with anyone before.

I know it's a tenuous connection that Hokzuh and I share, and that I hardly know him. Yet a part of me has waited seventeen years to meet him. Our fates were meant to cross, and now they have.

"Hokzuh was brought to me for a reason," I say finally. "If there's any chance that he can help me save Vanna, I have to take it. I have to trust him."

I steer back to the beach, knowing Ukar will catch up when he's ready.

# CHAPTER TWENTY-TWO

Hokzuh is still asleep when we return.

Ukar harrumphs at the sight, and he's about to nip the dragon awake when I stomp on his tail to stop him.

"Don't. He's wounded. Worse than he'll admit."

I crouch beside the dragon. His scales are darker when he slumbers, and it's beautiful how they gleam under the pale sun, almost like obsidian. He must not have aged during the century that he slept; he doesn't look much older than me— his scales are symmetrical and vibrant with youth. And his voice—he tries to keep it low and gruff, but when he forgets, it's a boyish tenor not too different from Oshli's.

A school of tiny fishes has made a home in the watery crevices of his wing. I scoop them back into the sea with my hands.

His bleeding's stopped, but apart from that, he doesn't look much better. I touch one of the cuts on his cheek. Dragons are known to heal quickly. So are demons. But Hokzuh does not seem to have this ability. I wonder if it's because the two sides of him, dragon and demon, war against each other—even in his blood.

I fan leaves over his face to block out the sun, then set to work. I break up the spindlebeard in my fingers, scaling off the thorns and smashing them with the white petals. I pound the gingerroot with a rock and mash the two ingredients together. Moistening the mixture with fresh water, I carefully rub the paste into Hokzuh's wings.

His arms twitch in his sleep, and I stay clear of them, mindful of the spikes on his elbows. As I roll him onto his side, I notice the scars along his spine. Some are from small cuts, like the wounds on his face and torso, while others look more serious. I have my own scars—mostly from Adah's lashings—but none so deep as his.

It makes me wonder about his past. About *his* nightmares. Whether they haunt his waking hours, as mine do.

Over the next hour, I smear his wounds with the spindlebeard paste. I work quickly, careful not to wake him, but he really *is* a deep sleeper. Even as I reset his broken wing against a branch, tying it with strips from my skirt, he barely moves. To pass the time, I start singing. Mama's old lullaby loosens from my throat. I like to think it's my voice, low and soft, that keeps Hokzuh in the realm of dreams.

Finally, he begins to stir, and I shuffle back as he sits up, letting out a grunt when he sees what I've done to his wings.

"Don't touch it. The stick will help set it straight." I purse my lips, watching him struggle to stand. His injured wings unbalance him. "How's the pain?"

"I'll manage." Hokzuh doesn't thank me for tending to his wounds.

*When can you fly again?* Ukar doesn't bother hiding our mercenary intentions.

"Not today." Hokzuh scans the waters. "With these tides, we'll have to leave before dusk if you want to rescue your sister from the Witch Mother."

"Demon Witch—"

"Whatever." Hokzuh knots his black hair behind his nape. "We need to find a boat. Should be one or two for sale in the village."

"For sale? I figured you'd steal one."

"I would, but Nakri wouldn't like that. She enjoys feeding thieves to the crocodiles."

"What do we do, then? We don't have any money."

He reaches into his pocket and reveals the white moonstone King Meguh always wore about his neck. There's still blood on it.

My eyes go wide. "You—"

"Plucked it off his neck after you murdered him," Hokzuh says without an ounce of remorse. He swings the chain. "Should fetch good coin. Nakri's always been soft for gold." He taps his temple with his knuckles. "Be thankful someone thinks ahead."

With that, he finds his stride and starts into the jungle.

I rush after him. "How do you know this is her island?"

"Because I've traveled most of Tambu, unlike you. I recognized the village." He waves me along. "Come, Yappang can't be far. Pick up your feet."

It's easy for him to say, when his legs are twice the length of mine. I have to run to keep up with him.

"Thanks, by the way," he says, abruptly stopping mid-stride. He waits until I'm at his side. "For whatever you put on my wing." A pause. "And for the singing. You've got a good voice, you know. Maybe when your demon-hunting days are over, you could join a troupe, become a singer."

"Don't mock me."

"Why do you think I'm mocking you?"

The dragon's gaze becomes piercing. He's genuinely curious.

"Because . . . because . . . ," I stammer, "no one says things like that to me."

"They say you look like a demon. To them, that is the truth. I say you have a fine voice. To me, that is also the truth. Fact is that you're a snake girl, immune to venom. Why do you let a few poisonous words hurt you?"

I don't know how to respond. "How are you so comfortable around people like that?" I blurt out. "They're cruel to you too."

"I don't have a heart," Hokzuh replies matter-of-factly. "I don't care whether people like me. You, on the other hand, do have a heart. And it isn't as strong as you pretend it to be."

My retort shrivels in my throat as I remember my own father's betrayal. Maybe it had been Dakuok's idea to sell me off. Maybe Adah had been reluctant to agree. All the same, in the end, I wasn't worth more to him than a small sack of coins.

I push forward into the jungle. "I'll lead the way."

Summer is in full blaze, and I coat my arms and neck with a thin layer of mud, motioning for the dragon to do the same before we go. It'll help with the heat and, for Hokzuh, the mosquitoes.

It's strange having Hokzuh in the jungle with Ukar and me. He's surprisingly light-footed for such a large creature, but his wings make it hard for him to move unseen. The spiked edges skim the undergrowth, occasionally getting caught on bulging roots and vines. But in spite of that, he doesn't slow us down too much.

Ukar keeps ten paces behind, wriggling through ravines and eating little mice. I don't worry about him lagging. If he eats now, he won't be hungry for days, and he's always less cranky when he's full.

The only person who ever came to the jungle with me was Vanna. I remember strapping her to my back when she was little, and taking her to feed a nest of snakes.

"These are my friends," I told her when Ukar and his cousins came to greet me.

"They're snakes!" Vanna exclaimed.

"No, they're my friends. You know all the names of the children in the village, and I know all the names of the snakes in the jungle."

Vanna wrapped her small arms around my neck, pressing her cheek against my back. She was afraid.

"They won't bite," I promised her. I pointed at a freckled

green snake near the nest. "Look, this one is Ukar. He's my best friend."

"Your best friend?" Vanna rapped on my back for me to put her down.

"Well, my best friend aside from you. Don't be scared."

"I'm not!" She slid down my back and reached for Ukar. To my surprise, she kissed him. "If you're Channi's friend, then you're mine too."

Ever since that day, Ukar's had a soft spot for Vanna. He wants to save her as much as I do, and right now it shows—especially with how hard he's trying to tolerate Hokzuh.

"Want some?" Hokzuh plucks purple berries from a bush. "They're sweet."

"They're poisonous," I reply. "Bristleberries. They make purple blood spew from your mouth and worms sprout from your insides."

Hokzuh stares for a minute, then pops the berry into his mouth. "Very funny."

Ukar and I are chuckling.

"Aren't you hungry?" asks the dragon.

"I ate already. How are *you* so hungry? I thought immortals didn't have to eat."

"I'm not immortal."

*Is that why you chose to stay with Meguh so long?* Ukar asks, unable to help his acid tongue. *For the royal feasts?*

Hokzuh's nostrils flare. Ukar's hit a nerve. "Meguh didn't feed me much at all."

*It didn't look that way at the banquet.*

"You think I dined at his special table every evening?" he barks at Ukar. "Last night was all for show. For *her*."

His steps quicken out of agitation, and I realize he speaks the truth. His spine protrudes from his back, and when he leans forward, I see a sharpness to his face from lack of flesh.

My mouth tastes suddenly bitter. I swallow and find my way to Hokzuh's side. I say gently, "You never told me how you ended up in Shenlani."

He is quiet for so long I don't think he'll reply. Then finally he speaks. "I had friends, once. A crew of men who took me in when I was barely grown. Call us pirates, but we never hurt anyone who didn't deserve it. We raided ships for money, used most of it for food and drink. No, I take that back. We used most of it for drink." A wan smile. "On one voyage, we got caught in a monsoon. Lost everything—my ship, my cargo, almost all my crew. One of Meguh's ships found us. Next thing I knew, I was in a cage."

"Angma trapped you," I whisper.

"Maybe. But it was Meguh who reveled in my torment. He kept me starved for over a year." Hokzuh's red eye glints. "He liked what I became when I lost control."

"Couldn't you fly away?" I ask.

"He broke my wings," says the dragon through clenched teeth. "Took a hot iron to the flesh, then shattered the bones. Then he put me and my men in the arena the next day. When I wouldn't fight them, he had his guards slaughter them. He left their corpses in my cell."

What can I say to that? My legs turn leaden and I stop, twigs snapping under my feet. "I'm sorry. I didn't know."

"I don't need your pity."

Words I've said so many times they sound strange coming from someone else.

I still don't know what to say, so we walk in silence, crunching through the underbrush before I finally change the topic. "Are you really a prince of dragons?"

"My father is the king of dragons," he says tightly.

*King Nazayun?* Ukar asks. He lifts his head in interest, his slit-shaped pupils widening like he is piecing together the clues of a profound mystery.

"Not the Sea King," barks Hokzuh. "The one who resides in the heavens."

"The Sky King," I say. Hanum'anya's secondborn.

Ukar's told me plenty of tales about Hanum'anya's heirs: how the two brothers once ruled the sea together until jealousy split the dragon throne, and one remained in the sea and one left for the sky.

"What about your mother?" I ask.

"A demon," Hokzuh says. "Don't ask me how it happened. She's dead."

He's waiting for my reaction, and I disappoint him with my lack of surprise.

"What?" I shrug. "It wasn't difficult to guess, considering your red eye . . . and what your pearl's done to Angma. You could have told me from the start. Demon blood or not, I'm not afraid of you."

"That's because I'm not a demon right now," he says darkly.

Here I thought Ukar was the dramatic one. "If that's

true, and your father is the king of the sky dragons, can't he help you go home?"

"No." Hokzuh's eyes are hard. "He hates me. I'm a reminder of his mistakes."

The way he says it brings a pang to my heart. I know something about being unwanted.

"Then how can you go home?" I ask softly.

"I have to find both halves of my pearl. Once they're united, I can become a full dragon. Until then, these wings are to remind me I can fly only high enough to touch the clouds, but not high enough to go home."

I feel my steps sink more heavily into the earth. His wings are like my mask: a cruel reminder of what I cannot have.

"What does your pearl look like?" I ask.

"If I knew, I'd have found it years ago." A note of resentment creeps into his voice, and he touches the white moonstone he stole from Meguh. It hangs on a simple gold chain, stopping just short of his chest.

*Why'd you stay?* Ukar cuts in. *You could've left Shenlani easily, from the looks of it.*

The question makes Hokzuh tense. "Because of your Demon Witch."

It's the first time that he's acknowledged that Queen Ishirya is Angma. "If you knew she had your pearl, why not take it from her?" I ask. "Why pretend to be under her thrall?"

Hokzuh's eyes dilate with displeasure. "You think it's as easy as stabbing her in the heart and cutting out my pearl?"

He snorts. "Maybe if I had the other half—the *dragon* half— I'd stand a chance. . . . But only Angma knows where that is."

"The dragon half," I repeat. "Did she give any hints about where it might be?"

"If she had, I wouldn't be here." Hokzuh forges ahead. We're almost at the hills, and I can see the rooftops that make up the village of Yappang. "She loved to torment me with what she knew, and what I didn't. In the end, she only said she'd have it soon." He scoffs. "Who knows? She's been so preoccupied with making Meguh attend your sister's auction, she's hardly mentioned it."

My mind is reeling. There's something to be unearthed here—I can feel it. A weakness or a secret that the Demon Witch has buried. "Going to the auction was the queen's idea?"

"She encouraged Meguh to go. Told him to offer as much gold as needed."

Hokzuh pushes aside tall elephant grass as we climb up a low hill. The grass tickles my arms, and wind sweeps over the sweat beading on the nape of my neck.

"Did she say what she wanted with Vanna?"

"Isn't it obvious?" says Hokzuh. "A young and beautiful maiden who's captured the attention of every king in the isles. My guess is the Golden One was going to be her next body. Ishirya's was getting . . . worn."

I remember how Ishirya's skin melted when I destroyed her shell. It makes sense that Angma would covet my sister's youth and beauty. But Angma has wanted my sister since she was a baby. Any idiot would guess it has to do with the light in Vanna's heart. It's strange that Hokzuh hasn't once mentioned it.

Strange indeed. My ribs pinch with sudden revelation.

"Who'd think a Demon Witch would be so vain?" I say, as casually as I can. My heart is thundering, and I hope Hokzuh doesn't hear.

He snorts. "I told you she was a witch. Beauty and youth are all those old crones ever care about."

"You didn't see anything . . . special about Vanna?"

"Special?" The dragon frowns. "What I saw was a spoiled, vapid girl who didn't even stand up for her sister, let alone herself."

Ukar and I exchange a look. Could Hokzuh not see the golden light bursting from Vanna's heart?

Ukar coils himself around my shoulders, his skin pulsing against my neck. I don't dare speak to him, in case Hokzuh hears.

I lengthen my stride, so the dragon and I can walk side by side. "You said you didn't know what your pearl looked like. What if the dragon half's deep in the bottom of the ocean or tucked away in a cloud? How will you know it?"

"That's the cruelty of this," says Hokzuh with a pained laugh. "I wouldn't know it even if it were right in front of me. It's my curse."

"But you found the demon half."

His nostrils flare. "Only because of what it did to Angma."

"What would the dragon half do to someone?"

"A dragon pearl is the very essence of pure and perfect

power," he replies. "Should any creature possess that half of my heart, they'd become . . . extraordinary."

Extraordinary. Like Vanna.

That gnawing feeling inside me intensifies. I can barely steady my voice as I speak, "And to get it back, you'd have to . . . to . . ."

"Kill them," Hokzuh states coldly. "I'm counting on your blood to help me slay Angma. With any luck, we'll get the bastard holding my dragon half too."

I force a smile, but inside, my world is crumbling. I am sure of it, as sure that the sun brings day and the moon harkens night, that the pearl Hokzuh so desperately seeks . . . is the light in Vanna's heart.

Of course, Hokzuh has no idea what I'm thinking. He regards me curiously. "Why so glum, Channari? You're no stranger to sacrifice. You've killed to get where you are today."

It becomes hard to breathe, even harder to hide what I'm thinking and look him in the eye. "Only Meguh and the captain," I reply, "and they deserved it. I'm not the monster I look like. I wouldn't kill just anyone."

"Not even to save your sister?"

I flinch, and Hokzuh knows he's struck a chord. "It won't come to that," I reply. "Angma is the only enemy I have left."

Even as I say it, I know it isn't true. As word of Vanna's light spreads, many more will covet her. Many more will seek her power.

"Let's hope you're right," says Hokzuh. "When it's my

time, *I* will have no hesitation. I'll do anything to possess my pearl once more."

"You'll kill and murder innocents."

"Whatever needs to be done."

"Would you have killed your friends?" I ask quietly. "The ones who sailed with you."

The scales on Hokzuh's face darken. He won't look at me. "Whatever needs to be done," he repeats.

He picks up his pace, but I touch his arm. "You say that," I whisper, "yet I don't believe you. You're not the monster you look like, either."

I expect him to brush me away, to mutter that I'm a fool, but he doesn't. Instead, his shoulders fall. There's a crack in his voice when he speaks: "I don't want to be."

They are words I can understand better than anyone. They are words that erase the apprehension building inside me and replace it with a familiar hope. The tightness in my chest eases, and I inhale a deep breath.

"We'll help each other," I promise. "We'll find a way."

Hokzuh gives a single nod, and it is as though the air between us changes, lifts. He gestures toward the village, and rather than taking off on his own as he did before, he walks with me, side by side.

In the back of my mind, I know it will be a dangerous path to tread—becoming friends with the dragon who seeks my sister's heart. But I don't turn.

# CHAPTER TWENTY-THREE

The village of Yappang looks like any other fishing town. There are about thirty houses built along the shore, with steeply sloped roofs designed to save rainwater. In the middle of the day, women are hanging clothes to dry and men stoke a fire while children toss a ball and kick it across the sand. Half a dozen wooden workboats litter the beach, anchored to bungalows that stand on stilts over the shallow sea. Nothing odd at all.

Except, if you look closely, in the murky water seethes a congregation of crocodiles.

Hokzuh strides ahead, but I crouch down by the reeds. "Give me a minute," I say, adjusting the ties to secure my mask.

The dragon raises an unruly eyebrow. "Yesterday you wrestled a demon *and* you impaled a king through the heart. Don't tell me you're afraid of a bunch of hapless villagers."

"It's just to avoid a scene. I don't do well around strangers."

"Do *I* look like I inspire the warmest of welcomes?"

No, but at least with his branched horns, his claws, his spiked black wings, he looks formidable. No one in their right mind would dare to throw stones at him, or strike at his head with the end of a fishing spear.

Me? I might have the face of a monster, but my body's still that of a scrawny girl.

"Put down the mask," says Hokzuh. "You have nothing to worry about. Nakri's a friend; I've done business with her. The villagers will remember me. They might even bring gifts."

"Gifts?" It's my turn to raise an eyebrow. "For you?"

He grins. "Plenty of villages worship dragons, you know."

"Not ones that look like you. Most dragons don't walk on legs and have arms and wings. . . ."

Hokzuh makes a point of ignoring me. "The grilled catfish here is scrumptious," he goes on, smacking his lips. "A local specialty. They'll probably bring a few platters, maybe with pearl necklaces and yellow orchids for your hair. Trust me, I'm popular here."

I lower my mask. He sounds confident, so why does apprehension churn inside me?

*Because you've developed a snake's sixth sense,* Ukar informs me.

*And what is that?*

*Pessimism.*

I let out a laugh as I trail Hokzuh into Yappang.

Within minutes we arrive. It's gone quiet. No one's on the shore, and the crocodiles are eerily silent. There's mist rising from the water, turning the air musty and thick. Just as I open my mouth to tell Hokzuh we should turn back, a thick net is cast over my head.

I dive onto the sand. The net falls short of my heels, but other nets come flying. Hokzuh spreads his injured wings. None are large enough to ensnare him.

Ukar crawls onto my shoulder and hides behind my neck. He glares at Hokzuh. *Well done, dragon. Still think this is a friendly village?*

The residents of Yappang creep out of the mist, coming out from behind their boats and wagons. I don't want anyone to get hurt. I lower my spear and open my hands. "We're not here to—"

"I'm a friend of Nakri's!" yells Hokzuh, interrupting me. He switches to a dialect I don't know, but the villagers cut him off with shouts, and jab their fishing spears at his broken wings.

Hokzuh retreats to my side. He flashes an uneasy grin. "Seems they *do* remember me. I think I was extra charming here."

I don't get to make a retort. More strikes are directed at Hokzuh, and at me too.

"Demons!" they shout. We could easily overpower them, but my companion's not attacking. If he won't, neither will I. I back up, same as him, until we're dangerously close to the edge of the village pier.

*One more step and we'll be a crocodile's lunch,* Ukar says, both a warning and a lament. *Maybe they won't find you tasty, but I'm a very fleshy snake. My meat is sweet.*

I try not to roll my eyes at my best friend, but I do glare at Hokzuh. "I thought you were friends with the witch."

"She'll come," Hokzuh insists, but he doesn't sound as confident as he did earlier.

At this rate, we'll be dead before she arrives.

Crocodiles snap their teeth under my feet. Their jaws are as long as my entire leg, and in defense, I thrust the end of my spear below the deck—

"You jab that spear one more time, and that pretty arm of yours will go flying into their gullets," warns a thin voice.

An old woman trundles down the narrow boardwalk connecting the bungalows, rapping a cane across the crooked boards as she walks.

"The Nine-Eyed Witch," I murmur as the villagers make way for her to cross.

*Indeed, look,* Ukar says, bringing my attention back to the crocodiles. They're lifting their heads in respect.

I've heard stories that she can speak to crocodiles the way I can speak to snakes. That she's a suiyak herself but, unlike Angma and her followers, has kept her bloodlust under control.

Up close, she is far shorter than I'd imagined, and so old that the lines in her face have deep shadows. A string of seven amber beads hangs around her neck, each with a teardrop-shaped black pupil. In her hand is a cane spiked with razor-sharp crocodile teeth. Just like in the stories.

"Nakri," cries one of the townswomen, "they came out of the mist. Demons, both of them—"

The witch silences her with a raised hand, long fingers fluttering. "This one is a pest." She points at Hokzuh. "But sometimes a useful pest. They are my guests until I say otherwise."

The weapons come down, and Nakri waves the villagers away with a flick of her fingers.

Once they are gone, she turns to me. "One of our hunters saw a tiger this morning. I had a hunch that it meant Angma's daughter would come to pay a visit."

I balk. "I'm not Angma's daughter."

"Can you prove otherwise?" She raises her cane at the white in my hair. "You bear her mark. Not to mention this one is at your side." Her gaze sweeps over to Hokzuh, and she pokes her cane at the spikes on his wings, the markings on his arms. "Still cursed, I see. I told you that you would be, the next time you came back."

Hokzuh's red eye flares, and he jerks his arm away. "We need help. I can pay this time."

"My ears deceive—did you say you can *pay*?"

"We need a boat," says Hokzuh, skipping over her. "And something to heal my wings. Channari needs to reach Tai'yanan to save her sister."

"I know why she's here." Nakri lifts Hokzuh's moonstone off his neck and holds it up to her eyes. "Are you sure you want to give this up so close to dusk, hmm?" She tilts her head. "I won't make it easy for you to steal it back."

Hokzuh's shoulders tense, and I have no idea what they're talking about. "I didn't offer the stone."

225

"And I didn't say I wanted it. I've no use for a tenth eye, especially one as large as that. The gold chain, then?" Nakri inhales. "It smells of rich blood."

"The king of Shenlani was wearing it when Channari killed him."

"Ah, so I'm in the presence of a kingslayer."

"Does that mean you'll help us?"

"Her," Nakri says. "I'll help *her*." She meets his glare, and the two are locked in what feels like an hours-long contest of wills. The crocodiles sink back under the boardwalk, their yellow-green eyes floating above the water.

"A boat and a potion," she says at last, "and I have sight to bestow upon the girl. Dragon and snake will wait outside."

Hokzuh's jaw tenses, but he nods. So does Ukar.

For someone who looks a thousand years old, the witch is fast. She hobbles for the last bungalow, already halfway there when I realize I'm supposed to follow.

Her house stands out from the rest; it sits on crooked bamboo legs, with a pointed thatch as hairy as an old man's beard. Crocodiles are packed densely around it, and their wary eyes follow me.

And the smell! I can't help wrinkling my nose.

Nakri tosses the gold chain into a cooking pot, then offers me a bowl of water that stinks of fish, but I'm too thirsty to mind. I finish it in a single gulp, then set the bowl down.

"I'm not Angma's daughter," I say again.

"And I'm not the Nine-Eyed Witch. But we don't get to pick the names they call us, do we?"

"What is your point?"

"I've heard the tales they tell about your sister. You don't even exist in them." She wipes her chin, tosses her bowl behind her. "In a hundred years, you might as well never have existed."

"I would be glad to be forgotten."

Nakri rests her chin on the jagged head of her cane. "A girl who hunts her nightmares yet cowers from her dreams. But that will change. You're quite different from how we saw you, Channari."

"We?"

The beads around her neck move in unison, until all seven pupils face me. Nine pupils, including the witch's own. *We*.

"What sight did you want to share with me?" I ask, as respectfully as I can.

"'One sister must fall for the other to rise,'" Nakri replies. "Do you remember those words?"

The Serpent King's prophecy sends a shiver dancing down my spine. I haven't heard it in years, and I don't appreciate the reminder. "Yes."

"The Serpent King wouldn't give his life for just anyone." Nakri's eyes roll from side to side, the various beads sending me furtive looks in turn. "We've been puzzling for years why he'd sacrifice so much to protect you. And why he told you that you would need Hokzuh."

"He foresaw that Hokzuh would help me."

"Help you?" Nakri repeats. "Do you truly think Hokzuh would help you . . . if he knew the true source of your sister's light?"

All of me goes rigid. *She knows.*

"You needn't fret. I won't tell him." Nakri leans forward on her cane. "I wouldn't recommend you do, either."

"I'm not a fool." A knot tightens in my chest. "He'd kill her."

"Angma has been toying with the two of you," she says. "Bringing you together as allies, when she knows you are destined to become enemies. Clever tiger."

I press my lips together. "So the prophecy was wrong."

"The serpents are keepers of ancient magic," replies Nakri. "Magic not even they understand anymore. Their visions of the future may come in pieces, often difficult to put together, but they will come to pass . . . in one way or another. My theory is that he foresaw your sister would need protection from Angma. Someone who would sacrifice what was necessary."

"He decided that someone was me," I say hollowly. I've always known that I'm the one who must fall.

"Indeed. That is why he poisoned your blood—to give you the strength you'll need to fight Angma."

Nakri takes our two empty drinking bowls and presses them together to make a sphere: an impression of the pearl. "Tomorrow, when Vanna turns seventeen, she will at last come into the full power of her pearl. As soon as that happens, Angma will kill her. If Angma can claim both halves of the pearl as her own, she will wield the tremendous powers of both dragon and demon. She would become the greatest sorceress of all Lor'yan."

It's my turn to lean forward. "Tell me how to stop her."

Nakri's eyes roll back until they are completely white. "The threads of past and present are already irrevocably stitched and cannot be undone. But the threads of tomorrow may yet weave a different path. Choose the right threads, and your sister will live."

That doesn't answer my question. "Then what? If Vanna lives, Hokzuh will come for her."

"So long as the pearl is broken, there will always be those who seek it," murmurs Nakri. "That is its misfortune."

My heart speeds up. "Then I'll kill Angma and give Vanna *her* pearl. Its power will go to my sister."

Nakri nods. "That is the only way she will have the strength to defeat Hokzuh. It is the only way she will live."

I start to rise, but Nakri grips my shoulder. Her eyes are still white. "Be warned. The pearl is no one's salvation except Hokzuh's. Powerful it may be, but it has a mind of its own—and will be more of a curse than a blessing to bear."

I won't be deterred. After all, none of this is news to me. Hokzuh has said the same thing, about the pearl being alive in its own way.

"Vanna is strong," I reply. "That's why the pearl chose her."

The two bowls in Nakri's hand snap in half. Her voice falls to a whisper. "Who said that the pearl chose *her*?"

I don't get a chance to ask what she means. Outside, the crocodiles lash at the boardwalk with their tails, hissing with an undercurrent of terror.

Nakri blinks, and her eyes are cinder-black once more. The beads on her necklace roll and roll, growing alarmingly fast. "Suiyaks," she whispers. "Suiyaks are here!"

# CHAPTER TWENTY-FOUR

Nakri shoves me aside and opens the wooden trunk I've been sitting on. Inside are bundles of dried shrubs, bags of ground teeth and severed fish fins, and jars labeled with animal secretions that I wished I hadn't read. No wonder the house smells so terrible.

She plucks out a thin vial. The liquid within is a questionable shade of green. "Give this to Hokzuh."

I tuck the bottle in my pocket, and Nakri shoves me out the door. "I've a boat under my house. Take it and go. My crocodiles will keep the suiyaks at bay, but not for long."

A suiyak smashes through the straw walls, and her chalky eyes take us in with glee. "I smelled you, sister," she greets Nakri, levitating as she speaks. "Mother Angma bids you well."

Nakri's greeting is a hard swing of her cane. She misses, and with a laugh, the suiyak bounces back. But Nakri's spry. The old woman leaps onto one of her old chests, and without mercy, she clubs at the suiyak's neck, neatly severing her head.

"It's the fastest way to kill them," Nakri explains between breaths. At my feet, the suiyak's white hair is fizzling into mist, bones turning soft as a fish's. She melts into a murky puddle, which Nakri mops into a crack on the ground. "Go!"

In the distance, the villagers start screaming. More suiyaks are coming.

Nakri's brow pinches with distress. "Go!" she urges again. "They're after you, not Yappang."

I grab my spear. A suiyak drops by the door, and I don't hesitate. On my way out, I bash her skull in—with a satisfying crunch.

Hokzuh is waiting for me in Nakri's fishing boat. I jump in and immediately pick up an oar.

"There she is!" the suiyaks call to one another. They gather in the sky, massing like a cloud of white birds.

Hokzuh and I row as fast as we can, leading the fight away from the village. I don't slow down, not even when my muscles start burning and the wind stings my eyes. We're offshore, nearly at sea, when the suiyaks descend upon us. By now they know about my blood. They ignore the gash I score upon my leg and grab me by the arms, lifting me off the boat.

Ukar is at my defense immediately. He sinks his fangs into the closest suiyak while I go at their necks, but they grab my wrists, twisting until I howl with pain. My spear drops from my grasp, and I have nothing. Nothing to protect me, as the suiyaks lift me higher and higher, out of Ukar's reach with my feet kicking at the wind.

I bite and scratch, drawing blood black as tar. Still they fly. I rip out clumps of white hair. Still they fly. Damn it, without my spear I cannot rip out their pale throats.

Thankfully, I'm not alone.

Below, Hokzuh and Ukar are surrounded. "Go for their heads!" I yell to them. "That's the only way to kill them."

The dragon gets to work. He shoots up, decapitating the monsters with his bare claws. Heads fly, bursting like rotting fruits, their black juices dripping—and the suiyaks surrounding me start to flitter away out of fear. They spread their arms, white hair flaring like wings.

That's when I seize my chance. I bite down on my lip until I taste blood, and spit at the closest suiyak. Her cheek sizzles, leaking mist as she shrieks in outrage. Or at least, she tries to shriek. I bash her skull with my own, as hard as I can. I'm not sure how it happens, but there's a rush of black scales and spikes, and next thing I know, I'm falling.

Hokzuh catches me neatly in his arms. He brings me down to the boat, where my spear has landed.

We're of the same mind. I slather my weapon with blood. "Here. Be careful."

With a nod, he launches high into the air. His left wing is still broken, but with his right, he cuts a deadly arc through the sky, guiding my spear expertly through a frenzied swarm of suiyaks. Left, right, left, right, he strikes a dozen of them, and their bodies arch back. One by one, their white hair fizzles into the sea foam.

The remaining suiyaks hiss.

"Come at me," I goad. I raise my bloodied palms. "Come!"

They don't dare. They hover several feet away, and as one they speak: "This is your victory today, but there is still tomorrow.

"We will see you soon," the suiyaks promise. "Let us go, sisters. She has been warned. Mother Angma will take care of the rest."

Then they are gone, and Hokzuh lands back in the boat with a thud. His muscles go slack with exhaustion, and I have to pull his injured wing out of the water before it drags us off course.

"Never a dull moment with you," he says, stretching out his legs. "You're a special girl, Channari Jin'aiti. Never met anyone like you."

*I could say the same of you,* I almost say. But instead, I reply, "Careful of Ukar." I kick his ankle away from my best friend, who's curled up in the bow. Biting always makes him sleepy. "He needs his rest."

"So do you."

I do. I'm tired, and my arms burn as I row, but every second is precious. I don't even look back until the island of Yappang has vanished beyond the curve of the earth.

Finally, setting my oar across my lap, I turn to the dragon. "Thanks for flying after the suiyaks. Your wing must've hurt."

"Couldn't let you and the snake become lunch." Hokzuh tosses my spear back. "You got the medicine from Nakri?"

"Yes."

"You should take the first sip. You'll need it if you're going to face Angma again."

"It's for your injured wing."

"Don't argue with me, Serpent Queen."

At the nickname, I glare, but I uncork the stopper to Nakri's vial and drink. I was expecting the medicine to taste like fish, but it's pleasantly sour, like a kumquat a few days shy of ripeness.

I lick my lips. "Done. You drink the rest."

I hold out the vial, and the dragon pinches his claws around it. He hesitates. "Will you help me?"

It takes me a moment to realize the vial's too small and fragile for him to handle. He's afraid of crushing it.

"Tilt your head back," I say.

He obeys, and gingerly I pour the medicine down his throat. "Better?"

He hasn't even had a chance to swallow yet. He chuckles. "Eager, aren't we? It's medicine, not magic, Channari. Don't worry, we'll get to your sister in time." He opens his wings carefully. As they billow in the wind like sails, he resumes rowing.

I row too, and our strokes naturally synchronize. We speed across the water, and it becomes an unspoken competition not to be the first to tire. It helps pass the time, since there isn't much to watch aside from the rise and fall of the waves, the rivers of clouds drifting above us. To my surprise, after an hour or so Hokzuh sets aside his oar. He lets out a groan.

"What's the matter? Are you in pain?"

"Acutely." His face contorts into a grimace. A beat. "I just realized I forgot to collect my earnings at the Bone-maker."

My shoulders fall. I can't decide whether to laugh or whack him with my oar. "You're impossible."

"I bet on you." He flashes me a grin, fangs and all. "Would've made a good thirty coppers."

Thirty coppers? "What a fortune," I say dryly. "Happy to know my life was worth two chickens. Maybe three. Shall we turn back to collect them?"

"And face that army of suiyaks again? Even I'm not that deranged." Hokzuh picks up his oar. His humor fades, and he meets my gaze. "I would've bet more if I'd had the money. I've seen you fight before."

I'm not sure what he's getting at, but there's an unfamiliar heat rising to my cheeks, and I don't like it. "It's a good thing Meguh didn't pit me against you in the arena."

That makes Hokzuh laugh. "That would've been awkward, wouldn't it? Though we do make a good team—Dragon Prince and Serpent Queen." A pause. "You know, I was thinking . . . maybe once this is all over, you can come adventuring with me."

I slip him a sidelong glance. "You want me to become one of your pirate lackeys?"

"It'd be a step up from backwater bumpkin. At least you'd get to see the world."

"I'm no backwater bumpkin," I retort. "And I have a sister, in case you've forgotten. I'm going to live with her."

235

"In Tai'ya?" Hokzuh scoffs. "I know you, Channari. A day fenced up in those high ivory towers and you'll be scaling the walls to get out, just like you did at Bonemaker's. A prison's still a prison, no matter how good the food is."

I cross my arms. "You talk from experience."

"I talk because I'm like you."

The words linger in my ears. *I'm like you.*

I bite down on my lip. The truth is, I've never given much thought to my future after Angma is dead. Never given much thought to what *I'd* want to do once Vanna was safe. The possibilities make my head spin.

"You don't have to make up your mind now," says Hokzuh. "But trust me, shared misery is better than misery alone."

*I wouldn't be alone with Vanna,* I almost say. But the words don't come. I know Hokzuh has a point. I always imagined I'd be content living out my days with my sister. But our paths are diverging in ways she cannot reconcile, no matter how hard she tries. She'll be a princess, I'll be . . . *me.*

What if I took Hokzuh up on his offer to sail the world? The idea of joining my fate with someone who understands what it is to be seen as a monster buzzes inside me in a way I can't ignore.

The boat rocks, and I let myself tilt closer to him. "Where will you go, now that you're free of Meguh?"

"Ideally, treasure hunting in the canyons of Guimon. Chasing phoenix feathers, drinking cases of stolen wine." He sighs. "But first, I'll find my pearl."

His pearl. Right.

*Stupid question, Channi,* I berate myself. I'd almost forgotten about his pearl. Guilt sharpens in my gut, and I turn to the sea, unable to face him.

"What's the matter?" he says. "Did Nakri tell you something you're not sharing?"

"No," I lie, far too quickly. I resume rowing, harder than before, falling out of sync with the dragon. "No."

He doesn't question me, which makes it worse. He believes me. He trusts me.

Hokzuh isn't my friend, I remind myself. We made a deal, and I owe him nothing outside of that. Whereas Vanna is my sister; I will protect her until my very last breath.

I bury my secret deep. With every stroke of my oar, that future with Hokzuh drifts further away. The dragon starts whistling, and it's the song that I sang to him while I nursed his wounds.

I bite down on my lip and pretend not to hear.

# CHAPTER TWENTY-FIVE

I don't remember falling asleep, but it's dawn when I awaken, and Hokzuh is flying. His wings, mostly healed, beat force-fully as he tows our boat across the sea using a rope tied to his ankle.

Ukar flicks my cheek with his tail. *Finally! I was about to try to choke you awake.*

My eyelids are crusty, and my hair sticks to my face, glu-tinous with sweat. *You let me sleep?*

*The dragon told me to. Said you needed to be fresh to kill the Demon Witch.*

I flick a glance at Hokzuh. *How considerate.* "Where are we?" I call out.

Hokzuh answers, "Tai'yanan, just ahead." He swats away a seagull that perches on his shoulder.

We must be close to land if there are birds.

I shield my eyes with my hand and stretch my gaze as far as it will go.

To the north is Tai'yanan, Island of the Sky Mountains. The air is clear and blue, and the mountains are perfect domes lining the horizon. Foam from the sea rushes against the crags, indeed making it look like they are floating on the clouds. It's beautiful.

"We're nearly there," Hokzuh says, closing his wings and causing the boat to rock as he lands. "The wind will take us the rest of the way."

"You look better," I say, bowing my head low in thanks. "The potion worked."

It worked for me too. The gash on my leg is gone.

I reach for the fishing net at my feet and slice off a length of cord. It's a ragged thing, nowhere as sturdy as the gold chain that Hokzuh used to have, but I offer it to him. "For your moonstone."

I've caught him off guard, and from the way his shoulders fall, I wonder how long it's been since someone has shown kindness to him.

His hands are too big to thread the cord through the moonstone, so I take over for him, then tie it around his neck.

"It's more than a trophy off Meguh's neck, isn't it?" I say as I hold the stone. "There's magic in it."

Hokzuh's shoulders stiffen. "They say snakes are sensitive to magic. Should've guessed that included you."

I recognize his flat tone. Adah speaks in such a voice when a matter is closed and I'm not to broach it again. But Hokzuh simply changes the topic. He reaches for his ankle, where he's strapped a dagger.

"Take this," he says, thrusting the weapon into my hand. It's double-edged, the same dagger he used to kill the suiyaks. "I doubt they'll let you bring your spear into the palace."

The dagger's hilt smells of fish, which makes sense given that's all we've had to eat for the last day.

"When you see a demon, don't aim for the heart. Go for the eyes or the throat."

"Why not the heart?"

"It's unbeatable."

He waits until I get the joke. "Gods, Hokzuh," I splutter, laughing even though it's not funny. "That was awful."

Hokzuh allows a small smile to reach his face. "In truth, not all demons have a heart, and even if they do, it could be in their foot, their head, their eyes. It's better to aim else-where."

My humor fades. "You talk as though you're not coming with me."

"I'll take you as far as the Port of Kimai. From there you'll find your sister easily." It's not an answer. He inclines his chin at my new blade. "Why don't you test it out?"

"The dagger?"

"No, the oar." Hokzuh rolls his eyes. "Obviously the dagger." He hovers above the stern of the boat and motions for me to advance at him. "Fight me. Pretend I'm Angma."

I twirl the dagger in my hand. "What if I hurt you?"

Hokzuh flashes his teeth and grins. "I hope that you do."

The dragon's smile sends an unwelcome rush of warmth to my stomach. I don't like it, so I leap forward and make the first attack.

Our space is cramped, which makes it a tricky fight. He

blocks me right away, but I expected that. I take no mercy. The first chance I get, I jab him in the groin with my knee. As he crumples, I pin him down with my full weight. I could easily take his throat next, a point I make clear by gliding the tip of my weapon across the tender part of his neck, just above the artery.

We're a breath apart, and it's an odd sort of intimacy: how well I know the chart of his veins, the throbbing pulse points across his body, the lean muscles cording his arms. How much I want to best him in a fight.

I purse my lips, feeling that stupid flutter in my stomach again.

Hokzuh attempts to get up, but I dig my elbow into his neck and make a show of sliding my dagger back into its sheath.

"I win," I say.

"Do you now?" Still lying supine, Hokzuh spreads his enormous wings. He cocks his head, a mischievous glint in his blue eye. "You know if I weren't injured, you'd be the one on your back."

His gaze unsteadies me. I hate it. "Unclear," I reply curtly. "You're fast, I'll give you that. But injured or not, your reflexes are like a slug's. And your attacks are predictable. You rely too much on your wings."

"Do I?" Hokzuh throws me off him with his tail, and I curse as I land on my back.

I always forget about the damned tail.

"At least I don't hesitate before I act. As you do"—he seizes my mask—"especially when you wear this."

My hair falls in a dark cascade over my eyes. "Give it back."

"Why? If people want to be afraid of your face, let them be. Why should you be the one who's afraid?"

"Give it here!"

"No!" Hokzuh holds my mask out of reach. "You're a monster to them. That will never change, no matter how thick your mask is."

I pick up my spear and lunge at him, but the attack is sloppy and impulsive.

Hokzuh checks it easily. He blocks my spear with his arm. Only a blink of his mismatched eyes warns me in advance of his tail whipping at my ankles again, sending me reeling back.

In seconds, he's the one pinning me down, armed with a complacent grin.

"I always forget about your stupid tail," I mumble.

"You forget because you're distracted." Hokzuh crouches until his breath is on my ear. "Gods, Channari. I've never met anyone as fixated as you are on one person."

"Angma is—"

"I'm not talking about Angma," he interrupts. "I'm talking about your sister. Vanna is your weakness. She holds you back from your true potential. Would she fight for you the way you fight for her?"

A retort dies on my lips. It's a question I've wondered before, and I'm unsettled that I cannot say yes.

"As I thought," says Hokzuh, letting me go. "I've seen what you can do. Few have my respect, but you! You're fearless, you're strong—you could be unstoppable, except, Gadda be damned, why won't you fight for yourself?"

The reprimand is all too familiar. I was giving it to Vanna only a few days ago, right before her selection. I never thought I'd hear it aimed at me.

I sit up. "What is there to fight for?" I say acidly. "What I want most I can't have. A family, a normal life, a chance at . . ."

"At love?" he says when my voice trails.

My cheeks suddenly go hot, and I look away, loathing that he's read such a vulnerable part of me so easily. "You've seen what people do when they see my face. I'm a monster."

"To the Nine Hells what people say! Do *you* think you're a monster?"

I swallow hard. I shake my head.

"Good." He touches my shoulder. "Because you're not one to me."

I look up at the half-dragon, heat rushing to my face, and I hold myself together with a breath. Here is someone like me. Someone who knows what it's like to feel misplaced, to be hurt by others simply for not belonging. We're monsters on the outside. Outcasts. But inside?

I'd be lying if I said I didn't feel the pull toward him. Whether it's the gods twisting our threads of fate together, or prophecy, or something else entirely—it's a small miracle that we've found each other.

"You're no monster, either," I say. "Not to me."

A shadow touches his eyes. It lasts only an instant before he blinks it away. As if nothing happened, he blows at his bangs and wears his usual grin. "Finally, you admit you like me."

"I didn't say I liked—"

"You're going to be the doom of me, aren't you?"

"What?"

He winks. "It's those snake eyes. I can't resist them."

I know he's joking, and I roll my snake eyes in mock exasperation, but there's a skip in my heart as Hokzuh offers me my mask back. When, for the briefest moment, our fingertips touch.

"Thank you," I mumble, practically snatching it.

"You can thank me by not dying."

I twist away, but as I raise the mask to my face, I hesitate. I bend over the side of the boat to face the Channi in the water, and I run my fingers over the rough surface of my skin. Scales crackle under my nails until I reach the nape of my neck, which is where my human skin takes over. The sound has always made me cringe, except today I raise my chin.

*This is the face I have,* I tell my reflection fiercely. *Nothing will change that. Nothing.*

Before I lose my courage, I fling my mask into the sea.

It drifts away on the current before the wood darkens and it starts to sink. For years and years I've worn a mask. No more.

With a slow exhale, I turn to Hokzuh, who's wearing an approving smile.

With that look, the loneliness etched inside me fades. A tickle buds in my nose, and when I let it free, it turns out to be a laugh. A laugh, coming deep from my belly and my heart. Even when I stop for breath, it doesn't taste bitter at all.

Hokzuh side-eyes me, not understanding what I find so funny. Then he shakes his head and starts laughing too.

It's nice, I discover, laughing together. My blood hums with warmth—different from the buzzy adrenaline I get during a hunt, and I feel light enough to sing.

"Congratulations," says Hokzuh. "No more masks. No more hiding. You are ready to fight, Channari. You are ready to win."

I let out a long exhale. "You can call me Channi."

He actually beams. It changes his face, softening the hardness of his jaw and brightening his mismatched eyes, so that he looks almost boyish. And the way the sunlight skates across his back, making his blue-green scales shine . . . it's beautiful.

"This means we're friends now, yes?" he says. "This calls for a celebration."

Before I can protest, he plucks Ukar and me up and bursts into the sky, leaving our boat far, far behind.

# CHAPTER TWENTY-SIX

Within the hour we reach Tai'yanan. In the very center of the island stands a silver palace, small in the distance. Sunlight spins off its spires in every direction, bathing everything—the villages and the farms, the forests, the coasts—in its radiance. What a fitting realm for Vanna to rule.

For once, I'm not worrying about my sister. Every time Hokzuh's wings catch the wind, giving us a boost of speed, I whoop with delight. He laughs when I do, and barrel-rolls through a cloud to make the ride even more thrilling.

It's exhilarating: soaring over the Kumala Sea, letting the breeze toss my hair as the birds gawk in surprise, leaving every fear and worry behind me. I can't remember the last time I've felt so free, so happy. I don't want it to end.

*It has to end*, Ukar slips into my thoughts. The snake's wrapped around my neck, practically strangling me every time the dragon makes a dip. *Or have you forgotten what Nakri told you?*

My laugh dries up in my throat. Ukar, ever the killjoy—

of course he was eavesdropping. *We don't have to become enemies,* I say, as quietly as I can. *I've thought about it. I'm going to tell him the truth.*

*Are you out of your mind?*

*He deserves to know.*

*He'll kill her.*

*Not if we make a deal,* I insist. *A new deal. I need him, Ukar. I can't defeat Angma on my own.*

Ukar's scales turn red to show his disapproval. *It's a mistake, Channi. An infatuation.*

*I am not infatuated.*

*That flush on your cheeks would suggest otherwise. And the speed of your heart.*

*That's from flying.*

*Lies.*

I want to throw up my hands in frustration. *Is it so bad to want a friend? Is it so bad to not want to be alone?*

*No,* Ukar admits. *What* is *bad is letting those desires deprive you of reason. Be careful, Channi. There will be consequences.*

*I am careful.*

I think of how Hokzuh rescued me from Angma, how he looked me in the eye and said, *You've earned my respect, Lady Green Snake.* My heart gives a twinge at the possibility that I might not be alone after all. That maybe there is some kindness left in the world—for me.

Ukar must think me a fool, and I can't blame him. Yet he doesn't understand what it's like for me to have found

Hokzuh. Ever since our duel on Sundau—when our minds touched for the first time—I've felt that our fates are inextricably tied.

With him, there's a sense of total acceptance and belonging that I've never had before, even among the snakes. Even with Vanna.

In his eyes I am not someone different. I am like him. If there's anyone I *shouldn't* lie to, it's him.

*He trusts me,* I tell Ukar, *and I can trust him. You watch and see. I'll show you.*

Ukar doesn't get to respond, because Hokzuh twists his head to glance at us.

"Everything all right?" he asks.

His attention makes me start. "Yes," I lie quickly. "Just Ukar grumbling that he's airsick."

"Then I've got good news for him. We're descending soon."

"Already?"

Hokzuh grins at my dismay. "Most snakes hate flying; makes them feel like they've been snatched up by a bird. But you're not a snake, Channi. You'd like to have wings of your own, wouldn't you?"

I would. It's true, I love seeing the clouds beneath me, I love latching on to the wind and letting it take us where it wills. But most of all I love how free I feel here in the sky, unencumbered by rules or walls or prying eyes.

"It doesn't have to be your last flight," says Hokzuh.

I say nothing, pretending instead to look at the clouds.

"You know what *my* favorite thing is about having wings?" he goes on. "You never have to fall."

*You never have to fall.* It's a throwaway remark, but I'm instantly thrust seventeen years into the past, to the Serpent King's prophecy: *One sister must fall for the other to rise.*

"Wait," I say, but the winds are too loud. They swallow my words. "Hokzuh, wait!"

He can't hear me, for he's begun his descent toward Rongyo's palace.

Ukar sends me a mincing glare. *Don't.*

I'm torn. Hokzuh is my friend. He's proved himself to me over the past few days, and we've made a pact to fight Angma together. I need to tell him the truth.

*I know where your pearl is,* I say, barging into the dragon's mind. *I know what Angma isn't telling you.*

Hokzuh turns and stares at me like I've gone delirious, but I don't flinch. That's when he realizes that I'm serious, and all of him stiffens. He stops his descent abruptly, practically choking us in midair.

We hang just below the clouds. "Speak."

The word is gruff, but he's not angry. Not yet, anyway.

"I'm telling you because you're my friend," I begin. "I trust you."

"I appreciate that," replies the dragon. He's cautious, as he should be. But he can't hide the eager glow in his eyes. They're hot and cold at once. I don't know which one to focus on, but the blue one's never a poor bet. It's like looking into the ocean, waters swirling and brimming with hope.

Seeing it makes me tense, but I forge on. "Half your pearl is inside my sister. Vanna. It's her heart."

It takes a beat before the words sink in, and Hokzuh's thick brows furrow. "Your sister?"

"When you said that the owner of your pearl would be imbued with the air of something extraordinary, I . . ." I bite down on my lip, summoning courage. "I suspected it was my sister."

Hokzuh dismisses me with a wave. "Enough with the jokes, Channi. You're the one who said we're in a rush, and now you—"

"Vanna's called the Golden One for a reason," I blurt out. "*You* can't see it, but she glows, radiant as the sun. That light is your pearl."

Slowly Hokzuh's scales darken, their blue-green edges turning black, as though singed by an invisible fire. It is a sinister transformation, and Ukar takes cover behind my hair.

"The Golden One," he murmurs. "She was in front of me the entire time." He growls, and it's alarming how swiftly his voice turns. The warmth and geniality are gone in a snap. "You kept this from me."

"I didn't tell you because you'd want her dead. Nakri warned me—"

"You said you didn't speak to Nakri about my pearl."

I'm caught, and I can't deny it. "I lied. I'm sorry. But I'm telling you the truth now."

"Why? No—I know why." His red eye glows as he draws out his words. "To beg me not to kill her."

I won't let him rattle me. "Listen," I say. "You have dragon blood. Even without your pearl, you'll live many more years than Vanna. Let her live her life, then claim her heart when she passes."

"What about Angma?"

"Stay and help me defeat her. You'll retrieve half your pearl when we kill her."

"The demon half," he says flatly. He clutches Meguh's moonstone. "I need both. This is not negotiable."

"Why?"

Instead of answering, he descends to earth with the force of a slingshot. My stomach drops, and I hold in a scream. I can't breathe. The air is rushing past too fast for me to inhale, and Ukar wraps himself around my face. He's shuddering with fear, the colors of his scales flickering uncontrollably.

Without warning, Hokzuh drops me, and Ukar and I tumble onto a rocky beach. I crawl onto my knees, shaking as I catch my breath.

When I look up, my view is all coastline, peppered with white-marbled rocks. The clouds are dark and low-hanging, and though the spray that tickles my cheeks comes from the sea, I smell imminent rain.

This isn't Tai'ya. The palace is faint in the distance, its silver spires and white walls framed by a horizon of tree-covered hills. The Sky Mountains.

"This is where our journey ends," Hokzuh says coldly. "Our deal is done."

"Wait," I begin, springing to my feet. "You said you'd—"

"I said I'd take you to your sister. You're on Tai'yanan. We're done."

He turns his back and starts for the sky.

"Wait." I catch him by the wing. "What about fighting Angma together? What about helping me, like you promised?"

Hokzuh parts his lips, and for a moment, I dare to hope that he's reconsidered.

"Help me," I whisper. "Please. We'll get your pearl *and* save my sister. Didn't you tell me we make a good team? There's a reason the Serpent King foresaw us together. We'll find a way."

That's when Hokzuh shakes his head. His red eye is glowing fiercely, wilder than I've ever seen it before.

"I liked you, Channi," he says. "You made me smile, after years of having nothing to smile about. That's why I'm letting you go." He lets out a quiet grunt. "Trust me, I *am* helping you."

Never have I heard words so tender yet cruel at the same time. I ball my fists, disappointment rising like a tide inside me. "Are we enemies, then?"

A muscle ticks in his jaw. "Enemies want to hurt each other. I don't want to hurt you."

I can read between his words. "But you'll hurt my sister, won't you?" My voice turns to ice. "If you so much as *touch* her, you won't live to regret it."

Hokzuh simply bows his head. "Angma will be coming for her today. So will I." He tosses me my spear. "You're far from the palace. I'd hurry if I were you."

With that, he leaps into the air, his wings beating a torrential wind into my face. I shield my eyes as he disappears into the clouds.

I kick the sand, cursing the dragon. Anger and betrayal twist into a fiery knot in my chest, and I could scream. I'd believed in him, I'd trusted him.

Ukar pokes his head out of my hair. *Well, what did I tell you? Consequences.*

*I don't need this right now, Ukar,* I reply, cheeks burning. I storm through the sand, wrestling my emotions away from my heart, forging them into a weapon.

I was naïve to think Hokzuh was my friend, but I don't regret telling him the truth.

His betrayal actually makes things easier. Now, when I have to fight him, I won't hold back. If I have to hurt him or even kill him, there will be no hesitation.

I pivot, marking the silver spires of Tai'ya Palace as my destination.

No matter the cost, I will win.

# CHAPTER TWENTY-SEVEN

My sandals squeak as I run. The straw soles are still wet, but, though a storm is coming, the sun is fierce, burning my footprints in the sand. Ukar hides under my shirt, clinging to my shoulders, as though my body were a warm rock.

Together we make for Tai'ya. In contrast to the rolling hills that overlook it, the city is a manicured plot of smooth stone roads, lavish gardens, and bell-shaped temples that spiral into the sky. People say it's the most beautiful city in all of the Tambu Isles, but every building could be made of gold and the canals could flow with quicksilver, and still I would not notice. My only focus is on finding my sister.

My pulse drums erratically in my neck. I carry my spear low, refusing to let its bulk slow me down. Vanna was born during the high morn, when the sun was near its zenith. If I were to guess, I have two hours. It's not easy to tell, with the threads of gray weaving across the sky. A storm is racing me to the city.

I push harder. I must get to Vanna.

For seventeen years, I've tortured my imagination with

all the ways Angma might strike today. Snapping Vanna's neck with a swipe of her paws, slitting her throat with a claw, ripping out her heart with those pearl-white fangs. . . .

My worst fear of all? That I am not there to stop it.

I run faster, until my sandals start to fall apart, and my knees are so wobbly I do not feel their pain. The Port of Kimai is long behind me, the sparrow hawks above are squawking about the snake on my back, and the farmers in the rice paddies call out to ask, "Where are you going, girl?" I breeze past them; they cannot see my hideousness, only a girl racing the gathering storm.

I run until I hear the chants of "Princess, Princess!" The ground trembles, and the beat of Vanna's name vibrates the grass under my feet. The palm trees on either side of me become terra-cotta houses, the trampled grass paths turn into dirt roads, and the wildflowers bloom into people—thousands of them.

I cannot run anymore. It isn't possible. I'm squeezing through crowds, cutting through alleys. I snatch a fan from someone's back pocket and use it to cover my face. Firecrackers pop, kites fly, squids sizzle, and peddlers thrust coral necklaces at me, promising they're giving me the best price. I shoulder through them all, keeping an eye on the sun.

Every time an old woman jostles me, I grip my spear tighter. Angma could be anyone in this crowd. She could be anywhere.

I weave deeper into the city. It's a maze of red banners and gold-painted windows, flowers on every door. At last I make it to the main arcade, where everyone is gathered to catch a glimpse of my sister. But all I see are scarlet-sashed servants throwing rice and hibiscus petals, and monks in bright orange robes chanting prayers. The crowd is broken into clusters, all the women and men are complaining—"Did you see her?" "No, she was in that palanquin, how could I?" "I saw the veil. That's all. Pretty veil."—and I can tell I've missed her.

I need to get to the front, closer to the palace.

Toward the middle of the procession, Ukar recognizes a familiar face. *Look there—isn't that—*

"Oshli!" I shout.

If Oshli is here, then Vanna must be too. But the shaman doesn't hear me. I shout again, louder, and at the last moment his brown eyes dart in my direction. He doesn't see me. Grim-faced, he's marching in step with the other priests and priestesses.

Finally come sedan chairs—carrying Adah and Lintang! Behind them is a scarlet palanquin carried by servants. Vanna's light is emanating from within the silk canopy. I glimpse her golden headdress, pink and purple orchids cascading down her cheeks.

I weave through the crowds, following as the procession approaches the palace gates. Once the royal party enters the imperial grounds, I'll lose my chance.

Desperation grants me courage, and I push through the tight gathering of onlookers until I am on the road. "Vanna!" I shout, chasing after her palanquin. "Vanna!"

The priestesses trailing Vanna block my path, and guards immediately descend upon me. Their swords flick toward my throat, but I don't stop. I shove one of the priestesses into their path and scrabble away.

"Vanna!"

She doesn't hear me. The closer to her I get, the more fanatical the mobs. They spill into the road, throwing betel flowers from their baskets at her for good luck and a good future with her husband.

"Happiness to our prince! Happiness to the new princess!"

She's passing through the gate. I'm about to lose her. "Vanna! Vanna!"

There's no use shouting. She can't hear me. And if I show my face, it's the crowds that will see me first. They'll turn on me, rather than let me through.

Someone grabs my arm from behind. The gesture is so sudden and unexpected that my hand goes immediately to my dagger, and I whirl, ready to fight.

It's Oshli.

He drapes his orange scarf over my head as a veil. His grip on my arm is firm, and as people swarm us, he pushes me toward Vanna's palanquin, waving his ritual staff.

"Let her through!" he commands.

The guards hesitate, but only for an instant. That instant is enough, and Oshli—who's never been helpful to me before—shoves me through the gate, right before it closes.

I bolt toward Vanna. Before I can cry out her name, a hard blow catches the back of my legs, and I fly forward.

The drumming stops. Footsteps pound in my direction— a group of guards with raised swords. I'm halfway up on my palms when I realize I've lost my spear. It's rolling under a wagon, far out of reach.

*Channi, watch out!*

Ukar's warning comes too late, and a guard delivers another blow to my back. My muscles constrict with pain, and my chin slams against the dirt. I'm up faster this time, taking in a blur of sandals and knees before I spy the wooden cane coming down once more. I catch it in my hand and twist, smashing the guard's face with his own stick. His friends come from behind, grabbing me by the waist and lifting me. Ukar springs at the guards, fangs dripping with venom.

"Stop it!" Vanna jumps out of the carriage and lifts her veil. "I order you to release her."

The guards drop me at once. A familiar awe ripples across the road, enchanting all who lay eyes on my sister.

"Bring her to me," she commands, and the guards obey, suddenly docile as lambs. I'm escorted to Vanna, and they circle us so the future princess might have a moment of privacy.

"Channi!" Vanna cries, hugging me. "You're here! It's really you!"

I melt into her embrace, and in my own relief I'm unable to speak. I touch my cheek to hers, treasuring this uninterrupted moment together.

She holds me by the shoulders. Under her veil, her eyes are pink and puffy, and she looks like she's been crying. "I was so worried. No one knew where you had gone, whether you'd been hurt or taken." She strokes my hair, not caring that it's dirty and matted with sand. "I'm glad you're here. I missed you."

She hugs me again, and I rest my chin on her shoulder. The orchids dangling from her headdress tickle my cheeks. Never have I been so aware of how utterly our paths have diverged.

Three days apart feels like three years. Vanna looks and sounds older. It's not just her confidence—how she ordered the guards to stop beating me—or her courtly finery. It's everything. Even her light is brighter, more radiant. Has she finally learned how to use the power of the pearl?

"You've grown up in three days," I say. "You look like a queen."

"I've probably lost a decade of life worrying about you," says Vanna wryly. She won't let go of my hand. "But now you're here."

I have to blink the moisture out of my eyes. What happened to my little sister, who used to chase after me, catching lizards with her bare hands? Who braided ribbons in my hair while I slept so I'd smile when I woke up? *You've been looking so gloomy, sister,* she would say. *This will bring a smile to your face.*

Those days are long gone, but the memories are etched in my heart forever.

"Listen, Vanna," I say, hooking my arm through hers. "I haven't come just for your wedding. It's your birthday, and I saw Angma—"

"Later, Channi," Vanna cuts me off. "Rongyo is waiting

with his mother. The queen! We were delayed at the port because she was furious at him when she found out he'd gone to Sundau. But she's blessed the wedding now!"

The drums resume, and I can barely hear my sister. The guards usher her back into the palanquin, but Vanna won't leave without me.

"Sit with me, sister." She pats the orange cushioned seat beside her. "Come, there's room for both of us. Ukar too. I know he's hiding under your shirt."

I squeeze onto the seat next to her. As the palanquin moves again, Vanna pets Ukar's head. "You've gotten thin, dearest Ukar. Are mice still your favorite? I'll see to it that you're brought a buffet of tasty rodents."

While she chatters on, I remember my spear. I scan the road, trying to find the weapon. But it's gone.

Wind sweeps the betel flowers and rice away from the carriage. Wind, and then a mist so gentle it tickles my skin.

"They promised it wouldn't rain today," Vanna says, tugging me away from the window.

Her nails accidentally graze a still-healing wound, and I recoil. "You shouldn't sit so close. I might have blood—"

"I don't care how dirty you are," interrupts my sister. "I missed you. Just wait until you see the new wardrobe I ordered for you. Your new robes won't be as itchy as mine or as heavy—I hope you'll like them. We'll get you straight to the bath, and I'll send someone to help you with your hair. I'll have one of the servants carve you a new mask too, just in time for the banquet—"

"I don't need a new mask."

Her smile falters. "I know that." She bites down on her lip, the same way I do when I'm nervous. "But Adah will insist. It'll make things easier with him. He won't be pleased to hear that you've come back."

"Is he *ever* pleased to see me?"

"Well . . ." Vanna's brown eyes lift to mine. "It's just that he . . . he says that you killed Dakuok."

I lean back. Oh, the things I would do to Adah if he weren't my father. After selling me to Meguh, he spins lies that I murdered Dakuok?

"I didn't," I reply coldly. "You have King Meguh to thank for that."

"I don't need an explanation," says Vanna. "I told him there's no way you could have done it. I know you would never hurt anyone."

I think of the spear I staked into Meguh's heart and the captain I brutally murdered in Shenlani, the countless guards and suiyaks I've slain to return to my sister's side. Let Vanna believe what she wants. I'm tired, and I don't want to talk about monsters anymore.

As our palanquin ascends the palace steps, I press Hok-zuh's dagger into her hand. "Take this. Angma is coming for you."

"A knife?" Vanna raises her brows. "Very funny, Channi. Is this a birthday gift? It's not auspicious to give knives, you know."

"It's for you to protect yourself."

"Serpents of Hell." Vanna shakes her head, refusing the blade. "You still think Angma is coming for me."

I grab my sister's arm, clutching the embroidered silk. "I *saw* her. She's strong, and she has an army of suiyaks—"

"Look outside," Vanna interrupts. "See the hundreds of soldiers in the palace? Each one has sworn to protect me with their life. Be happy for me. It's my birthday, and my wedding day. A double celebration."

"Vanna, Ang—"

"I don't want to hear about Angma anymore," she says, her voice rising.

The light in Vanna's heart extends to her eyes, and I lean back, staggered that I cannot say another word about Angma.

*It's the pearl,* Ukar murmurs. *She's using it on you.*

I shouldn't be surprised. Nakri did warn that Vanna would come into the pearl's full power on her birthday. It makes sense that she's gotten stronger since I've been away.

"I know it's hard for you to understand," continues Vanna quietly, "but you don't have to worry about me. I have guards aplenty now, and my very own prince to protect me."

Ukar's scales turn purple to match the cushions. *I'd like to see that princeling fend off Angma's demons. You should tell her what you went through to get here today.*

I don't reply. I can't.

"Will you brush my hair, for old times' sake?" Vanna asks. "Will you give me your blessing?"

It's a long-held tradition on Sundau, but probably considered backward on an island like Tai'yanan.

I hesitate. "I found a note in your pocket last month," I say softly. "It said, *You are the light that makes my lantern shine.*"

Vanna bunches up the folds of her skirt, the only sign that I've caught her off guard. "It's nothing and it's from nobody. Just a silly love note. I get them all the time."

She's lying.

"Was it from Oshli?" I ask.

Vanna flinches. "It doesn't matter. Please don't mention it again." A flash of gold sparkles in her eyes, and she lifts a comb from her hair. "Brush my hair. Please. You're the only one left who hasn't."

I take the comb. There's not a tangle in her cascade of silken black hair, and as I stroke down, carefully working around the flowers braided into her crown, the familiar motion calms my nerves. We both used to have trouble sleeping, and we'd take turns combing each other's hair, counting aloud until the sleep spirits claimed us.

"One . . . two . . . ," I murmur.

I make it to seventeen when Vanna turns and squeezes my hand. She takes a breath. "Forgive me if I sounded ungrateful, Channi. I know how much you've given up for me." She presses our fingertips together. "All I want is to take care of you, for us to be together always. I love you."

My heart goes soft. In the beginning, when Vanna was a baby, I protected her because of my promise to Mama. Now I protect her because I cannot imagine life without her. "I love you too."

I return the comb to her and note the flowers in her hair. Hibiscuses and lilies. A beautiful combination. But they're not her favorites.

"What can I bring you for your birthday?" I used to ask her every year.

"A moon orchid, like the ones you pluck from the pond. The butterflies like them."

"Just one?"

"I'll treasure it more if there's only one."

Our tradition began when she was five, when I first took her to the pond and showed her the flowers there. Since then, for twelve birthdays, I've scoured the jungle with Sundau's snakes for the most perfect moon orchid in bloom— and brought it to Vanna. For twelve years, one entire cycle through Tambu's calendar of animals, the tradition has gone unbroken.

As we enter Prince Rongyo's palace, surrounded by statues of guardian dragons and pillars of protection, it's all I can think about: that I've forgotten to bring her an orchid today.

How fitting that it is the year of the tiger.

# CHAPTER TWENTY-EIGHT

Rain leaks from the clouds. A few drops at first, then in drenching sheets, like water flowing from a jug.

An umbrella blooms over my sister, just wide enough to cover me too. Hand in hand, Vanna and I disembark from the carriage and enter the royal garden. I keep my head bowed, watching the rain drown the hibiscus petals that the servant girls toss at Prince Rongyo's slippered feet. He's rushing toward us. His headdress, even taller than Vanna's, is sliding off his head in a very unprincely manner. It makes me like him more than I want to.

"Are you harmed?" he asks, sounding genuinely concerned. "I heard a commotion."

The adoring way Rongyo looks at my sister reminds me of a lamb. There is little depth to his affection, but it's innocent and free of malice. I have no doubt he'd be good to her. But no lamb can protect her from a tiger.

"No commotion," Vanna replies. "Only Channi's arrival."

He shifts his attention to me. The sight of my unmasked face makes him blink, but he's polite enough to smile.

"Welcome back, Channari," he greets me. "Now that you've returned, this truly will be the happiest day of Vanna's life."

Vanna beams as she links arms with the prince. I've gone so stiff I cannot even bow. She hardly knows him, yet she's acting like they've been in love for years.

I know it isn't real. Like me, Vanna has grown up wearing a mask, only hers conceals not her face but her heart. I worry she has gotten so good at pretending that she can fool even herself.

"Have Lady Channari dressed," Rongyo commands one of the servants. "When she is ready, we'll reconvene for the banquet."

"I don't need to—"

"Go with them," Vanna says, cupping my cheek in her hand. "Rest, and enjoy what the palace has to offer, Channi. You deserve it." Her voice becomes swathed in power again. "I'll see you once you are bathed and changed."

Caught in the spell of her words, I obey.

Vanna and her prince vanish into one of the outdoor galleries, leaving me alone with two servants around my age. The way their faces pale at my appearance is a familiar sight, and I know I'll be the subject of cruel gossip later on. But it doesn't hurt, not anymore. I bet all three of us would rather be anywhere but here.

In silence they escort me through a torment of galleries and gardens, and I am aware of every minute wasted before we arrive at my apartments. The instant we enter, I dismiss them.

The taller girl protests. "But His Highness requested that you be bathed and—"

266

"I can bathe myself," I tell her. "Now go."

They bow hastily and scuttle out of view, and I confront my surroundings alone. Gilded bedposts, an excess of silken drapery—it's a generous space, befitting a princess's sister. I immediately dislike it. The walls are too white, and the air too sweet. No lizards crawl up the chair legs, every tree in its pot is pruned to the leaf, and I can't help but feel guilty about the dirt my sandals leave on the floors.

As I wander toward the bath, I spy a table with a wooden bowl full of fresh fruit. The bowl is wide and heavy, and the smallest smile touches my lips.

Vanna sleeps with a bowl just like this one over her heart, so that her own radiance won't wake her in the middle of the night. It was my idea, long ago when we were children.

*"Back again?" I ask when little Vanna peeks into my room. It's late, and even the snakes are asleep. But not me. I always know if my sister is awake.*

*She fidgets with the blanket wrapped over her chest and rubs at her eyes. "I can't sleep. Can I have spindlebeard?"*

*"I wish I'd never told you about that. No. You might end up sleeping forever." I glance about the kitchen, seeking inspiration. I grab the big bowl I keep by the stove. It's made of walnut, a dense, dark wood, and I often use it to put out small fires. "Try this."*

*"Don't be silly. I'm not wearing a bowl to bed."*

*"It'll be like a shield," I say. "Let's try." I lay her down on my cot and place the bowl over her chest. Sure enough, it captures most of her light. And its weight calms her restless heart.*

*Her eyelids grow heavy, and I tease her: "Still silly?"*

*She sticks her tongue out at me, her only admission that the bowl works. Then I sing to her, quietly, the way Mama used to sing to me, and brush my fingertips through the stray hairs that fall upon her forehead.*

*Under our blanket, she reaches for my hand. Squeezes it. "Good night, Channi."*

I set down the fruit bowl, my throat suddenly clogged with emotion. It's been years since I last sang my sister to sleep.

Footsteps thud from an inner chamber I haven't yet explored. I hear water. Someone must be inside drawing a bath.

At first, I assume it's Lintang. Then a short, scarless shaman with curls steps into view, and I let out a silent groan.

"I'll see to her," says Oshli to the other servants emerging from the bath chamber. "Her spirit needs cleansing."

The servants bow, clearly relieved that they won't have to tend me. "Yes, sir."

They leave, and my mood instantly sours.

Oshli, who used to throw stones at my face with the other children, who tried to exorcise me with nonsense prayers his father taught him. Then who became infatuated with Vanna like everyone else, and spent every waking moment he could with her, pretending I didn't exist.

Obviously, I'm not fond of the young priest, but I *am* curious why he has come. About the way Vanna's expression changed when I mentioned him in the carriage. . . .

"What are you doing here?" I greet him blandly. "Have

you come to accuse me of murdering your father? Well, I hate to disappoint you. It wasn't me."

"I wouldn't have helped you through the gates if I thought you'd murdered the High Priest of Sundau."

Oshli never refers to Dakuok as his father, even now that he's dead. I can understand what it's like having a father you don't respect. We used to confide in each other about ours, back when Oshli was my friend, not Vanna's. When we used to dig holes in the dirt and search for worms, when I lived in my old house and knew no one else my own age. So long ago the memory's all but a dream. I tuck it away, bury it deep. I doubt he remembers.

"Then what do you want?" I say.

The young shaman observes Ukar. To my surprise, he gives the snake a respectful nod—then he turns to me, and simply replies, "You lost my scarf."

"Ask Vanna's guards where it is," I reply tartly. "They're the ones who tore it off."

Little perturbs Dakuok's son. I might as well have told him that pigeons flew away with it. He changes the subject. "I hear you've been ordered to bathe."

So he knows about Vanna's newfound power. It seems she's acquired it just in time to be a princess.

Oshli gestures at the tub, filled with steaming water, fragrant with freshly plucked jasmine petals and lotus blossoms. It's supposed to be a luxury, but the only time I've bathed with flowers is in a pond full of frogs.

"I don't need any spirit cleansing."

"I don't think you have a choice."

He's right. No matter how I fight, I cannot resist Vanna's command to bathe. As the water rises, so does my resentment. I should be out scouring the palace, hunting for Angma, not lounging in a lacquered tub, soaking away my dirt and stink with perfumed bubbles.

Ukar doesn't hesitate. He slithers into the bath, letting out a pleasurable sigh. *It's warm,* he says. *And bubbly. Are you just going to stand there trading barbs with the shaman? Get in here.*

I tug at my clothes. "I might look like a snake," I snap at Oshli, "but I'm still a woman. I could use some privacy."

My remark succeeds in breaking the shaman's stony demeanor. He whirls, retreating behind a wooden folding screen. "I'll stand watch from here."

"I can protect myself."

"That's not the story I heard from home."

I have an itch to throw him in the tub and drown him. But he is a priest, so I mind my manners. Well, my hands mind their manners. My mouth has different ideas: "Aren't you the head shaman now that your father is dead?"

"I am."

"Then shouldn't you be at the temple with my sister? Or does she not want you there?"

The outline of Oshli's form goes straight and tense. I can practically hear him gritting his teeth. "I'll wait for you outside."

Finally, he exits the bathing chamber, and I disrobe in peace. His departure makes me feel victorious and rotten at the same time, but I don't dwell on it. Flicking a flower out of the tub, I dip a toe into the water.

Ukar is completely submerged, his scales glimmering to match the tub's blue tiles. I immerse my head too and clear my mind. Much as I hate to admit it, it's wonderfully cleansing.

A tingle comes over my face. Snakes might be the ones sensitive to magic, but I too can feel the power of Vanna's compulsion. As I bathe, complying with her order, the pressure washes off like the dirt on my skin.

Once I am free of it, I don't linger. I rise and dry myself. A silk dress is waiting for me, ornately embroidered, just as Vanna promised. I'm loath to wear it, but there's nothing else.

The silk is cool against my rough skin, and lighter than anything I've ever worn. Its turquoise is a rich hue, as vibrant as the water in a lagoon.

A pity I'll soil it with Angma's blood.

Once I'm clothed and have sandals on, Oshli reappears with a new scarf folded in his arms. It's orange, with golden tasseled ends that look like mop heads.

"To conceal the snake," he explains, motioning at Ukar on my shoulder.

I don't thank him. He's trying to chip away years of mistrust, trying to make me forget the relentless torment he heaped upon me as a child. Too bad I'm good at holding a grudge.

I wrap the scarf around my head, and Ukar slips underneath. Then I start for the door, but Oshli's not finished. He purposefully blocks my way.

What in the Nine Hells does Vanna see in this man?

"Move aside, priest," I say, straining to hold my temper in check. "I have places to be."

Oshli doesn't move. His voice goes low. "Angma is here," he says. "Isn't she?"

That, I was not expecting. "What?"

"It was a few years ago, when I noticed that demons were drawn to the light in Vanna's heart. Demons, like Angma." He tilts his staff, a subtle reminder that he has trained as a shaman. "Let me help you today."

"You?" I shake my head. "You used to laugh at my warnings. What was it you called me? 'A delusional little snake girl.' "

Oshli flinches, finally. "I was young. I was wrong."

I eye him warily, hiding my surprise. "If you want to protect her, why aren't you with her now?"

"I tried to warn her, but she thinks I'm trying to stop her marriage, so she sent me away. I'm not able to see her until she calls for me."

"She used her power on you."

Oshli's silence confirms my suspicion.

I wasn't imagining it, then. In the few days we've been apart, she *has* grown stronger. And more stubborn, it appears.

But I don't say any of this. "It's probably for the best you stay away from her." I scoff. "You'll just get yourself killed."

"You might think that all I have are my prayers," says Oshli, lifting his staff, "a few incantations that protect

272

against common demons. It's true, I don't have great magic against the Demon Witch. But I'm not entirely useless."

He isn't going to convince me. I start to shoulder past him, when he reaches behind a curtain and brings out my spear.

"I believe this is yours," he says.

My eyes widen. I practically snatch the weapon from him, but silently I'm grateful. The dagger Hokzuh gave me is better than nothing, but I fight best with length. The spear was an extension of me.

"Thank you," I mumble.

"I watched you fight for her," he says. "I didn't know you could move like that. You defeated a dragon. It's a good thing you've returned. Vanna will need you today. Everyone will."

It feels strange to hear Oshli speak of me with approval, and against my will his words whittle away at my grudge. There's no dismissing the intention in his voice, the intensity. Like me, he will stop at nothing to save Vanna.

"My sister gave you up for a palace and a prince she barely knows," I say. "Still you love her?"

Oshli's brow pinches. "You think she's doing this for a prince and a palace?"

"What else?"

The shaman shakes his head, making it clear he thinks I'm dense. "She has many reasons. Chief is you."

The words take a moment to land. "Me?"

"We argued about you before the selection. She said her marriage was the best way to protect you. If she married

273

into power, she'd find a way to get you what you want most. She'd break your curse."

Vanna has told me this before, but I always thought she was justifying her own desire to become a queen. I was wrong. My throat suddenly hurts. *Oh, Vanna.*

I have to go. But first, I hike up my skirt for the dagger I hid on my calf. I have a feeling Oshli has the mettle, if not the training, to use it if necessary.

"Vanna wouldn't take this," I say, handing him the dagger. "You have it."

He grips the hilt. His eyes are unyielding and hard, confirming my assessment of him. "Please, ask her to call for me once you find her."

"I will. Where is she now?"

"She's going to the temple for prayers with the royal family. It's the building with the golden roofs. You can't miss it."

"Aren't you coming too?"

"I doubt I'll be able to keep up with you. I'll find my own way."

Fair enough.

"Watch the sky," I say, pushing out the door. "Angma will be here before long."

It's still pouring as I tear across the palace grounds. The rain-washed paths are slippery, and the trees quake as the weather grows more violent. I do not stop until I reach the temple.

I find Adah and Lintang under a pavilion, kneeling before an altar. Behind them is a retinue of priestesses, each carrying a basket of yellow orchids. The oldest wears a blue scarf over her hair and leads the prayer.

Against my better judgment, I slow down. Vanna warned that Adah wouldn't be happy to see me, but sometimes I really can be delusional. Maybe the bruises on my arms, the cuts on my face, will soften his heart. Maybe he'll regret selling me to Meguh.

I am so naïve.

"The princess's sister," greets the priestess with the blue scarf. She inclines her head at me. "Would you like to join our prayer?"

At my arrival, my stepmother rises with ceremonial elegance. She tilts her head, and I can't tell whether she is relieved or shocked to see me. With Adah, I need not guess.

While he rises, my knees instinctively buckle, but Ukar slaps my back with his tail and I straighten, raising my chin with newfound defiance. "I'm back, Adah."

"At least have the decency to put on your mask," he hisses. He notes my weapon. "You bring a spear to your sister's wedding rites?"

He tries to seize it from me, but I do not let him. The brazen display of my superior strength infuriates him, and in spite of the priestesses and servants around us, he raises his hand to strike me.

Funny how small I used to feel around Adah. I'm as tall as he is. I'm stronger than he is. Yet in his presence, my instincts always told me to cower. My shoulders would curl in, and I would hunch . . . like a mouse.

Not today.

For the first time, I block him, catching his wrist easily in my grasp. He gasps. His anger freezes into fear. I could snap his bones with one hand, and he knows it.

"Channi, please." Lintang steps nervously between my father and me. "Don't make a scene. This is your sister's wedding day." Out of courtesy to her, I let go of Adah's hand.

She holds her umbrella over my head, but I step back into the downpour.

"Me? A scene?" Frustration cannons against my chest, making it hurt to breathe. "You allowed Dakuok to sell me to Meguh, and now that I'm here, all you care about is . . . is . . ."

Bile rises to my throat, and my words sputter out. I can see that explaining myself to Adah and Lintang will only be a waste of time.

I turn on my heel.

"Wait, Channi!" Lintang calls, raising her voice to be heard over the storm. "Channi, come back!"

She's still yelling when I turn the corner, but I ignore her. After years of wishing that she'd be a mother to me, that for once Adah might actually show he cares, I've learned the hard way that it'll never happen.

I don't turn back.

# CHAPTER TWENTY-NINE

The royal temple is framed by statues of the gods. It has five walls—each meant to represent a petal in a lotus bud.

Outside, before the temple stairs, umbrellas are hoisted high. They look like clusters of kites, and they crowd my view. I'm cursing because I cannot see the sun, hidden behind the storm clouds, inching close to its zenith. Darkness clings to every eave in spite of the hour, and shadows drape over the temple's sloped roofs, oozing into corners that not even Vanna's light can reach.

I have only minutes left.

Drums pound from the music pavilion across the courtyard, trying to rival the booming thunder. To their beat, Vanna and Prince Rongyo ascend the grand stairs of the temple, personally greeting each member of Tai'yanan's court.

I'm on a hunt, and from experience I know that most of it will involve waiting and being invisible. In hindsight, I'm glad Vanna forced me to take the bath. Best that I don't call attention to myself by reeking of fish.

I wrap Oshli's scarf around my head and dip into the crowds, mostly unseen. My spear draws a few concerned glances, but I'm gone before they reach my snake eyes.

As I plow past the lords, ladies, and ministers, I become vividly aware of every shift of the wind, every murmur and whisper, every flinch and step. The air grows colder by the minute, but my body is hot with panic. Angma is here, somewhere, lurking in plain sight. I can feel it.

We are moments from the exact hour of Vanna's birth. The light in her heart gives nothing away, bathing her in a golden crown as always—but I can feel the threads of her power vibrating, their pulse accelerating. When she reaches the top of the stairs, the rain finally begins to lift. Thunder still rumbles, but light leaks through cracks between the clouds.

The sun reaches its summit.

Framed by the Sky Mountains of Tai'yanan, Vanna turns to face the crowd. I am mere steps away. So close I can smell the hibiscus in her hair. If Angma comes, I will be ready.

"Seventeen years ago on this day," Vanna is addressing the court, "I was born with this light inside me. It has brought me great happiness—and great distress. A radiant curse, I've always thought it." Her voice goes subdued. "I know not where this light comes from, but I promise I will spread only its joy, only its hope." As she touches her heart, its radiance grows, fanning across the entire temple and beyond. Even I feel it, a tickle of warm air upon my lashes. I blink it away. "Thank you for welcoming me to your beautiful kingdom. I will be honored to call it home."

It is an odd speech, but Vanna could be reciting the Eternal Sorrows and no one would notice. Her light has the courtiers transfixed, and they murmur words of devotion to her, bowing as they would to the queen. I alone am scanning the garden, the temple, the sky. A trio of birds squawk in the far distance.

Ukar pops out of my scarf to get a better look. *They're flying too high for birds,* he says.

I squint, taking in their long wings and dangling feet. My body goes tight with dread. *They're not birds.*

"Suiyaks!" I shout. *"Suiyaks!"*

No one listens. In fact, people gasp at my rudeness for pushing through the crowd. I push harder. With the precious seconds I have, I shove my way to the stairs.

I'm halfway up when the crowd recognizes the suiyaks for what they are, and panic erupts. The royal guards spring into action, but they're woefully unprepared. It's going to be a bloodbath.

As the guards stagger back in shock, I grab the nearest bow and quiver. Four arrows.

*You've never been good at shooting,* says Ukar unhelpfully.

*This is not the time, Ukar. Not the time.*

I release the first arrow, but the suiyak catches it. Snaps it in her mouth, cackling like a crow.

Ukar's right, I'm not good at shooting. But I do learn quickly. This time, I press a second arrow to my skin, dabbing it with my blood before I nock it to my bow. When the same suiyak catches it, she doesn't laugh.

Good. One fewer.

By now, Vanna, Rongyo, and the queen have retreated into the temple. They probably think they're safe there, but the suiyaks are threading through the palace arches, shattering windows, and clawing anybody that gets in their way. Before long, they surround the temple, searching for a path inside. I run after them, until I hear Adah and Lintang's shrieks.

I've played this scene in my head a thousand times, promising myself that if Adah were ever in trouble, I wouldn't lift a finger to help him. That I'd remember all the times he struck me, and all the times he told me I was hateful.

Yet in this moment of reckoning, I advance toward him. There's nothing that can right the wrongs he has wrought upon me. No matter how much I might hate him, he is still my father.

And so, a beat before a suiyak will drain Adah's life, I throw myself at the creature and gouge her neck with my spear. Thick black blood splatters over my face, and the creature's eyes go blank. Her body turns limp in my arms.

"Run!" I yell at Adah and Lintang.

They scamper toward the temple doors. The blue priestess is there, helping everyone inside. "Hurry!" she shouts, ushering Adah and Lintang within. They are the last to seek sanctuary.

The priestess starts to close the doors. Standing alone at the top of the temple steps, she is vulnerable to attack, yet the suiyaks avoid her completely. They are feeding on the dead.

Before she locks the temple doors, the priestess takes a moment to survey the attack. With one hand, she undoes the blue scarf over her head. Her hair billows in the wind, white as bone, and as the sun gilds her face, her eyes gleam. Yellow and bright as a tiger's.

Angma!

I bolt for the temple, charging up three steps at a time to the top. The heavy wooden doors slam in my face, but I wedge my spear between them and pry until I open a gap wide enough to slide through. There, I tackle the priestess.

No sooner do I touch her than the yellow in her eyes fades and her face crumbles into ash. As I stagger back in horror, the rest of her dissolves too, and is swept away by a gust of wind that's followed me through the doors.

"May the gods see your spirit home," I murmur, hoping that wherever the real priestess's soul has gone, she can hear me. At least her body will no longer be a shell for the Demon Witch.

"Get out of here!" I shout at the crowd, but thunderclaps swallow my voice. The entire temple shudders, and with an ominous sweep of the wind, every candle goes out.

Darkness bathes the walls. I can barely make out my shadow or even the outline of Ukar's tail. But it's easy to know where to go—in the farthest corner, a golden light shines like a beacon. Vanna can't smother her heart's radiance the way one blows out a candle. Unless I do something, her light is going to get her killed.

*They're coming,* Ukar whispers.

Claws scratch the other side of the walls, nails shrieking

against the wood. The doors are rattling, and the guards huddle around them, their swords raised and ready.

"Get away!" I shout. "Away from the doors!"

There's an explosion. Men fly back, and debris shoots everywhere, pelting the people inside. I shield my face, and when I look up, the wooden doors are smashed and crackling with flame.

Smoke floods the temple. Everyone is panicking—I hear Lintang's voice among the chorus of screams—but I have never been calmer. The next few seconds will determine all our fates, and I don't waste them. I grab Vanna.

She is numb with shock, and the glow in her heart ebbs and flickers as I drape my scarf over her, wrapping it around her to cover her light. She doesn't stop me.

When we were children, she believed the story of Angma. She'd lie for me when I went to the jungle to search for tigers; she'd even help me train to become stronger. Only after we moved to Puntalo Village and she became friends with people like Oshli did she start to think my stories were tall tales.

Where would we be if she'd kept believing? It's pointless to wonder, yet my mind can't resist torturing itself.

I drag her into an anteroom, behind a statue of Niur. With a swift slash, I cut into my arm and sprinkle some of my blood onto Vanna's dress and on the flowers in her hair.

My sister gasps. "What are you—?"

"Don't touch it," I remind her sharply. "It'll burn you if you do."

*The suiyaks aren't attacking anymore,* Ukar announces, crawling to my side. *Do you think Angma is coming?*

"She's already here."

Across the temple, everyone has gathered around an altar, and the priests and priestesses chant, summoning protection wards. They only postpone the inevitable.

A silken purr makes the walls vibrate. At first it's barely perceptible—a drone beneath the chanting. "It's just the wind," Rongyo says, trying to calm everyone down.

Then the purr escalates into a growl. What's most unsettling about it is that it does not stop for breath. Soon the crowd realizes that it belongs to neither human nor beast.

But demon.

Rongyo has only a ceremonial sword, with more beads and tassels than sharp edges. He cannot protect Vanna. Nor can his soldiers and bodyguards. They are ill equipped to fight demons. They are barely equipped to fight me.

While everyone else speculates on the source of the growling, I scan the temple. I take in the three anterooms in the back, the wide pillars, the beamed ceiling. I note the statues of Gadda and Su Dano and watch their eyes to see if they move.

A hulking shape steals across the anterior wall of the temple, concealed by clouds of smoke. I don't see her, but I can smell her. Hers is a scent I would recognize anywhere.

I clamp my hand over Vanna's mouth, holding her still. Then I change my mind and cover her eyes so she can't see what happens next. In three beats, the tiger fells two royal guards, slitting their throats with her claws before they can swing their swords. The air goes taut, and the chanting stops.

"Step forward," the tiger speaks. Her voice is deep and viscous; it clings to the air and makes the walls tremble. "Family of the Golden One, show yourselves."

I pick out the sound of Lintang praying to Gadda for mercy.

"Help them," Vanna whispers. "Channi!"

I give a vigorous shake of my head. I won't leave her.

"Help them," she utters again, a shimmer of power in her words. "Please."

My sister knows exactly what she is doing.

But so do I. I've experienced her power once before. Now that I'm aware of it, I steel my mind against her compulsion. I can't completely ignore the command she's made, but I can work around it.

"Call for Oshli," I say. Vanna blinks with confusion, but I don't have time to explain. My tone goes harsh. "Do it. Now."

"Oshli," she says in a small voice. "Oshli, come back."

"Stay here," I tell her. "Don't turn around, and don't make a sound." I exchange a look with Ukar, ordering him to watch over her.

As Ukar coils himself around my sister's ankles, the power of her command makes me lurch to attention. But the best way to save Adah and Lintang is to hunt the tiger. And that is what I do.

Angma melds seamlessly into the smoke, disappearing into its folds so that only her blood-red pupils are visible. They burn through the shadows, and I follow their reflection in the fallen swords by my feet.

I pretend I am in the jungle, but instead of trees, here are walls carved with stories of the heavens and the hells, with wooden statues of immortals and gods with hollow eyes. The floorboards creak under my weight, but I don't bother moving with stealth. I know Angma can smell me.

I'm just about to lunge, when Rongyo, the fool, decides to seize the moment and get himself killed.

"Come out, demon!" he shouts, brandishing his sword at the smoke—nowhere near Angma's location. "Show yourself!"

"As you wish."

Angma pounces from behind him, but I'm one step ahead of her. I spring at the prince, shoving him into a cluster of clay vases. His head hits the wall. It lists to the side as he falls, dazed.

Saving Rongyo comes at a cost. When Angma marks me as her next target, I'm only half prepared.

She tackles me. Strikes and pins me down with her weight. It happens so fast I can't position my spear to mount an attack, but the spear isn't my only weapon. I sweep my fingers across the cut on my arm and bury my arm in Angma's fur. I can almost hear her flesh burn, and through the pain ringing in my ears, it is the most delightful sound.

"Troublesome child," she rasps, pressing down on my chest with all her weight. I wheeze, feeling my ribs crack, and my lungs fight for air. "Look at me."

I won't. I am not a child anymore. I know what power Angma's gaze holds.

I shut my eyes as her voice enters my mind. *You think I*

*don't understand you, Channi. You think I am a monster. I wasn't always one.*

"I don't care what you were," I reply.

*Your mother was dying. Had your father brought me the right sister, I might have saved your mother—but only for a few years at most. She was weak, like all humans. Even you were weak, but look at you now. Look what I've made you.*

*You want your face back so you can see your mother in the mirror,* she says, lifting the very words from my most secret heart. *You want your father to love you. But what then? Will you be happy?*

"I'll be happy when you are dead," I say between clenched teeth.

*What we want is not so different.* Angma sounds closer. Her voice is soft, almost a caress. *I can be a mother . . . to you.*

The words are so vile that I cannot believe I've heard them correctly.

*I'll not leave you, the way your mother did,* Angma is saying. *The way your sister will. We will be family. The family you always wanted.*

*The snakes are her family!* Ukar says, springing onto Angma's neck. He sinks his fangs into her hide with a hiss.

I twist out of Angma's grip, stabbing upward at her throat. My spear finds her shoulder instead, and I hold the shaft with both hands and slash up, ripping through muscle and bone.

Her cry is a terrifying sound, accentuated by a crack

of thunder. She retreats, shifting into the shadows. Black smoking blood gushes from the wound I've made, but she reaches into the darkness and peels a slip of shadow to patch her wound.

And that simply, she is whole once more.

At my shock, she twists her lips into a feral smile. "Your blood is potent, but it's not enough to end me." Her paws clutch the pulsing fur over her heart, which hides a writhing darkness I've never noticed before. It is like a patch of night against the whiteness of her chest. Her half of Hokzuh's pearl.

"I gave you a chance, but now I must deliver on my promise. Consider it a mercy you won't be there to see your sister die—"

An arrow shoots out of the smoke, piercing Angma in the cheek. She lets out a howl and whirls to face her attacker.

It seems I've underestimated Oshli's skill with a bow. His fingers are practiced as they nock a new arrow. But before he can release it, Angma pounces. She's about to snap his neck with a powerful swing of her arms, when Vanna's light flares.

"Stop!" my sister cries, throwing herself in front of Oshli. "If you want me, take me."

"No, Vanna!" I holler, but either she can't hear me or she chooses not to listen. The intricate braids of her hair have come undone, and her gown is blighted with dark spots of my blood. The glow in her heart blazes brighter than ever before.

"Take me," Vanna speaks. "Let the others live."

"As you wish." The corners of Angma's lips twitch into a smile. She turns, slowly, to confront my sister. "Golden One."

As if by magic, the doors burst open, and people pour out of the temple. Rongyo tries to go to Vanna, but the guards drag him out, assisted by his mother.

Within a minute, the temple is empty but for me, Ukar, Oshli, and my sister. At a supple flick of Angma's wrist, the remaining suiyaks pounce.

At least, they *try* to. But they cannot advance on Vanna; her light is too bright. They recoil, as if burned by its touch.

I take advantage of the suiyaks' confusion and tackle two at once, finding the tender spot between their milky eyes and driving my spear into their skulls. Experience lends me skill, and I kill three more easily, while Oshli stabs my dagger into a fourth.

But more suiyaks cluster outside the temple as we're wasting precious seconds fending them off.

For the first time, I witness the true and awesome power of Vanna's pearl. Light blazes from her heart, countering the shadows that rise out of Angma's. Where the two converge, a tremendous force is born. It cannot last. The walls throb, the ground quakes.

A shock wave ripples across the temple. And my instincts tell me to get out.

I seize Ukar and Vanna. "Run!" I shout to Oshli. The temple is collapsing.

I'm choking on dust as I run. Pillars topple; the roof is

caving in. We're not going to make it out in time, but I shove Vanna as hard as I can toward the doors.

I'm bracing myself for the temple's collapse when out of nowhere, black wings swoop in from the cracks in the roof. Hokzuh. I hear him grunt when a pillar topples against his back, but he throws it off as if it were a pesky tree branch and not solid stone. Then he plucks me, Vanna, and Oshli out of the temple a breath before the walls come tumbling down.

I barely notice that we're flying. I'm too busy spitting out debris and coughing. But it's really him. *Hokzuh!*

*You were about to become a pancake. And not the tasty kind.* He spares me a wry glance. *Guess the Serpent King was right. You do need me.*

I'm numb all over—and honestly shocked that I'm still alive. Lightning strikes dangerously close, but the thunder is growing fainter.

When Hokzuh lands in the garden, beyond the orchards and the lily ponds, I don't thank him. I reach for my sister. She's unconscious, and the light in her heart has gone pale, quavering with each breath. But Hokzuh doesn't release his grip on her.

There's a stench of betrayal in the air, and I dare not breathe. "Give her to me."

The dragon reads my fear with a click of his tongue. "To think I missed those snake eyes of yours." He glances at Oshli. "Tell me, shaman, did she always have such a poisonous glare?"

"Give her to me," I repeat.

Hokzuh drops his humor. "You won't outrun the monsters on foot," he says quietly. He spreads his wings, lifting into the air. "I'll take your sister someplace safe. I promise."

I don't get a chance to respond.

*Behind you,* says Ukar, nodding his head at the crumbling temple.

Angma is stalking out of its remains. Her fur is coated in dust, and she shakes it clean with a toss of her massive head. Then she parts her jaws and lets out an earth-splitting roar.

It's a command. The suiyaks assemble above her, and they slip into the lingering storm clouds, disappearing into the field of gray.

"Go!" I shout to Hokzuh. "Hurry!"

He launches into the sky.

It's staggering how fast the suiyaks catch up with Hokzuh. If he didn't have Vanna, he probably would be able to fend them off, but his wings are still healing, and her weight throws off his balance. He'll hardly be able to outfly the demons.

*Damn it,* I curse. *Fight them, Hokzuh. Fight!*

I'm running to keep them in sight, but there's nothing I can do.

Then, with one last crackle of thunder, the suiyaks vanish. And against the expanse of stark, empty sky is Hokzuh, looking smaller than a bird, his raven-black wings folded over him.

He is plummeting, and with him drops my stomach.

Vanna is nowhere to be seen.

# CHAPTER THIRTY

Lightning streaks the sky. Each bone-white flash is like a ghostly finger, clawing after Hokzuh as he falls through the clouds.

I don't see Vanna in his arms. My heart stops in terror, and my mind's gone numb, but my feet are moving. I'm running, blood rushing to my ears in a deafening cascade.

Reason screams that there's no possibility I can reach Hokzuh in time. That in all likelihood, my sister lies broken somewhere in the royal garden.

I move faster.

*Look at the sky, Channi,* Ukar says as I run. *He's not falling. He's diving.*

The storm has returned. The rain is fierce, and when I look skyward, it pricks my eyes like needles. But Ukar is right. Hokzuh *isn't* falling. He's swerving for the ground while the suiyaks flee.

My fists ball at my sides. What would cause him to abandon Vanna?

The temple has collapsed, and its dust and debris obscure

the scene before me in a dark gray cloud. I have to hold my breath as I run, my lungs threatening to explode. I cut through the remains of the courtyard, searching for Hokzuh and Vanna. So single-minded is my focus that I don't see my father lumber out from behind a prayer pillar.

"You!" he screams, tackling me from the side. "You did this!"

He pins me to the ground. The first slap comes, but I don't even feel it. My head doesn't jerk back, as it always did before. He's yelling, but I can't hear his words.

I fall on my back against the grass and come face-to-face with the sky.

There's no Hokzuh in it.

Which means Vanna is gone.

Gone.

Rain drums the top of Adah's head. It drenches his beard and his long umber sleeves, and water leaks out as his arm arcs toward me. Another slap.

This time I feel it. It doesn't hurt, but my ears ring from the impact, and I see the imprint of my scales on Adah's palm.

Anger surges up my chest. How is this my fault?

My inhibitions are gone, and I summon my full strength against my father, breaking his grip on me. I snap his wrist with a loud crack, and his breath turns into a wheeze as I hurl him into the bushes, where Lintang has been hiding from the suiyaks.

My stepmother rushes to him, cradling his broken wrist like an egg. Her stricken eyes meet mine, and they're filled with fear at what I'm capable of doing.

I part my lips, an apology on the tip of my tongue. But my cheek burns where Adah slapped it, and I lock my teeth so no words will pass. Never will I apologize for being the monster they made me.

I gather Ukar around my neck. This time, when I turn on my heel, no one calls after me.

*Where are you?* I shout for the dragon in my thoughts. *Hokzuh?*

My spear lies on the fringes of the royal garden, nestled between ferns. I pick it up and cut through the bracken, searching and shouting.

I don't know where I'm going. Because of Adah, I've lost sight of Hokzuh. I'm about to climb a tree for a better vantage point when I come across a reflecting pool. The water is overflowing onto the grass. Then I see the half-dragon floating inside.

Hokzuh's eyes are shut, and his wings are spread wide. He's grasping his moonstone with both claws, the tension in his broad knuckles the only clue that he's still alive.

Where is Vanna?

I leap into the pool, wading past the carp to fish out Hokzuh's limp form. He's damned heavy, but it turns out I *can* lift him after all.

The talons on his feet scrape against the grass, crushing the water lilies that have spilled out of the pool. His body is riddled with new cuts and bites. Once I lay him on the ground, I thump the heel of my palm into his chest, hard.

Hokzuh coughs to life. "Serpents of Hell, Channari!"

"Where is Vanna?" I demand.

He coughs again. I don't have time for this. I strike once more, this time with the flat of my spearhead. *"Where is she?"*

"The suiyaks took her."

"Took her? How? You were holding her!"

He bats my spear away. It's then that I spy that his moonstone is no longer on the cord I gave him—and there's a bloody gash on his neck.

No, that doesn't make sense. That can't be!

I dig my spear into his open wound, and he howls in pain. "You let go of Vanna for your moonstone," I say, fuming. "What is it, really? Tell me."

He won't answer, and I have to restrain myself from impaling him. The dragon owes me answers, but they can wait. There are more important matters at hand.

"Get up," I say. "We have to find her."

"You waste your efforts. She's gone."

"I meant Angma!" I snap.

As I say her name, a tiger's growl stings the air, close enough that particles of dust shudder.

My blood goes cold, and the rest of the world blurs as I follow the sound of the tiger.

Seventeen years, I've waited to kill Angma. This time, I won't let her go.

# CHAPTER THIRTY-ONE

I bolt into the garden, chasing Angma through a tangle of jasmine shrubs, following the faint supernatural rustling through the bushes.

I'm not in pursuit for long.

To my surprise, she stops at a pool, where she brazenly takes a sip of water—as if my pursuit means nothing to her.

With any other tiger, I would take my time. Would duck into the bushes and inch toward her, keeping a distance to disguise my scent. But not with Angma.

I launch at her full speed. Every step is charged, and I'm a breath from stabbing her in the back when her whiskers go taut, and she lifts her head. Swivels.

Her eyes are liquid amber, but I'm prepared this time. I've marked the precise location of her heart. I look away. Calling upon all my strength, I thrust with my spear.

"Channi!" Angma bursts out. "Don't!"

Her cry catches me off guard, but I don't hesitate. I strike. I almost have her, until she leaps into the water. I pierce her side instead of her heart.

Her holler is a song to my ears. But I won't celebrate until she's dead.

While she spasms in pain, I hook her neck under my arm. "Where is my sister?"

"Channi!" Angma croaks. "Channi, it's me."

The voice is Angma's; her inflections are gentle and melodic—the way Vanna speaks. I know better than to listen. Angma's tried to fool me before. I push her head into the water, intending to drown her.

Warm rain streams down my temples as I feel Angma's blood pulsing wildly under my fingers. She's shaking, barely resisting me.

This is not the Demon Witch I've fought before.

Still, I do not let go. I yank her dripping head out of the pool, only to demand: "Where is my sister?"

"It's me," Angma cries again, gasping for air. "*I'm* your sister!"

She flails, finally summoning her strength to pull herself out of the water.

*No, you don't.* I leap onto her back and fold both arms around her neck. She's yelling, but even if I could understand her words, I wouldn't listen. I have only one mission, and it ends with her death.

We tumble into the flowers, struggling against each other. Ukar sinks his fangs into her neck while I hold her down, strangling her with my bare hands. Then she rasps out a word that makes my breath catch.

"Cake."

Never has a single word been freighted with more meaning. I lower my lips to her ear. "What did you say?" I whisper harshly.

"Cake," she splutters. "Cake."

"What about cake?"

"The secret . . . secret ingredient is . . . white sesame."

My arms go limp, and as they drop to my sides, I let go of her neck.

It can't be.

This is Angma. The tiger that has haunted me for seventeen years. Rust-orange fur with thick black stripes, and white hair, matted across the ridge of her back.

It can't be Vanna.

But it is. I would have known if I had looked at her heart. It still glows, and as the pond water from her fur drips onto my skin, I kneel beside her.

"Vanna?" I whisper. "*Vanna?*"

A soft beleaguered cry crawls out of her throat, and I could weep. What have I done?

All of me trembles as I roll her carefully out of the dirt. She's bleeding from her side. It's an ugly gash, long and wet, but thank Gadda, it's not too deep.

I bury my face in Vanna's fur. "I'm sorry."

There's no time to ask what happened. Her whiskers go taut again, alerting me a second before swords hack through the bushes and footsteps come clomping our way.

The palace soldiers have found us.

There's a legion of them—and they're armored heavily. Where can we go? If we leave the garden, archers will shoot Vanna the instant we step onto the red-bricked paths.

I shield my sister with my body. "Don't touch her."

"Step aside, sister of Lady Vanna," says one of the guards. "The Demon Witch has enthralled you with her sorcery. If you will not move, we will be forced to harm you."

"This *is* the Lady Vanna!" I hiss, raising my spear. "Angma has taken her body. If anyone attacks her, they will answer to me."

"And me," says Hokzuh, who descends from the sky to my side. The ground shudders under his weight, and he opens his great black wings dramatically.

The soldiers back away, unsure whom to fear more: the dragon or the tiger.

Ukar flicks his tongue at me. *Go.*

I don't need to be told twice. While Hokzuh deals with the soldiers, I usher Vanna into the trees. Tai'ya Royal Garden is one of the wonders of Tambu. It is as wide as all of Sundau, interspersed with lush orchards of plump fruit. The perfect place to hide. Together, we skim past lime and breadfruit trees, but Vanna is breathing hard. She needs rest.

We take shelter under a wide palm, not far from a grove of durian trees. From experience, I know the spiked fruits make excellent weapons. Their pungent smell will deter people from finding us—at least for a little while.

Vanna's never liked durian, and the way she grunts at the smell erases any lingering doubts that this is my sister.

I collapse at her side, dabbing her wound with my sleeve. The blood's already drying. The light in her heart makes her coat glow, and though she wears Angma's stripes and fur, Angma's white hair and horns, she does not bear the shadows that clung to the Demon Witch. She is majestic, she is beautiful.

Rain streams down my face, more than a few drops catching in my eyes. They prick like tears. "I'm sorry I hurt you."

"I deserved it." Vanna's mouth curves into the semblance of a smile. It is terrible to look at, full of curved teeth and a massive pink tongue—yet somehow, in the softness around the corners, I see a hint of my sister. "It was stupid of me, going straight to the pool. But this body's heavy, and I was thirsty."

Try as she might, no smile can hide her sorrow. Her light's always given away her emotions, and though still radiant, it is dimmer than usual. I tuck her head under my chin, and she breathes heavily against my tunic. It is the hardest thing to swallow my rage. "What happened?"

"She won," Vanna whispers. "It was like a game, her heart against mine. Hers was stronger, but not strong enough to kill me. So she took my body instead and gave me hers."

I punch the dirt. Clever of Angma, switching bodies with my sister. She knows I will not kill her while she wears Vanna's shell.

"I'm going after her," I seethe.

"No!" Vanna exclaims with a roar. "You can't."

I'm not listening. I will find Angma. I will force my blood down her throat and watch her shrivel and die.

"Channi . . . ," begs Vanna. "Don't. I can live with this. What I can't live without is you. If you go up against her—"

"I was meant to fight her," I say, each word as heavy as the most solemn of vows. "To fight for *you*. That's why the Serpent King bit me."

Vanna replies with a sigh. She lies low. "I should have believed you," she says softly. "I should have come with you into the jungle all those mornings you asked."

I pretend to scoff. "You in the morning? You never could have gotten up in time. And training in midday is the worst. You'd have fainted from the heat."

She laughs, and the deepness of her tiger voice makes goose bumps rise on my skin. I thumb her cheeks, trying to dry them of rainwater, and find a streak of black fur among the white. The opposite of the white streak in my hair.

What a family we are, now. She a tiger, me a snake.

"All my life you've protected me, Channi," says Vanna softly. "I used to hope that the curse wasn't real, so you'd finally get to live your own life. So we could disappear into the trees together and not care what anyone thought of our faces. That was all I really wanted."

"Then that's what we'll have," I promise her. "After Angma is gone." I sweep the hair from her eyes. She doesn't look convinced.

"Could you fight her again?" I ask. "Angma has your body. If you win, you'd get it back."

"I wouldn't win," Vanna whispers.

"Vanna, you have half a dragon pearl in your heart. You have magic!"

She flinches, as if she's suspected this before but never dared believe it. She shakes her head. "Don't look at me like that. I've seen what she has planned, and we can't win against her."

"What does she plan?"

"She's going to rally the demons in Mount Hanum'anya. There will be hundreds of them. Thousands. Once they've been summoned, she will paint the world with ash and thunder—and . . ."

I'm unmoved. "And what?"

Vanna's pupils turn black and hollow under her hooded eyelids. "And she'll return home. Back where it all began. That is where all this will end."

Sundau. To the jungle with the crooked tree.

"What an event that will be," I say dryly as I scrape mud off my sandals' soles. The rain is finally stopping. "We'll have to go." I tilt my head. "We can ask Rongyo for help."

At the suggestion, Vanna cringes. "You go. I'll stay."

"Under the durian tree?" I almost laugh again, but my humor flees when I imagine the guards finding her and killing her. "Come with me," I say gently. "He'll understand."

Vanna makes an adamant growl. She won't budge.

I take a different tack. "What about Oshli?" I ask.

At the name, my sister's head lifts. Just a hair. "Where is he?"

So. She does care about him.

I shouldn't be surprised. Oshli, has always been there. It was Oshli who sneaked Vanna her favorite shrimp noodles when Lintang decided they were too greasy for the family, Oshli who painstakingly transcribed by hand Vanna's favorite romances and epics from the temple library so she

301

might have her own copy to read at home with me. Oshli, the only other person who looks after Vanna's best interest, even if it displeases her.

"I don't know where he is," I say at last. "Let's go find him."

I know she's tempted, but her lower lip quivers, and she shuts her giant, furred eyes tight. "Can I tell you a secret?"

"You can tell me anything."

She hangs her head low. "I was praying this morning . . . that I wouldn't have to go through with it. The wedding, I mean. Do you think . . ."

"That all this is your fault?" I shake my head vehemently. "No."

"I thought I wanted to be a queen, Channi," she says ruefully. "It was what I dreamed of for years. But I think what I truly wanted . . . was to be my own. To not be defined by . . . by this—" She makes a low growl at the light pulsing in her chest.

Her confession silences me. I've always known that Vanna's light is a curse of sorts, predetermining her worth in the eyes of others. But until now, I never realized how unhappy she must have been. I never realized how much she *fears* it.

"I did think about running away—from the contest and from today," she admits. "But I wasn't brave enough. I thought I'd get caught and dragged back."

"You underestimate yourself," I reply. "You have more power than you know. I would've helped you." I pause. "I still can."

She doesn't reply. I know she's doesn't want to disappoint Lintang and Adah. Her whole life, she's pleased everyone simply by existing. She isn't used to being a source of disappointment.

I wrap my arm around her back, press my cheek to hers, scale to fur. "Find the light that makes your lantern shine," I say softly. "Hold on to it, even when the dark surrounds you. Not even the strongest wind will blow out the flame."

She goes very still. Not a single strand of fur stirs.

"Oshli is that light, isn't he?" I say in a low voice. "And you are his, just like he wrote in that letter."

Twice now, I've asked her about the letter I found in her pocket. This time, she finally gives the barest nod.

"He told me you fought over me," I say. "But that's not the only reason you cast him away, is it?"

"You two have more in common than you think," she replies. "Like you, he hardly ever smiles." She snorts. Then she turns somber. "And like you, Sundau's the place he loves most. He was born and raised to become shaman of the temple there." A pause. "If he ties himself to me . . . he'll never have that quiet life. He might have to leave Tambu. Maybe forever."

"If he is like me, he will not mind it," I say. "He would choose to be with you."

Vanna inhales. "You know, what I always wanted was for you two to be friends. He told me once that you were, as children. He said you were his first friend."

*And he was mine.* I lift my head, surprised that he remembers.

"I used to ask him what you were like before your face was cursed," Vanna confesses.

It's my turn to go still. "What did he say?"

"He said that our house was the farthest from the village, his favorite to visit with his father. He said you used to race each other across the roads, and that you poked at worms together, and one time you flooded the kitchen."

"We did," I say, almost smiling. "Even after my curse, he didn't mock me like the other children did—not at first, anyway. He'd hold my hand while I cried, and I used to think it wouldn't be so bad since I had a friend."

I don't share the rest. That one day, Oshli changed. He stopped looking for me when he visited Adah's house, stopped acknowledging that I existed. It hurt, but at least I had my sister. Vanna, who loved me no matter what I looked like.

I stroke Vanna's ears. "You're right that he and I have much in common," I tell her. "Wherever you go, he will go with you. If you're ever lost, he will find you. I will be the same, right there with him."

I've never seen a tiger cry. I didn't think they could. But Vanna's pupils turn glassy, and the tears moisten the rims of her amber eyes, making the fur around them wet too.

My own sight goes misty, and wiping at my eyes and my nose, I pull her up by a hairy paw. My hand is small in hers, almost like a child's. "Come on. Let's go find him."

Her whiskers tilt up again, and her face brightens with hope, more like a stray cat in the village that's just been given milk than a fearsome tiger demon. "All right, I'll come."

My heart swells for her, and hand in paw we rise.

# CHAPTER THIRTY-TWO

The archers nock their arrows as soon as Vanna emerges from the garden. It's a miracle they don't shoot. The true miracle is the light in her heart. With each step she takes, it glimmers brighter, fanning over the flowers and the grass.

The soldiers hesitate. They're confused. They can sense she's different. No longer is she wreathed in shadow, and her presence does not inspire fear.

"Drop your weapons," I say. "This is the Golden One."

The guards' attention snaps to me.

"This is the Golden One," I say again. "Angma has taken her body. She needs to see Prince Rongyo."

"You cannot take that . . . that *beast* to the royal prince," blusters one of the guards.

"Watch me." I advance, but the guards block my way. *Now* their weapons are raised.

I'm battle-weary and exhausted, but I am ready to fight. I wave my spear high, until Vanna pushes me back by her tail.

"Let us pass," she commands.

Simple as that, the air goes still. There's a power to her

voice that makes me stand taller, and the guards part like two waves around the prow of a boat.

"You'll find His Highness at the healing houses behind the temple," says a guard in an awestruck tone. Enthralled by Vanna's spell, he adds, "Prince Rongyo and the queen are tending to the wounded."

Vanna dips her head in thanks, and back toward the temple we go. Except Vanna's hurt. Her breathing grows short and heavy, and I practically have to push her forward. Then suddenly, in the middle of the road, she stops. Her whiskers straighten, and she sniffs.

The hedges surrounding us rustle. I start to aim my spear, but there's no need.

It's Oshli. When he sees the tiger at my side, his composure falters. He runs to Vanna and kneels down beside her, and the two share a rueful look.

He knows.

I've assumed Oshli loved Vanna for her beauty, not for the person she is. There's a twinge in my chest, but I'm glad that I was wrong.

"I'm taking her to see Prince Rongyo," I tell him. "We need a ship to return to Sundau."

"She's hurt."

"It's just a graze," says Vanna.

Oshli says nothing, but the way he unravels his orange scarf and sweeps it over her wound, then touches her, his hand sinking into her fur . . .

"The prince can wait," he says. "I've some training as a healer. Let me."

Forgetting about me entirely, Oshli opens his palm, and magic pulses from his fingers. While he begins work on my sister's wound, she lowers herself onto the grass.

"I'm sorry, Oshli," she says, so softly I almost don't hear.

"I am too."

It doesn't matter what they are apologizing for. Vanna leaving him to marry a prince she'd never met, Oshli for some secret that only they share—there's something fateful and right about the two of them together, and as if the gods agree with me, they send two butterflies fluttering above their heads. One lands on Oshli's shoulder, and the other on Vanna's nose.

I look away, feeling like an outsider in their tale. I can't help the jealousy stirring inside me. How I crave a love like theirs. Seeing Oshli forgive my sister for her mistakes and love her even as a tiger, I'm forced to see the brightness in the world and not only its darkness.

They're so absorbed in each other that they don't see Prince Rongyo striding toward us, with Hokzuh a few steps behind. The prince's fine clothes are ripped, and from his anxious grimace, it looks like his heart has been torn as well.

I start to bow, but Rongyo grips my forearms, shaking them. "Is it true—the Demon Witch has her body?"

"And Vanna has hers."

His face turns ashen, and his eyes drift to Vanna. Unlike Oshli, he won't go near her. He can barely even look at her without flinching.

"What is it?" I speak without thinking. "Is she no longer worthy of you now?"

"No," Rongyo says, looking wounded. "Of course that isn't so."

His shoulders fall, and I regret snapping at him. It's no easy thing for anyone to see Vanna in Angma's body. My irritation fades, and if I were better with people I might say a few comforting words, but that is not who I am.

"Can it be undone?" the prince asks.

"We'll have to find the Demon Witch first," I reply. "Vanna says she's gone to Sundau."

"Then that is where we must go. The winds are strong, and my vessel is fleet. If we depart this evening, we can be there in two days."

"*One* day," I counter. "If my dragon pulls the ship, we can get there by tomorrow."

Vanna lifts her head off Oshli's lap. Her ears perk up.

It takes a second before I understand why, and then my cheeks blaze with embarrassment. "*My* dragon," I'd said. Curse him, Hokzuh caught it too. He raises a thick, bemused eyebrow, but at least he doesn't refuse.

"Tomorrow," he says airily. "I guarantee it."

He looks to me to confirm. For appearances' sake, I give a solemn nod. But if Hokzuh thinks I've forgiven him for abandoning Vanna, then he is fatally mistaken.

I stop listening as the prince and Hokzuh deliberate over logistics. I'm thinking about Oshli. How his expression, impassive as always, softened when he saw Vanna as a tiger. How his eyes flooded not with sorrow but with relief. Plain, pure relief.

Oblivious to the prince, Oshli is sitting cross-legged on

the bricked path, with my sister's furred head on his lap. Magic hums from his hands, hovering above Vanna's injured side. It's clear from his face that there's nowhere else he'd rather be.

"We'll bring Oshli," I interrupt.

Rongyo blinks. "Who?"

"Oshli." I gesture. "The late shaman's son. He came from our village with my parents."

Rongyo frowns, as if seeing him for the first time. "He isn't one of the palace healers?"

I can't decide whether Rongyo is young or dense. "He *is* a healer, but he's from Sundau," I say as patiently as I can. "He knows Vanna well, and she trusts him."

The prince's gaze drifts to the butterflies flying over the shaman and my sister. Sensing Rongyo's jealousy rise, I add, "He's her sworn brother."

It's a lie, but it does the trick.

"Very well," the prince agrees. "He may come."

"No one is going anywhere." The queen of Tai'yanan's voice rings out from behind the trees. Modest in height but formidable in presence, she storms into the garden unannounced. "I forbid it."

Rongyo whirls. "Mother!"

"The girl has bewitched you," she says. "I forbade you from going to that accursed selection, and yet you went. You bid the hard-earned fortune of our people to win her hand, and you risked displacing Tai'yanan from Tambu's fellowship of kings and queens. Yet in spite of my misgivings, I accepted her, and I permitted you to wed her. But now—"

The queen gestures to the royal temple, at its broken statues and crumbling arches. Servants are still gathering the dead, placing white sheaths of muslin over their bodies. There are so many the red-bricked path looks like it's covered in snow.

All of a sudden, I cannot blame her.

"Vanna is to be my wife," Prince Rongyo says. "She has been cursed, and I must find a way to undo that curse."

"Will you endanger your people for a girl you barely know?" says the queen. "Look at these bodies, Rongyo. Have sense!"

I keep quiet, but I know that Vanna's radiance has enraptured Rongyo too deeply. I've seen it in the village children and their parents, in Adah and Lintang, in the butterflies and birds and lizards even, in everyone whose lives are touched by my sister's light.

There is no depth or nuance to Rongyo's love; he will be loyal until the day he dies.

As Oshli will be.

As I will be.

"I cannot have sense," says Rongyo, taking the very words from my thoughts. "Please forgive me. But I will go with or without your permission, Mother."

The queen's silence is fraught with anger, with disappointment. "If you will not listen, then I will act. King Meguh is dead. Queen Ishirya too. Shenlani ships are on their way now—for her head." She points at me. "I will not have war on my shores."

She glances at the guards, who quickly surround Vanna and me.

"Stop!" growls my sister.

She shields me with her body, and her light intensifies, forcing the guards to stagger back, their eyes watering. In my periphery, Hokzuh is staring at Vanna, squinting at the light in her heart that only he cannot see.

"You need not force us," Vanna warns the guards. "My sister and I will leave, and we will not come back. We only ask for one ship."

"Vanna—" begins Rongyo.

"Let me speak." Vanna's light dims to a less forceful radiance, and she dips her head respectfully at the queen, then at Rongyo. "Prince Rongyo," she says, as gently as a tiger can speak, "I thank you for showing me kindness these past few days, but I cannot marry you. I do not want to spend my life pretending to love someone whom I do not. It would be a lie to both of us."

Vanna backs up until she stands between me and Oshli.

Rongyo is staring at the shaman, a progression of realizations crossing his boyish face.

I expect him to become enraged, to throw a fit. After all, he is a king's son. A prince, whose royal upbringing has probably instilled in him the expectation that he can have whatever—or whomever—he desires. His noble mien and robust build are exactly as Vanna would have conjured from her dreams, while Oshli . . . Oshli is like a copper coin next to a pile of gold.

He needs a moment to wrestle his pride, but in the end, he is more honorable than I've given him credit for. "Your heart is a special one, Lady Vanna," he says at last. "I am privileged to have known it—and you."

The queen exhales audibly, a sigh of relief. "We'll have a ship for you within the hour. Guards, take them to the port—"

"I would see the Lady Vanna and her sister home," Rongyo says over his mother. "If the Shenlani are coming, as you say, then Vanna and Channari will need the swiftest vessel in our navy, the best crew too."

"You and your ship are not going anywhere," the queen reminds her son frostily. "You are not king yet. You may not become king for quite some time, if you continue to challenge me thus."

"I beseech you," says Rongyo. "If I have brought misfortune upon Tai'yanan, let me be the one to do right by my country. Let me be the one to seek redemption in the eyes of the gods."

At the mention of the gods, the queen hesitates. She actually is a pious woman. I can tell from her humble brown dress, her simple braid—tied with a lone gold pin—and the charms of protection she wears around her wrist and ankles.

If there's one thing Oshli has inherited from his father, it's knowing when to seize an opportunity. He says, "Shenlani is without king or queen. Their ships are the least of your worries. But Prince Rongyo *is* right about quelling the gods' ire." The metal rings on Oshli's staff tinkle as he points skyward. "Look."

At first, I don't see anything. The lightning and the rain have stopped. But when I squint, there are strokes of orange between the clouds. They're far away, gathering most strongly over Mount Hanum'anya.

*I've not seen that before,* murmurs Ukar.

My chest goes tight. "Angma is rallying the demons at Mount Hanum'anya," I say. "If my sister and I don't return to Sundau . . ."

I let my voice trail off, because truthfully I don't know what will happen. But all of us have imaginations, and we know it can be nothing good.

The queen's eyes linger on the burning sky.

She finally relents. "Take your ship, Rongyo. You will escort them home, but that is all. You shall not step upon Sundau's shores. Both sisters are cursed. I shall not allow them to be the fall of our kingdom."

"I understand, Mother," says Rongyo.

The queen isn't finished. Her gaze falls on me, so sharp I feel an imaginary pressure in my ribs.

"I've already lost my husband," she warns me. "If I lose my son, there is nowhere in this world you will be able to hide from my wrath. Not even in the afterlife will you be safe."

I believe her. A mother's love is special; it is the purest love. Boundless, unconditional, unyielding. It is the love that I've missed most.

"Yes, Your Majesty." I bow low.

The queen turns back toward the temple, followed by her retinue of guards. Once she is out of earshot, I grab

313

Hokzuh by the wing and slice off the cord he's re-knotted around his neck.

His moonstone falls neatly into my hand.

"What are you doing?" he snarls. "I helped you, I saved you from the temple—"

"Quiet!" I cut him off. "If you want your stone back, then come with me. You owe me answers."

# CHAPTER THIRTY-THREE

I don't actually know where I'm going, only that I have an hour until the ship is ready and I'm not going to waste it sweltering in the middle of Tai'yanan's royal garden.

I'm inside one of the most magnificent palaces in all Tambu: I have my pick of gilded pavilions, outdoor galleries depicting scenes from the epics of Gadda, and towering belfries with carved floral tiles. Such beauty is lost on me. I'm more interested in the thin jet of smoke trailing behind the temple. I don't know much about palaces, but where there is smoke, there is fire. And where there is fire, there is oft a kitchen.

"This way," I say, starting out of the garden.

But Oshli makes no move to follow. "I need to finish treating her."

I don't argue. I bend down and touch my forehead to my sister's, untraining my mind from years of fearing those liquid amber eyes.

"Do you want any cakes?" I ask her gently.

My sister shakes her head.

It seems too cruel to remind her that it's her birthday. "I guess tigers don't eat cakes," I say, awkwardly trying to make her smile. "Soup?"

"I'm not hungry." Vanna's light makes an agitated flicker. "You go. I'll rest here. Oshli will take me to the port."

"All right." I hug her. She smells of rain and moon orchids and—I hide a smile.

"You should have Oshli wash your fur," I whisper into her ear. "You smell like durian."

Finally, I'm rewarded with a laugh. Even as a tiger, Vanna has a laugh like music. It sounds like a mellow horn, and I could listen to it for hours. I almost forget my hunger.

Almost.

Fighting always makes me hungry. Until I fill the hollow of my belly, I'm useless. I need to replenish my strength before the next battle with Angma.

The smoke does indeed indicate a kitchen. It's vast enough to accommodate even Hokzuh, who follows me inside without a word. The servants flee upon our arrival, and I make myself at home.

Most of the celebration food has gone to the injured in the healing houses, but there are baskets of eggs and yams and peppers, of freshly steamed bread under a mesh net, and skewers of uncooked meats.

I hover beside a pot of fish soup. I toss carrots inside to sweeten the flavor, then throw a few pieces of bread onto a copper pan and crack an egg over them.

"What are you making?" says Hokzuh, sniffing hungrily.

"For a dragon demon, you certainly have an appetite for human food."

He smacks his thick lips. "Is that lard for pork noodles?"

"It's for frying the bread."

"The carrots?"

There's a note of revulsion in his tone as he glances into my pot. Guess the dragon demon doesn't like vegetables. "Just trust me."

Bread for greasy, fried goodness, and soup to warm up my cold blood. An ideal breakfast. I'll make an extra portion for Vanna and pack it for our ride across the sea.

"You like cooking."

I do. It calms me and gives me a sense of purpose.

"I grew up in a kitchen." I scrape off bits of fried bread clinging to the pan. "Vanna used to say it wasn't fair that I had to sleep with all the pots and dishes. She'd try to ask Adah to give me my own room."

"But he didn't."

"I always stopped her from asking. I figured if I was going to be surrounded by walls, then let it be a kitchen. After all—"

"It's where all the knives are," Hokzuh finishes for me.

*Yes. Exactly.* That flip in my stomach again, and it's not from hunger.

Pressing my lips tight, I impale a slice of bread with a stick. "Well, we had only one good knife back then."

As hot oil spits and crackles in the pan, Hokzuh stuffs his face with skewered meats. "Maybe you can be a singer *and* a cook. A singing cook. I'd pay to see that."

"Stop trying to charm me, demon. You're not getting your moonstone back."

Hokzuh smothers his smile. "I thought you had questions."

"I do. But if you lie to me—" I hold up an egg and crush it in my fist, illustrating my point.

"Don't I get any credit for coming back?" Hokzuh protests. "I saved you."

"But not my sister." I pluck a slice of bread straight from the pan's crackling heat, knowing the yeasty aroma of fat tantalizes the dragon. I take a loud bite, nodding with satisfaction as I chew.

Then I begin my interrogation: "What is your moonstone? It's not just some morbid keepsake. It's magic. For what?"

"It's a talisman," confesses Hokzuh. "An enchanter in Cipang made it in exchange for . . . a price. So long as I am near it, I can suppress my demon side."

"Your demon side." This is the first time I've heard him refer to it as such. "What do you mean?"

"Without a talisman, I would turn into a demon when the sun sets," he explains. "That is my curse as a dragon without a pearl."

I lean against a table, noting how his scales flicker, changing between black and blue-green depending on where the shadows fall. It's a subtle effect, but now that I know to look, I can't unsee it.

"Angma lured you to Shenlani," I realize. "She knew who you were."

Hokzuh sinks onto a bench. "She took away my moonstone."

"Then had Meguh kill your men."

"No." Hokzuh's voice is thick. "I told you that Meguh's guards killed my men, but it's not true. I wish it were."

I wait, giving him time.

"When we wouldn't fight in the arena, Meguh put us all in the same cell." His tail curls in as he stares at the ground. "He knew what would happen that night. Without my moonstone, I couldn't control myself. I killed my own men. My friends."

I've completely forgotten about my bread.

Hokzuh inhales. "Sometimes, in the dark when I'm alone, I can still hear them screaming."

I turn so I don't have to face him, and busy myself by transferring the rest of the bread to a plate. But inwardly, it's hard to pretend I'm unmoved. I know what it's like to be haunted by the same dream night after night. To fear what I might do if my darkness were unleashed.

"You see?" A hoarse laugh scrapes out of him. "I told you I'd kill my best friends for the pearl. I made good on my word."

I say nothing. I ladle fish soup into a bowl, but I don't taste it. "What happened after?"

"Ishirya gave me to Meguh. He starved me for weeks, then put me in the arena. Said he'd feed me for every win I made. At first, I resisted, but then he stopped leaving the moonstone near my cell at night. Dead bodies showed up in the morning, and to this day, I still don't know who they were. Only that they were innocent. And that their deaths were my fault."

Gods, I hope Meguh's rotting in the Ninth Hell. "So you became his champion."

"Yes. I killed. I slaughtered. I've lost count how many. Some were demons, others were not." His wings fold. "I always tried to make it quick."

I sit beside him on the bench and take his arm, turning it so I can see the names inked deep into his flesh. Now that I know his story, each line has new meaning.

Much as I'm angry at him for choosing his moonstone over Vanna, I can understand his fear. "You aren't alone," I say at last, repeating what he once told me. "I know what it's like to be afraid of yourself."

"No, you don't," he says stolidly. "*Your* mind is your own. That isn't your curse."

I part my lips, but Hokzuh doesn't give me a chance.

"Do you know what it's like turning into a demon against your will?" He growls. "It's like having drunk far too much wine and being pushed by someone you hate to do things you despise. All while barely remembering your own name."

I remember the demon that helped me flee Bonemaker's Arena. I can't believe the words that I end up uttering: "Not all demons are murderers. Some fear humans more than we fear them."

"Those demons have a heart," Hokzuh replies. "A darker, different kind of heart than yours. But a heart all the same. I have none."

"Then work with me to find your heart. Accept my offer. . . . I won't ask again."

"Your offer?" His wide brow furrows. "To wait until Vanna dies?"

"A natural death," I affirm. "You've dragon blood and demon blood—a few decades are nothing to you. And you will help us kill Angma."

"I can't have only the demon half," he says darkly.

"You won't. Vanna will take it. She will bear both halves until she dies, and then you may have them."

"Both halves?" Hokzuh nearly knocks over a table in his disbelief. "That would keep her alive for far longer than a few decades."

"Then you'll have to wait a little longer—" I preempt his protests with a dismissive wave. "I'm not negotiating."

Hokzuh's jaw tightens. "You're impossible."

"And you don't have a choice. You don't want to fight against me, Hokzuh."

"All right," he mutters. "All right. I accept."

"It's not a deal. It's a promise. You will swear it to me."

*Make him swear on his true name,* says Ukar, slithering inside through one of the windows. His scales match the wooden frame, and I wouldn't be surprised if he's been there the whole time, eavesdropping. *The name he was born with.*

Hokzuh glares at the snake. "I don't need to swear on my true name. If Vanna has the entire pearl, she'll be a thousand times stronger than she is now. She'd be able to fend me off easily."

"Then it'll cost you nothing to swear," I say. "I'm not taking any chances. Make the oath. Now. On your true name."

After a long pause, he inhales. "Khramelan," he says finally, so quietly I have to strain to hear it. "Don't repeat it. Names gather power only when they're kept secret. When they're forgotten."

I nod, feeling the power of *Khramelan* tingle against the nape of my neck. I wonder how long it's been since he's uttered it.

"To Channari Jin'aiti, I make this inviolable oath: I swear on my true name, Khramelan, that I shall not harm Vanna Jin'aiti of Sundau, and that I shall help her slay the Demon Witch."

There's no bolt of lightning, no spark of fire from the stove as he makes his promise. But the air between us goes still, heavy with shared intention.

*A promise is not a kiss in the wind, Channi,* Mama used to tell me. *It is a piece of yourself that is given away and will not return until your pledge is fulfilled.*

On her last night on this earth, Mama bound me to a promise with Vanna. And now I am bound to Hokzuh.

I lob over a piece of fried bread. "Eat."

While Hokzuh chews, I help him knot the moonstone around his neck. The talisman is more fragile than it looks. "Why did you come back?" I ask.

Another bite. He takes a sudden interest in his plate, and I almost think he won't answer. Then he says: "Isn't it obvious?"

"No."

His mouth hangs open for a breath. "For your cooking," he says at last, plastering on the ghost of a grin. "Bread's delicious, by the way. Is that pork fat you used? I must get the recipe."

I roll my eyes and try to snatch the bread back. But Hokzuh's fast. He tosses the last scrap into his mouth, and I end up grabbing his empty hand.

It's as if the air has gone out of the room. I hold my breath as our fingers uncurl at the same time, palms flat against each other. It's as intimate as a kiss, standing like this, locked by our hands.

"Thank you for coming back," I say finally. "I'm glad you changed your mind."

"I am too."

We've both forgotten about Ukar. The snake glides between us, slithering over my arm. He sends me a disapproving look as Hokzuh steps back.

The moment's ruined, and I have never been more relieved and nettled at the same time.

*The ship is ready,* says Ukar, as drums pound in the distance.

Outside the window, the sun grows dim. It's high in the sky, but a mantle of night is falling upon the island, hours too early. And the strange fiery veins still permeate the clouds, spreading like a disease. I know where they will gather.

"Come," I say, touching Hokzuh on the arm. "The race to Sundau has begun."

# CHAPTER THIRTY-FOUR

It is dusk when we set sail. The sea is a pool of ink, black as far as the eye can see, but by nightfall there is so much fire in the sky that even the sea foam churns orange.

On a normal night, Mount Hanum'anya would be far behind us, and out of sight. Yet its dragon head is aglow with molten rock, and fire spews continuously from its maw. The seas rumble with aftershocks, and ashes coat the ship's deck.

No one with sense would volunteer for our voyage, but Rongyo wasn't lying when he said his crew was loyal. How he convinced each man to come is a mystery Ukar has been trying to solve all night.

Hokzuh has nicknamed our galley the *Centipede,* for all the oars together look like a hundred little feet skittering across the ocean. As one, we wage war against the seas, rowing until our palms are blistered. But we forge on, and before long my eyelids are heavier than iron, and Ukar has to nip me in the shin every time I nod off. In my half-dream state, I wish I'd made cakes.

"Take a rest," says Hokzuh, landing on the deck for a break. "You're the only one who hasn't."

*Finally, we agree on something,* says Ukar with a huff. *Go on.*

"I'm not tired," I lie. My words slur together, betraying my fatigue.

"It's an order, Channi."

It's not the first time Hokzuh's called me by that name, so I don't know why I'm taken aback. I look up and see his wing over my head, covering me from the shower of ash. Such a small gesture, yet a lump hardens in my throat. There are scorch marks on his flesh from falling embers.

The boat rocks as I rise, and Hokzuh steadies me with a hand. His fingers are warm. "Come on," he says. "I'll walk you to the cabin."

Mutely, I nod. I'm shivering and drenched with seawater, but there's no use drying myself until I'm belowdecks. The wind carries ash. No matter how I spit, I cannot get its taste out of my mouth.

"Did you keep any spindlebeard?" Hokzuh asks. "Take some to sleep, if you need it."

I have a sprig of the herb in my pocket, but I won't need it. "Thanks."

When I enter the hold, Oshli is there, asleep and curled up against my sister, breathing softly.

No matter how tired I am, I'm not sharing a room with Oshli and my sister. I turn to leave, but the young shaman stirs. "You stay with her," he whispers, rising creakily to his feet. "I'll row."

"Don't forget your scarf," I say when he leaves it behind. "It's cold out."

Oshli looks up at me. Gray circles ring his eyes, and his cheeks are sallow. He's aged years in just a few hours. As he picks up his scarf, I note a spot of fresh blood on the brightly woven fabric. Oshli quickly folds the spot away and mumbles, "Thank you."

"Why orange?" I ask the young shaman. I've always wondered.

There's a beat of surprised silence, and then he responds, "It's bright even in the dark. It reminds me of Vanna."

When the hatch shuts behind him, Vanna lays a paw on my shoulder. "See? He's not that bad."

I whirl. "I thought you were asleep."

"I was pretending. You taught me that."

"He's not that bad for a shaman," I agree belatedly. I can't help teasing her: "But you could have had a king— even the high queen of Agoria."

Vanna snorts. "The high queen didn't come. If she had, perhaps I would have picked her over Rongyo. Just think, what a better world ours would be if it were ruled by women. Not pigs like Meguh or Dakuok."

"I would be glad for whatever choice you made, whether it was the prince, the shaman, or no one. So long as it is yours."

"I would choose you above all, sister," Vanna says, and I know she means it.

"Doubtless you would," I reply, "but in this life, you're meant to be with a penniless shaman."

She chuckles. "Adah will have a fit."

"Who cares?" I certainly don't. "All the riches and power in the world cannot buy someone who loves you truly." I pause meaningfully. "That's the greatest treasure."

"Have you found such a treasure?" Vanna asks, her eyes twinkling faintly. "You and the dragon are quite a—"

"We're sparring partners."

"Sparring partners," Vanna repeats. Her eyes are sly. "That's one way to put it."

She's about to tease me more, but she starts choking. I pat her back, my good humor overcome by the wretched smell of bile on her breath.

"Are you feeling unwell?" I ask worriedly.

"I'm just seasick. I was ill during the voyage to Tai'yanan too." A whistling sound escapes from behind her teeth, and it takes me a moment to recognize it as her stomach grumbling. "Ironic, isn't it? All my life I've wanted to see the world, but my body just wants to go home."

"Go back to sleep," I say. "That will help."

"I can't." Vanna tilts her head sheepishly. "I haven't figured out what to do with my horns."

I chuckle out of relief. Even in times of despair, she finds something to laugh about. This is her strength.

"How about I tell you a story?" I say. "How about your favorite? About the moon goddess and her rabbits and cakes—"

"That'll only make me hungry," Vanna says darkly. "It won't be good for me to be hungry."

At first, I don't grasp her meaning. Then, *of course*. Angma's body sustains itself on human life. No wonder Vanna's fur is dull and lackluster—I noticed right away when I saw her in the cabin. No wonder she's walled herself away from everyone except Oshli.

She's starving.

I purse my lips, remembering the spot of blood on Oshli's scarf and his wan appearance. I know without asking that he fed her his blood to sustain her. But it won't be enough. Not nearly enough. *She needs her body back.*

The dagger I gave him is on the floor, close to where he was sleeping. I pick it up and tuck it by my side.

Vanna lounges down onto her forelegs. "Sit, and stop looking at me like that, or I'm going to call you Mother." She stifles a yawn. "You'd make a good mother, you know—if you were just a little bit less overbearing."

Vanna always knows how to make me smile. It's true, I love children. The young snakelets back home adore it when I visit, and the babies in the village don't cry when I coo and make faces at them. They know that they are safe with me. I'd die before breaking such trust.

I sit.

"Now, tell me a story, like you promised," says Vanna. "Tell me about the light of Gadda."

"Why that one?"

Vanna smiles faintly. "It always helps me sleep."

A soft snort escapes me, and I begin the tale. "Niur is our creator god, father of the world as we know it, but it is Gadda we love most, for he loved humankind despite our faults, and had mercy on us when his brother Niur tried to remake the world with a great monsoon."

I stroke Vanna's fur tenderly. "Gadda saved us. He asked the dragons to let humans ride on their backs as the world flooded with rain and sea, and Gadda sprinkled seeds into the sea, so the Tambu Isles were formed—a hundred islands of verdant, fertile land for us to thrive on."

"Sundau was the first island created," Vanna adds. "That's why the serpents of Sundau have magic in their blood."

"Indeed," I murmur. If Ukar were telling the story, he'd give some screed about the heroic deeds of his royal ancestors. But Ukar is asleep in an empty barrel somewhere, wisely banking his strength for what is to come.

"Niur was furious when he found out what Gadda did and turned him into a mortal as punishment. But before Gadda left for earth, he stole the brightest star from Heaven and gave its magic to humans. Now we believe the sparks of the first enchantments are what illuminate that star—Gadda's light—a reminder of all he sacrificed so we might live."

By the time I'm finished, Vanna is snoring quietly, wheezing slightly with each exhale. I press my face to the fur on her snow-white chest, rising and falling with her breath.

Ukar and I used to think the light in her heart was the same light that burned in Gadda's star.

I press a kiss on my sister's head and adjust her blanket. She doesn't need one, but it makes me feel better to shield her.

I lie by her side. I miss the nights we used to sleep together like this. The nights Vanna would sneak into the kitchen, always with her wooden bowl under her arm. I'd keep a bag of peanuts for us to snack on, and fried fish skins too—when I had time to make them—and Mama's cakes, to sweeten our dreams. Together, cocooned under our blankets, we'd gossip and complain and giggle until dawn.

"What'd you learn today?" I'd ask routinely, out of curiosity.

"I read an entire book on my own. It was about two lovers who turn into butterflies—"

I rolled my eyes. "Let me guess—the Epics of Su Dano. Ukar says books only get half the legends right, Vanna. Only the serpents know the truth."

"It isn't only the truth that's worth reading about, Channi." Vanna's eyes were bright. "Come, I'll show you."

Even then, Vanna was always looking for an escape. She told me stories about worlds beyond our little kitchen on Sundau; she brought me books and, by candlelight, taught me to read and write. *Today's lesson was a bore,* she'd say, *but if I can share my assignments with you, that makes them a little more bearable.*

*So I get to be bored too?*

*That's what sisters are for. My joys are your joys—*

*—and your miseries are my miseries.* I made a face, but my heart hummed with warmth. *I guess I ought to learn, if only so I can write down Ukar's histories.*

Learn I did, thanks to Vanna. And with her, night after

night, we did escape to new worlds. Some I still visit when I sleep.

But tonight, when I close my eyes, I know that there is no place I can escape where Angma will not find me.

It is a small gift from the gods that I do not dream.

# CHAPTER THIRTY-FIVE

I've lived my whole life on Sundau, yet never have I seen it from the vantage of a ship approaching port. I see anew the landmarks I've known my whole life: the giant tree with its mushroom flare at the top, the white-sand beach with the gulls sitting on the hooked crag, the ravine that takes me to my first home, where Mama died.

Yet as my homeland emerges out of mist and fog, my gaze is fixed on the fiery firmament above. The moon is swollen red, and the sun has a bluish tinge as it fades into the clouds. The sight sends a shiver trailing down my spine.

All night, we've warred against the Kumala Sea, but now the waters taunt us with their silence. Not one fishing boat dots the coast. There are only shadows that creep over the land and sea, as thick and dark as the fear enfolding my heart.

I find Oshli by the rowers. The hollows under his eyes have deepened. How much blood did he give Vanna?

I pass him the last of my fried bread. He tries to give it

back, but I shake my head. "You used to bring breakfast for me when you visited."

He looks up. He *does* remember.

"Channi . . ."

I shake my head. This isn't the time for reminiscing. "Eat," I say, closing his fingers over the bread.

We're minutes from making landfall. I can smell the trees, the dirt, the flowers. It's a scent that calls to me. It beckons me. *Home, Channi. You are home.*

Even before our ship scrapes shore, I'm climbing off the rear deck. I lower myself into the shallow sea and wade across to the beach, almost running. Smoke presses down on me with every breath. Angma's power is strong here. I can sense it permeating the entire island. But I don't care. I could kiss the white sand under my feet.

Ukar is eager too. He burrows into the beach, burying himself until only his eyes are visible. Usually he loves the sand, loves disappearing under its grains, but now he resurfaces quickly and skitters onto a rock—his scales trembling, his color flickering. He is rattled, and I know why.

"Angma," I murmur. I can feel it too. As can Hokzuh.

Since we've arrived on Sundau, his scales have become near black, his demon red eye bright against the smoke. The way he clutches at his moonstone makes Ukar nervous.

"I wouldn't go any farther if I were you," I tell Rongyo, before he steps off the gangway and onto the beach. "You should turn around and go home."

The prince obviously wants to come with us. He's young

and craves an opportunity to prove himself. But he's a future king, not a demon fighter.

"Your crew is tired," I continue, "and your mother is waiting. You promised her."

The stubborn prince shakes his head.

Vanna stalks soundlessly to my side. "Rongyo," she speaks, so gently that she almost sounds like her old self.

There's a long pause, and I expect her to use her power on him, but she does not. Instead, she touches her forehead to the back of his hand. Her breath catches in her throat as she says, simply, "Thank you. I am glad to have known you."

She turns quickly, before Rongyo can reply, and nudges me forward with her head.

She doesn't look back, and neither do I.

For the first time, it is Vanna who leads the way into the jungle, not I. She sets an urgent pace, and all of us but Hok-zuh have to run to keep up. Not once does she hesitate, not once does she look from side to side to make sure she is on the right path.

I, on the other hand, can't stop looking. The jungle is like an old friend who's become a stranger. Its soil is cold under my feet, and the air, which usually clings to my skin in a sticky haze, prickles like tiny ice chips. Oddest of all, not one snake comes out to greet Ukar and me.

"This isn't the way to the rock," I say between breaths

when Vanna veers into a grove of bamboo. Nestled in the shadows, its stalks have become a graveyard of spines.

"It's the way she wants us to take," Vanna replies.

I swallow. "Angma?"

"Yes."

"You can hear her?"

"I can *feel* her." As she says this, the faint light pulsing in her chest gains intensity.

"Angma's heart and yours are part of one whole," remarks Hokzuh. "It makes sense that you are drawn to each other."

Vanna prowls forward without reply, but I can read what she is thinking: that if one of them must die, it won't be her.

At midday, hours after we've begun, she leads us across the rice paddies and the low hills. I would rather avoid Puntalo Village, but it's the fastest way to the crooked tree.

On the outskirts of the village, she suddenly turns to me. "Stay close," she says, her tone almost a plea.

"I won't let Angma hurt you."

Vanna wrinkles her nose. "That isn't it." She looks ahead to the clay roofs peeking out of the trees and the beginnings of Puntalo's dirt road. "Angma's the least of my worries right now."

I fail to understand. "Then what?"

"Stay close so I can smell your blood," says Vanna. "It helps me lose my appetite."

*Oh.* A hiccup rises to my heart. She's hungry.

I tighten my hold on her neck, stretching my arm until I

can cup my hand over her light and she can smell the poison in my blood.

Vanna takes a long inhale, then a shudder rolls down her spine. I can feel her pulse slowing, steadying. "Thank you," she says.

I climb onto her back and put on a wry smile. "Never thought I'd get to ride a tiger. Usually they're too busy trying to throw me off."

That makes her laugh, and me too. The sound of us together is music, causing Vanna's light to flicker with some of its old brilliance.

*You see, Angma?* I think. *No matter how dark you paint our world, Vanna will always bring the light.*

All the same, I wish Vanna didn't have to come. But only she has the power to defeat Angma. That's been true since the day she was born.

"Come on," I say. "Let's go home."

~⁓∽

The demons have beaten us to Puntalo.

Everything lies in ruins. The marketplace, the temple, the row of red wooden houses where Oshli's family lived, and even the statue of Su Dano by the washing pond. All that's left are smashed poles, broken wheels, and a road sticky with rotting fruit and spoiled meat.

It stirs deep emotion within me. I like to say that I don't care about Puntalo Village. That if a tiger were to attack, I'd only fight it to save my sister. But that's not true.

In spite of my snake face, my heart is human. Though Sundau has not always been good to me, I would never wish ill upon it. It is my home, and Ukar's too.

My body goes hot with anger, and Ukar coils his body around my shoulder, cooling me down with his skin.

*There's nothing you could've done,* he says.

Demons have never beset our village before. I shudder, noting the long claw marks rending rooftops. The temple was hit hardest. Its walls are scorched, and candles and broken statues are strewn about the dirt path.

"Hello?" Oshli calls, picking up a fallen lantern. No vultures circle, and no bodies litter the streets. That's enough to spark hope. With more urgency, he raises the light toward the temple.

"Hello?" I shout. "It's Channari, Khuan's daughter. I'm back."

A few lanterns flicker in the distance, and I pick out voices. As we make our way toward them, it starts to rain. Heavily.

"This way," I say, leading us down the road.

Such showers are common on Sundau. They won't last long, but we need shelter. Hokzuh shields us with his wings while we run, and Vanna's heart illuminates the way.

We head to Adah's house. It sits at the intersection of two roads, the largest in the village. The gate is broken, and a few trees in the courtyard have toppled over. Tiles from the roof lie shattered over the wide stones.

"I pity the demons who did this," Vanna murmurs. "Lintang is going to break their necks with her broom."

I have to laugh. We used to joke that the house is our stepmother's true love, not Adah. "Or she'll scream so loud they shrivel up and die."

"No one can scream like Lintang."

"No one," I murmur in agreement. "At least the rest of the house is still standing." I climb over a fallen tree, then head toward the kitchen. I have weapons stashed in my room.

"Wait." Halfway into the garden, Vanna stops midstride, her nostrils flared. "We're not alone."

I'm instantly on my guard. "Demons?"

"No." A low chuckle huffs out of her. "Children . . . in the kitchen. You and Oshli go to them. I'd just frighten them."

Words she's never spoken before in her life.

Hokzuh stays with her. "I'd have to break my bones to fit through that tiny door," he says, nodding at the kitchen. "I'll wait out here with your sister and come up with a plan."

Together, Vanna and Hokzuh retreat into the storerooms, and I wonder what they'll talk about while I'm gone. Will Hokzuh tell my sister one of his terrible jokes, or will he simply stare covetously at the pearl he cannot see but knows is there? When I hear her laugh, I know it's the former. And I breathe a little easier.

The kitchen smells of open sugar jars, and flies hum merrily over the table. Oshli picks a broken wooden bowl off the ground. It's the one Vanna used to cover her heart when she slept.

My sister's right. This isn't the work of demons. It's the

work of children. Five of them, hiding on the other side of the muslin curtain—their ten tiny feet just visible.

"It's me," I say, as gently as I can. "Channari. And Oshli."

Silence.

I bite down on my lip. "Remember?" I sing hoarsely:

*Channi, Channi, Monster Channi.*
*Rain and wind and gloom all day.*
*When the sun sees your face,*
*it goes away. . . .*

One brave face peeks out from behind the curtain. The oldest, from what I can tell. When she spies Ukar on my shoulder, she steps out. "Look! It *is* her."

She's a girl of eight or nine whose mother used to shake her lizard-hitting stick at me whenever I passed their house—but this girl does what no child of Puntalo has done before. She runs *toward* me, nearly toppling us both with an unexpected embrace.

"Channi!" she cries.

I don't know what to do other than hug her back, and as she cries into my tunic, I hold her small shoulders still. "Are you hurt?"

She shakes her head mutely.

"Your family?"

"Asleep, in the next house. Almost everyone is asleep."

Oshli and I exchange glances. He crouches next to us and touches the girl's arm gently. "You've been very brave,

Liyen, and I'm grateful you are here. Will you tell us what has happened?"

Quietly, the other children start coming out from behind the curtain to join Liyen, who sits on a cushion. "Demons came last night and tore the village apart." She lowers her lashes. "They didn't hurt anyone. Yet. But they said they'd kill us if Channi didn't give the Golden One to Angma. Then everyone fell asleep. Except us." She glances nervously at her friends. "We ran here—the mist didn't touch this house."

I can picture it all. The foul mist that toys with people's thoughts. I grind my teeth, furious that Angma has resorted to threats against my village.

I stroke Liyen's short black hair. "Nothing will happen to you," I swear to her. "I'll keep you safe. All of you." I draw back my hand. "Once the rain passes, I'm going to Angma."

"With the Golden One?" Liyen's a sharp girl, and she must have caught sight of Vanna's light when we were outside.

"Why is she a tiger like Angma?" one of the boys asks, his voice small.

"It's only temporary," replies Oshli. "She won't harm you."

I offer a smile at the children still by the curtain, then turn to Liyen. "Are you and your friends hungry?"

She shakes her head sheepishly. "We ate the cakes that were in the cupboard. Sorry."

She means the cakes I steamed for Vanna before the selection. I'd forgotten about them.

"Did you find the ones in the tin box too?" I ask, reaching for the second stash I kept by the oven.

At the possibility of extra cakes, the younger children's eyes brighten.

I open the box and pass out the slices. Oshli takes one, then starts to tinker with the broken bowl under his arm. A sense of peace occupies his face. I let him have the moment.

"We didn't know you made cakes," Liyen's sister says. There's sugar on her cheek, and I thumb it off. "They're delicious. Better than my mama's."

I almost laugh. "I won't tell her so. But yes, I make cakes."

Another little boy leans his head against my shoulder. "We weren't scared yesterday. Well, only a little. We knew you'd come back. We were waiting for you."

I blink with surprise. "You were?"

"They saw you fight Hokzuh," says Oshli. "You've become a hero, especially with the children." He pauses. "I didn't tell you because I knew you wouldn't believe me."

This is so, I wouldn't have.

Except it's true. There's no fear of me in the children's eyes. Instead, there is wonder and awe. And something more valuable: a shining film of hope.

The last girl to come out from behind the curtain is the child who shouted for the mobs not to hurt me. Without warning, she throws her little arms around my neck, and the others follow. I hug them all tight, even kiss a few of them on the cheek. Just knowing that they're unharmed by the evils that have befallen Sundau makes my heart lighter.

341

"You're going to fight the Demon Witch, like you did the dragon!"

"Can we come, Channi? Please?"

"No," I reply. "It'll be too dangerous." Their faces fall, so I offer the next best thing. "But you can hold Ukar."

Ukar sticks out his tongue at me to show he resents being made into a pet, but I know deep down he enjoys the attention. While the children stroke his head and coo over his multicolored tail, he coils with happiness.

Liyen doesn't play with Ukar. Instead, she takes a nibble of her cake before giving the rest to her little sister. Seeing this brings back memories of Vanna and me.

For years, Dakuok and Adah forbade me from going into the village. They convinced me that no one could ever overcome their fear of my face, that I was a demon, a blight upon the island. But now my heart throbs with what could have been, had I been a little braver, a little less obedient. Not everyone would have thrown stones and sticks at me. I might have found friends.

I always thought my fight against Angma was for Vanna. The truth is, I'll be fighting for myself, too. *My* life. *My* future.

While the children eat, I slip into the nook where I used to sleep, rifling under my bed for fresh trousers and a clean pair of sandals. The rain is tapering off, and I quickly sharpen my spear before dipping into the secret collection of weapons I've hoarded. It isn't much. Two fighting sticks, an odd assortment of blades and arrows, a rusting sword that I stole from a visiting soldier. I'm hardly equipped to slay Angma.

But I will. In my bones, I know I must.

As the rain ends, heavy smoke envelops Sundau like a cage. The whole island smells like tinder, a spark away from combusting. Behind the billowing gray, the sun begins its descent.

"Wait!" cry the children, sensing I'm about to leave. "We have something for you."

They press paper charms into my hands for luck and protection, and they bring offerings: bananas, a packet of sticky rice, a doll, a wooden snake. The gifts are meager, but I'm touched. Ukar especially likes the wooden snake. He insists it's him.

I draw all the children into a hug. "Thank you," I say, my voice thick with emotion. "Try to sleep tonight, and no matter what you see or hear, don't leave this house."

I make each of them promise, and then I head outside. Oshli and Hokzuh are waiting, torches in hand.

In the short time I've been with the children, Vanna has grown even more gaunt, her light muted. But her eyes are as bright as ever.

"Your dragon's quite the character," she says when I join her. "He found where Adah hides his wine."

I eye her. "Are you drunk?"

"You think *this* body can become inebriated on one measly cup?" Vanna exclaims, rightfully so. She lowers her voice. "No. Besides, I wanted to hear every word the dragon said about you. Clearly."

"What did he say?"

"That your father keeps *horrible* wine," interrupts

Hokzuh. "It's barely fit to fertilize the trees. It's a miracle that with such terrible spirits we were able to come up with a plan."

I glance at Vanna, who's smiling. Curse them, becoming allies behind my back. But I will take whatever bonds we four can form tonight. They may be the only thing keeping us alive.

They lay out their plan: once we approach the crooked tree, I will seek Angma out first and weaken her with my blood, then Vanna will come. Should everything go in our favor, together we'll slay the Demon Witch and take her heart. Should everything *not* go in our favor . . . I don't want to think about what this means.

Vanna has always been lucky, so maybe my worries are for naught, and everything will turn out all right.

Only one thing is certain: it is going to be a long night.

# CHAPTER THIRTY-SIX

Soon after twilight, the fire in our torches surrenders to the presence of demons, and our only light is the feeble glow of Vanna's heart. It doesn't slow us down. Even in utter darkness, I would know my way to the rock. Come the end of this earth, I would still be able to find it.

The mangrove trees are the first marker that we're on the right path. There aren't many monkeys on Sundau, but they like to play among the twisted roots and dip into the shiny stream curving through the densely packed trees.

There are no monkeys now. I've stolen along this path on nights darker than this, and even then there would be frogs in the ponds with their low mating calls, bats clicking over the tree canopies, demons humming from within their hollows.

I cannot remember the jungle so quiet. It disquiets *me*.

While I ride astride my sister's back, Ukar slithers off my shoulders, weaving through the thick layers of mossy undergrowth. We move through the forest. He is joined by his many brothers and sisters, my brave army of snakes. They hiss often at Hokzuh, and chatter about him as they follow. *Has our Lady Green Snake gone out of her mind? Allying herself with a dragon demon?* they mutter. *No, no. We must trust her. And Ukar.*

Snakes, always such gossips. More than ever, I find their nattering a comfort. It fills the eerie silence between footsteps. The loudest silence of all is my sister's.

I cling to Vanna's back, wondering what can be on her mind as she leads us through the forest, passing by the waterfall where she taught me to swim. "To the left," I murmur into her ear. "Straight past the hidden hills."

I've never taken her to the crooked tree where Angma cursed me, but she's heard the story so many times, she never asks me to repeat my directions. Like me, she instinctively knows the way.

Finally, the air becomes cold, and I slide off my sister's back.

I smell cloves.

The odor is faint, buried beneath layers of smoke and fungus and rot. But it is unmistakable.

I catch my breath, sucking it in. Vanna's pearl barely illuminates what lies ahead—a grove of headless clove trees, all diseased and withered. Lights dance within, low and in a wavering pattern. They look like fireflies buzzing over puddles of rain, but fireflies do not glow red in the dark.

Suiyaks pop out of the dead trees, their white tresses catching in the brittle branches like webs.

"Vanna!" I shout.

They begin to swarm us, their snarls surging into a violent cacophony. And they aren't alone. Demons leap out of the dark, joining them in staggering numbers.

I know these demons. They live in the dark crevices of the forest, inside the tree hollows, under the waterfall overhangs. At first glance, most look like ordinary beasts, except with a few peculiar traits: an extra ear, lizard skin instead of fur, a mismatched tail. Always, red eyes. They thrive on mischief, stealing glittery trinkets from our cupboards and inviting ants to raid our kitchens. It isn't like them to attack.

But these creatures aren't like other demons; their eyes are glazed with gold. They're under Angma's control, and they must do her bidding. Unfortunately, that means they're out to kill us.

I fight wildly. I don't want to hurt them, but we have to get to the crooked tree.

While Hokzuh and Oshli focus on the demons, I turn my attention to the suiyaks. They've clustered around Vanna and are trying to carry her up into the sky. Together, my sister and I fight back. Vanna, who's never so much as swatted a mosquito, surprises me with her violence. She tears into their necks and rips out their throats. The next time I glance over, she's drinking one of the suiyaks' blood.

If I had free hands, I would clap. I have no idea whether suiyak blood will satiate my sister's hunger, but it is quite satisfying to watch.

More demons keep coming, and in spite of our small

victories, it's an unpleasant truth that when the enemy is stronger, fights in greater numbers, and is near impossible to kill, the odds are in their favor.

"Stay together!" I yell, rounding Vanna to my side and grabbing Oshli by the arm.

The young shaman pants as he runs. He's out of arrows, and the fighting edge of his ritual staff has been broken off. I'm surprised he's still alive. Even more surprised that he's still whole. Perhaps all his praying has paid off after all.

While Hokzuh barrels through the demons, clearing a path so we can continue forward, I wave on the snakes.

*It's time,* I inform them.

Ukar's kin never cease to amaze me. In a fluid motion, they use their bodies to form a ring around Vanna and Oshli, braiding their tails and looping their necks until the snakes form a continuous circle.

Once the circle is made, the demons cannot cross it, no matter how they try. The suiyaks too are blocked. I've always known that snakes have some mysterious power against demons. But now I'm guessing it's a sort of divine amends against Hanum'anya's Great Betrayal.

"They'll protect you," I tell Vanna. "Stay here until Hokzuh gives the signal."

*Our protections won't last,* Ukar warns me. *Go now.*

Quickly, I race beyond the treeline, toward the rock. On the way, the demons swarm me. If they can't get to Vanna, then I'm the next best option. I tear through their ranks, choking on the acrid smell of demon blood. Yet no matter how hard I fight to press on, more demons come. My arms grow tired, my muscles strained. I let out a cry. I haven't come so far and gotten so close just to lose everything.

Someone grabs my wrist. I whirl, ready to attack, but it's Hokzuh. Without a word, he folds his arms around my shoulders and flies me forward.

The island is on fire, and there are demon marks all over his flesh, but for once, for a precious instant, I'm glad he came. I'm glad not to be alone.

"I'm afraid," I confess quietly as Hokzuh lands in the clearing. Just ahead is the valley, the crooked tree, the rock.

"Shall I come with you?"

I shake my head. "I have to go alone."

He's holding my hand. Mine is small compared with his, but just as callused, as rough, and as strong. I start to draw it back, but he hangs on.

"Every time I let someone close, they die," he says in a barely audible whisper. "I won't have to worry about that with you, Channi. You'll win."

With a numb nod, I start to turn, but Hokzuh's not finished.

*Look into her eyes when you stab her,* he says, speaking into my mind. *Twist your knife deep, until the shadows bleed out of her heart. Then cut out my pearl.*

I give a single nod, and then it's my turn to speak. "When this is over, I want to sail with you. I'll be one of your pirates—so long as I get first pick of whatever treasure you find."

"First pick?" Hokzuh raises a thick eyebrow. He cocks his head. "What will you do with your treasure?"

I shrug, trying to sound carefree, but my voice is husky. "Sell cakes, build a temple for my mother. I'll have time to think about it."

Hokzuh clasps both his hands over mine. "I'll be waiting."

Waiting be damned, I wrap my arm around his neck and touch my forehead to his. It takes him aback, but not for long. He raises his fingers to my face, traces the contour of my cheek. His skin is cool, like mine, each scale like a smooth shard of obsidian against my own.

"Did I ever tell you that green is my favorite color?" he whispers.

I could swear my heart stops then, and I cannot find my words. I don't need them, for Hokzuh's mouth finds mine—or maybe it is the other way around. We kiss. It is one that neither of us expects—sweet and clumsy and fierce all at once, but I don't pull away, and he doesn't, either. It is not a long moment that we can capture, but it is one that I will crystallize into my memory. Even when we let go, the warmth of his breath lingers on my lips.

"I'll see you, Channi," he says, still touching my cheek. Then he recedes into the shadowed woods, and I give myself a moment, a breath, before raising the dagger at my side.

Countless times I've used my blood as a weapon, but that doesn't change the fact that every time I make a cut, it hurts. I bite my cheek, holding in a cry as I slice the blade across my thigh.

As I work, a leaf-green snake coils around my ankle. "Ukar!" I exclaim. Did he fly with us? I flush. "What are you doing here?"

*I'm coming with you.*

"Absolutely not," I hiss.

Ukar travels up my leg and around my waist, finally coming to rest around my shoulders. *Do not insult a snake so. Especially this snake.*

Snakes are stubborn, and Ukar the most stubborn of all. "All right, but if you get hurt, I'm throwing you out."

*I'll say the same for you.* He dives into the undergrowth.

It's like old times. Smothering a smile, I hold my spear slightly over my head. Its heavy wood is a familiar weight in my palm, but how I wish I'd had the chance to add an extra blade.

No time for idle wishing, for regrets or second chances. Angma is waiting, and I am ready for her.

With my free arm I sweep aside a curtain of hanging vines, and I enter the heart of Sundau.

# CHAPTER THIRTY-SEVEN

It's hard to imagine that there was a time when I couldn't feel the magic of this place—this cursed valley in the middle of Sundau. It is quiet here, as if I've entered a world far from the one I know. The air shimmers with a cold, wet mist that hums against my skin.

I breathe in, and the smell of clove, high and strong, stings my nostrils. Ahead is the crooked tree where everything began.

The flat rocks are smaller than I remember, and they're blanketed by moss. I've come here countless times, searching for Angma. But today is the first time I know with certainty she is here.

I stand on the largest rock—the one where Adah left me to die. Ukar slithers into the ferns while I turn slowly, scanning for Angma. I know she is watching.

"I'm here," I whisper.

No sooner do I speak than the wind presses an icy kiss on the back of my neck.

"Hello, Channari."

All day I've braced myself for this moment, for the sight

of Angma wearing Vanna's face, Angma speaking with Vanna's voice. But to actually see it and hear it?

Nothing could have prepared me.

She looks exactly like my sister. Hair black as obsidian, skin as luminous as the sun, and lips like the pinkest lily buds. The smaller details are there: the mole on her left shoulder that I used to pinch when we were children, the twin eyebrows, always in expressive sync with one another, the willowy line of her back as she walks.

Adah would be fooled. Lintang too.

But not me. I know it is darkness smoldering in her heart, not light. And I know that if I meet her eyes, they will glow like burning sand, red in the center.

With a cry, I aim my spearhead, and ram it straight at her ribs with the force of every muscle in my body. But Angma simply glides to the side, and my spear pierces only mist.

I pivot to face her. She's tittering, and the sound rankles me. Vanna never titters.

*Calm, Channi,* warns Ukar. *Don't lose your focus.*

I've never been more focused. Again, I charge. Again, Angma ducks my attack.

Back and forth we go, but damn Angma, she floats like a feather in a storm. She's had a full day to recover since her last encounter with Vanna, and it's clear that during the time her power has grown tenfold. Not only has she retained her tiger strength, but her every movement is a murderous dance, a cruel defilement of Vanna's natural grace.

She drives me back against the clove tree, grabbing my braid and turning me by the shoulder until I face the other side of the valley, where my sister and friends are fighting. And losing.

Wave after wave of demons pour in—from the sky, the sea, rising from the ground. Already, the circle of protection around Vanna is splintering. Many of the snakes are dead, which weakens the chain. Oshli is out of arrows, and Hok-zuh cannot fight all the demons of Tambu alone.

"It will be over by midnight," Angma prophesies, her voice humming against my ear. "Not long from now your sister's heart will be mine."

Ukar's been waiting for the perfect chance to strike, and he has found it. He emerges from a nearby tree, flinging his body through the air and landing on Angma's shoulder. His white fangs glint against the glow of her eyes as his jaws clamp down on her neck.

With a whirl, I slice my braid free and swing my spear into Angma's chest, sending her reeling. Before I can deliver another strike, the darkness in her heart unlocks. Long shadows froth out of her body like eyeless worms, born of the blackest night.

"Ukar!" I scream as the shadows overwhelm him.

He disappears into the mist, and I'm swiftly surrounded myself. The shadow worms slither up my spear handle. They clamber up my legs to immobilize me. They are wraiths of darkness, not flesh, and they do not flinch at the poison leaking from the open cuts on my skin.

I throw my weight at Angma, but her strength is great. Mimicking my own attack, she claps the end of my spear in her hands before I can thrust it forward.

A sharp sizzle kisses the air. It is the sound of Angma's flesh meeting the blood on my blade. Her fingers are blistering, turning red and raw. But I'm the one who winces.

"Careful, Channari," she chides, "you wouldn't want to destroy your sister's body." She claps the blade harder, and I smell Vanna's skin burning. "Then that'd make you the monster, not me. Wouldn't it?"

I forget how fast she is. The crown of her head comes crashing into my face. I manage to evade the brunt of her blow, but as I duck, she wrangles the spear from my grip. With a swing of her hips, she knocks me down to my knees.

She looms over me, holding my spear upright.

I expect her to end me here and now, the way I have dreamed countless nights of ending her. But to my utter astonishment, she kneels beside me.

She lifts her hand to my cheek. I must be delirious, for her touch is tender. Gently, she caresses the streak of white hair that she marked me with, all those years ago.

"You came to this place often, Channi," she says. "Filled with all that hate, that stubborn will. In a way, I raised you more than your own mother did. I made you the fighter that you are."

*The snakes raised me,* I want to hiss, but it hurts too much. *I only came here to find you. To kill you.*

"So you did. But for seventeen years, you thought about me more than anyone, even your sister. I gave you purpose. I shaped you."

I *am* delirious, I decide. I bite down on my collar, stemming the rising tide of pain as I lunge uselessly for my spear.

Angma doesn't even have to move. The shadow worms fold tighter around my arms, restraining me.

This is hardly the epic fight I envisioned I'd have with the Demon Witch.

"You blame me for taking your mother away from you, but it is not my fault she died. You blame me for taking your sister from you, but I have kept her secret. I've protected her."

"*I* protected her."

"On Sundau, yes." Angma wears a sideways smile I've never seen on my sister's face. "But from the rest of the world? You did not have the foresight to consider anyone but me an enemy—until it was too late."

Understanding chills me. For years I dreaded Meguh, yet I didn't consider him a threat. Has Angma always known what a monster he was? Is that why she positioned herself as the queen of Shenlani?

"Enchanters, demons—even gods—would have come for her," says Angma. "Extracting that pretty pearl from her heart would have been an easy task when she was a child. Hokzuh would not have hesitated."

"You want to kill her too."

"I must. Or she will kill me," replies Angma. "The pearl has driven us to war."

I see my error now. All these years I've spent training to hunt, to fight and kill, to become strong so I could protect Vanna, when it was Vanna who should have been training. She was always the only one with the power to kill Angma.

"You were taught by legend to fear me," Angma continues, "but legends are steeped in untruths. You think I took the pearl because I wanted to live forever, to rule all of Tambu? No. I was a healing witch, Channari.

"I had a daughter. She was curious as a bird, and clever. Cleverer than her mother. Brave too. She wasn't afraid of spiders or snakes—or tigers." A pause. "You reminded me of her when I first came to you. You saw a fearsome tiger and stared me down instead of running.

"One day my little girl fell sick, and nothing I did would make her better. Until I chanced upon Hokzuh's pearl.

"It was like a piece of broken obsidian," Angma says wistfully. "That's why I picked it up—I thought I could sell it or use it to decant my medicines. But at night it spoke to me. It told me it could make my every wish come true. And so I wished my daughter to be well again, and I devoured the pearl, as it bade me to."

"What happened to your daughter?" I ask.

"She was healed," replies Angma, "just as the pearl promised. I was overjoyed."

"But then?"

"Over the next few days, I grew ravenous. I'd always been poor, and during the worst monsoons, I'd gone a week without food . . . but I had never known a hunger like this. Rice would not fill the emptiness in my belly, nor meat nor leaf nor drink. It depleted my senses and installed a monster in its place."

I shiver, remembering this part of the legend. "You killed your own daughter."

"I did." A muscle throbs in Angma's cheek. Her voice breaks. "I did."

I feel sorrow only for her daughter, not for Angma. "The pearl lied to you."

"The pearl does not lie. It shapes the truth as it sees it. I asked for my daughter to be well, not for her to live a long life."

"I imagine you've learned to be more careful with your words," I say coldly.

Angma lets out a bitter laugh. "Since then, the pearl has granted my every wish. Except when it comes to you."

Me?

A beam of faint golden light seeps through the dead grass under my feet, traveling slowly toward the shadow worms that lock around my ankles. I hold my breath, a tickle of hope rising inside. Angma will notice it before long. I have to keep her talking.

"Me?" I say aloud.

"Look at me, Channi. On my honor, I will not bespell you."

*You have no honor,* I want to say. But I don't. Instinct tells me that Angma is speaking the truth.

Ever so slowly, I lift my gaze to meet hers, those same amber eyes that have haunted my dreams for years. There is no demon red, no malice, no magic spinning in them. "What do you want with me?"

Angma hesitates. She lowers the spear to the stone. "I am not the monster you think I am. I am not without compassion. You wish for the face you should have had—I can grant that."

"At the cost of my sister's life," I snap.

"You think that giving my pearl to the Golden One will save her. No—it would doom her to a curse she can never break. I'm sure Nakri warned you just as much. It would be a *mercy* for me to kill Vanna. A mercy you ought to allow."

*Where is Ukar?* If he were here, I'm sure he would have gnawed out Angma's eyes by now.

But the light is close. I have to keep Angma distracted. I school the harshness out of my features and open my palms. I lean forward. As if I'm listening. Considering.

She latches on to my silence. "Had you given me your sister, I would have raised her as my own until her pearl matured. Then, in return for the pearl, I'd have seen her reincarnated into a new life. A happier life. Such will be the pearl's power, when both halves are reunited."

"Could the pearl truly be so formidable?" I ask, genuinely curious.

"It can do whatever the bearer wishes of it, for a price." Her voice falls, turning subdued. "I've told you before, I want the same as you. To have another chance." She meets my gaze. "I lost my daughter, and you lost your mother. Let us be the ones we've lost for each other."

The first time she made such an offer, I was stunned. I was sure it was a cruel, preposterous trick. This time, I believe her. Angma has unmasked herself to me, showing me a glimmer of the woman she used to be.

It is the most perverse proposition I have ever heard, and never have I hated her more—yet never have I felt sorrier for someone, either.

The flat stone beneath me grows warm, a narrow stream

of light gilding its veins. "I won't be the redemption for your mistakes," I say quietly. "I'm not your daughter, and I never will be."

I bolt for my spear, but Angma's too fast. With a rancorous cry, she twists it from my reach and raises it high. I'm a beat away from being staked in the chest when a dazzling flare of light explodes over the valley.

Vanna.

She bursts toward us, the pearl in her heart shining brighter than I have ever seen. "Do not touch my sister," she commands, her tiger voice booming with power.

Oshli rides on her back, followed by Hokzuh on foot. My friends aren't alone. They've brought an army: Angma's army. I never thought I'd be happy to see demons, but I am. Their eyes are red, freed from Angma's thrall. The first thing they do is turn on the suiyaks.

And my sister confronts Angma, raising her claws with a blast of light.

Angma staggers back, taking me with her. The spear flies out of her grasp, and I try to wrestle free to grab it— but she holds me close, using me as a shield. Shadows tear out of her body, wrapping around me.

Light and darkness meet head-on, clashing like warring tidal waves. I am thrust between them, my body slammed by cold and heat in the greatest extremes, as both halves of the pearl struggle for dominion.

As Angma's shadows creep over Vanna's light, I fly forward, closer and closer to my sister. I know I'm screaming, but I can't feel my lungs. I'm drowning in white, dazzling pain.

"Let her go!" Vanna shouts. "Channi, get out of here!"

My sister's eyes are pained; she knows she's hurting me with her light.

*Don't stop,* I plead with a look. *If you do, Angma wins.*

Angma is counting on the bond that we sisters share. She's betting that Vanna will hold back her power to spare me the pain. She knows Vanna won't sacrifice my life.

But I will.

My body is heavy as lead, and every movement that I make feels like I'm pushing a mountain. Futile. Pointless. But I don't give up. Muscle by muscle, I twist back toward the Demon Witch. Her shadows lock around my shoulders and stab through me like phantom knives. I will bear it. I must.

Time itself sways. I am in the eye of a storm, but I am moving, fighting to obliterate the distance between Angma and myself. We might as well be worlds apart. The space feels infinite, impossible to overcome. But thank the gods for Ukar.

He springs through the mist, coming out of nowhere. Even I don't see where he was hiding. He bites Angma on the ankle, the way the Serpent King bit me years ago. The Demon Witch draws a sharp breath, and for a precious instant, her power falters.

Thanks to Ukar's diversion, I tear free of Angma's darkness. I stumble into the bushes. My body no longer shields the witch, and Vanna is free to release the full power of her light.

It's a sign we're winning when Angma starts to change back into a tiger, whiskers springing from her cheeks, fur rising from her pores. I drag my gaze to my sister, who's turning human at the same time.

But I don't dare rejoice.

I know that Angma has had years to master her pearl, and she can sustain its power longer. She will outlast Vanna. Unless I do something.

My body is still shaking with shock. It's madness to throw myself back in Angma's way, but I don't care. I bite into my palm, tearing through my calluses. Pain chokes me. I swallow and bite deeper. Again and again—until blood floods my mouth and all I can taste is iron.

With my teeth, I gnash into Angma's fur. My poison is not enough to kill a monster like her, but I feel her muscles jerk and her heart leap. That's all I need. The shadows spiral back, just long enough so I can lurch out of their path and retrieve my spear.

I pick it up, right as Angma springs for me. Sharp curved claws shoot out of her fingers, and before I can attack, she snaps my weapon in half.

The last time I fought a tiger and she broke my weapon, I dropped it out of surprise. Not this time. Even as the splinters of wood explode in my face, I hold fast to the pieces of my broken spear. First chance I get, I jab one end into Angma's belly. Her fur hisses from contact with my blood, but I don't pierce her flesh. I ram the other half of the spear into her back. Deeper and deeper into her heart until I feel the hardness of the pearl lodged inside.

Then I twist.

A scream careens out of Angma's lungs. The sound is like thunder; my entire body goes numb, and my ears are deafened.

I twist and twist, my eyes watering as her tattered hide hemorrhages smoke. Nothing in the world can stop me. Layer after layer, I unfold shadow and blood until, finally, the broken pearl tumbles out of her chest. I scoop it up with my bare hand.

Shaped like a half moon, it looks no more extraordinary than a stone from a riverbed. But I can feel the terrible power it holds, humming as it rests on my palm, fitting there as neatly as a small rice bowl.

I stumble to my feet, senses still reeling, but I'm trembling with joy. Angma lies under the clove tree, in a puddle of bleeding darkness. The glow of her eyes is fading, and her white hair is lank against the dirt. She's dying.

"It's over," I whisper to her.

Across the mist, the golden beams fanning out of my sister's heart recede into a gentle glow. With a smile, she leans tiredly against Oshli. She's human again, and I thank Gadda under my breath. Everything will be all right.

"Not so," Angma rasps, jolting me from my peace. "You think I am your sister's greatest enemy, but you are wrong." A brittle laugh. "Look, Channi."

She's wheezing, bleeding out on her back, and yet she uses her last strength to point at the sky. I look up, but it's hazy still, and I can't see much. Gradually, a divine brush sweeps away the fire, and the smoke pressing against the jungle dissipates. Angma's curse on the island lifts.

"You see now?" she whispers.

There, up against the high moon, is Hokzuh. He's alone, pitted against an army of suiyaks. There have to be over a hundred of them, so many that their masses of white hair resemble a thick cloud. I don't know what's happening, but all the joy I felt earlier is gone, replaced by a creeping dread.

"This is my last wish to the pearl," Angma whispers with a growl. "Let my pain be yours."

Then, with one final spurt of strength, she leaps—and throws me to the ground.

I'm caught off guard. I fall forward, landing on the bulging roots of the crooked clove tree. As Angma holds me down with her massive weight, I turn onto my back. The suiyaks are there, winging behind her, too many to count. I hold the black half of the pearl close, ready to fight to keep it. But no attack comes—from Angma or from the suiyaks.

Instead, the suiyaks crowd around the Demon Witch. Then, as the remaining light from the fire dissipates behind the trees, one of them drops something white and shimmering into Angma's mouth.

My dread calcifies into horror. Too late, I know what Angma wished for.

I'll never forget her smile, all teeth, as she widens her maw, revealing Hokzuh's moonstone trapped inside.

"No," I choke, screaming. "No!"

Angma folds over me, as if diving for an embrace. She crushes me with her tiger weight, but her muscles go soft, and her fur turns limp. She begins to shrink as though her insides are leaking out. As I squirm out of her arms, Vanna calls for me.

"Channi, Channi, I'm coming!"

My sister is trying to rescue me, and that means charging through a wall of suiyaks.

"Vanna, get away!" I yell. "Get out of here!"

"Would she fight for you the way you fight for her?" Hokzuh asked me once.

The answer is yes, Vanna would. And gods, I wish I didn't know it.

Mist thickens the air, blotting Vanna and the suiyaks from my view. A rush of cold nips at my ankles. It's Angma. All that's left of her is a shadow upon the flat rock. Then nothing.

This time I don't gloat.

I scramble to my feet, retrieve what remains of my spear. Night has come, and the suiyaks withdraw to the sky, joining the exodus of demons freed from Angma's command.

Except for one demon. I can see only his profile, but he's larger than the rest, with great black wings and two horns that curve like scythes. He hangs against the night, as if waiting for something. Or someone.

He turns slowly, and I see his eyes—one blue, growing dimmer by the second until it's lost to the night, and one red, dazzling against the pale white moon.

I'm already running, but gods help me, there's no way I will make it in time.

*Hokzuh, don't,* I warn. *You promised.*

The demon does not hear me.

With a roar, he dives to where I last saw my sister.

And her light goes dark.

# CHAPTER THIRTY-EIGHT

Time stops. I cannot breathe, and it's only by the grace of Gadda that I'm running, for all of me is numb, too numb to remember how.

*Do you know what it's like turning into a demon against your will?* Hokzuh asked me. *It's like having drunk far too much wine and being pushed by someone you hate to do things you despise. All while barely remembering your own name.*

Gone is every trace of the Hokzuh who held my hand and kissed me. Who made me think he could be something more.

Hokzuh is a demon.

The world is spinning, and all I see is that glob of light burning in his grasp. My sister's light. My sister's heart.

"Vanna!" I cry when at last I reach her.

She's lying on her side, her head in Oshli's lap. She's still breathing. Still alive.

Oshli is murmuring frantic words of healing, and magic stutters out of his cracked staff, but I know it's in vain.

Angma lasted only minutes without her heart. The same will be so for Vanna. Unless—

"I'm here," I tell my sister. "I have Angma's pearl."

Vanna reaches for me. For the first time I can remember, my fingers are warmer than hers. "I tried to stop him, Channi," she says. "But I . . . I let my guard down. I was weak."

Only my sister would apologize for Hokzuh's betrayal. It isn't fair. Vanna just got her body back. Angma is dead. We should be rejoicing. We should be going home together, holding hands, singing and dancing on our tired, aching feet.

"Not weak," I whisper. "You fought bravely against Angma. You'll fight bravely now. You're strong. You're going to be all right." I hold up the darkly shimmering half-pearl. "Look."

I press it toward Vanna's chest, expecting it to fill the hole where her heart used to be. But her body won't receive it, and she jerks away.

"It's cold," she cries. "It hurts."

*She needs her own heart,* Ukar says, appearing from behind the bushes. *The dragon half.*

I grit my teeth. "Don't go anywhere," I order Oshli and Ukar. My voice breaks. "Keep her alive."

I crane my neck skyward. With Vanna's light in his possession, Hokzuh no longer blends into the night. But why hasn't he devoured his half of the pearl yet? I see him hovering above me, angling for Angma's pearl. If he wants it, he'll have to pry it from my corpse.

The wind buffets my back as I raise the demon pearl

high. What did Angma say about how she'd wielded it? Nothing, except that it granted her wishes.

I don't have time to hesitate. If I don't act, if I don't wish, my sister will die.

"Bring me Vanna's heart," I command the pearl, my voice trembling. Again, louder: "Bring me my sister's heart!"

There comes a howl of wind against my neck, and I duck, clutching the pearl under my ribs. Hokzuh's red eye is bright against the darkness, and he flies like a wraith, shredding everything in his path. Even as I shout his name, yelling for him to stop, he does not hear me. He does not know me.

Instead, his enormous wing scrapes against my back, its barbed edge close enough to skin my elbows raw.

One more dive like that and I'll be dead. There is only one thing I can do.

I hold the demon pearl close. Shadows waft up from its dark surface, caressing my mouth. I speak: "Khramelan."

Hokzuh's true name is heavy on my tongue. Even after it leaves my lips, I can feel its power. I repeat the name over and over.

"Khramelan," I say again, stronger now. "You swore an oath that you would not harm my sister. Now you will pay the consequences for breaking that oath."

Hokzuh dives again, but this time I'm ready. I retrieve the spindlebeard from my pocket and hurl it into the forest, mouthing a silent command. *Grow.*

Spindlebeard bushes burst from the earth, branches springing forth like arms. They wrap around the dragon, stronger than any iron chain. Big, fat thorns pierce out of the vines and hook downward like stakes, pinning his wings in place.

A wounded cry scrapes out of Hokzuh. He groans from the pain, but I do not flinch.

"Restrain him," I command.

More thorns emerge, the sharpest, most sinister thorns I've ever seen. They slice into Hokzuh's flesh, producing a sound that's visceral and wet as they release their poison into his veins. Slowly. Painfully. With a hiss.

His body goes limp, and his hooded eyes close in sleep. His fist uncurls. His wings flatten against the earth.

I bend to retrieve Vanna's heart. Hokzuh lets out a ragged grunt, which I ignore. I'll deal with him later.

Right now, Vanna needs me.

# CHAPTER THIRTY-NINE

Vanna is right where I left her, lying on the grass, her head upon Oshli's lap.

Oshli cradles her to his chest. He's given up trying to save her with magic, and his dark eyes swirl with anguish. When he sees me arriving with both halves of the pearl, he wipes his cheek. "Save her," he says hoarsely. "Please."

A lump swells in my throat as he gives my sister to me.

Vanna wilts against my arm. Her eyes are closed, but her chest rises and falls, so I know she is still breathing. Some of the weight inside me lifts.

"Wake up," I whisper, stroking her cheek. "Look, I have your light."

My sister's eyes twitch, then flutter open. They are the same eyes I have always known, warm and familiar. They gaze at me, unwavering, with the unconditional love of a sister. My favorite eyes.

Vanna reaches for her heart. "It's warm."

"It's yours." I tilt the dragon pearl to her chest. It's been inside her all her life. It knows her. Yet as I dip it toward her, its gilded light flickers hesitantly, then dims.

No matter how we try, it refuses to take its place in her chest.

"It doesn't want me," Vanna says quietly. "I can hear it. It's no longer mine."

A tide of alarm washes over me. "I don't understand. I have both halves. I've seen what Angma did with only half a pearl. Two . . ."

*Two should be able to save you.* In frustration, I force the pearl halves together, but like opposite ends of this earth, they repel each other. They will not come together.

"Heal my sister," I order them. "Heal her. Save her. I command you."

The pearl halves hum, and Nakri's words come back to me unbidden: the pearl has a mind of its own.

What did she mean by that? Is the pearl *choosing* not to save Vanna? I let out a frustrated cry. Time is running out, and I don't know how to use this magic. I don't know how to save Vanna.

"Enough, Channi," she says, pulling on my arm. "It's all right. Let go."

I won't set the pearl down. I know it has the power to heal her. Even if it won't take her back, it can help her. It must.

*Listen to your sister,* says Ukar. *She has a request to make of you.*

Vanna places her hand over mine. The radiance from the pearl halves fans over her skin, as if giving her strength.

372

"Take me to the water," she says. "I want to dip my feet in the sea. I always loved that. I've missed it."

How can I refuse?

I rise to my knees, still holding Vanna, but Oshli backs away. I incline my chin at him. *Are you coming?*

He gives a pained shake of his head.

"Just you and me, Channi." Vanna smiles at me, a particular smile I haven't seen in years. "Like old times."

I remember the day she was born, to the moment she first opened her eyes and saw me—newly a monster—and smiled. Oh, how her little face beamed and shone at the sight of me, with pure happiness I've seldom seen on her face since.

I think of all the times I've clucked my tongue at Vanna for giving in to what Adah asks of her, never fighting for the future she wants, never chasing the love she deserves. I thought her weak, I thought her shallow and selfish.

I do not deserve her.

I lift her carefully, and she does not move. Her face is turned to my chest, and as I carry her, I can feel the ridges of her spine, the fragile intake of her breath as her ribs go in and out. More than anything, I wish my blood had the power to heal, not hurt. I would give my life for that to be true.

"Stay with me, Vanna," I whisper. "Stay strong."

The sea is too far, so I settle for a nearby pond. It's one I know intimately, where Ukar and his siblings swim often, and where I used to practice on days when I could bear the sight of my own reflection. It's also the pool where I come to pluck orchids for Vanna's birthday. I rue the fact that I don't see any now.

I lay her against the trunk of a tree that overlooks the water. She's lost her slippers, and there are leaves between her toes. I brush them off before I slide her feet into the cool pond.

"This is beautiful," Vanna whispers. "It reminds me of home. Remember our little hut near the beach? It was so close, but I always made you carry me there."

It hurts to swallow. "I remember." I pretend to tease her. "You were so spoiled back then. You made me take you almost every day."

"We'd sculpt snakes in the sand, and then Ukar would blend in until we couldn't tell what was sand and what was snake." Vanna chuckles. "Then I'd run up and down the beach, and nothing I did could make you come into the sea with me."

"Except for that one time you pretended to drown."

Vanna smiles. "That was cruel. I didn't understand why you hated the water back then."

She falls quiet, watching the currents dance past her toes. A butterfly lands on her wrist, and I wave the creature away, but Vanna raises her fingers to stop me. "Don't. I've been waiting for them to come."

"The butterflies?"

A nod. "They're my favorite."

"You never told me why you love them so much."

Vanna smiles to herself. "There's a story I learned in

school, about a pair of lovers that couldn't be together. They prayed and prayed to Su Dano, and out of mercy she turned them into butterflies. Every year when spring comes, they're reborn and find each other, and they're happier than in any other life."

I take her hand in mine.

"Butterflies celebrate all love, Channi, because every love is precious. And mine for you, above all. That love is forever."

Heat rushes up my throat to my eyes, and I can no longer hold back the tears. "Don't talk like this," I scold her, but my words tremble. "We're going to leave Tambu together. Remember? You wanted to sail across the nine Emerald Seas, and hear the yawnbirds of the Suma Desert, and climb the thousand steps to Gadda's Temple on Jhor. . . ."

"In another life." Vanna caresses my cheek with her fingertips. "In another life, we will do these things. Together." She leans against the tree, her face utterly serene. "Stay good, sister. Love more, for me."

Her eyes start to close, and awful sister that I am, I shake her. I clasp her hand. "Don't go."

Vanna smiles, a softer smile than before. "I'm only taking a rest. I'm tired."

I will go to the Nine Hells for this, but I grab her wrist. "No."

Bless Vanna for humoring me. "So many times you've helped me sleep—with your stories and your songs. Will you sing to me now?"

I have no songs in my memory now. My mind is numb. But for the hope of keeping Vanna awake, I make something up:

> Channi and Vanna lived by the sea,
> And kept the fire with a spoon and pot.
> Stir, stir, a soup for lovely skin,
> Simmer, simmer, a stew for thick black hair.
> But what did they make for two happy smiles?

"What?" breathes Vanna.

I smile.

> Cakes, cakes with coconut and peanuts.

Vanna laughs gently, and the sound is music.

Night ages, but I hardly notice. I keep singing, even as her lashes droop down over her eyes, falling into a delicate black curtain.

When at last my voice grows tired, and my song ends, words coming to a gentle cadence, Vanna's eyes open once more. They see a realm beyond ours.

"Vanna?" I whisper, a leap in my heart.

"Channi, your scales are turning white," she says, peering up at me.

The transformation is reflected in her eyes, the green of my scales paling into a milky white. "It happens to the snakes of Sundau." My ribs go tight. *When they lose someone they love.*

"You look beautiful." She reaches for my hand and holds it. "Look, like the moon."

I fall for the trick and look up, but before I can find the moon, Vanna sags against the tree, and I catch her just before she falls. She's gone. So gracefully, she's slipped from this world and entered the next.

A sob wrenches out of my chest, and I stare at my beautiful sister, swearing that I will never forget her face. Never forget a single hair or line. Never forget her voice or the sound of her laugh.

I weep and weep, certain that I will weep forevermore. I fold my body over hers, clinging to her as long as I can before she begins to glow. Vanna's skin shimmers gold, like when she was born, and softly she goes into the earth.

Then she is gone, and she will never shine again.

# CHAPTER FORTY

After sorrow comes anger. Anger like I have never felt before. It consumes me, a fiery poison that burns down my
throat. Nothing can quench the heat.

"You!" I rasp at the pearl. The halves lie still, innocent as
river stones. But I know better.

They've taken everything from me. The person I loved
most, and who loved me most. I loom over them with a rock
in my fist, ready to shatter them into dust—when suddenly
they quiver to life.

They rise from the ground, lifted by invisible wings. Side
by side, they circle me wildly, one dark as night and one
bright as the sun. I hate them both, and I slam down my rock.

I miss. I curse.

"Stay still!" I shout. I try again. I miss again. "Haven't
you brought enough misery to this world? This is the end.
Begone!"

The pearl halves hum insistently, buzzing around me. I
snap a thick branch off a tree and swing with all my might,
but instead of hitting the pearls, I hit . . . a thread.

It dangles between the pearl halves, shimmering. It's the thread of Hokzuh's soul, a token of the promise he made me. The promise he has now broken.

The thread weaves toward me. One end loops around my wrist, and tugs, beckoning me to follow. I cannot see where it leads, but I have a feeling.

I tear through the trees, following the thread to its end: a wide thicket drenched in shadow. The night has gathered here, but there is no darkness that can protect the traitor who's taken my sister from me.

"Khramelan." The anger blistering inside me boils. "Awaken."

At the sound of his true name, the demon stirs. His wings rustle against the vines of spindlebeard that immure him, and his red eye burns through the shadows. This is not the Hokzuh I knew.

When he sees me, he snarls. I meet him with a cold and unfeeling glare.

He struggles against the vines, but even a demon like him cannot fight the magic of the pearl.

He will hear what I've come to say, and witness what I've come to do.

He draws a sharp breath when the two halves of the pearl emerge from behind me.

One dragon half, one demon half. Together, they make up the heart he has so desperately sought. Yet they trail me, not him. And I'm beginning to understand why.

"A promise is not a kiss in the wind," I say in my lowest, darkest voice. "It is a piece of yourself that is given away and will not return until your pledge is fulfilled. You have broken your promise to me. For that, I am owed a piece of your soul."

The pearl halves float above my hand, spinning slowly, orbiting one another. "You have taken from me what I treasured most in this life. And so, shall I take from you. I claim your pearl, Khramelan."

The invisible thread around my wrist suddenly snaps. It spools long, spinning itself around the two pearl halves, and with a great unseen force, it draws them together in a cocoon. In a blur of light the halves are united in one last flash, forming a broken sphere. A broken *pearl*.

Khramelan reaches out for it, but I take the pearl first. It turns black in my hand, and a sharp golden light emanates from its fissures.

"No," he whispers. "Channi."

The sound of my name jolts me. It sounds like Hokzuh.

The *real* Hokzuh. His blue dragon eye is throbbing, as though it wars against the other for control. "Channi," he says again. He's whispering, the words crawling out of his throat as though he's fighting to speak. "Don't do this. Forgive me. Channi."

My shoulders fall. Never has the sound of my name made my heart ache as it does now. He sounds small and broken. Only hours ago, I held his hand, I held him to me. I trusted him.

A trace of sorrow slips through the cracks of my fury. What happened to Vanna wasn't his fault; it was Angma's, for unleashing the demon inside him.

*Stay good, sister,* Vanna told me. *Love more, for me.*

I lower my hands, bringing the pearl down to my side. It has been the longest night of my life, and my body beseeches me to succumb to slumber, in hopes that my dreams might somehow bring me closer to Vanna.

For Vanna, I hold the pearl out to Hokzuh. "You want it? Then use it to bring back my sister."

Hokzuh is the master of the pearl. If anyone can wield its full power, *he* can.

He takes the pearl as though it's a goblet of water and he is a man who's been parched for weeks. But where his fingers touch upon the pearl's surface, it sparks, and he draws back in pain. Again he tries. Again the pearl sends him reeling.

It will not have him. Just as it would not have Vanna.

The demon in Hokzuh resurfaces. His blue eye dulls into shadow, and he turns wrathful. "Give it back to me!" he roars, finally breaking free of the thorns with a burst of monstrous strength. "Give me the pearl!"

No matter how he strikes, he cannot touch me. The pearl has erected a wall of light between us. He takes out his anger upon the forest.

*"Stop!"* I shout as his wings raze the trees. *"Enough."*

But he does not stop. His moonstone is gone, destroyed. His demon is unleashed. I know that if I let him go, he will not be able to control himself. He will destroy the island.

And if I could not save Vanna, I must at least protect Sundau.

My jaw goes hard. I have no choice.

"The pearl will not have you," I say. "It demands that you pay for breaking your promise to me."

I half close my eyes. "A curse," I decide. "A curse was what began all this, and a curse shall end it." I turn to Hokzuh, power gathering in my words. "I banish you, Khramelan, to the forgotten corners of this world. Never will you be free, and never will you escape—for only I can release you, and where I go, you cannot follow. Until I die, you will live in darkness. Only then will you awaken and be free. That is the price you shall pay, for taking away my sister."

"Channi!"

I cannot tell whether it is Hokzuh or the demon within him that shouts my name. It is the last sound he makes before he begins to writhe, his flesh contorting in ways I did not know were possible. The earth beneath him quakes violently; water gushes up higher than the trees, swooping down to devour him.

I turn away, holding a tree for support as the force of the water slams back into the earth. All that's left of Hokzuh is a mark in the mud. I do not know where he has gone.

My heart goes tight. I cannot breathe.

I've lost my sister, and now I've lost my friend. All because of the pearl.

I unclench my fists at my sides, and crawl toward it. The cursed thing is waiting for me to claim it.

"I don't want you," I tell it. "I don't want anything to do with you. Go, for all I care. Roam the whole of Lor'yan, causing whatever havoc you wish. But now, in this moment that you're mine, you will do something for me."

I seize the pearl. "You will bring my sister back," I command it. I *beg* it. "Please. I cannot live without seeing her face again, without hearing her voice again. Do this for me, and it will be all I ask of you." I press my face to the dirt. "Please. Do what you must. Let me be a monster forever. Or take me instead. Only bring me back my sister."

The pearl wrestles free of my grip. It shoots above me, light spilling out of its crack and washing over my face. Its radiance is a warm tickle at first, and then it grows so bright that my eyes water and my chest goes tight. Tighter.

*Stop,* I plead. *I can't breathe.*

The light doesn't stop. It grows in brilliance. It gains in power. I cannot stand it anymore. My lips part, and as a fiery heat comes over my face, I scream.

# CHAPTER FORTY-ONE

"Vanna?"

I blink. It's morning, and Oshli's face blurs into view, the brightness of his orange scarf stinging my eyes.

"Vanna?" he tries again, softly, his voice thick with hope.

I gasp and sit up. Nausea rises inside me, and simply keeping my eyes open is so disorienting that everything in my stomach roils up and wants to come out. I clench every muscle, willing myself to hold it down, hold it together. Then I lift my head.

Oshli is staring at me. He's saying things. Things meant for Vanna. There are tears in his eyes, but I push him away.

"Stop calling me that, have you gone ma—" My tongue goes leaden, and all words flee me.

*My voice* . . . It doesn't sound like mine. There's a new lilt to it, almost like a song. This is not me.

I hear it even in my breathing—something is very, very wrong.

My clothes are the same—the ripped gray tunic I borrowed from one of Rongyo's sailors, the musty striped pants I put on back at Adah's house.

But my hands! I gasp. My fingers are long and slender, my nails are clean, no blood or dirt crusted beneath. No calluses, no scratches or cuts. Not even the two puncture scars I got once from one of Ukar's cousins, who bit me for accidentally scaring off his breakfast. As my pulse thunders in my ears, I drag my gaze upward to find my reflection in Oshli's eyes—and my heart stops.

No. I choke on my breath. No, it can't be.

"I am not Vanna," I cry hoarsely. I start to push Oshli away, but his fingers graze my arm.

"Let me help you—"

"Don't touch me!" I shout. Light flares from my chest, and Oshli is frozen, his mouth still wide.

"Vanna?" he whispers.

All it takes is that one word, that one name, and I wish the earth would devour me whole, the way it did Hokzuh.

"Never will you speak that name again," I say, my voice trembling with power and trepidation.

His mouth clamps shut, and I twist from him to run through the trees. I run until I stumble upon a narrow stream, and there I kneel slowly, grabbing myself by the arms, forcing myself to breathe. I count to ten before I face my reflection.

What I saw in Oshli's eyes was no illusion. No nightmare—or dream.

I have lips. Soft, lily-bud lips that are pink, even as I curl them in dismay.

I have eyes the color of teakwood, warm and umber. And my pupils—they're round. They're human.

Lastly, my skin . . . My scales are gone. I have cheeks and a nose, just as I've always wished. They are smooth and firm, and perfect—except for one thing.

This face—*my* face—is Vanna's.

All the bile I've forced down threatens to surge up again. *It can't be.*

But my face is as unmistakable as the light shimmering in my heart. A light that reflects my every thought and feeling, just as it did for Vanna. Whereas my sister's light was gold, mine is silver. Still, it's radiant—even more radiant than before—and casts a mesmerizing glow on my skin. I loathe it.

I press my palm to my chest, where Hokzuh's pearl pulses. Every beat hurts. Was it this way for Vanna, or does it hurt because the pearl is broken inside me?

"Why did you do this to me?" I whisper to it. "Why did you give me my sister's face?"

As soon as I ask, I know the answer. *Bring my sister back,* I begged the pearl. *I cannot live without seeing her face again, without hearing her voice again.*

And so, the pearl granted my wish. It granted both my wishes: to see my sister again and to finally be rid of my cursed snakeskin . . . but in the cruelest way imaginable.

Enough! I dig into my chest, trying to wrench out the pearl. My nails cannot even pierce the flesh. Fortified by the pearl's magic, my skin is thick as armor.

I fall to my hands and beat the earth, letting out a frustrated, strangled cry.

*What foolishness is this?* Ukar's head pops out of a leafy fern. *Channi, enough.*

The sound of my real name startles me, and I look up. "You . . . you know me?"

*What kind of idiotic question is that?* Ukar huffs, and his scales ripple red with mild irritation. *Of course I know you, Channi. You could wear a donkey's hide and I would still know you.*

Without another word, I scoop him into my arms. I want to cry, but there are no tears left in me. My eyes are so dry they sting even when I blink.

*Cry as much as you need to,* Ukar says gently, *but don't despair. Your face might be Vanna's, but the rest of you is still Channi. Your strength, your heart . . . your blood too, from the smell of it.*

It's meant to cheer me, but I cannot be cheered. "Your king lied," I tell Ukar. "He said that 'one sister must fall for the other to rise.' *I* was meant to fall. Not Vanna. *Me.*"

*What makes you think you haven't?* Ukar prods. He tilts his head skyward. *Vanna has risen, and you . . . you still carry the burden of life. There are many ways yet to fall, and you will have years ahead of you.*

"I don't want years with this face."

*After bearing Angma's curse for so long, you will let this one defeat you? Vanna wouldn't want that.*

"She doesn't get a say in what she wants anymore," I

snap. As soon as the words leave me, I wish I could take them back. My mouth tastes bitter, and I stare at my hands. "It's not only a face I have to bear, Ukar," I say thickly. "It's the pearl, too."

*Yes, and you'd be a fool not to be wary of it. Your sister barely wielded its power. That won't be the same for you, Channi. It will ruin you—if you aren't careful. But it may also save you.*

The pearl thumps in my chest. It is a sly and loathsome thing; I can't imagine how it might save me. "You're speaking in prophecies."

*You'll have to get used to that, I'm afraid.* Ukar blinks. His pupils are larger than I remember, deeper too. They look ancient, almost.

"Ukar . . . you look different."

*Do I?* Amusement edges his voice. *I was hoping you wouldn't notice.*

There's a hood along his neck that wasn't there before. He's grown wider and longer, and his scales have a vibrancy to them that makes their surroundings blur. It's like an invisible aura, and I gasp with awe. "You're . . . you're the Serpent King!"

*Don't bow,* Ukar warns. But it's too late, and he groans when I do.

"How . . . when?"

*When I woke, I was like this. Changed . . . but not as changed as you.*

A lump lodges itself in the back of my mouth, and I cannot speak.

*You are stronger than the pearl, Channi. That is why it chose you. That is why the last king said what he did. Because everything was leading to this: you and the pearl together.*

"I don't want it," I say vehemently.

*And I don't want this,* he says, flaring his hood. *But some roles are cast upon us, and we must play them until death. This is only the beginning of our burden.*

I exhale a ragged breath. *You sound more like a father now than a best friend.*

*It's all that royal poison in my throat,* Ukar grumbles.

I might not be able to muster a smile or a laugh, but a touch of the heaviness in my heart is lifted. For now, that's enough.

I place a kiss on his head and drape him over my shoulders. "Come, Your Majesty, let's see what mess the demons made of Adah's house."

# CHAPTER FORTY-TWO

I am sweeping ash in the courtyard when my father returns to Sundau. At first, I don't hear him. I've been alone for over a week. So except for Ukar and his kin, I'm not expecting anyone.

The gate groans open, and Adah's footsteps clip down the stone pathway into the courtyard. I stop sweeping, but I don't look up.

"So many snakes," Adah mutters, kicking at them until they scatter into the garden.

I rap the end of my broom against the ground. "Stop."

That is when Adah sees me, and the look he gives is one I've seen only in my dreams: there is tenderness in his eyes, and his arms open for an embrace.

"Daughter! Will you not welcome your father home?"

I don't move. I may wear Vanna's face, but my memories are my own. I remember each time Adah flinched at the sight of me, each time he took a fishing rod and beat me across my back. In my coldest voice, I say, "Welcome home."

His gaze falls upon my unkempt hair and dirty face,

which seem to upset him more than my brusque tone. "You cut your hair," he blurts.

I clutch the end of my broom so I don't lash out and break his other wrist. For the sake of Vanna's memory, I bridle the anger inside me.

But even the tamest snake can still bite.

"My sister is dead," I say piercingly. "It is appropriate."

Adah summons just the right amount of sorrow on his face. I suspect he practiced on his way. "Forgive me. I heard about Channari. We will make suitable arrangements at the temple—"

"She has already been buried," I lie. This is the last thing I want to discuss with my father. "She is with the gods. Let us not speak of her again."

"Certainly," Adah agrees quickly. He doesn't even try to hide his relief. Then he hesitates. It is a rare moment that he bares his emotions. "I know you must think I was cruel to her," he says in a quiet voice. "Your sister."

I dare not breathe.

"I know it myself. Every time I saw her, I couldn't help it. I didn't hate her, Vanna. But what was I supposed to do, when she returned with the face of a snake demon—because of me? When her mother died, because I could not save her?"

I am silent. This might have meant something seventeen years ago, but not anymore. I offer no words of solace, no forgiveness.

In return, he buries the specter of the past. "Come with me now. Lintang is waiting for us on the ship—"

"The ship? You're not staying?"

"No, I came only to fetch you." Adah wrinkles his nose at our old house. "It's time we left Sundau. I have decided we shall stay in Tai'yanan."

"But why?" I frown. "The engagement to Prince Rongyo is dissolved."

"Even so. We aren't the only ones leaving. Many of our neighbors have gone already. As you should have, after that tiger witch attacked—"

"I'm staying," I interrupt. My voice is Vanna's, but every inflection is wrong. Vanna was never this harsh. "I will not go. I need time to grieve."

My request puts Adah on edge. "Be reasonable. There is talk of war with Shenlani, and after what your sister did to King Meguh, they are bound to come after our family. We must take refuge in Tai'yanan."

I don't budge. I'm shrewder than Vanna was, and I don't believe anything Adah says. "No one is coming after us," I reply calmly. "Shenlani has fallen, *thanks* to my sister. She rid Tambu of a brutal king—and queen—and she deserves a proper mourning. I will not bend on this."

With a grimace, Adah takes off his hat and fans himself. "How long do you require?"

"A hundred days. Maybe more."

"What will I tell them? They're already inquiring after you—"

*Them.* It takes me a moment to realize Adah doesn't mean Lintang or Prince Rongyo, or whoever may be waiting for me in Tai'yanan. *Them* means the new suitors that will come clamoring for Vanna's hand—*my* hand, now that it is no longer promised to Rongyo.

They're gnats, the lot of them. As long as my heart shines like a flame, they will always be drawn to it. Nothing I can do will stop that—this is the pearl's curse, as well as its blessing.

"Tell them I wish for ten thousand mosquito hearts on silver trays, a bridge of gold built across the Sundau Strait that leads up to the sun, a warship painted entirely with royal blood."

Adah blanches. "Vanna!"

*Vanna.* I could ask for a temple of bones and still Adah would not see that I am Channi.

"Tell them to rot in the lowest Hell," I say. "I will see no one, and I wish to be left alone. I will grieve in peace."

Adah lifts his arm, and I instinctively brace myself to be struck, but I am even more stricken when he simply touches my shoulder. Squeezes it. "A hundred days, then. Do what you must to be happy." A tender pause. "I've missed your smile, daughter."

Against my will, my chest caves in. For so long, I've trained myself to not feel anything for my father, but nothing could have prepared me for this. This was what I wished for, wasn't it? For him to finally love me and see me the way he sees Vanna.

The irony is sharper than a needle.

The next time I speak, power hums in my throat. "Do not speak to me again of suitors or of leaving Sundau."

"Yes, daughter," Adah says, his eyes sprinkled with silver. "It shall be as you say."

"Good." I pick up my broom again and resume sweeping. "Fetch Lintang. Bring her home. We will stay awhile."

A hundred days, a hundred years. Never will I get used to waking up and realizing I have no sister to cook breakfast for. That if I want to see her smile, I will have to confront my own reflection. I cannot do it. Seeing myself brings only sorrow, and I cannot smile. My sole comfort, as the days stretch into weeks, is that every morning without fail I visit Vanna.

I've planted moon orchids over where she rests. Seventeen flowers have bloomed, one for every year she lived. The number is the same every day, but I count them anyway.

"I missed your birthday once, sister," I murmur, keeping a respectful distance. "I'll never forget another."

Each day, I speak the words. Each day, they hurt just as much. I will never stop wishing that I had brought her an orchid for her last birthday. It is a small thing, but it will haunt me for years.

I crouch, sinking my knuckles into the earth. Ants crawl between my fingers, but I ignore them. I'm concentrating.

The pearl inside me stirs to life. I can feel it spinning as its power intensifies, and my skin prickles with a now-familiar pain. I cover my face with my hands, cupping away the light. It's taken time, but I am learning to control it. The pearl's power comes naturally, a realization that is both exhilarating and terrifying.

When my light recedes, the pond beside me ripples with a shadow of silver. And I look within the water.

"Hello, Channari," I murmur.

Yellow eyes stare back at me, and all is as it was: the narrow slits of my pupils, the ridges between my ears and neck, that pale streak of hair Angma once marked me with. The only difference is the color of my scales. They are white, the color of loss.

The spell won't last long, but it is necessary. I will not visit Vanna while wearing her face.

With a deep breath, I move forward to the orchids.

This is the hardest part of my day—finding the words to greet my sister. Sometimes I cannot even muster a hello. Sometimes I release a waterfall of regrets. Sometimes I simply weep.

Today, I turn to the butterflies fluttering about the flowers. They are always here, as constant as the air and the trees, and the ache in my heart swells. They know Vanna, the way the snakes know me.

I bow to them, deeply. *Thank you for keeping her company when I cannot.*

Then I kneel beside my sister.

"I got a letter yesterday," I begin. "From Nakri—she's invited me to become her apprentice. She thinks I need to leave Sundau, but I don't want to. What do you think?"

Of course, there's no reply. I falter at the silence, nearly ready to leave, when two of the butterflies land on my knuckles. Their wings, beautiful and bright, open as if to say, *Go on.*

And so I do. I tell my sister everything, from Lintang's new gray hairs to the serpents from Yappang that have come to swear fealty to Ukar, to Mama's cakes, which I've started to make again. An hour slips away, and I do not hear the footsteps behind me.

"Channari?"

I freeze.

"It is you."

When I turn, I wear Vanna's face once more. "You are mistaken. And you will forget whatever you—"

"Stop." Oshli shakes his ritual staff at me. "Have some respect. I've known the truth for a while. I guessed it soon after you woke as . . . as *her.*"

I spare the shaman a dispassionate glance. "And so you've confirmed what you already know. Now leave. I wish to be left alone."

"Your stepmother came to see me at the temple," he says, ignoring my command. "She's worried about you. She says you haven't smiled in weeks, that you won't speak to her or your father. That you disappear into the jungle every morning."

I make a mental note to confront Lintang when I go home.

"For weeks I've tried to come see you," he goes on. "But every time I near your house, my mind descends into a fog and I forget why I am there."

I'm silent. This is by design, but Oshli shouldn't be aware of it. No one else is.

He lowers his staff. Two lanterns hang from the top, both unlit. "You cannot hide from the world forever, Channari," he says quietly. "You haven't asked me why I'm here. It's because I made a promise. To your sister."

My eyes fly up. I look Oshli up and down. His hair is uncut, and he's wearing his shaman's robes and his orange scarf instead of mourning white. Yet any fool can see he is grieving. It's in the harsh lines on his face, the hollows under his eyes, even the way his feet fall on the earth, heavy and final.

"What promise?"

"I will tell you," he says. "But first, allow me to speak her name again."

Suddenly, shame heats my cheeks, and I'm sorry for being peevish to Oshli, for ignoring him, for keeping Vanna to myself when he has as much right as I do to see her and honor her. For cursing him so he cannot speak her name.

*I've been afraid,* I want to tell him, but I cannot. So I do the best that I can, and touch my chest, lifting the silence I cast upon him. "You may speak her name."

In my life, I have never seen anyone look so grateful. "Vanna," he says, as though the name were a key that unlocks the very air he breathes. "Thank you."

"She is buried there." I gesture at the orchids. "Go, speak to her."

I start to turn for Adah's house, but Oshli lifts one of the lanterns from his staff. "Wait." A small smile touches his face, turning it boyish. "Did you know I used to call Vanna 'my lantern'? Because of how her heart shone." He looks at me, for the first time without faltering. "You were the light that made it shine brightest, Channi."

I swallow hard. "Don't flatter me. She loved you."

"She didn't love me until the end. She loved you from the beginning."

There is no bitterness in his tone, no envy or resentment. He merely speaks truth.

Butterflies flock to him, landing on his arm in such numbers that they resemble a ruffled sleeve. He strikes a flame and lights one of the lanterns.

"Why did you bring two?" I ask.

"For the two sisters," he replies. He offers me his candle so I may light the second lantern. "Gadda says that this life is merely a stepping-stone to the next. I have faith that in your next one you will find each other again. The lanterns will guide you."

I take more comfort in his words than he can know. The lantern in my hand sways.

"Do you want to know now what I promised her?" Oshli asks.

When I nod, he sets down his lantern. "I promised to tell you that she will wait for you. That she wants you to take your time."

They are the simplest words, but also the words that break me. My shoulders shake, and the tears begin to fall.

"I promised her you wouldn't be alone, that I would be a friend if you needed me." His voice falls soft. "She wanted you to be happy."

"She didn't know about my . . . my *face*."

"She couldn't have. But she knew life hasn't been easy for you, Channi. She wanted you to find your way, however you must."

"I don't know how."

"Nor do I," he admits. "But every day I get a little closer. It is a journey, and it begins once you walk past the walls you've built around your heart." He pauses. "Can you leave those walls behind—for her, for yourself?"

I finally remember the lantern in my hand. I set it down beside Oshli's. Their glow is a mirror of my own light. "I will try."

It is well into the night when I pad into my old room in Adah's house and reach under my cot. There I find the broken spear that I stabbed Hokzuh with. I hold it upright, and the tip of the blade comes only to my chin.

All day, I've thought about Vanna's request. I've thought about the walls I've always hated—not just the walls of this house, but also the walls forced upon me by my face.

*My face*. For years, a serpent's. Now, until I die, my sister's.

I might not be able to break down those walls, but Oshli's

right. If I cannot find a way to walk past them, I will always be trapped. And there is only one way I can think of to set myself free.

Still holding my spear, I turn to Mama's shrine. There is a white orchid next to the sculpture I made of Mama, and it bobs along with my movements.

I catch it in my hand, hold it by the stem to my cheek. My throat swells, making it hard to breathe. It is a moon orchid, Vanna's favorite.

"Sister," I say softly to the flower, "your face was the one I loved most in this life. Never did I dream it might bring me pain to see. But it does. Because it is *your* face, not mine." The words crawl out of me, and I pause before I can speak again. "I would not disrespect you, so I ask for your permission. Please." I grip my spear tighter. "Will you let me be free?"

The orchid sits on my hand. For a long while, it does not move, and I exhale, ready to set aside my blade. Then, as I start to turn, the wind plucks the flower from my palm and sweeps its petals up across my cheek to my forehead. The motion is tender, like the brush of Vanna's fingers on my skin.

Then the orchid falls on my spear.

Before, I would dismiss such a gesture as merely the wind. But there's a tingle that races across my skin, and I know it is more than mere chance.

"Thank you, sister," I utter, still softly. "And forgive me. This will be the last time I put blade to skin. The last time I shall bring forth the poison in my blood. I will be good, as you asked of me. I will love more."

I look skyward, and I bow once to Mama, once to Vanna. Then I raise the blade to my forehead, just above my eyebrow, and wait until my hands stop shaking. For all my strength, my spear has never felt as heavy as it does now.

With a deep breath, I pierce into my flesh. And cut.

The pain doesn't come right away. I get as far as across the ridge of my nose before the backs of my eyes begin to burn, and my skin sings in protest. I finish quickly, moving down across my cheek before I drop the spear and hurry to the water bowl.

Blood clings to my lashes and mixes with my tears. All the times I've cut into my scales to gouge them out, I have never cried. This time, I cannot hold back the pain.

I bite down on my lip and watch my reflection in the bowl. The pearl's silvery light bathes my face, already working to heal its wound.

*No,* I seethe, fighting against the light. *Let me have this.*

With my spear, I trace the cut on my face. My blood bubbles up again, thicker than before. So many times I tried using its poison to burn away my scales, always in vain. Then again, I have never tried to use it as a cure.

I drag my finger down, smearing blood across my gash. The pearl hisses, its light trying to stitch up my broken skin, but it cannot touch the rivulet of blood that streams down my face. Every time it comes close, I retrace the line in blood. I hold on to the lesson the snakes taught me when I was young: Not all poisons are bad. Sometimes, they can make for the most unexpected medicines.

I never thought my poison—the strongest known on

earth—could heal anything. But Gadda help me, if I'm to live, I will not be a prisoner to my own skin.

"You will not win," I whisper to the pearl through my teeth. "This is not . . . my . . . face!"

Finally, the light recedes into my heart, defeated.

On my face, a shiny white scar forms. I touch it. It is slightly raised, with rough ridges that remind me of the scales I once bore. The scales I once wished so hard to be rid of.

It's ghastly. Impossible to hide. But to me, it is victory enough. It's a tear in the mask, a piece of the real me for all to see.

I will never let it go.

# CHAPTER FORTY-THREE

Word of my scar travels across Sundau, then Tambu, then the rest of Lor'yan. If I thought it would stamp out any interest in me, I was wrong. The stories spread, and everyone wonders why my light has changed. Why it is now silver like the moon instead of golden like the sun. Slowly, they stop calling me the Golden One, and new names for me appear in songs and tales. I would list them, but I despise them all.

Before long, the suitors come swarming again. Ships upon ships visit Sundau. Merchants, lords—even a gang of bandits who try to kidnap me in my sleep. They gagged my mouth and carried me out of my bed, trying to smother my light with blankets. They got as far as my door before I turned them into rats. Ukar and his kin had a heavy breakfast that morning.

Anyone can see that I *am* different. I'm not the docile, exuberant daughter Adah has touted to the world. No. I never smile, I never bow—even to the kings and queens who come to visit—and I rarely even speak, unless I must.

In private, Adah pleads with me to be warmer. "You will

start a war with that grimace," he says. "I know you mourn your sister, but how long must you stay sequestered in your room? You must marry, Vanna. Do you wish our fortunes to crumble?"

"I don't give a damn about our fortunes."

Adah is stricken by my words. In the past, he wouldn't have tolerated such defiance, but now he does not dare to argue. He fears me, though he does not know why.

In the past few months, I've begun to master the pearl's power. I can make a dozen minds yield to me with just a look, and I have even begun to meddle with memories. I know this is just the beginning. The glow of my light is harsh; it is more brilliant, more intense, than Vanna's ever was. Cross me, and it'll burn.

It would be easy for me to fashion myself a sorcerer queen, formidable beyond anything Angma could have dreamed. But that is not what I want.

I regard my father. "You wish me to marry, Adah?"

A fervent nod.

"Then begin the selection once more. I will choose whoever can make me smile."

Adah blinks, as if the task is far too simple. "No more trays of mosquito hearts or bridges of gold and that nonsense?"

"Whoever can make me smile," I repeat. "Will you agree to this?"

Adah's elation shines through his eyes. "Yes, yes."

*I wouldn't be so hopeful if I were you,* I think as he runs off to tell Lintang the good news. The inklings of a plan are taking shape in my mind, and they will not be to my father's liking.

<hr />

Vanna's room once brimmed with storybooks and maps, with hanging bouquets of dried flowers and incense that smelled like jasmine. All that is gone or shipped to Tai'yanan. Now there's only a stack of unwashed tunics, and a pile of unwanted gifts that Adah plans to donate to the needy in our village. Among those presents is the sculpted crane from Emperor Hanriyu.

The humidity has made the milky paint on its feathers turn yellow, and darkened its crown to crimson, but it's still an elegant bird. When I touch it, I could swear its wings lift. Like me, it wants to fly away from this place.

*Why do you bother with gnats when you can easily swat them away?* Ukar asks, slithering into the room. *Why encourage them?*

"Because I must leave Sundau."

*You could go to Yappang. Nakri's asked you more than once to become her apprentice.*

I shake my head. "Then the suitors would go to Yappang too. Their numbers will only grow. I won't be a burden to her."

Ukar knows it's true. Right now, it's kings who seek my hand. Soon, others will come. Demons, enchanters, perhaps even gods.

*Why a selection, then? You could easily leave Tambu for any corner of the world you wish.*

And I would. I would disappear into the deserts of Samaran or the backwaters of Balar. The last thing I want is to take part in a selection. But there's only one place where the light in my heart might be forgotten, and where it might cease to haunt me. The problem is, its borders are magically sealed. I cannot go there—unless I am invited.

I turn to my friend. "What do you know of Kiata? The kingdom of the crimson crane."

*Kiata?* Ukar's tail flicks. *That's on the other side of this world.*

"Not quite as far as that. There are no dragons there, no demons . . . no magic. There, the pearl's power will be weakened, if not subdued completely." I gather my breath. "I've considered this with great care, Ukar. It is the only place I can go."

*So you'll ask Hanriyu,* Ukar says. *No offense to your allure, Channi, but he didn't seem particularly interested the first time.*

"He found the selection abhorrent," I say softly. "That is a point in his favor. More than that, he lost the person dearest to him, as I did. We'll understand each other."

Ukar looks skeptical. *Doesn't he also have six daughters and a son? Or was it the other way around?*

"I like children."

*Seven is too many.*

I roll my eyes at him. "*Your* mother had seven."

*Like I said, it's too many.*

"I want to go to Kiata," I say. *I want to keep the world*

*safe from me.* "I'll ask Rongyo to invite the emperor . . . as a mediator for the selection."

*And then? You'll use the pearl to make him marry you?*

"No," I say sharply. "Never. I will leave with him only if we are suited to each other. *If* I do marry, it will be on my terms. And when I leave Tambu, it will not be to escape, but to have a new beginning." I inhale sharply. "I'll use the pearl to erase every trace of my name—and Vanna's—across the whole of Lor'yan. What do you think, Your Majesty?"

*Call me "Your Majesty" again and I'll bite you.*

It's the closest I've come to smiling since Vanna died.

*Are you sure this is what you want?* asks my best friend. His eyes dilate as they scrutinize me. *You're a formidable sorceress. You could be greater than Lor'yan's most famous enchanters. You don't have to hide on some snow-ridden wasteland. You don't have to marry.*

"All the power in the world cannot bring me what I desire most," I reply dully.

*And what is that?*

"Peace."

At my answer, Ukar's green scales fade into a more muted shade. He lets out a sigh. *Then do what you must. But when you cast your spell, leave me and my kin untouched. Not everyone should forget you. And I . . . I most of all want to remember.*

It hurts to speak. "I thought you might come with me."

*I cannot,* says Ukar. *I am king now, and I am needed here.* He flicks out his tongue. *Besides, I would not be happy in a land full of cranes.* There's a hint of his old dry humor. *Cranes eat snakes, you know.*

My shoulders shake with mirth, even though I am not laughing. I kiss the top of his head. "I will miss you, you cantankerous creature. Wherever I may go, I will think of you every day. You are my only family left here."

*The snakes will be your family no matter where you go. From this life to the next, they will remember you.* Ukar dips his head. *Lady White Snake.*

At the name, my chest swells with the pearl's light. It bathes Ukar and me, but its warmth is bittersweet.

Her "radiant curse," Vanna called it. I'm beginning to understand what she meant—that its light brings as much pain as it brings hope.

Now until my last breath, it will be mine.

# EPILOGUE

*One year later*

Hanriyu and I stand side by side on his ship. Below, the servants are loading our possessions and the sailors are preparing the vessel for departure. In minutes, we will set sail.

My months on Tai'yanan are a story for another time. I did indeed host a new selection, one that lasted a year, a far cry from the single-day event that Vanna experienced. In this year, I became a new Channi. Instead of wielding spears and knives, I pored over maps and scrolls. I studied language and history, I learned to dance and embroider birds and butterflies with richly colored thread, I perfected my penmanship.

For the entire year, I did not smile. I thought I had forgotten how.

Until Hanriyu returned to Tambu.

There were no machinations on my part. I did not enchant him into seeking me out, or even into becoming my friend. But we did become friends; slowly, our trust in each other built over a long month. I was not even aware that I smiled for him, *with* him, when I finally did.

"Why did you smile for me?" Hanriyu asks now, seeing my mouth tilt to a bemused angle. He's asked many times before, and I've never answered.

The wind sweeps my hair off my back as I turn to him. "It was a story you told me about your daughter. About how she found a caterpillar and thought it was a snake, so she put it under her brother's pillow." I cluck my tongue. "Two years old and already such a mischief-maker. It reminded me of my sister when she was young. That was why I smiled." My shoulders go soft. "And now I smile because I still don't know your daughter's name."

Hanriyu blinks with surprise. "I haven't told you?"

"You've told me your sons': Andahai, Benkai, Reiji, Yotan, Wandei, and Hasho." Hanriyu looks impressed that I've remembered all six, and in order of age. "You haven't told me your daughter's."

"Shiori," he replies slowly. "It means 'knot.' My wife chose it. She'd wanted a girl for so long, but after six boys she'd nearly lost hope." He wipes the perspiration from his neck. "When Shiori finally arrived, she chose the name to signify that Shiori would be the last."

He chuckles, and I picture his wife in my mind. A woman whose laugh touched the corners of her eyes, who hugged each of her children in the morning and at night and counted the stars with her hair unpinned and her feet un-slippered. Like her, I sense, her daughter is special.

"Are you sure you want to come with me?" Hanriyu asks suddenly. "A hundred sovereigns across Lor'yan have declared their undying love for you. You should choose one of them, not a man whose heart is with his dead wife."

"You've asked me this enough times. My answer hasn't changed."

"Even so. You are young. You've a chance at love."

I say nothing. All my life, I wished to be loved. I dreamed of a mother's arm around my shoulders while I slept, of a lover's stolen kisses and the warmth of a body pressed to mine. But not anymore.

I will not lie when it comes to Hanriyu. We will never love each other the way Oshli and Vanna did, and we will never have the connection that Hokzuh and I shared. But there are many different kinds of love.

"Your love is with your wife, and mine is with my sister. The fractures in our hearts will never heal. But I at least seek to make mine whole again. It is not a lover or a husband who can do that, but a family." I pause, more certain of this than of anything. "Let us be family for one another."

Hanriyu is taken aback. Then he nods. "I warn you, my children are quite a handful."

"I'd be disappointed if they weren't," I reply. I grasp at the railing to keep from swaying with the wind. "All I want is to love someone the way I loved Channari. Unconditionally, fully, and with every fiber of my being." Heat rises to my throat. "I have a feeling your children will fill her absence in my heart."

Hanriyu touches my arm. "I remember your sister," he says quietly. "She had the saddest eyes. Those eyes are in you now."

For the longest moment, I could swear he knows that it is me. Me, *Channari,* trapped in my sister's body. But it can't be so. Such is the power of my pearl.

"Will you do something for me?" I say, rather abruptly.

"What is it?"

"I would ask that you never speak of my sister again."

Hanriyu's brows knit. "Did I say something to offend you?"

"No, far from it."

I inhale. I've long pondered the words I'm about to speak, and the broken pearl inside me shimmers, giving away my nervousness.

"I have told you before, my sister's death changed me. I no longer wish to be a queen, and I no longer wish for the burden of *this.*" I cup the light in my chest with my hand.

"I know," says Hanriyu gently. "Any magic that passes into Kiata is suppressed by the gods. You will be free there."

It will be a new start. A new everything, really: a new family, a new land, even new seasons. I am nervous most of all for the snow. I have never seen it before, and though Hanriyu tells me it is beautiful and lasts only a season, I shiver in anticipation of the cold.

"I ask that you never speak of my sister again," I repeat. "Or of the time you've known me in Tambu. I wish to leave my past behind. All of it. Even my name."

"Your name?"

"Yes. I don't wish to be called Vanna any longer."

There are questions in Hanriyu's dark eyes, but I appreciate that he doesn't ask them. "It will be against convention . . .

but my people will accept it if I do. Still, you must have a title. What will we call you?"

I hadn't thought this far ahead. Lady White Snake. Serpent Queen.

"Her Radiance," I pluck out of nowhere.

"Her Radiance," Hanriyu repeats.

I don't explain myself. Let him think that I mean the brilliance within me. But no, I'm thinking of the light that makes the lanterns glow at night. The light that poured from Vanna's heart and into my own when she was alive. That light I will never forget. I wish to carry it until my last day, until I see her again.

"It suits you," he says when I am quiet. "So it shall be. Her Radiance."

~⁓~

It is time.

Night has fallen, and Hanriyu is asleep in the cabin adjacent to mine.

One knee at a time, I lower myself beside my window. I run my fingers down the scar on my face, following it to the end.

My gaze wanders out over the water. Somewhere across the sea is Puntalo Village, Adah's house, the little hut by the jungle where I grew up. Ukar and the snakes.

I didn't say goodbye to Lintang or to Adah. I'll never see them again, but I have no regrets. When I am done, they will hardly remember me.

"When will you cast the spell?" Oshli asked, before I left.

"When I am on the ship to depart Tambu."

"Your father will forget you? Your stepmother too?"

"They'll only remember that they had a daughter who went away and won't be coming back." I pause. "They won't remember Channari at all."

Oshli is quiet. "It's hard for me to fathom such power."

"As it is for me," I admit. "But it will be done."

"I'm sorry that I cast stones at you," he blurts. "I'm sorry I abandoned you when you needed me. I was a child—a stupid child—and I've been sorry for years. I know you'll not forgive me, but I want you to know this before you leave. Before I forget you."

The apology is late, yet it unwinds a thread inside me, tied tight for years. I almost smile. "You won't forget all of me."

We bow to each other, and all I can think is how Oshli and I have misjudged each other. How I am glad that we will part as friends.

"Here," he says, giving me the broken wooden bowl from my childhood home. He's repaired it, mending the cracks with melted gold. "My father kept for himself the coins that Vanna's suitors gave to the temple. I used part of one to make this. The rest, I'll share among the villagers. We'll rebuild." A pause. "You must too, Channi."

"I will." I touch his shoulder, lingering before I leave. "Thank you, my friend."

They will be my last words to him.

It is time now, and my voice carries across the sea: "You

will forget Vanna Jin'aiti, and you will forget her sister, Channari. Everyone you speak to will also forget, and it will be as if they never existed. As if they were a tale from a time long forgotten."

My words coalesce into a cloud of gold and silver dust, and it disperses across the islands. I see it sprinkle down over Yappang, where Nakri is wrenching out a crocodile's rotten tooth. She lifts her head, as if she senses me, and grins just before the gold dust passes her eyes. I see it come to rest upon Lintang and Adah, the children of Puntalo, my neighbors and those who once knew me. They blink, momentarily disoriented, before resuming their lives.

The dust passes next through Oshli's eyes. His body sags against his broom, but his face does not go blank like the rest. His ties to Vanna are strong. I can muddy his memories, but he will always sense the shadows of truth behind the lies I've spread. Until I die, these lies will unsettle him.

The dust does not reach Ukar and the snakes. Only they will remember the full truth.

Tears pool in my eyes. *Be well, my friend,* I whisper to Ukar, knowing that even across this vast distance, he can hear. *Rule wisely and dream well.*

Ukar shifts his scales to look like the sea, and in a gift of enchantment, I can almost see him outside my window. He lifts his scales to my cheek, one last time, before the moment is gone, and the sea separates us once more.

Lastly, the dust settles upon Hanriyu's ship, erasing the final traces of my past. Come morning, the stories about the two sisters—one the monster and one the beauty—will be splintered from truth. They will be legends, and few will remember that they were real.

As the last of the dust dissipates in the wind, I murmur my true name, so I don't forget it.

"Channari." My moon-faced girl.

My spell is done, and I am more tired than I ever have been. My every muscle feels like a stone weighing me down, and it is the hardest thing, turning back into my cabin. I lie on a small cot hardly made for a queen, with hastily decorated silk cushions. Hanriyu didn't expect me to come home with him.

I reach for the wooden bowl at my side. It is one of few possessions I've brought from Sundau, its delicate cracks carefully sealed with gold. I rest it on my palms. As Vanna did, I use it to cover the light inside me, so I may sleep.

When I arrive in Kiata, I'll no longer need this bowl. My light will soften. It will fade into a spark, and over time, it will be forgotten.

In its place, I will have six sons and a daughter. A family, at last.

The thought fills me with hope. I drift into my dreams, meeting the ghost of my sister with a smile.

# ACKNOWLEDGMENTS

This book has been a long time coming. I began it before writing *Six Crimson Cranes,* and it's been on my mind for many years since.

Thank you to my editor, Katherine, for your invaluable guidance and support on this book, and for helping it find its heart. Thank you to my agent, Gina, who read the early drafts of Channi's story and urged me to finish it. I needed that extra push.

To Lili, my publicist, for always being a step ahead in all ways of getting my books out to my readers. To Melanie, Gianna, Kelly, Elizabeth, Dominique, John, Natali, Shannon, Alison, Artie, Kayla, Barbara, and the fantastic team at Knopf Books for Young Readers. I am so grateful for everything that you have done to get *Her Radiant Curse* out into the world.

To Tran, for bringing Channi and Vanna to life in as perfect a way as I could have imagined, for brilliantly capturing the tone and vividness of this book.

To Alix, for expressing all the beauty and epic-ness of

this story in three simple words of text. I love the lettering so much.

To Virginia, for Tambu's absolutely stunning map. Having your beautiful art grace my books is a gift.

To my team in the UK: Molly, Natasha, Kate, and Lydia, thank you again for your amazing care for, and dedication to, my stories and for bringing *Her Radiant Curse* across the world. And to Kelly Chong for another glorious cover. I'm obsessed with the butterflies and the snake—they are so beautiful!

To my beta readers: Leslie and Doug, who believed in Channi and loved her from the start, and Victoria, Amaris, and Eva for your keen eyes and honest critiques, and for always being sounding boards for new ideas.

To my parents and my sister, for supporting my writing from the beginning and encouraging me to follow my dreams. To Adrian, for your love and tireless support, and for alpha-reading every one of my books while also helping raise our daughters. I couldn't have dreamt of a better partner in life. To my girls, my stories are for you, and I love you so much.

Lastly, a heartfelt thank-you to my readers. Without you, my stories would have no home—so thank you.

# ABOUT THE AUTHOR

**ELIZABETH LIM** grew up in the San Francisco Bay Area, where she was raised on a hearty diet of fairy tales, myths, and songs. Before becoming an author, Elizabeth was a professional film and video game composer, and she still tends to come up with her best book ideas when writing near a piano. An alumna of Harvard College and the Juilliard School, she now lives in New York City with her husband and daughters.

Elizabeth's bestselling Legends of Lor'yan novels include *Spin the Dawn*, *Unravel the Dusk*, *Six Crimson Cranes*, and *The Dragon's Promise*. She is also a contributor to Disney's A Twisted Tale series.

elizabethlim.com